Praise for Peter May

'Peter May is a writer I'd follow to the ends of the earth'
New York Times

'Tightly plotted, with no skimping on either the nuances of character or the wonderfully evocative descriptions . . . a true pleasure to read'
Guardian

'One of the best regarded crime series of recent years'
Boyd Tonkin, *Independent*, on the Lewis Trilogy

'May's novels are strong on place and the wounds left by old relationships'
Sunday Times

'Will have the reader relishing every tendency of description and characterization'
Barry Forshaw, *Independent*

'Lyrical, empathetic and moving'
Alex Gray

'Dark, exciting and atmospheric'
Scotland on Sunday

'Powerful and authentic'
Glasgow Sunday Herald

By Peter May

FICTION

The Lewis Trilogy

The Blackhouse

The Lewis Man

The Chessmen

The China Thrillers

The Firemaker

The Fourth Sacrifice

The Killing Room

Snakehead

The Runner

Chinese Whispers

The Enzo Files

Extraordinary People

The Critic

Blacklight Blue

Freeze Frame

Blowback

Standalone Novels

Entry Island

Virtually Dead

The Noble Path

Hidden Faces

Fallen Hero

The Reporter

NON-FICTION

Hebrides (with David Wilson)

First published in the USA in 2007
by Poisoned Pen Press

First published in Great Britain in 2014 by

Quercus Editions Ltd
55 Baker Street
7th Floor, South Block
London W1U 8EW

A CIP catalogue record for this book is available
from the British Library

PB ISBN 978 1 78206 209 7
EBOOK ISBN 978 1 78206 886 0

10 9 8 7 6 5 4

inted and bound in Great Britain by Clays Ltd, St Ives plc

Typeset by Ellipsis Digital Limited, Glasgow

Peter May was an award-winning journalist at the age of just twenty-one. He left newspapers for television and screen-writing, creating three prime-time British drama series and accruing more than 1,000 television credits. Peter now lives in France where he focuses on writing novels.

The Critic is the second book in the Enzo series.

PETER M
THE CRI

Quercus

This book is dedicated to the memory of Tom Smyth

Whoever fights monsters should see to it that in the process he does not become a monster. When you look into the abyss, the abyss also looks into you.

Friedrich Nietzsche, *Beyond Good and Evil*

PROLOGUE

There is a smell among the vines. Of grape juice and leaves and trod-
den earth. And something else. A black smell edged by the yellow of
the harvest moon, which spills its light across the neat, manicured
rows that march side by side across this gentle slope. A smell which
has none of the sweetness of fruit at maturity. It is rotten, and carries
the unmistakable stench of death.

The air is warm, soft on the skin, and full of the sound of grapes
dropping into plastic buckets. A gentle plop, plop. A rustle of leaves,
the snipping of secateurs. Beams of light from flashlights on helmets
criss-cross in the dark, then pierce the sky as if searching for stars as
heads lift for air.

Annie is young. Just sixteen. It is her first vendange. A night pick
by hand to harvest the cool, white mauzac grape for the vin mous-
seux. She knows nothing of how it is made – a secret stolen centuries
before by a monk called Dom Perignon, and made famous in another
place on the far side of France. She is young, and ripe like the grapes.
Ready for picking. And she knows that Christian is watching her, bid-
ing his time with growing impatience. He is in the next row. She can
hear him breathing as he examines each bunch in the light, before
paring away any mould and then dropping it in his bucket. They have

made a tryst, to meet at the source of the stream that tumbles down the hillside to water the vines, clear and sparkling in the moonlight. A place in the woods where lovers have met for hundreds of years, in the shadow of a château that is no more, beneath the abandoned church that dominates the hilltop. Far below, the river Tarn forms a seam of gold traversing the night.

It is almost time. Annie glances at her watch. Just after three. And then she hears the tractor as it makes its way back from the chai to collect the next load of grapes for the pressoir. She looks down the row. The others are dragging their buckets towards the big red bins for loading on to the trailer. There is an urgent hissing, and she turns to see Christian signalling through the leaves. Her heart nearly fills her throat and her breath comes with difficulty. They'll never miss us, he had said. We'll just switch off our lamps and drift away in the dark, like ghosts.

With sticky fingers she finds the switch and darkness wraps itself around her. She ducks beneath the wire and feels his hands pull her through, sticky like hers, sweeter than sugar. And his lips find her lips, and she tastes the grapes he has been eating as he picked.

They lock hands and, crouching beneath the level of the vines, scamper away up the slope towards the dark line of the trees above. This is fun. The fear has gone now, to be replaced by the thrill of anticipation, the approach, finally, of womanhood. She laughs, and he presses a finger to her lips to shoosh her, and she hears him fight to restrain his own laughter.

They are far enough away now to rise above the vines and run for cover. But even as they turn towards the woods, a figure casts its long, dark shadow towards them, arms outstretched as if to block their way and herd them back to their task.

They stop, and she hears Christian curse. Putain! They are caught. But the man does not move. A long gown hangs from his arms, stirring in the night breeze, a harbinger of the vent d'autan to come. White gloves catch the light. A strange, triangular hat shadows his face. And still he does not move.

'Who is it?' Annie whispers, an odd foreboding descending on her, like the darkness of the night as a cloud momentarily masks the moon. The light from Christian's lamp pierces it, startling and bright, and finds a face, sunken and wrinkled, and stretched back across an impossibly prominent skull. Black holes where once there were eyes. Skin, teeth, hair, the deep, red colour of grape juice, matching the crimson of the gown. The mouth hangs open as if frozen in some dying scream. But it is Annie's scream that fills the night, full of the fear of mortality that comes from a first encounter with death.

CHAPTER ONE

I

'Petty must have been one of the most unpopular men in France, Monsieur Macleod.' The Préfet waved his hand airily, as if all of France lay before him. 'Imagine. An American who told Frenchmen if their wine was any good.'

Enzo couldn't resist a tiny smile. 'I'm sure those *châteaux* in Bordeaux, whose wines sell for a hundred dollars a bottle or more, were very happy with the ratings Monsieur Petty gave them.'

'Yes, but that didn't mean they liked him. Feared him, more like. After all, one bad rating could spell ruin. And there's been more than one winemaker destroyed by Petty's disapproval.'

Distaste curled the Préfet's lip.

The Cathedral of Sainte Cecile, the largest brick building in the world, loomed above them, its basilica dominating the skyline of the city of Albi, a feat of mediaeval engineering yet to be surpassed by twenty-first century architects. The Préfet strolled across the cobbled cathedral square as if he owned it, which he very nearly did. On the far side, there were already queues at the gate of the Toulouse-Lautrec museum.

'Of course, one critic passes, another fills his shoes. Robert Parker is king now. And the journalists of *The Wine Spectator*. More Americans.' The Préfet's distaste was wrinkling his nose now. 'But none of them has ever come to Gaillac to taste our local wines. Parker was rumoured to have once rated a Château Lastours. I don't know if that is true or not, but Petty was the only one to come to do a comprehensive tasting.' He sighed and turned a look of curiosity towards Enzo as if it was only just occurring to him to wonder why he was even discussing the matter with this strange, pony-tailed Scotsman. 'But then we'll never know what he thought, since his tasting notes were never found. Although I'm sure you know all this already.'

Enzo nodded. He knew every detail of Petty's disappearance and murder. Not only from what he had read in Raffin's book, but from the briefing Raffin himself had given him. Originally, there were only to have been six unsolved murders in the book. The Petty case had been a last-minute inclusion. A Stop Press.

'So I'm not exactly sure how it is I can help you. My opposite number in the Lot spoke very highly of you. We were at ENA together, you know.'

'Yes, I know, Monsieur le Préfet. I was hoping you might be able to put me in touch with someone at Gaillac. Someone who could help me go undercover. Grape-picking, perhaps.'

'So you think you're going to solve Petty's murder as well as Gaillard's, do you? Another bet?'

It had been widely reported that Enzo had cracked

the Gaillard case as the result of a three-way bet with his local Préfet and the police chief in his home town of Cahors. Albi was two hours south of Cahors, high up above the River Tarn – fast-flowing water coruscating in the slanting September sunlight.

Enzo glanced along the tree-lined river bank, brick-built houses with shallow, red, Roman-tiled roofs rising above turning leaves. 'Not this time, Monsieur le Préfet. I'm trying to raise funds for the new forensics department at my university in Toulouse. We attracted a lot of publicity with the Gaillard case, so I'm working my way through the other unsolved cases in Raffin's book.'

They stopped at the foot of steps leading to the elaborate gothic stone entrance that abutted the towering brick edifice of the cathedral. The Préfet was on his way to morning prayers, a religious man filled with piety outside the secular confines of his political office. He turned a speculative eye on Enzo. 'I'm not sure I approve of amateur sleuths working outside of the law.'

'I'm hardly an amateur, Monsieur le Préfet. I'm well qualified in the art of forensic science.' And before the Préfet could point out that it was an art he had not practised for twenty years, he added, 'And besides, there wouldn't be any need for amateur sleuths if the police were doing their job.'

The Préfet raised an eyebrow. 'Préfet Verne said you were a plain-speaking man.' There was an almost imperceptible hesitation before he reached a decision. He took out a small, leather-bound notebook and scribbled a name and number on a blank page. He tore it out and handed it to Enzo. 'I wish you the best of luck, Monsieur Macleod. You'll need it.' And he turned and ran up the steps, late for his appointment with God.

II

'I made the initial identification at the morgue three years ago.' Laurent de Bonneval was a man in his early fifties. He was, perhaps, a year or two older than Enzo. He was tall, and willowy thin, with thick, black, curly hair, shot through with an odd streak of silver. His friendly, liquid brown eyes were melancholy now with the memory of the moment. 'It was shocking. I've never seen a human being in a state like that. It was almost as if he had been pickled by the wine, like something preserved in a jar. I suppose the alcohol retarded the process of decay. He must have been completely submerged in it for most of the twelve months he was missing.'

Bonneval turned away from the window. The blood had drained from his face, leaving his tanned skin a sickly yellow. Beyond him, fifty feet below the battlement walls of the old abbey, the River Tarn continued on its stately route west from Albi, now thirty miles upstream.

They were in the offices of the *Commission Interprofessionnelle des Vins de Gaillac* in the *Maison des Vins*, part of the thirteenth-century brick-built Abbaye Saint-Michel in the millennium town of Gaillac. Enzo felt a thousand years of history encased in the red brick walls around them. 'Why wasn't he identified by a relative?'

'Because no one bothered to come over from the States when they found him. He'd been divorced for several years and estranged from his daughter, apparently.'

Enzo cleared his throat self-consciously. These were uncomfortable parallels with his own life. But, then Monsieur de Bonneval wasn't to know that. 'So why did they ask you?'

'He'd been tasting my wines at Château Saint-Michel the week before he went missing. So I'd met him. But also, I suppose, because I was president of the CIVG. I represented all the winemakers of Gaillac. Still do.'

Enzo looked at his blue-ribbed pullover with its faded elbow patches, and his baggy cord trousers, and thought he looked like an unlikely representative of winemakers. But there was something attractive about him, an avuncular quality that made him instantly likeable. 'Police reports said he'd been dressed up in the ceremonial garb of some local brotherhood of winemakers.'

'Yes, the order of the divine bottle – *l'Ordre de la Dive Bouteille*. Quite bizarre, really. The order is a brotherhood of bon viveurs in the mould of François Rabelais.'

Enzo knew of the famous sixteenth-century French writer's predilection for wine, and also of his infamous one-line will: *I have nothing, I owe a great deal, and the rest I leave to the poor*.

Bonneval said, 'The brotherhood is rooted in an ancient society that existed five hundred years ago called *La Companha de la Poda*. A *poda* was a short hand-axe they used to use for pruning the vines. But nowadays it seems the *confrérie* has only two purposes. The promotion of wine, and the drinking of it.'

'You're not a member, then?'

'Good God, no. I'm a serious winemaker, Monsieur. I don't have time for dressing up in crimson gowns and pointed hats.' Bonneval smiled. 'I don't mind drinking the stuff, though.'

Enzo nodded. He wasn't averse to a glass or two himself. 'So what was Petty's connection to the organisation?'

'He'd been inducted into the *confrérie* shortly after his arrival here. Made a *chevalier* of the order.'

'Was that unusual?'

'Not for someone of his standing. He was, after all, just about the biggest name in the world of wine, Monsieur Macleod. And he'd come to taste *our* wines. Maybe even put us on the map. Good ratings from Petty could have made some of our *vignerons* a lot of money'

'And bad ratings could have ruined them.'

Bonneval shrugged. 'If you're looking for a motive, then I suppose that's true.'

'So,' Enzo said. 'Do you think you can help me?'

'Oh, I think so, yes.' He took a business card from his wallet and handed it to Enzo. 'Look, why don't you come to the *château* this evening, have dinner with my wife and me. Are you familiar with wine-making, Monsieur Macleod?'

'I understand the process. But I'm not familiar with all the mechanics.'

'You do enjoy a glass, though?'

'Oh, yes.'

'Good. We'll have a bottle or two, and then I'll show you around. And in the meantime, I'll see if I can't get you placed for a little grape-picking.' He smiled. 'I hope you don't have back problems.'

III

Gaillac, Enzo reflected, as he crossed the freshly re-cobbled Place du Griffoul, was not a beautiful town. It had neither the scale nor dignity of the departmental capital of Albi, but it had a certain dusty charm. It was a working town, filled with working people. Red bricks and grapes. The smell of them filled the air, a rich, heady, fruity scent carried in waves on the breeze. It was harvest time, and the lifeblood of the town and the vineyards that climbed both banks of the river around it was being gathered and squeezed and fermented in towering stainless steel tanks at more than one hundred and twenty *domaines* and *châteaux*.

Diners were gathering in restaurants and cafés around the old *bastide*, and Enzo climbed the narrow Rue Charles Portal, with its ancient cantilevered buildings leaning at odd angles, oak beams and brick, glass and neon. A strange amalgam of old and new. The sun was high and hot in an early autumn sky, burnt-out and shimmering in the haze of its own heat, and people hurried home to lunch clutching warm, freshly-baked loaves. It was hard to believe that in this somnolent town in south-west France, a killer still walked free – long after his victim had been buried and all but forgotten.

The entrance to the *gendarmerie* was in Avenue Jean Calvet, an electronic gate opening into a hot, asphalt courtyard, bounded on its east side by an apartment block that housed *gendarmes* and their families. Enzo pressed the buzzer and told the girl who responded over the loudspeaker that he wanted to talk to Gendarme David Roussel.

Roussel's office was off a corridor beyond a faded, green shuttered door on the far side of the courtyard. *Gendarmes* stood around in groups, smoking and chatting and watching Enzo with idle curiosity as he crossed it. He was clearly not local. A tall man, over six feet, with an odd silver streak running back through greying, dark hair.

Roussel himself was a short man in his mid-thirties with a fine stubble of dark hair growing like velvet across a bullet skull. He had big, dark, suspicious eyes and hands that would make fists the size of Belfast hams. His dark blue trousers were tucked into black leather boots, a pale blue, short-sleeved polo shirt tucked into the trousers above a white belt and holstered gun. Just beneath the buttons at his neck, a dark blue square bore two silver stripes, and on his left arm, a lion rampant rose proudly on a grey shield. Both were attached to the shirt by velcro, removable for washing, and Enzo reflected on how practical the French could be.

Roussel ushered him into the gloom of his office, a small cluttered space with three desks, both windows shuttered against the glare of the outside world. A life-size cardboard cut-out of Lara Croft leaned against the back wall, thrusting outsized breasts into the room. A U2 poster was a visual counterpart to the music that played through the speakers of Roussel's computer. Roussel positioned himself behind his desk, hands on hips. 'Best rock group in the world.' He allowed time for Enzo to absorb this wisdom, then added, 'You know, there are people out there campaigning to stop prisoners being kept three to a cell. Cells bigger than this.' He waved a hand around his office. 'There are three of us in here – and we're *gendarmes!*' He barely allowed himself time to draw breath. 'What do you want, Monsieur Macleod?'

'You received a fax from Madame Taillard, the police chief in Cahors?'

'I did.'

'Then you'll know I'm here about the murder of Gil Petty.'

Roussel allowed himself to drop into his seat, and he folded his arms across his chest. Enzo noticed a foot-high plastic model of Lara Croft standing to one side of the computer, the cardboard box it had come in discarded amongst the detritus piled up on the floor behind the desk. 'I don't like the *Police Nationale*, monsieur. They're civilians, we're army. They get funded, we don't.' He picked a pen out of a jar of them standing on his desk and scribbled with it on his inkpad. It left nothing but an indentation in the paper. '*Gendarme*-issue. Doesn't work.' He picked up a file on his desk and pulled off the paper clip that bound it, holding it up for Enzo to see.

'Paper clips? Got to buy them ourselves. You think the *Police Nationale* buy their own paper clips?'

'I have no idea.'

'No, of course you don't. And I have no idea how I can help you.'

'I'd like access to your files on the Petty case.'

Roussel gazed at him very directly for a long time. Then his face broke into an unexpected smile of genuine amusement. 'I like a man with a sense of humour, Monsieur Macleod. What makes you think I would give you access to the files?' But before Enzo could reply, he lifted a hand to stop him. 'No, tell me this first. Who are you?'

Enzo was taken aback. 'Well, you know who I am.'

'Do I?'

Enzo sighed. 'My name's Enzo—'

Rousell cut him of. 'No, I know who you are. Or, rather, I know who you tell me you are.' He reached across the desk. 'And what I read in a fax from someone purporting to be the chief of police in Cahors. You could be the killer for all I know. And you want me to hand over my files?'

Enzo was at a loss.

'And in any case, the *Gendarmerie Nationale* doesn't give out information to private investigators.'

'I'm not exactly a private investigator.'

'No, you're not.' Roussel opened a slim file on his desk and lifted a sheet of paper to examine it. 'You're a former forensics officer from Scotland. You've lived in France for twenty years and you teach biology at Paul Sabatier University in Toulouse.'

'I thought you didn't know anything about me.'

'I did some checking. In my business it pays.'

Roussel had done his homework, but it was time, Enzo thought, to turn defence into attack. 'It's easy enough, monsieur, to find facts that are readily available on the internet. It's quite another to solve a crime when none of the facts are apparent, and it requires some intelligence to unearth them.'

Colour rose high on Roussel's cheeks, marring a smooth, tanned complexion. 'Your point being?'

'Petty was missing for a year before his body turned up. Not only did you fail to find him, you didn't even know he'd been murdered until his killer decided to put him on public display.'

Roussel's anger was apparent only in the almost imperceptible clenching and unclenching of his jaw. He gazed at Enzo with steady dark eyes. 'People go missing all the time, Monsieur Macleod.' He tapped another file on his desk. A fat one this time. 'I have nearly half a dozen cases in my missing persons file. Very often people have their own reasons. Nothing sinister. A marital break-up, a secret affair, redundancy, mental illness. Sometimes they just want to disappear.' He opened the file and lifted out a sheaf of papers held together with a clip he had no doubt bought himself. 'This one I was at school with. Serge Coste. Just upped sticks and left a year ago. His wife says she has no idea why. But I figure they had a big bust up. They were childless. She wanted to adopt, he didn't.

That sort of thing can put people under all sorts of pressure. But we'll probably never know why he left, or where he went.' He closed the file and slapped his hand on top of it. 'We had no reason to suspect foul play when Petty disappeared. Even when we came under pressure – he was an international personality, after all – we could find no evidence that there had been any crime committed.'

'Even when he turned up strapped to a cross like a scarecrow in a vineyard?'

'That was twelve months later. The trail was cold as ice.'

'Not where he was found. He'd only been there a matter of hours. You had a fresh crime scene. And a killer always leaves something behind. Some clue. No matter how small. Always.'

Roussel pursed his lips to contain his anger. 'Officers from the *Police Scientifique* in Albi examined the scene in the minutest detail, Monsieur Macleod. If the killer had left some trace, we would have found it.' He pushed himself back in his seat and pulled open a drawer. He took out a book and dropped it on his desk.

Enzo inclined his head to look at it.

'Your friend, Roger Raffin is causing me no end of trouble, Macleod.' Enzo noticed that Roussel had dropped the *monsieur*. 'Especially now that it's been translated and published in the United States. Although no doubt only because it contains the Petty case. You just missed his daughter.'

This time Enzo's interest was piqued. "Michelle Petty? She's here?"

'Not for long. She was looking for his personal belongings.'

'After three years? She's taken her time.'

'Four years since he went missing. And it's the first contact we've had from any member of the family – apart from arranging to ship the body back for burial.'

'So what did you tell her?'

'That his personal effects are still regarded as evidence in an open case. So I don't think she'll be here for much longer.'

'I don't suppose you'd know where she's staying.'

Roussel fixed him with hard eyes. 'And why should I tell you?'

'To get me off your back.'

Which brought a smile to the *gendarme's* face. The first in a while. 'Now there's an offer. She's staying at the Château de Salettes, Monsieur Macleod. It's where all the really wealthy tourists stay. I'd say Michelle Petty has done pretty well from her father's death.'

CHAPTER TWO

I

The narrow road wound upwards amongst vineyards that stretched away through chalk hills north and south, as far as the eye could see. Some of the vines were still laden, heavy bunches of tightly packed black braucol or duras grapes, or the yellow-green mauzac or *loin de l'oeil* – romantically named 'far from the eye' because of its long stalk. Others had already been harvested and seemed naked somehow, stripped of their fruit under the hot September sun. The *vendange* was early this year after a heatwave in July and a warm, wet August. It promised a fine vintage.

The landscape was punctuated by tall, thin poplars, like exclamation marks, and the distinctive *pins parasols*, pine trees that spread their dark canopies like giant parasols to provide shade from the heat of the day. Hilltop villages in shimmering white stone were roofed with red Roman tiles set at shallow angles, in the Mediterranean style. Enzo's polished cream Citröen 2CV rolled on soft suspension as he steered it right at the crossroads. The car was his pride and joy, lovingly restored by a specialist in Belgium from the carcasses of cars long since extinct. It was quintessentially French and, with its roof rolled back like a sardine can, gave Enzo's big frame all the space he needed.

From its windows he had a panoramic view across the rolling hills to the valley below, and he reflected that this landscape would not have looked so very different in Roman times. Stone-built villas, poplars, vines. Land tamed and cultivated by men in skirts and sandals. The only difference now was that the roads were metalled, and the grapes were harvested for the most part by machines that shook them violently from their stalks. Enzo could see one now, in the distance, huge wheels straddling vines carefully pruned to accommodate them. A monster of a machine, towering over the vineyard as it made its steady progress up the hill, grapes drawn into huge containers on either side.

He passed a small, private chapel and graveyard, and turned towards the recently restored Château de Salettes on the crest above. The *château* was cradled in the heart of the vineyard which produced the wine that bore its name, white stone reflecting bright light around mediaeval towers and high walls built to defend against attack. Enzo pulled up in the car park and walked through an arched gate to a timeless courtyard beyond. A vast, milky, canvas sail was stretched across it to provide shade for diners at tables set below. Potted poplars lined the walls, modern sculptures echoing their theme outside a tasting room where *château* wines could be sampled and bought. A *dégustation*. Enzo turned into a cool, dark, reception room and asked the girl behind the desk if Michelle Petty was still a guest in the hotel.

*

She had her back to him when he emerged from the castle wall on to a lawn that ran the length of the building. It was south-facing and commanded spectacular views across the hills to the Tarn valley far below, a dusty road, laid like a ribbon of chalk over its undulations, vanishing finally into a haze of green. She sat reading at a mahogany table and raised her head as he cast his shadow across it. Her eyes were hidden behind dark glasses, and he could not at first detect her reaction to him, until she lowered her glasses and he saw the curiosity in their cool, green assessment. He was not the sort of guest you would expect to find in a place like this. A voluminous khaki shirt over baggy cargo trousers, a well-worn canvas bag hanging from his shoulder. And he was clearly not on the serving staff.

'Jeez,' she said unexpectedly. 'Is that real or an affectation?'

Enzo was taken by surprise. 'Is what an affectation?'

'The hair. That white stripe. You get that specially dyed?'

He smiled and shook his head. 'I've had it since I was a teenager. Waardenburg Syndrome.' He sat down opposite her. 'If you look closely you'll see one eye is a different colour from the other.'

She removed her glasses altogether and squinted at him in the sunlight. 'So they are. One brown, one blue. Is it serious?'

'Well, I haven't died from it yet.' He noticed for the first time that she was an attractive girl. He knew, from Raffin's notes, that she was twenty-five, had barely been out of her teens when her father went missing. Even though she was seated, he could see that she was tall – long, elegant legs in cut-off jeans, a white blouse partially unbuttoned and tied above her waist, revealing a taut, tanned belly. Long, chestnut hair was held back from her face in a clasp, and tumbled carelessly over square shoulders. Her face was handsome, without being pretty. Strong features, full lips, large eyes, and not a trace of make-up. She seemed only now to become aware that he had joined her uninvited, and she became self-conscious and wary.

'Is there something I can do for you, Mister . . . ?'

'Macleod. Enzo Macleod.'

She seemed amused. Her caution hadn't lasted long. Eroded, perhaps, by his charm. 'What kind of name is that?'

'My mother was Italian. Enzo is short for Lorenzo. My father was Scottish. I grew up in Glasgow.'

'So what are you doing here Mister Lorenzo Macleod?'

'I'm going to find out who murdered your father.'

She flinched, almost as if he had struck her, and all animation left her face. It was a moment or two before she found her voice, and when she spoke it was softly, in contrast to her words. 'Why don't you go fuck yourself?'

'I'm serious.'

'So am I.'

'Don't you want to know?'

'I couldn't care less.'

'But you're here to collect his things.'

'Only to put an end to it. Once and for all. Ever since that Goddamned book got published in the States, it's like he's come back from the dead to haunt me. Newspapers writing articles, wanting interviews. An hour-long documentary on 'Forty-Eight Hours'. He never had five minutes for me when he was alive. Now he won't let me be. I want it to stop.'

'There'll never be closure as long as his killer walks free.'

Some of her emotion spent, she took a moment to assess him a little more carefully. She slipped on her sunglasses to hide her eyes. 'What's it to you?'

'Before I came to France, I was a forensics expert in Scotland. I'm using my experience and my science to burst open some of those cold cases in Raffin's book. I've already laid one of them to rest.'

'And my father's just the next one on the list?' She couldn't keep the sarcasm out of her voice.

'You could put it that way.' He took a moment to compose his proposal. 'I know that *Gendarme* Roussel is reluctant to let go of your father's possessions. Maybe if you made me your official representative, I could do something about that.'

She held him in her gaze for a long time, impenetrable behind her dark lenses. When, finally, she spoke, it was in the same soft tone as before. 'I don't think so.' She picked up her book and started reading, or at least pretended to. Enzo was dismissed, and she wasn't going to engage him any further.

He sat for a full minute before standing up and dropping his card on the table. 'That's my mobile number. If you want to find me, I'll be staying at the *gîte* your father was renting when he disappeared.'

Her attention remained focused on the pages of her book, and he gazed out for a moment over the shimmering vineyards below before heading back to the carpark where his 2CV sat baking in the afternoon sun.

II

This was wine country. So it was not unnatural that Gil Petty would have stayed at a *château*. Except that he hadn't. He had rented a small country cottage in the shadow of a restored castle that dated back to the eleventh century. A tiny, cramped estate-worker's house with a single room serving as kitchen, dining and living area, and just one bedroom. It was a beautiful cottage, though, covered in autumn-red ivy. A small *terrasse* looked out over a fifteenth-century *pigeonnier* that stood on stilts of stone in the dappled shade of three massive chestnut trees. The towering walls and turrets of the imposing Château des Fleurs were a stone's throw away, catering for wealthy tourists in sumptuous *chambres d'hôtes* off the open gallery that ran all around the top of the building. The lady of the house was renowned for her cuisine. As Enzo drove up the long drive to the castle, he wondered not for the first time why a man of Petty's means had chosen to spend a month in a cramped and inexpensive *gîte* when he could have opted for the comfort and fine cuisine of the *château*.

A worker's white van was parked at the foot of the steps to the *gîte* and, as Enzo got out of his car, Pierric and Paulette Lefèvre hurried out from the tiny estate office they had made in its cellar. Paulette had struck Enzo as a tall, attractive, older woman when they first met. And then he realised she was probably the same age as he was, and wondered if that made him an 'older man' – attractive or otherwise. Certainly, it had been clear from Paulette's warmth, that *she* had found him attractive. Something of which Pierric had not been unaware. He had ill-concealed his irritation. A beanpole of a man with a loping gate, and thinning, grey hair, he had deeply etched lines on either cheek which gave him a somewhat simian look. He was irritated again now. He waved an arm towards the worker's van.

'I'm not at all sure about this, monsieur. There's bound to be damage to the wall.'

'I'll pay to have it fixed,' Enzo said. 'But I need my white-board. I think visually, you see.'

When he had first come to arrange the let, he had thought it might be useful to let them in on why he was here. It helped to have local knowledge on tap. And they had met Petty. They had been enthusiastic and helpful, anxious that the stain of the wine critic's disappearance and murder should be removed once and for all from their castle and cottage. Now, perhaps, Pierric at least was having second thoughts. Paulette stood anxiously in the background, gently wringing her hands. She gave Enzo a pale smile when he caught her eye, then winced as the sound of hammering reached them from inside.

'Petty's daughter is here,' Enzo said, as a way of distracting them. 'She's staying at Château de Salettes.' It worked. The whiteboard was suddenly forgotten.

'What has she come for?' Pierric wanted to know.

'Her father's things.'

'Some of his stuff was here for ages after he vanished,' Paulette said. 'The family never showed any interest at the time.'

'Maybe she'll want to come and talk to you.'

Neither of them seemed happy at the prospect. They were an odd couple. Parisians. He had been something big in insurance. Then twenty years ago they had given up everything to buy and restore what had been little more than a ruin when they bought it, living in the little cottage while the work was carried out on the *château*. Now they catered to wealthy tourists and made organic wine from fourteen hectares of vineyard they had planted themselves. They had given Enzo a bottle of their red and it wasn't bad.

Now he bounded up the steps to the door as the joiner emerged carrying his bag of tools. 'All done, Monsieur Macleod. I'll send the bill to the *château*, shall I?'

'No, I'll settle in cash. How much do I owe you?'

The *menuisier* thought for a moment. 'Two hundred.'

'Euros?'

'Well, it would hardly be francs now, would it?'

Reluctantly, Enzo counted out the notes. It was more than he had expected, and he only had a small, unofficial budget from the university.

When the joiner had gone, Enzo stood and surveyed his board, mounted squarely on the far wall. The Lefèvres appeared at his back, anxious to see what damage had been done. But the *menuisier* had been tidy and left no mess, and whatever damage there was to the wall was hidden from view. Enzo strode across the room, took out a blue marker pen and wrote 'Gil Petty' in the top left corner. In the middle of the board he wrote 'Ordre de la Dive Bouteille,' circled it and drew an arrow to it from Petty's name.

It was a start. But he needed help.

He fumbled in his trouser pockets for his mobile and cursed softly when he saw that the battery indicator was flashing. He turned to Paulette and Pierric. 'Is there any chance I could use a phone in your office?'

III

The old stone farmhouse on the hill above had been empty as long as Nicole could remember. As a child she had played inside it, until her father had hammered wooden boards across the door. It was dangerous, he had said.

She climbed the track towards it now, glad for a breath of air, past the wood her father had cut and stacked to dry. The collies ran about her legs, chasing each other, barking at the wind. Where the track turned into the old, abandoned farmyard, she stopped and looked out across the rolling, tree-covered hills of the Auvergne. Crystal clear streams cut deep through the rich, red soil so that it seemed the land was repeatedly folding over on itself. She loved the random nature of it; the way it changed through the seasons. The colour of the trees. A field ploughed one year, given over to pasture the next. She loved in equal measure the hot, summer wind that blew up from Africa and the icy winter blasts driven in from the Atlantic.

But most of all she loved her mother and her father, and her heart was filled with fear for them both.

She sat on an old tree-stump, and the collies frolicked around her, pushing against her legs as she tousled their heads in turn. She had spent most of the morning in her mother's darkened room, just holding her hand for comfort, then made her father's lunch when he brought the sheep down from the high grazing. Now she had a little time to herself. Time to think about the future. To fret about it. To fear for it. University would start again in just a few days, and she didn't know how her father was going to manage without her.

Even worse, she had no idea how he would manage without his wife. It had been a long, depressing summer since the doctor had diagnosed terminal cancer. It could be weeks, he'd said. Months, if she was lucky. Lucky! Nicole didn't think so.

The sound of the car came to her on the wind before she saw it, sunlight catching its roof as it wound its way up the track from the valley below, past the great pile of old tyres holding down the *bâche* that covered the silage. She watched as it drew up in the yard below, and her aunt got out to greet her elder brother, Nicole's father. They held each other for a long time before he took her case from the boot and they went into the house. She would be there now until the end, and Nicole had pangs of guilt at the relief she felt. It was like being let out of prison. Or like a runner, exhausted and failing, passing on the baton for someone else to run the final leg.

The dogs crowded around her, peering up anxiously into her face, sensing her distress. She spoke to them softly, running her hands back over upturned heads, and felt a comfort in their untiring love.

'Nicole!'

She looked up as she heard her name carried on the breeze. Her father stood on the stoop, the telephone held up in his hand. He was a big man, his ruddy complexion visible from here beneath the ubiquitous cloth cap pushed back on his bull head.

'A call for you!'

IV

Enzo watched as the tractor backed into the shed, manoeuvering the blue Rock trailer up to the *pressoir*. It rose on pneumatic cross-levers until its funnel slipped into the mouth of the press, and the giant screw inside the trailer started turning, gently mashing the grapes into their constituent parts of juice, skin, seed, and stalk. Somehow, somewhere in the machine, the stalks got separated from the grapes and were spat out into large plastic bins, while the juice and skins and seeds were pumped under pressure through a plastic tube leading into the next shed. A man crouched beneath the *pressoir*, gently feeding clear liquid from a plastic bottle into the mix.

'SO_2. Sulphur dioxide,' Laurent de Bonneval shouted above the roar of the motors. 'Kills the bad bacteria without

damaging the yeasts, and protects the wine from oxidation.'
He was wearing a wine-stained tee shirt, ragged shorts, and a
pair of green Wellington boots.

He turned back to sheafs of paper he was examining on
a table pushed up against the wall. A table littered with
charts and weather forecasts and handwritten notes, test
tubes and pipettes. A bin beside it was full of empty tins
labelled *Lafase He Grand Cru*. Idly, Enzo picked one up to read
that it had contained 'purified pectolytic enzymes' for increasing the 'selective extraction of compounds from grape
skins'.

Bonneval grinned. 'There's a lot of science in winemaking,
Monsieur Macleod. We balance sulphites against pH. We
measure sugar and acidity and alcohol. We use cold to inhibit
fermentation, heat to accelerate it. But, really, it's much more
than that. It's about instinct, and flair, and sophistry. A kind
of alchemy. Magic, if you will.' He turned towards the mixture
being squeezed out of the *pressoir*. 'Two winemakers can take
the same grapes, from the same vintage, and produce entirely
different wines. One might give you soft, vanilla fruit, the
other tannic green pepper. It could even be argued that a
wine reflects the personality of the winemaker.'

'And what do *you* make, Monsieur de Bonneval? Soft vanilla
fruit, or tannic green pepper?'

Bonneval smiled, brown eyes full of mischief and amusement. 'Oh, soft vanilla fruit, of course. These days winemakers
must pander to the tastes of critics who grew up drinking
Coca Cola and root beer.'

'Which says what about your personality?'

He threw his head back and laughed. 'Probably just that I'm a man keen to sell his wines.'

Enzo followed him through to the adjoining shed where red flexitubes, like giant worms, lay about the floor, attached to motorised pumps moving grape juice under pressure between tanks. Workers were dragging tubes from one black bucket full of foaming pink juice to another, then hauling them up ladders to grilled walkways overhead which provided access to the tops of two rows of huge stainless steel vats. The air was filled with the distinctive smell of mashed grapes and alcohol, thick and heady. And all the time the roar of the *pressoir* and the pulse of the pumps assaulted the ears.

Bonneval led Enzo up a steel staircase to the network of walkways above. He pointed to the tube feeding the incoming mix from the *pressoir*. It was tied to the rail beside the top of the nearest vat, and you could see the grape juice pulsing through its semi-translucent skin as it thundered up and then out and down again into the vast, black emptiness of a container that held one hundred and fifty hectolitres. Enzo did a quick calculation. That was fifteen thousand litres. Or twenty thousand bottles. A lot of wine.

'Once the *cuve* is filled, we let the juice settle,' Bonneval said. 'The skins and seeds rise to the top. So we extract the juice from the bottom and pump it back into the top, remixing the *must* to get the maximum flavour. Sometimes at high speed. Sometimes transferring the entire contents of one *cuve* to another. Which also helps to oxygenate it, which in turn combines with the yeast to produce more heat, and therefore more alcohol.' He grinned. 'Another reason why we want to pick the grapes at maximum maturity. Sugar plus heat equals alcohol. And wine wouldn't be quite the same without the alcohol now, would it?'

'So you measure the sugar content of the grapes before you pick?'

'Daily, as we get near harvest time. We also taste test them for sweetness and flavour. And when the seeds have turned brown, and you can crush them between your teeth, you know they are ripe.' He turned back towards the *cuve*. 'Of course, we also need to control the heat that gets generated during fermentation. Too much heat equals too much alcohol, and you ruin the wine.' He pointed to large black tubes running around the outer walls of the *chai*. 'Cold water. We run small-er tubes down into each tank to feed cold water through fila-ments like radiators that hang down inside them. That way we can stop the mixture from overheating.'

They went back down to the floor of the *chai* and walked through to a third shed. 'We have twenty stainless steel *cuves* now,' Bonneval said. Enzo did another calculation and blew a silent whistle through pursed lips. That was four hundred thousand bottles of wine! Bonneval was still talking. 'Before that we used resin tanks, made from fibreglass.' He indicated a row of half a dozen tan-coloured tanks with lids that were raised and lowered by an old-fashioned pulley system. 'But we don't use them for primary production any more. Before that, the *cuves* were made of concrete. We store some of our *rosé* in those now.' He turned to Enzo. 'But enough of that. Let's go and taste some of the finished product.'

They went out through huge sliding doors into the dying light. The air still carried the warmth of the day, and even outside was saturated with the smell of fermenting wine. The fields around the *chai* were full of ripening corn. Bonneval took them past a disused tennis court, weeds poking up through cracks in the tarmac, and a tall, brick *pigeonnier* built on arches.

'You see these *pigeonniers* everywhere,' Enzo said. 'People around here must have liked pigeons.'

The lord of the manor chuckled. 'In Gaillac, Monsieur Macleod, in the Middle Ages, they used pigeon shit as fertiliser in the vineyards. So most vineyards had at least one *pigeonnier*. Of course, they also ate the birds, and a girl with a dowry of pigeons was considered to be a real catch.'

They passed a kitchen garden whose season was nearly over, and went through an arched gate into a courtyard bounded by the main *château* on the south side and long, low wings to the east and west. The west wing had been the *chai*, or wine cellar, since the nineteenth century, Bonneval said. The east wing had been the original *chai*, then later provided stabling for the horses. The *château* itself, a patchwork of new and old brick, cement and stone, had seen better days. It was impressive nonetheless, standing foursquare at the end of a long, straight, tree-lined drive, its walled gardens just metres from the banks of the river Tarn. The original house was built on three levels, and then extended on two at either side some time later.

They went up steps to the main door and into a dark, stone-flagged hall. At the far end of it, tall wooden doors stood ajar, opening into a circular room whose walls were lined with elaborately framed mirrors and paintings. It was a clutter of antique furniture and family heirlooms.

But Bonneval took them east, down a long corridor lit by north-facing windows. All the doors opened into south-facing rooms. 'To harvest the summer sun, and protect us from the north wind,' Bonneval said. 'Our ancestors knew a thing or two about designing buildings.'

Enzo became aware now of the smell of good things cooking, and his host opened a door into the family apartment, where they were greeted by a soft, warm light and the gentle, welcoming smile of Jacqueline de Bonneval.

Enzo let the smooth velvety liquid fill his mouth, breathing in through his nose, and experiencing the wonderful flavours and aromas of toasted oak, rich red fruit, and spicy pepper. As he let it slip back over his throat, it left a slight acid freshness on his tongue and, long after his mouth was empty, there lingered hints of blackcurrant and liquorice. For several moments he was completely absorbed by it, before looking up to find Laurent de Bonneval watching him with wide-eyed anticipation. 'Well?'

Enzo shook his head, trying to find words to describe his feelings about the wine. He swirled the deep, garnet-red liquid in a wide-bottomed glass that tapered up to a narrower lip. And in the end, he gave up. 'Fabulous,' was all he could find to say, aware of how inadequate that was.

Bonneval beamed nonetheless. 'It's our *cuvée spéciale*, 2002. Petty liked it, too. A blend of cabernet, braucol, duras, and syrah. Aged in oak, of course. You know, we decant the wine from the barrels from time to time and move it around. Every barrel is different, you see, so it helps with the consistency. And the oxygenation improves the ageing.' He put a confidential finger to his lips. 'But don't tell anyone.' He grinned and filled Enzo's glass as his wife served up platters of *confit de canard* and cubed roast potatoes with garlic and *cèpe* mushrooms.

Jacqueline de Bonneval was not at all what Enzo had been expecting. She was a small, plump lady with an unlined, pretty face. Her hair was the colour of brushed steel, thick and luxuriant, and drawn back in a bushy ponytail at least six inches longer than Enzo's. It had been hard to put an age on Bonneval. Early fifties, Enzo had thought earlier. But meeting Madame de Bonneval he had been forced to reassess his first impression. She was nearer sixty than fifty and, unless she was a good deal older than Laurent, Enzo must have been about ten years out in his initial appraisal.

'I like your ponytail,' she said to Enzo as she pulled in a chair to the table.

Enzo said, 'You know, when I was first in France, and my French wasn't what it is now, I always used to mispronounce that, and I never knew why people were laughing.' Neither

Jacqueline nor her husband could guess at how me might have mispronounced it. So he demonstrated. '*Cul de cheval*,' he said, and they both burst out laughing. It only took a slight mispronunciation for 'horse's tail' to become 'horse's ass'. Enzo smiled ruefully. 'I'm older and wiser now.' He paused, and looked appreciatively at Madame de Bonneval. 'And you have a much more impressive ponytail than mine, madame.'

They started to eat. The duck was moist and fall-apart tender, with a crispy skin that melted in the mouth. And Enzo thought the potato, garlic, and *cèpe* mix was the best he had ever tasted.

A door opened from the hall, and a tall young man emerged from the gathering gloom of the *château*. His tee shirt was torn and stained, his green boots blackened by red grape juice. 'Papa?'

Enzo watched Bonneval's face light up as he turned towards his son, dark eyes brimful of affection. 'Come in, Charles, come in. Meet Monsieur Macleod. He's a Scotsman. Come to find out who murdered Gil Petty.'

Charles glanced distractedly towards Enzo. He nodded and offered a cursory handshake. '*Enchanté*, monsieur.' But his mind was on other things. He turned back to his father. 'Michel Vidal claims you said he could have the harvester tonight.'

Bonneval roared with laughter. 'What do *you* think?'

'I think Vidal knows the rain's on its way and he's trying to pull a fast one.'

Bonneval grinned at Enzo. 'The boy's not daft.'

Charles seemed embarrassed. His fresh, pink complexion darkened. Large-lobed ears poking out from a tangle of black curls glowed hot and red. He glanced self-consciously at Enzo.

But his father was oblivious to his discomfort. 'Just completed a degree course in viticulture at Bordeaux University. He's the future of the *château*, Monsieur Macleod. The future of the wine. But more than that, he loves driving that harvester. Am I right, son?'

'I'll tell Guillaume to send Vidal packing.'

'Sit at the table, Charles.' His mother pulled out a chair. 'There's enough for four.'

'I can't, *maman*, I've got to get the machine ready.'

'See?' Bonneval cocked an eyebrow at Enzo.

'It was nice to meet you, Monsieur Macleod.' Charles glanced at his watch. 'Excuse me.' And he beat a hasty retreat.

'He's going to be a much better winemaker than his father.' Bonneval's pride in his son was nearly palpable. 'Knows more about the science of it all than I ever did.'

Madame de Bonneval sighed. 'Just one more in a long line of Bonnevals who's going to sacrifice his life to the Château Saint-Michel.'

'It's his birthright,' Bonneval said. 'His inheritance.' He paused for momentary reflection. 'His duty.'

From where he was sitting at the big table in the kitchen, Enzo could see through a door into a sitting room dominated by a huge marble *cheminée*. 'Is this the only part of the château you live in?'

'Good God, yes,' Bonneval said. 'We could never heat the whole place. And in winter it's damned cold, I can tell you. My ancestors had notions of grandeur, but they must have been hardy souls, too.'

'How long has Château Saint-Michel been in your family?' Enzo sipped more wine.

'There have been Bonnevals on this land since the thirteenth century, Monsieur Macleod. More than seven hundred years. The *château* isn't quite that old, but the original building dates back to the fifteenth century. It was my ancestor, Hubert de Bonneval, who was responsible for most of its enlargement in the late seventeen hundreds.' He took another mouthful of wine, warming to his subject. 'He had grand plans for the place. Bought a brick factory, just to make bricks for the expansion. But it also made him a lot of money, which helped pay for it, too.' He paused, his face clouding at some unhappy memory. 'Sadly, he never finished it, and in fact the east wing of the house was almost destroyed by fire. It was his son who took up the project again in the early nineteenth century, and he's pretty much accountable for what you see today.'

'It's an enormous responsibility,' Madame de Bonneval said. 'I know that Laurent feels the weight of history on his shoulders. It's important that the wine of Château Saint-Michel is successful just so that we can afford the upkeep of the building.'

Enzo took another sip from his glass. 'With wine this good, I don't see how you can fail.'

But Bonneval just shrugged. 'At eight euros a bottle, monsieur, we're never going to get rich on it.'

Enzo shook his head. 'It's crazy. There are Bordeaux wines costing fifty and sixty euros a bottle that aren't a patch on this.'

'Yes, but ask any wine drinker in America if he's heard of Bordeaux and he'll laugh at the stupidity of your question. Ask him if he's ever heard of Gaillac, and you'll get a vacant look and a shake of the head.' The winemaker sipped thoughtfully on the product of his own vineyard. 'Gaillac is one of the great undiscovered wines of France, Monsieur Macleod. We've been making wine here for more than two thousand years, even before the Romans arrived. But very few people outside of the area have heard of it. We were victims of our own geography.' He waved a hand towards the window. 'Out there is the river Tarn. It was the only way people could get their wines out to the world. It was our bad luck that the Tarn runs into the Garonne, which takes it to Bordeaux. There, we were obliged to unload our wines before shipping them on to other destinations.

'Unfortunately, the Bordelaise didn't relish the competition. So they levied taxes on us, built weirs and damns across the river, and charged us to use the locks to bypass them. Effectively, they choked off our trading route to the rest of the world. Which today is why Americans have heard of Bordeaux and not of Gaillac.' He sighed. 'But we made good wines, Monsieur Macleod. The *vin du coq* was shipped in barrels branded with the symbol of the rooster, and drunk in royal households around Europe. It was a great favourite of François Premier.

But with the Bordelaise barring our way out, and then the phylloxera wiping out the vines, winemaking in Gaillac was all but finished by the end of the nineteenth century. It's only during the last thirty years that young, innovative wine-makers have restored our wines to their former glory. The trouble is, nobody knows about them. Which is why Petty's death was such a blow. He was about to introduce Gaillac wines to the rest of the world. Instead, they still languish in underpriced obscurity.'

The lights of the *chai* blazed out from open doors into the dark of the night. The sky was ink black, peppered with stars, the merest blush of colour still staining the western horizon. 'Where did you park?' Bonneval asked.

'I didn't. I walked.'

Bonneval looked at him with surprise. 'Walked? It's a good three kilometres back to Château des Fleurs.'

'I need the exercise, Monsieur de Bonneval. Besides, I've drunk a fair bit of your excellent wine tonight, and it might not have been a good idea to drive.'

'It's a long way in the dark, though.' He thought for a moment. 'You know, there's a shortcut through the vineyard. If you give me a few minutes, I'll walk part of the way with you. We have a night pick tonight. By hand. And the machine will be out as well.'

As he followed the winemaker into his *chai*, Enzo rubbed his chin thoughtfully. 'I read in Raffin's notes that Petty's body was discovered during a night pick. Why on earth do you harvest grapes in the dark?'

'Usually just the white ones, Monsieur Macleod. They generate more heat during fermentation, so it's better to pick them when they're cool. Also, at night, the sap rises in the vine and the grapes are fatter, juicier.' He grinned. 'More alchemy. Tonight, though, we'll be bringing in the red as well. With the big harvester. The weather is forecast to break in a few days, so I want to strip the vines before it rains.'

They passed the tasting room, and a tall wooden table littered with bottles and notes. There were used oak barrels, stained red from the wine, stacked up against the wall behind it.

'If you want to wait for me here,' Bonneval said, 'I just need to have a few words with my foreman.' And he headed off into the roar of pumps and *pressoir* in the adjoining sheds. If the harvester was going to be out in the dark, clearly that meant that grapes would be coming into the sheds all night. Enzo glanced at some of the paperwork on the desk. A jotter was filled with notes made in a small, tight hand. They looked like mathematical equations. But Enzo could make no sense of them. There was an official leaflet on new hygiene practices in winemaking, an analytical report on grapes sent to the Laboratoire Oenologique Départmentale in Gaillac, a *fiche de vinification* from the Centre Technique du Vin, with graphs charting levels of sugar and alcohol. There was a great deal more to winemaking, Enzo reflected, than simply crushing grapes.

He heard a thump that seemed to come from a room off the dark end of the shed. He listened for a few moments, wondering if there was someone there. But there were no further sounds. The door to the room lay ajar, and there was a light burning faintly from somewhere within. Curiosity got the better of him, and Enzo crossed the shed and pushed the door open to look inside.

Along the right-hand wall was a row of what looked like six ceramic chimneys rising out of a concrete apron, flexible pipes feeding into them from black tubing around the walls. Cold water. And Enzo realised that these were the tops of *cuves* which had been sunk into the ground. To the left of them, a red staircase went down at angles into a square pit below, where sealed hatches gave access to the bottoms of the tanks, presumably for cleaning. A railing ran around the top of the pit, and steps led up half a metre to another level where several more ceramic chimneys were sunk in concrete. There were hoses strewn everywhere, and tubing ran from a pump above the pit to an open door leading out to the castle courtyard, as well as into the pit itself. The source of the light was down in the pit, and the rest of the room was in darkness.

Enzo could not see what had made the thumping sound, but he was drawn in by his curiosity nonetheless. He made his way along the top edge of the pit, holding on to the rail, until he reached the staircase. He peered down into it, but could see no sign of life. 'Hello?' he called, and moved on to the top step.

'For Christ's sake man, don't move!'

Enzo turned, startled, to see Bonneval silhouetted in the doorway.

'Just step away from the stairs and come towards me.'

Bewildered, Enzo did as he was told, and Bonneval flicked on a light switch, flooding the room with a harsh, cold light.

'If you'd gone down there, you'd be dead before you reached the bottom of the stairs. There are accidents like that in wine cellars every year.'

Enzo was still none the wiser. 'I don't understand.'

Bonneval crouched to remove the lid from the nearest *cuve*. It was filled almost to the top with white, frothing grape juice. The top of a cold water radiator broke the surface, but the liquid looked as if it were boiling. 'It's in full fermentation,' Bonneval said, 'and when wine is fermenting, particularly the white, it produces copious amounts of carbonic gas.'

And suddenly Enzo understood why he had been in such danger. The gas in itself wasn't poisonous. It dissolved in water, and was what made fizzy drinks fizzy. It was what put the bubbles in champagne. But it was heavier than air, and would fill your lungs like water, displacing all oxygen, and killing you in seconds.

'The gas escapes from the tops of the *cuves* and sinks down into the pit. You can't see it, but it's down there. One lungful, my friend, and you're dead.'

It was with some relief that Enzo stepped back out into the safety of the shed. His legs had turned to jelly, and he became aware that his hands were trembling. And it wasn't the effects of the wine he'd had over dinner. Quite unwittingly, he had come uncomfortably close to killing himself. 'I'll never think about champagne the same way again,' he said. 'Although I could do with a glass right now.'

'I think you've had more than enough to drink already tonight, Monsieur Macleod. Especially if you're going to be walking home alone in the dark.'

'I thought you were coming with me? At least some of the way.'

'I'm afraid I can't. We have a problem with the *pressoir*. But I'll point you in the right direction.' And as they walked out into the courtyard, Bonneval said, 'By the way, I've got you a grape-picking job on a neighbouring *domaine*. It's a farm, not a *château*, but they have thirty-seven hectares of vines at La Croix Blanche, and a young winemaker, Fabien Marre, who's producing some very good wines.'

'Sounds ideal,' Enzo said.

'I've told him you're an old friend who wants to experience the *vendange*. They still do quite a bit of picking by hand, where most of ours is mechanised. It's just up the road from where you're staying. But here's the interesting thing. It was on the south-facing upper slopes of Marre's vineyard that Petty's body was found.'

V

The dusty track shone silver in the moonlight, as did the strips of chalky, stony soil between the rows of vines that stretched away into the darkness on either side. The track was raised a metre or more above the vines, and Enzo had a fine moon-lit view across the floodplain of the Tarn. Away to his right, he saw the lights of the *vendangeurs* hand-picking the mau-zac grapes for the *vin mousseux*, a wine produced in almost identical fashion to champagne, except that in Gaillac there was no final addition of sugar before the bottle was sealed. It was known as *méthode gaillacoise*, and had most of the at-tributes of champagne at a fraction of the price. Enzo had discovered it many years before. He could hear the voices of the grape-pickers in the distance, the lamps on their helmets dancing in the dark like demented fireflies.

The air was still balmy and soft, redolent with the heady scent of ripe fruit. Fresh from having consumed several glasses of it, Enzo reflected on what a fine creation wine really was. He was wondering how on earth man had first stumbled upon the secret processes of fermentation, when he was star-tled by the sudden roar of an engine off to his left. Lights from a massive mechanical harvester flooded the vineyard, and Enzo stopped for a moment to watch as it began its steady progress along the first row towards him. He felt the ground shaking beneath his feet, and thought that he preferred the gentler sounds of the *vendangeurs* picking by hand.

He carried on along the track and had covered less than twenty metres when a dark shadow loomed unexpectedly out of his peripheral vision. He had no time to turn before some-thing struck him hard on the side of his head. The pain was intense, but short-lived as the night burned out in a glare of bright light before plunging to black.

It was like struggling up through a sea of treacle, fighting to break the surface. And when, finally, he did, it brought only pain. And light. And noise. And confusion.

Enzo had no idea where he was. His head hurt like hell. Like the worst migraine he'd ever had. He smelled earth and leaves. And something sweet. Something rich and dark and seductive. Grapes. He tried to focus. But still he was blinded by the light. He blinked furiously to try to clear his vision without success. The roaring in his ears, he thought, must be the blood pulsing through his head. He put his hand to his face and felt something sticky and warm, and he could smell it, even above the scent of grapes. The blood wasn't in his head, it was coming out of it. He started to panic and tried to get to his feet, but his legs wouldn't support him. He found himself clutching vine leaves, searching for support. Grapes burst in his grasping hand, and he felt the juice running down his arm. And still the noise got louder.

He looked down and realised that he could see perfectly well. Blood and grape juice mixed together in his hands. He looked up again only to be blinded once more by the light. But this time, something was emerging from its glare. The dark, ridged tread of a tyre that stood a metre high and was turning relentlessly towards him. Somehow the light had risen above him now and, with a sudden clarity, he realised he was about to be crushed by the giant mechanical harvester he had been watching earlier. A machine probably driven by Bonneval's son, oblivious to the fact that he was about to kill the man he had been introduced to less than an hour before.

It was almost on top him, the thrum of its motor unbearably loud. The ground shook as if gripped by a seismic event of Richter scale magnitude. The vine was being rattled and shredded as interlocking bars on either side of it ripped the grapes from their stems. Some powerful suction drew them up into the body of the beast. And still Enzo's legs would not support him. He shouted at the thing in futile desperation, but there was nothing he could do to stop it from running over him. Then, at the very last moment, with a great effort, he rolled himself to one side, into the narrowest of gaps between the wheel and the adjoining row of vines. The rubber of the tyre grazed his face as it went past, and he was struck by a huge blast of hot air that carried in it stinging fragments of stalk and leaf and grape skin, and a fine mist of grape juice.

It left him sticky-wet and gasping for breath. The noise and the lights receded as the machine carried on towards the far end of the field, Charles de Bonneval unaware that he had very nearly crushed a man to death.

Enzo managed to get to his knees and started crawling back towards the path where he had been walking, some twenty or thirty metres away. He found his shoulder bag lying discarded to one side and, clutching a wire strung between posts to support the vines, finally succeeded in getting to his feet. For several minutes, he stood there, unsteady, gasping for breath, fighting the nausea that accompanied the pain in his head and realised that someone had just tried to murder him.

CHAPTER THREE

There were no lights on in the *château* when finally he got back, exhausted, head still pounding. It was after midnight. Clearly the Lefèvres had gone to bed, and as far as Enzo knew there were no guests staying in the *chambres d'hôtes*. Moonlight flooded the gravel courtyard and the garden beyond, the white stone of the *château* almost glowing in the dark. The entrance to the *gîte* was cast in profound shadow and, as he walked towards it through grass already wet with dew, he fumbled in his pockets for the key. He was one step from emerging into moonlight from the deep gloom of the chestnut trees, when a movement on the *terrasse* of the cottage caught his eye. Something glinting. The tiniest shard of reflected light. He stopped dead, every nerve and sinew in his body held in a state of extreme tension. In the absolute still of the night his own breathing seemed thunderous.

Fear wrapped itself around him like a cloak, raising goosebumps across his shoulders. He began to shiver in the warm night. Someone had tried to kill him little more than half an hour before. It had taken him that time to make his way home. Why wouldn't his would-be killer have got there ahead of him, having failed at the first attempt?

Enzo had no idea what to do. Confront his assailant and risk further injury or even death? Or retreat to somewhere safe where he could think? But where? In the end, he decided on a middle course – to try to get a closer look at whoever was waiting for him on the *terrasse*.

Away to his left was Pierric Lefèvre's *chai*, a long, low building covered in ivy. He backed off towards it, still in the shadow of the trees, until he was within a metre or two of the far end. Quickly, he ducked across the path and out of sight of the cottage. He stopped to listen for any sound of movement. But all he heard was the distant hooting of an owl.

He circled around the back of the *chai* until he reached the far end. From here he had a direct view across a short stretch of gravel path towards the steps of the cottage. It was still mired in darkness, but he could just make out the shape of a figure sitting at the table. Waiting for him.

Staying within the long shadow cast by the wine shed, he moved carefully across open ground to press himself against the gable end of the house. Anxious not to disturb the ivy, he craned his head around the wall to try to get a better look at his unwanted visitor. To his horror, the detector on the halogen lamp high up on the end of the *chai* picked up his movement and the whole area was flooded with light. He cursed under his breath. Run? Or attack while he still had the element of surprise? He decided in a fraction of a second to opt for the latter and ran for the steps, exposing himself to the full glare of the light.

Something soft and heavy caught him just above the knee

and he went toppling over it, sprawling across the lower steps. He looked back to see a large suitcase as it fell with a thud. It seemed strangely familiar.

A figure rose up above him as he turned.

'Monsieur Macleod! What on earth are you doing?' Nicole gawped at him in amazement as he scrambled to his feet.

He looked up at her, holding on to the rail to stop himself falling over again, and saw the look of incredulity verging on horror that wrote itself across her face. Were he able to see himself he would have realised why. He was spattered head to toe with red grape juice, trousers and shirt mud-stained and torn. Bits of leaf and dirt clung to him, fixed by the glue of the fruit. There was dried blood down one side of his face. His ponytail had long since lost the band that held it, and his hair was a shock of sticky clumps and curls tumbling wildly over his shoulders.

She opened her mouth to speak, but for several moments nothing came out. Then she said, 'Are you alright?'

Fear, which had given way to humiliation, now lurched towards anger. 'No, I'm not alright. Do I look alright?'

She shook her head slowly, still staring in wide-eyed astonishment. 'No. No, you don't.'

Nicole was a big girl of good farming stock, wide-hipped and large-breasted, the antithesis of the skinny, flat-chested French girls in the TV ads and on magazine covers. She had a pretty face, though, and long silky brown hair which she gathered loosely at her neck before leaving it to cascade down her back.

She was, by a long way, the brightest student in Enzo's biology class, perhaps the brightest student of her year. But her upbringing on a remote hill farm in the Auvergne had left her somewhat lacking in sophistication. She was gauche and shy and had suffered the gibes and taunts of her more streetwise peers during her first year of university in Toulouse.

Enzo had taken her on early that first summer to help him crack the Gaillard case. There was, it seemed, nothing she didn't know about computers, and she could surf and navigate her way around the internet like an experienced sailor. He needed help again, so he had asked her for a few days of her time before the first semester of the new university year got under way. He knew, too, that she had spent much of the summer nursing her dying mother, and that she could probably do with the break.

When he came out of the shower wrapped in a towelling robe, blood was running down the side of his head where the hot water had reopened his wound. She made him sit in a chair while she pressed a clean towel against his head to stop the bleeding. Her large breasts quivered at eye level, just centimetres from Enzo's face, and he tried hard not to look at them. They were, he reflected, Nicole's most outstanding feature, a subject of discussion on more than one occasion amongst male lecturers in the staffroom at the university. She always seemed intent on making the most of them, wearing tee shirts a size too small, or low-cut tops that revealed acres of cleavage. Hoping, perhaps, to attract attention. Which, of course, they did. Always of the wrong kind.

Enzo closed his eyes.

'Do we have any disinfectant, Monsieur Macleod?'

'Coping with the aftermath of an attempt on my life wasn't one of the things I considered when packing my bags, Nicole.'

'You should always be prepared.' Nicole was nothing if not practical.

'There's really nothing prepares you for someone trying to kill you.'

'You must be exaggerating. Are you sure you didn't just trip, or something, and fall in front of that harvester.'

Enzo contained his irritation by clenching his teeth. 'Someone hit me on the head, Nicole.'

'Had you been drinking?' She sniffed his breath.

'What's that got to do with it?'

'I thought as much.' She looked around the room. 'Ah, that'll do.'

Enzo turned to watch as she headed for the bottle of malt whisky on the table. 'Good idea. Make it a large one.'

She lifted the bottle and tutted. 'You've probably had more than enough already, Monsieur Macleod.' She unwrapped the seal and pulled out the cork. 'It'll make an ideal disinfectant.'

'Nicole, that's a thirty-year-old Glenlivet single malt!' Enzo watched in horror as she soaked the towel in the pale amber liquid and came back to press it once more to his head. 'Jesus!' He flinched from the pain. Not only was it a criminal waste of good whisky, but it hurt like hell.

Nicole held him firm. 'Don't be a baby.' She glanced up at the whiteboard. 'So this is the Petty case we're looking at?'

'You've read up on it, haven't you?'

She nodded. 'Disappeared four years ago.'

'From this very *gîte*!'

'Really? God, that's spooky.' She thought about it for a moment. 'The autopsy report said he'd drowned in wine, then twelve months later turned up in a Gaillac vineyard pickled red and partially preserved. Why would he do that?'

'Petty?'

'The killer. If he'd got away with it for a whole year, and no one even knew for sure that Petty was dead, why did he suddenly draw attention to it?'

'If we knew that, we'd probably know who did it.'

'Did you bring the laptop?'

He nodded, then winced from the pain. 'We'll set it up in the morning.' And, as an afterthought, 'Where are you staying?'

'Here, of course.'

He pulled away from the towel. 'Nicole, you can't!'

'Why not?'

'Because there's only one bedroom. And I don't want your father storming in here and accusing me of trying to have my wicked way with you.'

She blushed to the roots of her hair, and her eyes strayed away self-consciously towards a rickety open staircase leading up to a gloomy mezzanine built into the roof. 'What's up there?'

'A couple of kid's bunk beds that wouldn't do for either of us.'

She looked at the settee. 'That's a *clic-clac*. Folds down into a bed. You could have that.'

'Why couldn't *you* have that?'

'Monsieur Macleod! I need the privacy of my own room.'

Enzo sighed.

'And one other thing,' she made a face, 'I hate to ask, but . . . do you think you could bring my suitcase up the steps? It's too heavy for me.'

Enzo's frustration released itself in an explosion of air from between his lips. 'Nicole, why can't you ever travel light?'

'Because unlike you, Monsieur Macleod, I always come prepared.'

Enzo knew of old that when it came to things practical, there was no point in arguing with Nicole. She would make a fine wife and mother some day, if she could ever find a man. He eased himself to his feet and walked stiffly across the room, every muscle in his body complaining. In the doorway he stopped and turned. 'How's your mum?'

A shadow fell across Nicole's face as if the light had dimmed. 'Not so good.'

She lay in the dark, the bedroom window open to the night, and gazed up at the reflected moonlight on the ceiling. For a short time she had been able to forget, to occupy herself with Monsieur Macleod and his injuries. To listen to his story of attempted murder among the vines and feel the thrill of his danger. It hadn't occurred to her that if her mentor were in danger, then she might be too.

But any such thoughts were crowded out by the returning memory of her mother wasting away in the dark, holding her daughter's hand, like she was holding onto life. She felt hot tears filling her eyes and turned over to blink them away, spilling them onto the pillow. And for a moment she fantasised that maybe the door would open as she was drifting off and Monsieur Macleod would slip between the sheets beside her, folding himself into the curve of her back. And that he would just hold her. Just for the comfort of it.

CHAPTER FOUR

I

The early morning sky was a burnished gold, painting the edges of the leaves a fiery red and throwing long shadows from the *pigeonnier* towards the *gîte*. And as the sun slid slowly up above the distant treeline, it suffused the main room with a warm autumn light to accompany the rap of knuckles on glass.

Enzo lifted his head sharply, painfully, at the sound of knocking on the half-glazed front door, only to be blinded by the light that flooded through it. He could see the silhouette of a figure on the *terrasse* trying to see beyond the reflections in the glass.

He had slept soundly enough, but the *clic-clac* was hard and uncomfortable and had done his aching body no favours. He groaned as he swung his legs out from the covers and found the floor with his feet. He reached for his bathrobe and dragged it on, sweeping his hair back from his face and walking stiffly to the door. Blinking in the sunlight as he swung it open, he found himself looking into the quizzical green eyes of Michelle Petty.

She looked him up and down with naked curiosity, eyes

lingering a moment on the blood-stained lapel of his robe, before examining the dried blood around the wound high up on the side of his head. Then she focused on his eyes and he blinked self-consciously.

'Been in a fight?'

He unstuck his tongue from the roof of his mouth. 'You could say that.'

'Well, aren't you going to ask me in?'

'Sure.'

He opened the door wide, just as Nicole stepped out from the bedroom, stretching sleepily, her dressing gown hanging open over a flimsy nightdress. 'What's all the noise?'

Michelle looked at her, surprise giving way to . . . what? Disapproval? Enzo wasn't sure. But when she turned her eyes back towards him, all warmth in them had vanished. 'I think maybe I've made an error of judgment,' she said. 'I'll not bother you any further, Mister Macleod.' She turned to hurry down the steps.

'No, hang on . . .' Enzo started after her.

'Who was that?' Nicole said.

He turned back in the doorway and stabbed a finger in her direction. 'You. Make yourself decent and pack your bag. You're not staying here another night.'

'Well, where'll I go?'

'I don't know. Get yourself a cheap room somewhere.'

'The *château* does *chambres d'hôtes*.'

'Aye, at a hundred and twenty euros a night. *Cheap*, I said. I'm not made of money. And try and get somewhere close by. I don't want you sleeping over, but you're going to be spending most of your days here.'

Michelle had passed under the *pigeonnier* where a child's swing stirred slightly in the early morning breeze and was heading towards the parking at the end of the drive when Enzo caught up with her. 'Look, I'm sorry. Nicole . . . she's not what you think.'

Michele didn't miss a step. 'Why would it matter to you what I think?'

'Well, I wouldn't want you thinking I'm the sort of man who preys on young women.'

'She certainly is young. More girl than woman, I'd have said.'

'She's one of my students.'

They reached her rental car and she turned to face him. 'It just keeps getting worse.' She paused. 'I thought you were a forensics expert.'

'*Former* forensics expert. I'm a professor of biology now at a university in Toulouse. They asked me to set up a department of forensic science after we cracked the Gaillard case.'

'We?'

Enzo glanced back towards the *gîte*. 'Nicole's been working as my assistant for a bit of extra cash.' He added quickly, 'I'm not sleeping with her.'

'It's of absolutely no interest to me who you sleep with.' She looked down at his bare feet on the gravel path and then again at his bruised face and the dried blood matting his hair.

'You seem an unusual sort of man, Mister Macleod. Who were you fighting with?'

'Someone tried to murder me last night, Miss Petty. Cracked me on the skull and dumped me in the path of a mechanical harvester. I was very nearly just another elusive flavour in a bottle of wine.'

She frowned. A look of genuine shock in her eyes. 'Why would someone want to murder you?'

'Because they don't want me finding out who killed your father.' She drifted away into unspoken thought. 'Why did you come here?'

She dragged back her focus from some distant place. 'I didn't sleep much last night, thinking about what you said yesterday. I thought maybe . . .' Her voice tailed away.

'You might take me up on my offer?'

'I'm not sure, Mister Macleod. I mean, what do you really care about me or my father? I might be useful to you, that's all.'

'Someone tried to kill me last night, Miss Petty, which makes this very personal to me. I'm going to find your father's killer whether you help me or not.'

II

There was a weariness in Roussel's demeanour as he showed them into his office.

'I knew it was a mistake to tell you about Mademoiselle

Petty.' He glared at Enzo. 'Now you've come back to haunt me, like all mistakes do.'

'Could we do this in English?' Michelle said. Although she spoke passable French, she found Roussel's accent impenetrable.

Roussel looked to Enzo for elucidation, then shrugged when Enzo obliged. 'We did it through another *gendarme* last time whose English was pretty poor. I think yours is better, monsieur.'

Enzo explained to Michelle, then turned back to the Frenchman. 'Mademoiselle Petty has engaged me to represent her interests in the recovery of her father's personal belongings.' He ignored the *gendarme's* theatrical sigh. 'And to achieve closure on the unanswered question of who murdered him and why.'

'I've already told you, monsieur, we're not an information service for private investigators.'

'Mademoiselle Petty has an absolute right to take possession of her father's things. They are legally hers.'

'Then she is entitled to make her request through the proper channels.'

'What's he saying?' Michelle's frustration was patent.

'He's being an officious bastard,' Enzo told her. Then he turned back to Roussel. 'There's not a single reason in the world for you to hold onto that stuff. I'm quite sure the *Police Scientifique* at Albi went over everything with a fine-toothed comb at the time. No doubt the reports are in the file. Now we can do this the easy way, and you can sign release forms right here and now. Or we can do it the hard way, and I'll make a personal complaint to the Préfet about police obstruction.'

Roussel fixed him with a long hard stare, before his face slowly melted into a smile. Enzo had no idea what he found amusing. 'I admire your balls, monsieur. There are not many Frenchmen who would have spoken to a *gendarme* the way you've just spoken to me.'

'The Scots are renowned for being bolshie.'

'I know. I've watched your countrymen play rugby against *La France*. I shudder to think what goes on in the scrum.'

Enzo couldn't resist a smile. On whatever other subjects the Scots and the French might diverge, they always found common ground on the rugby pitch. Especially against the English.

'What, are we sharing a joke now?' Michelle's frustration was turning to irritation.

Roussel ignored her. 'Alright, monsieur. I'll let her take her father's things. But as for access to other evidence, my answer's still the same.'

'Well?' Michelle was impatient to know what was happening.

Enzo said, 'He's agreed. You can take your dad's stuff. But knowing the French, there'll be a blizzard of paperwork.'

Through a window that opened into the courtyard, Enzo could see Michelle fighting that blizzard at reception. Roussel lit a cigarette and blew smoke speculatively in Enzo's direction. The sun was rising above the shallow pitch of the roof, glancing brick-red off terracotta Roman tiles, and spilling across the courtyard towards the residences. A low-ranking *gendarme* in shirt sleeves was washing the boss's car. Roussel tipped his head towards Enzo's injuries. 'Too much to drink last night?'

'Someone tried to kill me.'

The cigarette paused halfway to the *gendarme's* mouth, the smoke hanging in the still morning air with the same sense of suspended animation. 'You're not serious.'

'I am.' Enzo told him what happened.

'No witnesses?'

Enzo shook his head, and Roussel looked at him for a long time, almost as if trying to decide whether he believed him or not. Finally he said, 'I was on the net last night, looking at your qualifications.'

'Impressive, huh?'

Roussel grinned. 'The piece I read credited you with many things, Monsieur Macleod. Modesty wasn't one of them.' He took a thoughtful pull from his cigarette. 'An honours degree in biochemistry, a masters in forensic science. Head of biology section, Strathclyde police. Blood pattern interpretation at crime scenes, DNA databasing . . .'

'And one of only four people in the UK to train as a Byford scientist. Which makes me an expert on serious serial crime analysis.' He met the *gendarme's* steady gaze. 'We don't have to be at odds, Gendarme Roussel. I can help you.'

Roussel took a final puff on his cigarette and threw it away. 'I appreciate the offer, monsieur. I really do. But we don't need your help. We have all the expertise we require within the service.'

For a moment, Enzo had felt he was making progress with the man. Now he sighed and changed the subject. 'Well, maybe you could tell me a little bit about *l'Ordre de la Dive Bouteille*.'

'What do you want to know?'

'How many members does it have?'

'Twenty-five.'

'That's all?'

Roussel nodded.

'So how come you couldn't track down the owner of the costume that Petty was wearing?'

'Every current member of the *Ordre* was still in possession of his robes. The society was formed more than half a century ago, Monsieur Macleod. There have been dozens of members over the years. When one dies, someone else takes his place. All the accoutrements go to the relatives of the deceased. There was no way of accounting for all of those.'

'So who's the head of the *Ordre*?'

'The president?'

'Ah, yes, there's always a *Monsieur le Président*, isn't there?'

'Why should I tell you?'

'It's not a secret, is it? I'll find out anyway.'

'So you will.' Roussel kicked at a stone on the ground with one of his big, black boots. 'His name's Jean-Marc Josse, a winemaker at Mas Causse near Cestayrols. He's been running the show for a long time. A real character.'

The sound of a door banging made them turn as a

triumphant Michelle strode out of the *gendarmerie* waving a sheaf of papers. 'I have the release forms, signed and sealed. A veritable Amazononian forest.' She beamed at Enzo. 'Thank you, Mister Macleod. Now all I have to do is go to somewhere in Albi to get the stuff.'

'The TGI,' Roussel said. 'The Tribunal de Grande Instance in the Place du Palais. It's a beautiful old building.'

III

Nicole sat on the *terrasse* of the Grand Café des Sports at a plastic table under a yellow awning. The tables at the Brasserie Saint-Pierre next door were empty for the moment, waiting in silent anticipation for the *midi* rush. There were only a couple of other tables occupied at the Café des Sports, a disabled man in a high wheelchair, and two farmers in from the country, greasy overalls and cloth caps and big fingers holding small glasses of red wine. Nicole's car was lined up among the others in the shade of the trees in the Place de la Libération, where old men sat on benches watching the traffic and sucking on nicotine-stained, hand-rolled cigarettes held precariously between dried lips. On the far side of the square a young girl was setting tables on the pavement outside the Cassis restaurant where lotus-eaters from England gathered to exercise their native tongue and complain about the French. A brown puppy with a huge head and big paws was flapping up and down the pavement, playfully chasing passers-by.

Nicole sipped her coffee and munched on the *chocolatine*

she had bought in a *boulangerie* across the square, and examined the map and the list of *chambres d'hôtes* she had acquired from the tourist office beside the abbey. There were dozens of them. The trick was going to be finding one close to Château des Fleurs, the cost of which would not send Monsieur Macleod into another fit of Scottish apoplexy. He could, she reflected, be seriously bad-tempered at times. She put it down to the lack of a woman in his life.

She highlighted the Château des Fleurs on the map with a marker pen, then drew a circle around it with a radius of around two kilometres. Now she tried to match the place names within the circle with place names on the list.

Her concentration was such that at first she didn't notice the tugging at her shoes. When she did, she tutted with irritation and looked under the table. The brown puppy was pulling at the laces of her running shoes and had somehow managed to undo both of them. When Nicole's head appeared beneath the level of the table it stopped, looking at her eagerly, as if for approval, but poised ready to back off if its achievement had the opposite effect. Nicole could not be angry. 'You little devil!' She reached down and ruffled its head, and it went springing delightedly around the table. She leaned over to retie her shoelaces.

'Sorry about that. He's been doing it all week.'

She looked up to see the waiter grinning at her. He was a young lad, with a shock of dark, curly hair shaved close around the back and sides of his head. Nicole was aware of his brown eyes being drawn involuntarily to her cleavage then darting quickly, self-consciously away. 'What, untying shoelaces?'

He nodded. 'It's a trick he's learned. Some of our customers are less tolerant of him than you. He's only narrowly avoided the toe-end of a few boots.'

'So who taught him the trick? You?'

The boy laughed. 'No, he's not mine. Or anybody's, I don't think. Probably too many pups in a litter, and he's been dropped out the back door of a car somewhere. At any rate, he seems to have adopted us. We call him Braucol.' The pup heard the familiar sound of his name and danced around the waiter's feet, trying to grab a shoelace. The boy nudged him away with his toe.

'Braucol?'

'It's a local red grape, one of the *cépages* that gives the Gaillac wine its distinctive flavour.'

'Braucol.' Nicole repeated the name, trying it out for size. 'I like it. It suits him.' She felt a tugging at her feet and looked down to see that her newly retied shoelaces had been undone again. Braucol went prancing off to a safe distance, eyes wide, watching for her reaction.

The waiter laughed. 'He's going to be a big one, too. Trouble is, the boss is fed up with him already. If he makes an official complaint the municipality will have to take him away, and he'll probably get put down. You don't want a puppy, do you?'

Nicole gave a little Gallic shrug of regret. 'I would if I could, but I can't.'

A couple sat down at an adjoining table, and the waiter went off to take their order. Nicole retied her laces for the second time and wagged a finger of admonishment at the watching Braucol. 'Go,' she said. 'If you hang around here you'll just end up in that big kennel in the sky.'

As if he understood her, Braucol went springing off, chasing after the wheels of a passing pram, and Nicole returned to her list and her map. Almost immediately, she spotted a *chambre d'hôte* on a farm that lay virtually next door to the Château des Fleurs estate. She drew a circle around the name, La Croix Blanche, and looked around for the waiter to ask if she could use their phone. But even as she caught his eye, she felt a tugging at her shoes. 'Braucol!' she hissed under the table in admonishment. The puppy lifted his eyebrows and seemed to smile, as if happy that she knew his name.

She turned her car off the narrow country road into the entrance to La Domaine de la Croix Blanche, past the small, white cross that gave the place its name. Countless rows of vines stretched away across the valley, rising up across chalk hills towards an old church commanding unparalleled views over the right bank of the Tarn. A mechanical harvester sat silent on a stony track, and there wasn't a soul moving amongst the vines in the midday sun.

Mature oaks cast their shadows across the drive towards the pale green shutters of what must once have been the original farmhouse. Now, it seemed, it was only used for storage, and a tasting room had been fashioned from the garage at the end of it. Washing hung listlessly in the heat, on a rope strung between the trees, and there were cars parked in the glare of a drive of crushed *castine* chippings.

Nicole left her suitcase in the boot of her car and walked up the drive to the modern two-storey house that had been built to replace the original farmhouse. The door of the *cave* lay ajar, and she could hear the sound of voices raised in animated conversation coming from within.

She stopped at the open door, and saw, in the cool, dark interior of the cellar, a dozen people or more sitting around a long table, eating starters of *crudités* served from large stainless steel platters. There were several open bottles of wine on the table. Conversation fizzled out as the diners became aware of Nicole in the doorway. A young man glanced around, before reluctantly leaving his place to come to the door. He was a big man, in shorts and a torn tee shirt, with thick, strong arms and calves like rugby balls. He had a tangle of dark, curly hair above a round face shining with perspiration and big eyes that seemed to Nicole to be almost black. She thought he was probably in his early thirties and that he was really quite handsome.

He stepped out into the sunshine, pulling the door closed behind him. He gave a short, sharp, upward flick of his head, one eyebrow raised in query. 'Can I help you?' But he didn't sound as if he wanted to, and Nicole quickly found herself reappraising her initial impression of him as handsome. He steadfastly avoided looking at her breasts.

'I called earlier. About the *chambre d'hôte.*'

'Oh, yeah.' He leaned back into the doorway. 'Maman! It's the girl about the room.'

Maman turned out to be a formidable old lady with sharp, suspicious eyes. Unlike her son, she was tiny, birdlike, and had a voice that could cut paper. She led Nicole upstairs to a landing of faded floral wallpaper, and a door off it leading to a small bedroom with shutters closed tight against the hot September sun. The young man followed them in and hefted Nicole's suitcase on to the bed with no apparent effort. The room seemed crowded with the three of them in it and so dark Nicole could only just make out the old framed family photographs on the wall. The inside of the door had the same floral wallpaper on it as the hall outside. Her immediate sense was one of depression. She had spent the last two months sitting in a darkened room at her mother's bedside, and her impulse was to open the windows and throw the shutters wide, letting life flood in. But she resisted the urge. 'This'll be fine.'

'We've never had any complaints,' Maman said.

'Have you eaten?' The young man spoke to her for the first time since greeting her at the door of the *cave*.

'No.'

He looked at his mother. 'There's enough for one more, isn't there?'

His mother shrugged. 'I suppose.'

'That's very kind of you,' Nicole said. And she stuck out a hand towards him. 'My name's Nicole.'

He seemed suddenly embarrassed. 'Fabien.' He took her

hand with reluctance, and it felt huge and rough, and she saw his eyes glance fleetingly towards her cleavage. Perhaps he wasn't so rude after all. Just shy, maybe.

His mother watched her with patent disapproval. 'Do you want to eat or not?'

A hush descended for a moment over the gathering at the table when Fabien and his mother returned with the girl who'd appeared briefly at the door a few minutes earlier.

Nicole found a free seat at the far end beside an old man whom everyone called Pappy, and who had none of Fabien's inhibitions about letting his eyes wander at will. He had a face as sharp as a blade, and fine, muscled arms exposed by a grape-stained sports vest. 'Come to pick grapes with us, mademoiselle?' he asked.

'Not exactly.'

'On holiday, then?' This from a ruddy-faced man across the table who poured her a glass of wine.

'No, my boss is staying in a *gîte* at the Château des Fleurs. He's the one going grape picking. Sort of undercover. He's here to investigate the death of the wine critic, you know, the American, Gil Petty?'

A silence you could touch fell across the table, and Nicole wondered what she had said wrong. All eyes were turned towards her.

'Grape picking where?' Fabien said.

Nicole was beginning to think it had been a mistake to say anything at all. But having started, she could hardly stop now. She said, with a lightness she did not feel, 'The vineyard where the body was discovered. He starts tomorrow.' She glanced anxiously around all the faces turned towards her. 'Do you know it?'

The long silence that followed was finally broken by Fabien, whose dark look was reflected in the ominous tone of his voice. 'We do. It's here. La Croix Blanche.' He paused. 'And you can tell your boss he needn't bother turning up tomorrow.'

CHAPTER FIVE

I

Enzo guided his 2CV through a narrow archway, to the front of a house built in the style of a Spanish *hacienda*. Steps led up through a garden of small trees and potted plants to double glass doors opening into a cool reception hall. Wisteria, long past its season of tearful, violet bloom, grew gnarled and twisted around the doorway, and vivid red geraniums overflowed from their *bacs à fleurs* to discourage mosquitoes. Beyond the house, a roof sloped steeply over the entrance to a darkened tasting room, and huge windows gave on the *chai*, where men were at work pumping freshly pressed *must* into stainless steel *cuves*.

Opposite the house, on a *terrasse* shaded by ancient oak trees, a white table and chairs looked out over a retaining wall to the valley below, fields of golden stubble shimmering off into a hazy distance. An old man in dark blue overalls and a chequered shirt sat in the shadow of the trees, the remains of a meal on the table in front of him, a nearly empty glass in his hand, a nearly empty bottle just within reach. He seemed lost in contemplation, and only turned as Enzo shut the car door and started towards him.

'I'm looking for Jean-Marc Josse,' Enzo said.

The old man grunted. 'Then you've found him.' His round face was covered with a fine, silver stubble, and in spite of nearly having finished a bottle of wine, his eyes were sharp and bright. 'Who wants him?'

'My name's Enzo Macleod.' Enzo held out a hand, and the old man reluctantly let go of his glass to shake it.

'What kind of a name's that?'

'Half Italian, half Scottish.'

'You're not English, then?'

'No.'

'You sound English.'

'I'm not.'

The old man thrust out his jaw. 'That's alright, then. You'd better sit down.'

Enzo pulled up a chair and seated himself opposite, placing his hands carefully on the table in front of him. In France it was considered bad manners to hide your hands from view, in your lap or below the table. A hangover, perhaps, from the days when a hidden hand might have held a weapon.

'So what can I do for you, monsieur?'

'I'm investigating the death of Gil Petty, and I wanted to talk to you about the l'Ordre de la Dive Bouteille.'

Jean-Marc Josse's face darkened. 'A damnable affair. Left a stain on the Ordre as impossible to remove as red wine on white silk. I wish he'd never come here.'

'You made him a chevalier of the Ordre.'

'He was the most influential wine critic in the world. The

aim of our organisation is to promote the richness and diversity of the wines of Gaillac. Who better to make a *chevalier*?'

'So you invited him.'

'We invited him to apply.'

'And what does an application entail?'

'A letter asking to be inducted into the *confrérie*, and a complete *curriculum vitae*, leaving nothing out. To be accepted, you must reveal absolutely everything about yourself.' He rubbed his stubble thoughtfully with the flat of a big hand. 'You know, there are more than two thousand *chevaliers* around the world.'

Enzo nodded and became aware of the hum of insects that filled the air around them. A slight breeze stirred the leaves above their heads and dappled sunlight danced across the table, a kaleidoscope of flickering light. 'Do you take photographs at these induction ceremonies?'

'Of course. Do you want to see them?' The old man's pride in his organisation was overcoming his initial reticence.

'I'd like that. Thank you.'

Jean-Marc Josse eased himself out of his seat, stretching stiffened limbs and headed off into the house with a slow, shuffling gait. He emerged some minutes later with a huge, hard-backed photo album, a thick manila file, and a bottle of red wine. 'Have you tried our Mas Causse reds?' He dumped the album in front of Enzo, laid down his folder, and began opening the bottle.

'I can't say I have.'

'This is our classic,' the old man said. 'Forty per cent

braucol, forty per cent duras, and ten per cent each of merlot and syrah to soften it.'

'Aged in oak?'

'Good God, no!' Old Josse was shocked. 'I don't believe in oak. I want to taste the grape. Too many winemakers these days hide their shortcomings behind the big, buttery flavours they get from aging the stuff in oak barrels. With the Mas Causse you taste the real thing. If we've made a bad wine, you'll know it.'

He poured a small quantity into his own glass and took out another from the deep pockets of his overalls to pour a little for Enzo. Enzo watched, and followed suit, as the old wine-maker held his glass up to the light, then peered into it before putting his nose almost entirely inside and breathing deeply.

'Powdered sugar,' he said. 'Raspberry.'

Enzo nodded. He could see what the old man meant, but perhaps his nose was not as well developed. It certainly wasn't as big.

Now the old man swirled his glass and breathed it in again. 'Big fruit. Plums. And the raspberry's still there.' Then he took a mouthful, sucking air over his tongue as slowly he let the wine slip back over his throat.

Raspberry and liquorice were the overwhelming flavours that filled Enzo's mouth. The wine was freshly acidic, not too heavy, and with a peppery taste that lingered pleasantly in the nasal cavity. 'Very nice,' he said, and the old man lifted an eyebrow as if Enzo had just damned his wine with faint praise.

Enzo opened the photo album. Its pages were filled with large, colourful prints that had been pasted on either side. Men and women in flowing crimson gowns edged in black. Jean-Marc Josse with his tri-pointed red Rabelaisian hat, brandishing a piece of gnarled and polished vine root that served as an induction rod. *Intronisation* into the *confrérie* was symbolised by the presentation of a gold-coloured representation of an *amphora*, the Greek urn in which Gaillac wines were originally stored and sold. This came in the form of a chunky medallion hung around the neck on a gold rope.

He flipped over a page, and there was Petty: a maroon apron over a red jacket, Josse hanging the amphora around his neck. Petty, Enzo knew, had been almost exactly the same age as himself, but he seemed much older. He was much more conservative, with his short cut, dyed black hair, a little silver left at the temples in an attempt to deceive the world into believing this was his natural colour. There were few things more unedifying than a man who dyed his hair and pretended not to.

Petty had been a private man, but vain. Biographers had found it hard to get background information about him. Most of their research material had come from his ex-wife and former friends. It was something Enzo had noticed in almost everything he had read. Petty seemed only to have *former* friends. In the end, it appeared, he had been a lonely and introverted soul, estranged from his family, never giving interviews, and turning up only rarely at public events.

The induction in the photograph was held in a place with

tiled floors and vaulted brick arches. 'Where is this?' Enzo asked.

'The vaults of the Abbey Saint-Michel. It's where we hold our chapters and many of our inductions.' Old Josse filled both their glasses, then held his up to contemplate the wine. 'Hard to believe that the vine started life as a forest creeper, climbing tree trunks, twenty, thirty metres, to reach the canopy. The fruit was for the birds, to carry the seeds off to germinate elsewhere. It's the great thing about Man, you know, that he can shape and bend nature to his will, cut a thirty-metre creeper down to a metre and a half and make it produce fruit to his specifications. And then turn it into something as wonderful as this.' He took a mouthful. His concentration was intense as he extracted every last moment of pleasure from the wine. Then he beamed, sharp eyes a little less sharp than before, his diction a little more slurred. He looked at Enzo. 'Who exactly are you, Monsieur Macleod?'

Enzo told him, and Josse thought briefly before taking a sheet of paper from his folder and slipping it across the table. Enzo picked it up. 'What's this?'

'Terms and conditions. If you want to apply to become a *chevalier*.'

Enzo glanced at the sheet. 'Don't I have to be someone who's done something to promote or advance the wines of Gaillac?'

'Monsieur, if you can find out who murdered Petty and put this thing to rest once and for all, you'll have done more for the wines of Gaillac than Petty ever did.' He took another mouthful of dark, seductive red, sunlight slanting through his glass to illuminate its limpidity. 'I love this place. I love the wines we make. My father made wine here before me, and now it's my son who's the *maître de chai*. There's poetry in the grape, you know. The essence of Man, of civilisation, of sophistication. We've done all manner of things. We have circumnavigated the globe, sent spaceships to Mars. But there's no higher achievement than the making of a fine wine, no greater pleasure than to drink it.'

He indulged in that pleasure once more and eyed Enzo with watery eyes. 'When I was a boy, we had a contract with the railway, and we sent barrels of a wine called *vin bourru* every year to Paris where it was drunk in all the bars. It was white, and cloudy and sweet, and still fermenting. Maybe only three per cent alcohol. But then, after the war, the Europeans told us we couldn't guarantee the consistency, so effectively it was banned.' He grinned wickedly. 'You want to taste it?'

'You're still making it?'

'No, not really. But the white wines in our *cuves* have just begun their fermentation. And that's the very stuff we would have sent by rail to Paris. A little taste of history, monsieur.'

No one paid any attention to them as old Josse led Enzo through the *chai* clutching a couple of fresh glasses. He stopped at one of the *cuves* and peered myopically at the hand-written label attached to the tap, then muttered his satisfaction. '*Loin de l'oeil.*' He opened up the tap and poured them each a half glass. The wine, still in its very early stages of fermentation, was indeed very cloudy, almost yellow. 'Try it.' He handed Enzo his glass.

It fizzed on the tongue, sweet and sharp and yeasty and still warm from the fermentation.

'I love to have a glass or two at harvest time.' The old man's eyes sparkled with mischief. 'It always feels like raising two fingers to the damned Europeans. They might be able to stop us selling it, but they can't stop us drinking it.'

The taste of it lingered in Enzo's mouth as they walked back along the drive to his car. He shook the old man's hand, and was about to get behind the wheel, when he had a thought. He stopped with one foot already in the car. 'You said that an application to become a *chevalier* had to be accompanied by a full CV, nothing left out.'

'That's right.'

'Do you still have Petty's application and CV?'

'Of course.'

'I suppose the police must have asked to see them at the time?'

'No. The police were only interested in the gown and the hat and gloves and whose they might have been.'

Enzo was almost afraid to ask. 'Would you let me see them?'

Old Josse grinned. 'Monsieur, we have drunk the *vin bourru* together. Of course you can see them.'

II

Enzo followed Paulette Lefèvre up the broad stone staircase, sunlight spilling through arrow-slit windows to fall in zigzags across the steps of the old *château*. The swing of her hips was emphasised by the fullness of her calf-length skirt. There was something innately sexual and provocative in it. He wondered if she was aware of it and decided she probably was. In his experience, women were almost always aware of the signals they sent out. Her heels clicked sharply on the stone flags of the first floor landing, then she turned right, through a huge, studded, wooden door, into a vast salon filled with the clutter of old furniture and cardboard boxes. Some of the pieces were covered with dust sheets. An old rocking horse, its paint eroded by time and history, stood in front of an enormous, moulded *cheminée*, the centrepiece of which was a faded fresco in the process of restoration. Motes of dust hung in the shafts of sunlight squinting in through small windows. Pierric Lefèvre looked up from a long, wooden table littered with papers and maps and ancient books with curling yellowed pages. He was riffling through an old ledger of some kind, mottled and stained by centuries of damp.

'I've been going through all this stuff ever since you called. We found most of it, you know, in an old *armoire* in the east turret when we first bought the place. God knows how it survived.'

Enzo had seen the photographs downstairs in the great dining hall. Pictures Pierric had taken showing the restoration of the Château des Fleurs at all its stages. But it was the earliest photographs which were the most dramatic. There had been no floorboards on the first or second floors, and it had been possible to stand in the dining hall and look straight up twenty-five metres to see torn pieces of sky through the roof.

He approached the table, and Pierric turned the age-brittled tome towards him so that he could see it. 'I think I've found what you want. It's a kind of employment ledger, listing the estate workers, where they lived, how much they were paid.' He flipped carefully back a couple of pages, and ran his finger down a list of names written in a flamboyant, old-fashioned French script. The ink had faded considerably and was in danger of being lost in the fog of discolouring paper. 'There.' He stabbed his finger at an entry. 'Georges Petit, estate manager. Lived with his family right across the way there in what is now the *gîte*. Right up until 1789, when his employment was terminated.'

Enzo peered at the final entry, which was dated August 12, 1789. It said simply, *Émigré*. Emigrated.

'Probably to the New World,' Pierric said. 'A lot of people left France for the Americas at the start of the French Revolution.'

Paulette was regarding Enzo with considerable curiosity. 'How did you know?'

Enzo took a photocopied wad of papers from his bag. 'Gil Petty's *curriculum vitae*, as presented to the *Ordre de la Dive Bouteille* to whom he was obliged to reveal all. He took that requirement literally, it seems. Because in it he disclosed that his interest in Gaillac was not just wine-related. His roots were here. His family had emigrated to the United States, he thought early in the nineteenth century. The name Petty is just a corruption of Petit. His ancestor was Georges Petit who lived, as your ledger attests, in the very *gîte* Petty rented when he came here four years ago. For him it was a voyage of discovery. A man in search of his history. Gil Petty was coming home. Although I doubt if he realised for one moment that he was coming home to die.'

CHAPTER SIX

I

Nicole looked up apprehensively from the laptop computer as Enzo came in. He was, she thought, looking very pleased with himself. For most of the last couple of hours she had been framing in her mind how to tell him that she'd blown his cover at La Croix Blanche and making herself ill at the thought. So it was with some relief that she decided, given his mood, that this was not the moment. 'You look like the cat that got the cream,' she said.

But he walked straight past the table where she'd set up the computer and took out a marker pen to write *Petit* up on his board, right below Gil Petty's name. Then he turned towards her. 'What does that mean to you?'

She shrugged and frowned her confusion. '*Petit*. Small.'

'Yes, but what else?'

She shook her head. 'I've no idea.'

'It's a name, Nicole. Petty's family name. Petit was corrupted to Petty when they emigrated to the United States during the French Revolution.'

Understanding dawned. 'So he was really French?'

'His ancestors were. And they lived in this very house. I

always wondered why he'd rented this place. Now we know.'

'Wow!' She thought for a moment. 'So how does that help us?'

Enzo's smile lost a little of its shine. He turned and looked at the board. 'I'm not sure. But it's information, Nicole. Something we know now that we didn't know before. It's what you learn about the application of forensic science to the examination of a crime scene. Every microscopic speck of evidence is important in piecing together a complete picture of what happened. But this is important, I think. It's something no one else seems to have known.'

He inclined his head towards the computer.

'Are we connected to the internet?'

'Yup.'

'How? Did the Lefèvres give us a telephone line?'

Nicole made a show of examining something on the screen. 'No.' Her response was too casual.

Enzo frowned. 'Then how are we connected?'

'They've got wi-fi downstairs in the estate office. It's not password-protected. So I just sort of . . . tapped into it. They'll never know.'

'That's stealing, Nicole.'

'No, it's not. We haven't taken anything from them. They've still got their own access.'

'We'll have to tell them.'

She shrugged. 'Suit yourself.' She started tapping at the keyboard.

'Did you get yourself a place to stay?'

She kept her eyes fixed on the screen. 'Uh-huh.'

He waited for her to tell him, but she just kept typing. 'Well, where?'

'On a farm. Just up the road. Hardly any distance.' Then she added quickly, 'I've been doing some research on Petty. There's still a lot of stuff out there on the internet about him. He really was the number one wine critic, wasn't he?'

'He had more power to determine people's tastes in wine, and the price of it, than any one man should ever have.' Enzo spoke with feeling. There were too many good wines out there that would always be beyond his means.

Nicole poked a finger at the screen. 'I found an article here that says his recommendation of one of the Bordeaux vintages in the nineteen-eighties sent prices skyrocketing four hundred per cent in three years!'

Enzo shook his head. 'That was the irony. When Petty first started publishing his newsletter, with detailed tasting notes and wine ratings, he wanted to be the consumers' champion. To tell them what wines were good and what weren't. Trouble was, he became so influential, that when he gave a wine a good score, the price of it soared way beyond the pocket of the ordinary consumer. He almost single-handedly turned the drinking of good wine into an elitist pursuit for the wealthy.'

Nicole scrolled down her screen. 'It says here that eighty per cent of wine sold in the US is bought by only twelve per cent of the population.'

Enzo shrugged. 'I rest my case.'

Nicole looked at him, forgetting for the moment her debacle at La Croix Blanche. 'That Michelle Petty . . .'

'What about her?'

'It seems they didn't talk, she and her papa.'

'No, they didn't.' But Enzo didn't want to discuss it with Nicole. It was all just a little too close to home for comfort. He changed the subject. 'Let's take a look at how he rated the wines he tasted.'

Nicole brightened. 'I was reading about that earlier.' She went into her browser's history and pulled up a previous page. 'He didn't go for the hundred-point scale that other critics like Robert Parker or the *Wine Spectator* use.'

'Why not?'

'It seems he thought that the difference between, say, a ninety-five and a ninety-six, would be so tiny, and so subjective, that it really wouldn't mean anything at all. That's why he grouped his ratings in fives, which he categorised by letters of the alphabet. "A" at the top end, "F" at the bottom. So that an "A" would be like ninety-five to a hundred, "B" would be ninety to ninety-five.'

'Which means it was the hundred point scale by any other name.'

'Except that it allowed room for personal interpretation. One man's meat, and all that. And . . .' she held up one finger as she scrolled down the page, 'he gave each wine a value rating, which Parker doesn't do – 1 to 5, with 1 being the best value, and 5 being pretty damned expensive. That way, an A5 would be a great wine that cost a fortune.'

'And an A1?'

Nicole grinned. 'The Holy Grail. He never awarded an A1, although apparently he was convinced that it was out there, and that one day he'd find it.'

Enzo eased himself into a wicker rocking chair facing the table and winced as bruised and overstretched muscles from the night before reminded him that he was not as young as he used to be. 'So do these numbers represent actual prices?'

'Broadly, yes. The best rating, A1, would be anything up to twenty-five dollars, scaling up to a 5, which was anything over three hundred. But most of his A wines were rated 3 or higher, which takes them up over seventy-five dollars.'

Enzo marvelled at the prices some people would pay for a bottle of wine. Twenty-five dollars to him would be seriously expensive. Most of the wines he bought were around five or six euros. He rubbed his fingers gently over the scab on his head wound and mused out loud, 'Petty was used to rating top wines from Bordeaux and Burgundy, Champagne and Chablis. How could he possibly have applied that kind of value scale to the wines he was tasting here? I've never *seen* a Gaillac that cost more than twenty-five dollars. Most of them are under ten euros.'

Nicole said, 'My papa gets his wine *en vrac*, in a big plastic container. It costs one-and-a-half euros a litre.'

He looked at her and realised that where she came from there would be something obscene about paying twenty-five dollars for a bottle of wine, never mind a hundred. The budget to feed the family was probably under fifty euros a week. Her father was hardly able to bear the cost of sending her to university. Enzo knew, because he had seen it, that Nicole shared a miserable bedsit in Toulouse with three other students, and her father could barely even manage that.

They heard a car pulling into the gravel parking area beyond the *pigeonnier*, and Enzo got up to look out of the window. 'It's Michelle Petty. She must have got her father's things.' He watched for a moment as she lifted a large suitcase out of the boot and a smaller bag, like a soft briefcase. She was wearing jeans and trainers and a tee shirt today, hair freed from its clasp and cascading over square shoulders. As she lifted the case and turned towards the cottage, braced to take the weight of the bags, he thought how attractive she was. Not at all like her father. And he remembered, from somewhere amongst all the notes he had read, that her mother had been a contestant on the beauty queen circuit in the States before meeting Petty at a party and marrying in haste. Only to repent at leisure. He turned to Nicole. 'You'd better go.'

Her disappointment was palpable. 'Why? I'd like to see what she's got, too.'

'Another time, Nicole. She's pretty fragile right now.'

Nicole raised a skeptical eyebrow. 'And it wouldn't have anything at all to do with the fact that she's young and attractive.'

'Nicole.' Enzo's warning tone was clear.

'Alright, alright.' She held up her hands. 'I'm out of here.'

II

Enzo watched as Michelle crouched to unzip her dead father's suitcase and throw back the lid. She stood up then, and looked down at the case lying open in front of her on the *clic-clac*. Neatly folded clothes, a toilet bag, shoes in a plastic carrier, unopened packs of socks held to the inside of the lid by a strap. And silent tears filled her eyes, teetering briefly on the lower lid, before tumbling down cheeks flushed with sudden colour. She sucked in a deep, tremulous breath. 'Oh, my God. There's still the smell of him in his clothes.' She wiped away hot tears with the backs of her hands. 'I don't know what it was. Aftershave, hair-cream. But I remember that smell from when I was a little girl, and he would sit me on his knee in the big armchair to watch TV. It was so him. Like a signature. When I came in from school I would know if he was home by the scent of him in the hall.' She turned to look at Enzo, eyes shining with tears of contradiction, happy memories fighting for ascendancy with sad ones.

He put a hand of comfort on her arm and was taken by surprise when she slipped her arms around his waist and pushed her face into his shoulder, clinging to him, pressing herself into all his curves, stifled sobs vibrating against his chest. Years of denial given sudden release to mourn. He held her for what seemed an inordinately long time before she finally released herself to stand back, self-conscious and embarrassed by a moment of emotional weakness she had never, perhaps, suspected was even possible.

'Sorry.' She couldn't meet his eye.

'We can do this later, if you like.'

'No!' A sudden fiery determination lit her from within. 'Let's get it over.'

And so they went through the suitcase, item by item. Shirts, pullovers, trousers, underwear. Everything seemed clean, freshly pressed, and Enzo wondered what had happened to Petty's dirty laundry. He had, after all, been at the *gîte* for over a week before he went missing.

He seemed to have only one pair of shoes, although perhaps he had been wearing another when they found the body. There was a pair of threadbare old slippers in a plastic bag at the bottom of the case.

In the toilet bag there was a half-empty tube of toothpaste for sensitive teeth and a soft toothbrush. Michelle opened a bottle of aftershave moisturising cream. She sniffed, pressing her lips together to contain some emotion that welled up inside, then screwed the lid back on. 'That's it. That's what he wore. I never knew before.'

There was a small pressurised container of shaving foam, a razor in a waterproof black bag, and a plastic box of fresh shaving heads. Enzo carefully examined the head which had been in use. There was a gluey dust of finely cut whiskers clogged between the blades, with the possibility that there could be dried blood in there from tiny nicks made while shaving. He set it aside. Michelle looked at him, the question in her eyes, but she didn't ask it.

There were some medicines. A nearly empty pack of Hedex,

paracetamol painkillers. Haemorrhoid cream and suppositories. Ranitidine tablets for a duodenal ulcer. A glycerine-based dry-skin product called Cuticura. A man suffering from the ailments of middle age.

Michelle picked up the skin cream. 'He had psoriasis. Not all the time. Bouts of it. I can remember his elbows breaking out, and sometimes he would have patches of dry skin on his face.'

All the symptoms of a man under stress. Psoriasis, headaches, acidity. Even haemorrhoids could be aggravated by stress. This was not a man at ease with himself or the world.

Michelle removed a plastic comb from the bottom of the bag, and Enzo took it from her, holding it up to the light. There were still hairs caught in the roots of the teeth. Short, black-dyed hairs. Enzo took it through to the bathroom, laid out a piece of white toilet paper beside the sink, and carefully teased out a few of those precious hairs. He became aware of Michelle's shadow at his shoulder. 'What are you doing?'

'Between these and the razor, we should be able to get a sample of his DNA.'

'Is that important?'

Enzo shrugged. 'It might be. But it's better to have it than not.'

'Won't the police already have done that?'

Enzo found it hard to resist a small, cynical smile. 'I doubt it. Things might have improved in the last four years. But at the time your father went missing, the French police were about twenty years behind the British and Americans in the use of DNA technology. There was no DNA database in France before the year 2000. There are only four hundred thousand names in it today. Compare that to the British, with a similar population, who have the DNA fingerprints of more than three million offenders.'

'It's weird.' In the mirror, Enzo saw her biting her lower lip. 'He's been dead for four years, and yet you can still extract the living essence of him from a hair.'

'Maybe.' Enzo carefully wrapped the hair in the toilet tissue and slipped it into a clear plastic ziplock bag. 'We'll see. What's in the other bag?'

'His laptop computer. But the battery will be dead.' They went back through to the *séjour*.

'If there's a power cable, we should still be able to fire it up.'

The laptop was a white G3 Macintosh Powerbook, the top model of its day. It was in a padded black nylon case, along with various cables, an instruction manual, and a book that Petty had clearly been reading. There was a bookmark at page 220. The book was called *A Superior Mystery*, by American writer Carl Brookins. Enzo turned it over and read the back cover. It was about a Seattle PR executive and his wife sailing amongst the Apostle Islands of Northern Wisconsin to solve old and new murders.

'My father loved to sail,' Michelle said. 'But for him it was a solitary thing. A one-man dinghy out on Lake Washington. He was a member of the local club in Sacramento. I would have loved to go sailing with him, but he wasn't interested in taking out a family membership.' Enzo heard the bitterness in her voice, and he looked up to see her fighting back more tears.

He returned to the bag and took out the power cable and unravelled it. It had an American plug on it, with a French adapter. He hooked it up to the computer and plugged it in, then opened up the laptop. He hit the power button, and they held their breaths for a moment before the computer's start-up chorus issued through tiny speakers, and the screen flickered and lit up to begin loading its system software.

'The police must have looked at all this,' Michelle said.

'I should think so.'

'So what are you hoping to find?'

'I don't know. Something they've missed.' The desktop appeared, along with the finder window, giving access to all of Petty's files. 'He must have kept his ratings on here.'

'Are they important?'

Enzo turned to her. 'Michelle, your father could make or break a winemaker by how he rated his wine. Those ratings could very well provide a motive for his murder.'

Enzo went into the documents file and found dozens of folders. And folders within folders within folders. Petty's whole working life was here. Wines he had tasted and rated going back to the mid-eighties. Articles he had written for his newsletter, *The Wine Critic*. Pieces he had done for the various newspaper columns he somehow managed to feed on a weekly basis. There were schedules for wine tastings in France, the US, Italy, and Spain, dating from the early nineties. Files imported and reimported from previous computers, previous lives.

Enzo scratched his head. 'Jeez. It could take weeks to go through all this stuff.'

'I'll bet the French police didn't. It's all in English, for a start.'

'They probably concentrated on finding his Gaillac ratings.'

'Well, where are they?' She scanned the screen.

But Enzo could only shake his head. There seemed to be no folder containing work in progress. 'They're not here. Unless they're somehow hidden on the hard disk. Although I'm pretty sure the *Police Scientifique* would have had an expert take a look at that.'

'Knowing Dad, he'd have some way of hiding them. He was good at hiding stuff. His emotions, mostly.' She paused. 'He was obsessed by secrecy, you know. When his newsletter came out each month, wines that got high ratings could double in price overnight. Anyone who knew in advance what those ratings were could make a killing. Buy cheap, sell expensive. He even wrote a punitive secrecy clause into the contract with his printer.'

'Well, wherever he kept them, they don't seem to be on his computer. There weren't any notebooks or diaries among his things?'

She shook her head.

He thought about it for a moment. 'Surely he made notes when he was tasting. The police must have kept them as evidence.' He pulled up the navigation bar from the bottom of the screen and clicked on the mailer. 'Let's have a look at his e-mails.'

Petty had organised his e-mail correspondence with the same meticulous care with which he had filed his back catalogue of wine ratings. There were thirty or forty folders containing two-way correspondence with wineries and *négociants*, journalists, printers, publishers. A huge file of several thousand e-mails under 'Miscellaneous.' Nothing personal. Except for a single folder above 'Miscellaneous' that was labelled 'Michelle'.

Enzo glanced round as she leaned over his shoulder to peer at the screen. She had seen it, too. 'Go on,' she said. 'Open it.'

He clicked on the folder, and they found themselves staring at an empty screen. Nothing. The folder was empty. He could feel her tension. 'Did you ever correspond by e-mail?'

'Never.'

'So why did he have a folder with your name on it?'

She shook her head, at a complete loss. 'I've no idea. Maybe he always meant to write. Don't they say that the road to hell is paved with good intentions?'

'Or maybe he was waiting for you to write to him.'

'Hell would have frozen over first.'

Enzo was shocked by the vitriol in her tone. He turned to look at her, but she moved back out of his field of vision. 'Why should I run to him? He was the one who never had time for me.'

He thought for several long moments. 'You know, sometimes you just have to swallow your pride and make the first move. If you love someone, you have to tell them today. Because they might not be here tomorrow.'

She looked at him curiously, forgetting for a moment her own selfish obsessions. 'That came from the heart. Personal experience?'

He glanced at his watch and looked out through the window to see the light dying in the east. 'Maybe we should eat,' he said. 'I know a place.'

III

The old square in Lisle-sur-Tarn was almost deserted as they walked across the dusty red blaize in the fading light. Lamps illuminated the dark interior of brick arcades around the thirteenth-century *bastide*. Shops were shut, but customers sat at tables outside Le Cépage restaurant and the Olivier bar in the far corner. There was a function of some kind in the Hôtel de Ville, lights blazing in tall windows all along the upper floor, the sound of accordion music drifting on the warm night air. The Musée du Chocolat was locked up tight, air-conditioning keeping chocolate sculptures safe from the heat.

At the south-west corner, they passed beneath enormous oak beams that held up ancient, sagging buildings. Beyond, a long narrow street ran between cantilevered houses down to the river. Lights from Le Romuald restaurant fell out into the evening gloom.

'So how do you know about this place if you're not from

around here?' Michelle inclined her head towards him quizzically.

Enzo could see her green eyes fixed on him, bright and interrogative. Gone was the pain that had clouded them earlier as they went through her father's belongings. 'It was a recommendation. From the proprietors of the Château des Fleurs. They said if I ever wanted to romance a young woman this was the place to come.'

She laughed. 'They did not.'

He grinned. 'No, they didn't. They said that the food gets cooked over the smoking embers of an open fire in a huge *cheminée*, and that the cuisine is excellent.'

A young man raked through the remains of oak logs on a hearth raised to waist height, pushing freshly burning chunks of wood to the back and dragging glowing remnants towards him. He set a grilling rack above the embers and marinated lamb cutlets hissed and sizzled, spitting garlic and blood, as he placed them over the heat.

Michelle watched, fascinated, as she finished her salad *entrée* of goat's cheese and *gésiers*. She looked at Enzo, a sudden question occurring to her. 'Why do the French call a starter an *entrée*?'

'Because that's what it is,' Enzo told her. 'The entry to the meal. It's a French word. It's Americans who have corrupted it to mean a main course.'

'I suppose you Europeans think Americans have corrupted everything.'

Enzo smiled. "Not *everything*. You make some pretty good wine in California.'

'My father thought so. Californian reds made up most of his top ten. That and a handful of Bordeaux.'

'No Burgundies?'

'He loved Burgundy. He just didn't rate it as highly. He adored pinot noir, but not as much as cabernet or merlot or syrah.'

'Which makes his ratings very much a matter of individual taste.'

'Of course. What else is a critic going to do, but say what it is he likes and what he doesn't? A lot of people followed my father's recommendations and found that they agreed with him. That's why he was so successful.'

'For someone who wasn't speaking to him, you seem to know a lot about your father.'

She shook her head in vigorous denial. 'That was his fault, not mine.'

Enzo let her sudden flame of anger die again before he said, 'You talked earlier about curling up with him on an armchair, watching television together.'

'That's when I was just a kid. He used to call me his little fish, and I would make these fish mouths at him and make him laugh. And he ended up calling me "fishface." My friends were horrified. But I was happy enough. I used to figure it meant he loved me.' She pushed the remains of her salad away, as if she had suddenly lost her appetite. 'But that was before his newsletter took off big time.'

A light came on in a central courtyard which was open to the sky beyond French windows. There were tables and chairs out there for summer diners, potted plants, crimson ivy creeping up brick walls, and a large woodstore at the back to feed the fire. Michelle was distracted for a moment before gathering her thoughts again.

'At the height of his celebrity, he had nearly sixty thousand subscribers. That's still more than Robert Parker has today. But he started off with just a handful. It was a hobby. He loved to drink wine. He and mum had friends round for blind tastings, and they'd all get drunk. And summer holidays were always spent wine-tasting, touring around *châteaux* in France in the cheapest rental car he could find. The great would-be connoisseur of fine wines pitched a tent every night and slept under canvas. He was a bank clerk, for God's sake. He couldn't afford any of it, and he was spending more than fifty per cent of his income on wine so that he could taste it and rate it for his precious newsletter. Mum had to get a job, and boy did she hate that!'

Enzo saw how the gentle glow of the fire was reflected in her face, soft hollows and flickering light. There was something touching, childlike in her intensity, but her eyes were feral, and at times when she turned them on him, he had a disconcerting sense of her sexuality. Something in the way she looked at him. Something predatory.

'Of course, when he got successful and subscriptions were going up every month, he never had to buy wine at all. It arrived on our doorstep. Cases of the stuff. Everyone wanted him to taste and rate their wines. What had started as a hobby turned into a passion, and then an obsession.' She examined the backs of her hands, as if they might provide some kind of window to the past. 'That's when we lost him. When he quit his job and the money began to come in, and we started being able to afford the things we'd only ever dreamed of.' She shook her head at the irony of it. 'Just as life should have begun to get good, it started falling apart.'

'How did he make his money?' Enzo was puzzled. 'He couldn't have earned that much from the newsletter, surely?'

'No, he didn't. There was a point when he got enough subscriptions that he could give up his job. But it was everything else that made him the money. The syndicated newspaper columns. The books – on Bordeaux, Burgundy, Rhône, Piedmont, Rioja. He was producing one a year, and they were all bestsellers. Then there were his radio slots, his half-hour weekly show on cable TV, speaking engagements.'

'I'm surprised he had any time left over to taste the wines.'

'Oh, he always had time for tasting wine. He had a custommade tasting room in the house. He would spend hours in there. And when he left to go on tasting trips he would be away for weeks on end. You know, he could taste a hundred wines in the morning, have lunch, then go on tasting in the afternoon.'

'If I tasted a hundred wines I wouldn't be able to stand up.'

Michelle laughed. 'He didn't swallow, Mister Macleod, just tasted and spat.'

Enzo shook his head in wonder. 'Even so. A hundred wines

in a morning? How on earth could he ever remember one from another?'

'He took notes, of course. But my father had an extraordinary memory. Some people have photographic memories. My father could remember smells and tastes. He could file them away then pull them back at will. He could pinpoint the grape, the year, and the *château* of a wine he hadn't tasted in ten years.' She was lost for several long moments in some sad reflection. 'He had a pretty good memory in general. He used to tell us about when he was a kid, just four or five years old. His parents forced him to learn by heart all the US presidents, and all the US states, and made him rhyme them off as a party-piece for visitors. All the same, he had to train his sense of smell and taste. I used to hold his hand as we walked down the street, and he would close his eyes and identify all the smells that came to him. Cut grass. Tar. Rotting garbage. Cherry blossom. He was good at it.' She drew a deep breath, and brought herself back to Enzo's original question. 'So, yes, he always had time for tasting wine, Mister Macleod. It was his family he had no time for.' She shrugged. 'You know the rest, I guess. Mum divorced him. Got the house and half his money. And his difficult, adolescent daughter refused to talk to him ever again.'

Their lamb came to the table then, along with potatoes that had been scooped out, mashed with cream and garlic, then stuffed back in their skins and roasted in the oven. The meat was smoky tender and perfectly pink. Enzo filled their glasses from a bottle of Domaine Sarrabelle Saint André, a hundred per cent braucol aged in oak. It was soft and smooth, fruit and vanilla on the tongue.

'So now you know our whole sordid little story,' Michelle said. 'But I don't know anything about you. Are you married, Mister Macleod?'

'Enzo.'

'Are you married, Enzo?'

He looked up and saw again that strange quality in her eyes, pupils dilated, a penetrating ring of green around black. She flicked her head to toss her hair back over her shoulders.

'I was once,' he said. 'A long time ago. Back in Scotland. A girl I was at university with.'

'Any children?'

He avoided her eyes and focused on cutting his lamb. 'A little girl. Kirsty. She's a couple of years older than you now.'

'So what happened?'

'I met someone else.'

'Uh-oh.'

He smiled ruefully. 'Yeah, not a very original story, is it?'

'She was French?'

'Good guess.'

'There had to be some reason you were here.'

He sipped some more Saint André. 'Her name was Pascale. I met her at a forensics conference in Nice. She was younger than me.'

'Aren't they always?'

He shrugged. 'I've always conformed to stereotypes. It's easier than being original.'

'So what happened?'

'Oh, you know, not that different from your dad. My wife divorced me, got the house and just about everything else. And my little girl wouldn't talk to me again.'

He looked up to find that her eyes had softened. There was sympathy in them. 'And there's me been banging on all day about *me* and *my* dad.' She reached out to put a hand over his, and he felt an electricity in her touch. 'I'm sorry. I didn't realise.'

'Of course not. Why should you?' She left her hand over his, and he began to feel uncomfortable. 'Anyway, we had a sort of rapprochement recently.'

'You're talking again?'

'Just about.'

'That's what you meant when you said earlier about telling people you love them, because they might not be around tomorrow.'

'Actually, I was thinking about Pascale.' He gently slipped his hand out from under hers to scoop up some potato with his fork. It was easier if he concentrated on his food.

He heard her small, sharp intake of breath. 'She died?'

'In childbirth. More than twenty years ago. Left me to bring up little Sophie all on my own.'

'So you have two daughters?'

He nodded.

'And there's never been anyone else?'

He shrugged. 'There've been women. Nothing lasting.' He thought about Charlotte. She was the only woman who had ever meant anything to him after Pascale. But he still had no idea what he meant to her. And he wasn't about to discuss that with Michelle.

'That's really hard to believe.'

He looked up, surprised. 'What is?'

'A good-looking man like you, without a woman.'

He felt trapped by her eyes and disconcerted by the hunger he saw in them. His mouth was dry, and there was a strange stab of desire in his loins. But she was far too young. 'I told you, I'm not the sort of man who preys on young women.'

'And there was me hoping you might just have been saying that to lull me into a false sense of security.' Still she fixed him with eyes that seemed to penetrate the very depths of his darkest desires, and he knew she would be difficult to resist.

IV

The balmy warm of the evening had given way to a slight autumn chill. It was carried in the humidity condensing on the grass as dew and gathering along the river to form a mist that would obscure the early sun of tomorrow morning. Enzo drew his 2CV alongside Michelle's rental car where she had parked it that afternoon. There was condensation forming on the windscreen.

They stepped into the wash of moonlight. She shivered and insinuated herself under his arm, running a hand across his chest in search of warmth. He felt her own warmth through her tee shirt and her breasts pressing into his side. Almost instinctively he put an arm around her shoulder. She turned her face upwards and pushed herself up on tip-toes to brush her lips against his in the lightest of kisses. 'Are you going to invite me in for a nightcap?'

'I only have whisky.'

'I love whisky. I love it on a man's breath when I kiss him. Sweet and smoky and sexy. But I've never tasted it on the lips of a real Scotsman before.'

Enzo felt blood rushing to that place between his legs that would steal away all reason.

They walked past the other cars parked there, and almost subliminally Enzo heard the tick, tick of a cooling radiator. A vehicle not long arrived. There were still lights on in the castle, and he assumed that the Lefèvres were recently returned from an evening out.

At the foot of the stairs, Michelle slipped out from under his arm and jumped on to the first step to turn and face him. Their eyes were on a level now. The green of hers almost glowed like a cat's in the moonlight. She took his face in both her hands and kissed him. A long, searching kiss that made his legs nearly fold beneath him. She broke away and smiled. 'Just wanted the before and after effect.'

Enzo was not sure he could restrain himself long enough for an after effect. He fumbled for the keys in his pocket and climbed the stairs ahead of her to search in the dark for the keyhole. When, finally, he found it, the key wouldn't turn. He had a moment of confusion. He was certain he could remember locking the door when they left. Then fear stole in to displace the desire that had occupied him only moments before. He pushed the door open and felt for the light switch, blinking in the sudden flood of light that it brought.

She was sitting in the rocker facing the door, legs crossed beneath a long, flowing black skirt, revealing black leather boots with pointed toes. A black, cotton top dipped from her long, ivory neck to the swell of her full breasts. A black lace shawl was draped across shoulders nearly obscured by the cascade of dark, curling hair. She was rocking very gently back and forth, and her dark, dark eyes regarded Enzo and the young woman at his shoulder with what appeared to be dispassionate interest.

'Charlotte!' Enzo was startled. 'How did—'

'The Lefèvres let me in. I think they thought I was your lover.' Her eyes flickered towards Michelle. 'Obviously they were wrong.'

Enzo glanced at Michelle, self-conscious and embarrassed. 'We were just going to have a nightcap.'

'Don't let me stop you.'

Michelle cleared her throat. 'Actually, it's late. I should really be going.' She looked at Charlotte. 'We only came back to get my car.'

'Of course.'

'This is Gil Petty's daughter, Michelle,' Enzo said.

'Pleased to meet you.'

'Charlotte's a forensic psychologist. From Paris. I'm not quite sure what she's . . .' he turned to Charlotte, 'what you're doing here.'

'I had no patients for a few days. I thought maybe I could help. But you seem to have things very well in hand.'

The tension in the room nearly crackled. Embarrassment flushed Michelle's face. 'Well, anyway. I should be getting back to the hotel.' And to Enzo. 'I'll come and get my father's things tomorrow.'

He nodded. 'Okay.'

'Good night.'

'Good night,' Charlotte called after her as she hurried down the steps, and Enzo closed the door.

He turned to face her and remembered why he found her so bewitching. She was a beautiful woman, a good ten years older than Michelle, smart and full of wit and barbed humour. A slight, quizzical smile played around her full lips, and the desire he had felt earlier returned, though now it had a different focus. One without guilt or apprehension. But, still, it was fighting for a place in his emotions with a spear of anger.

'Sorry to interrupt,' she said.

'You didn't.'

She smiled. Enzo had never been a convincing liar. 'No, of course not.'

'You have no right to be jealous, Charlotte. We *have* no relationship, remember? You're the one who's always made that clear to me.'

'Why on earth would you think I was jealous?'

He gave her a long, hard stare. Desire, frustration, anger, all in conflict. 'How long are you staying?'

'I think I should probably leave in the morning. There's nothing worse than being superfluous to requirements.'

'For God's sake, Charlotte . . .'

But she didn't want to hear it. She stood up and waved a dismissive hand. 'I'll take the bed, if that's alright. I see the *clic-clac's* already made up. You can have that.' And she went through to the bedroom and shut the door behind her.

Enzo remained standing for some moments in the harsh electric light, looking at the *clic-clac*, wondering how a night which had begun so promisingly, could have ended so bleakly. And he wondered, too, if he would ever get to sleep in the bed he was paying for.

CHAPTER SEVEN

I

Her hair fell across his face in the darkness. He felt her skin naked and warm against his. He smelled her breath, hot and sweet, her lips so very close. She reached down and held him, guiding him towards that place where he could lose himself in her forever. And the phone began to ring.

'Jesus!' he hissed. 'Just leave it.'

'We can't. It might be important.'

'Nothing's more important than this.' But already his ardour was diminishing.

'The moment's passed, Roger.'

He felt a stab of hurt. 'I'm not Roger, I'm Enzo.'

'Oh, shit,' he heard her say in the dark, and he woke up in a tangle of sheets, perspiring, lying face down, an erection pressed hard into his belly. The phone was still ringing, an insistent, warbling, electronic rendition of Beethoven's Ninth Symphony. He was torn between disappointment that her presence in his bed was only a dream and relief that she had not, after all, called him Roger. Somewhere deep in his subconscious, there must still have been a festering seed of jealousy over her relationship with Raffin. Which was ridiculous. It was months since she and Raffin had broken up. And it had been at Charlotte's bidding.

The phone stopped ringing. Either the caller had given up, or Enzo's answering service had kicked in. He had left the mobile on a charger somewhere in the room but couldn't remember where. Now he couldn't decide whether to get up and try to find it or to stay in bed and go in search of his lost dream. He had no idea how long he had slept, and it was too dark to see his watch. But he was wide awake now and lay on his back staring up into nothingness. It was no good. He was not going to get back to sleep in a hurry. He cursed softly and rolled over, finding cold floorboards with warm feet.

He got up and walked smack into the rocking chair. He heard the crack of wood on shinbone almost before he felt it and, this time, cursed more loudly. He fumbled around, grabbing for bits of furniture until he found the table and the small green desklamp that stood on it.

Its light hurt his eyes, and he blinked several times to clear his focus. The mobile was on the top of a bookcase behind the table. He looked at its display and saw that there was a message. As he dialled the *répondeur* the bedroom door opened, and a sleepy Charlotte emerged in her nightdress, the light from behind her outlining the shadow of the tall, elegant body he had been dreaming about only moments earlier.

'Who's calling at this hour?'

He looked at his watch. It was a little after two. Then he heard Nicole's breathless voice. 'Monsieur Macleod, where are you?' There was a desperation in it. 'They've found another body. In the same state as Gil Petty. Up in the woods, not far from where they found *him*.'

II

Three hundred metres past the turn-off to La Croix Blanche, a gate stood open to a track which left the road and made its stony progress up through the vineyard towards a brooding treeline. Moonlight spilled across the slope etching lines of silver between the dark rows of vines, as if a comb had been drawn through black hair revealing the white scalp beneath. Enzo's 2CV rolled and bounced over the uneven surface on its soft suspension. He had read once that 2CV owners congregated in annual competition to try to overturn their cars in bumpy fields. So giving was the suspension that it was almost impossible to do. He was grateful for that now as he steered his way towards the blaze of headlamps and the flash of blue and orange up ahead.

A *gendarme* stepped into the light of his headlamps, one hand raised, the other resting nervously on his holster. Enzo flipped up the window, and the *gendarme* leaned in, shining a flashlight in his face. 'You can't come up here.'

'I'm looking for Gendarme Roussel.'

The *gendarme* cocked his head suspiciously. 'And you would be . . . ?'

'Enzo Macleod. I'm a forensic specialist consulting on the Petty case.'

The police officer eyed him thoughtfully for a moment. 'Park up here and follow me.'

Enzo pulled his car into a tight space between two rows of vines and followed the *gendarme* up the slope. At the end of the track, where the land rose steeply to the woods, a small knot of people stood talking and smoking. There was a cluster of police vehicles, blue and orange lights flashing out of sync, and unmarked cars pulled up at odd angles, abandoned for the final climb on foot.

'Monsieur Macleod!' Nicole detached herself from the group and hurried towards him.

'Nicole, what are you *doing* here? How did you know about all this?'

'She just happened to be in the right place at the wrong time.'

Enzo had barely noticed the young man in the baseball cap who had followed behind her. He eyed Enzo with obvious dislike, the reflected light of police headlamps cutting deep shadows into a fleshy face. He was a big man, a powerful presence in the dark. He sucked at a cigarette and the shadows that masked his face glowed red in its light.

Nicole cleared her throat uncomfortably. 'Monsieur Macleod, this is Fabien Marre. He's the owner of La Croix Blanche.'

'My *family* owns the *vignoble*,' Fabien corrected her. 'I make the wine.'

Enzo looked again at the young man, then back at Nicole. 'So what are you doing here?'

'She's staying here, monsieur.'

Fabien Marre's insistence in answering for her was beginning to irritate Enzo. 'I'm not asking you.'

Nicole was almost beside herself with embarrassment. 'I
didn't know when I took the room, Monsieur Macleod, hon-
estly. I mean, I'd read all the stuff about Petty, but La Croix
Blanche is a pretty common name. I didn't realise until ...
well, until I'd blown your cover.'

Enzo sighed. He could imagine exactly how it had
happened. Nicole, he knew, enjoyed the sound of her own
voice.

'So you needn't bother turning up for the *vendange* tomorrow,' Fabien said. 'And you can tell Laurent de Bonneval that
we'll be having words.'

Enzo realised there was no point in recriminations. And,
in any case, everything had changed now. He looked at Nicole.
'You said they'd found another body.'

'Up there in the woods.' Nicole pointed vaguely towards
where they could see flashlights pricking the dark and the
shadows of officers moving among the trees. 'There's a *source*
up there. La Source de la Croix. Apparently it's been a rendez-
vous for young lovers for centuries.' She glanced at Fabien,
almost as if looking for his permission. But he just shrugged.
She turned back to Enzo. 'A young couple came banging on
the door of the house at La Croix Blanche just after midnight.
She was hysterical. By the time I'd got into my dressing gown
and slippers and gone down to see what all the noise was
about, Fabien and his mother were there and the girl was in
floods of tears. Her boyfriend could hardly stop shaking.'

'What had happened?'

'They'd gone up to the *source* to ... well, you know, do whatever it is young couples do in places like that.' Nicole had grown up on a farm. Animals had sex. People had sex. She'd never really drawn the distinction. But now, discussing it in the presence of Enzo and Fabien, she was suddenly self-conscious. 'Anyway, they heard someone moving about in the woods, and they thought it was a Peeping Tom. The boy got angry and went after him. That's when he found the body.'

'So you called the police?'

'Not right away. Fabien wanted to see for himself.'

Enzo looked at the young winemaker. 'Why?'

'I'm not going to go calling the police out on a wild goose-chase on the say-so of a couple of kids.'

'And I went with him.'

Anger flashed in Enzo's eyes. 'You took Nicole?'

Fabien shrugged dismissively. 'You know her better than me, monsieur. Have you ever tried saying no to her?'

Enzo glanced at Nicole with irritation and silently conceded the point.

'It was horrible, Monsieur Macleod. I mean, I read all the descriptions people gave of Petty's body when they found it. But nothing prepares you for the real thing.'

Enzo flicked a look at Fabien. 'So you trampled all over the crime scene before you called the police.'

'So?'

'So if they find your traces there, then there's a perfectly logical reason for it.'

Nicole frowned. 'Why wouldn't there be?'

Enzo didn't answer. He kept his eyes on Fabien. 'You were there when they found Petty.'

'I was.'

It was with a shock that Nicole suddenly realised where this was heading. 'Monsieur Macleod! You can't possibly think . . .'

But Fabien talked over her, his voice low and steady and filled with a latent anger. 'I never made a secret of the fact that I didn't like Petty, monsieur. Nothing personal. But there are those of us who produce the wine, and there are others who leech off it. Those who produce nothing but fancy words, impose their tastes and fill their pockets. They've never broken their backs during all the hours and weeks and months of pruning, or lost a crop to the vagaries of the weather. So if you want to know what I think, I think whoever killed Petty deserves a medal.' He drew a deep breath. 'But it wasn't me.'

Nicole turned to look at him, shocked by the intensity of his words and silenced by their virulence.

Enzo said, 'Murder is never to be congratulated, Monsieur Marre.' He paused for a moment's reflection. 'But it's an interesting coincidence, don't you think, that both bodies should turn up on your land?'

Fabien dropped his cigarette and ground it into the stones with the toe of his boot, refusing to meet Enzo's eyes.

Enzo gave Nicole a look that would have wilted flowers, and turned back towards the waiting *gendarme*. 'Where's Roussel?'

'Straight up to the treeline, monsieur.'

*

Roussel was on his way down as Enzo climbed up. They met halfway, and the investigator shone his flashlight in Enzo's face. 'How the hell did you get up here?'

'I told them I was a forensic expert consulting on the Petty case.'

Roussel glared at him. 'I could have you arrested for that.'

'Why? It's true. I *am* consulting on the Petty case – for his daughter.'

Enzo couldn't see his expression beyond the glare of his flashlight, but he could feel the intensity of Roussel's gaze before he heard his lips part in a smile. Roussel turned off the lamp, and as Enzo's eyes adjusted he saw a weary amusement in the palest of faces. 'You're a character, Monsieur Macleod. *Un vrai personnage*. I'll give you that.'

'You look like you've just seen a ghost.'

'Maybe because I have.' He drew a deep, tremulous breath, and wiped a thin film of perspiration away from his forehead with the back of a hand that Enzo noticed was shaking.

'You know the victim?'

'I spoke to you about him just a couple of days ago. One of my missing persons. The one I was at school with.'

Enzo remembered the file on Roussel's desk and his glib assertion that people went missing all the time. 'So there *was* something sinister about his disappearance after all?'

Roussel gave him a darting look. He did not miss the echo of his own words. 'He's not pleasant to look at, monsieur. Submerged in wine probably since the day he went missing. But there's only enough alcohol in red wine to inhibit decay, not prevent it entirely.'

Enzo said, 'When Admiral Lord Nelson was killed by you people at Trafalgar, they shipped him back to Gibraltar in a barrel of wine. There they changed the wine for brandy, and sent the body back to Britain for burial. It's how they preserved bodies for the long trip home in colonial days.' He rubbed a hand over the stubble on his jaw. 'Legend has it that, in Nelson's case, the barrel was nearly empty by the time the ship made port.'

Roussel pulled a face. 'Thank you for that thought, monsieur. It makes me feel so much better.'

Enzo nodded towards the woods. 'Who's up there?'

'Two *gendarmes* and an adjutant from the STIC.'

Enzo shook his head. 'Which is what?'

'*Section Technique d'investigation Criminelle*. The *Police Scientifique* from Albi. Officially known as the IRCGN these days. And a police photographer.'

'Can I have a look?'

'No.' Roussel was emphatic. 'You shouldn't be here at all.'

'You've seen my qualifications, Gendarme Roussel. You know that crime scene analysis is one of my specialities.'

'I know that I'd get shot if I let you anywhere near it. We have our own people, Macleod.'

'Just a glimpse. That's all.'

Roussel looked at him long and hard – although perhaps it was through him, rather than at him – as he engaged in some inner dialogue, a silent argument with himself. Then he delved into the pockets of his jacket and pulled out a couple of plastic shoe covers. 'Put these on. And touch nothing. This is strictly unofficial.'

The *source* was dry, moss-covered stones carefully built around the opening of an underground spring from which water would bubble when the water table was high and tumble down the hillside to irrigate the vines. It was only three or four metres inside the treeline, a path trodden through tangling saplings and briars. Enzo could not imagine what possessed young people to come here. If sex was the object of the exercise, he could think of many more appropriate places.

Almost as if reading his mind, Roussel said, 'It's the romance of the legend that draws the kids. I don't know the whole story, but needless to say it involves young lovers meeting in secret, defying families and fate. There was a *château* here in the woods at one time, but it was destroyed during the Albi crusades. The cellars and foundations still exist somewhere, pretty much buried by the centuries. The old church that served it is still up there on the hill looking out over the valley.'

He turned towards a path freshly beaten through the undergrowth.

'This is the way the boy went when he heard the killer and thought it was a Peeping Tom.'

'What exactly did he hear?'

'Someone moving through the undergrowth, he said. Making quite a noise, apparently.'

'Did he see anyone?'

'Not until he stumbled across the body.'

They followed his path through the trees, a chaos of decaying wood matted with moss, fresh saplings, broken branches, boots choked by ivy leaning one against the other. Leaves wet with condensation slapped their faces. In the distance, light shone through the mesh of vegetation, splintered and fragmented, hanging in the mist that now rose from the rotting forest bed beneath their feet.

Lamps powered by battery were raised on unsteady stands to throw light across a clearing where someone had broken the ground with a shovel, scraping fresh, rich earth to one side in a shallow pile that was peppered with fallen leaves. The outline of what looked like a grave was clearly marked out, but it was no more than a few centimetres deep. The clearing was delineated on the south side by the gnarled trunk of a huge chestnut tree that must have been three hundred years old. It was long dead, its twin trunks collapsed and rotten. One of them had fallen across the clearing at an angle, creating something like an arch, a natural entrance, old branches propping it up, like so many crumbling columns, to prevent complete collapse. It looked as if the tree might have received its fatal blow from a lightning strike, which had split the central trunk in two, creating a deep, natural cradle about two metres from the ground. It was this cradle that held the body, purple and shrivelled, naked legs dangling like withered sticks, arms stretched out on either side as if to hold it upright. The head was canted forward, grotesque in the harsh lamplight. There were no eyes, just deep, dark shadows, thin lips stretched back across red-stained teeth in a ghastly grimace. Black hair was smeared across the forehead. There was an odd stench of alcohol and decay in the air.

Several uniformed *gendarmes* hovered around the perimeter of the clearing, just beyond the light, in which three figures in white tyvek suits moved around in careful concert searching for evidence. The splat and whine of a flash camera filled the night air as a photographer took pictures of the corpse.

Roussel said, 'The killer entered the wood from the east side. You can follow his path through the trees. It's a pretty well-worn trail. I guess people must come up here quite a lot. It looks like he held the corpse under each arm and dragged it backwards. You can see the tracks the heels left through the fallen leaves.' He shone his flashlight in the direction from which the killer had come, and Enzo saw the grooves made by the heels. 'There's an old farm track runs along the east side of the forest, so it was easy for him to get up close with it.'

'Did the young couple hear him drive away?'

'They did. No lights, though. It's a nearly full moon, so I figure he wasn't taking any chances.'

'Tyre tracks?'

Roussel shook his head. 'It's stony ground up here, monsieur. And it hasn't rained in weeks.'

Enzo craned his neck and gazed up into the dark above them. The nearest leaves were illuminated by the light from the clearing, but beyond it was just blackness. The warm

September weather had retarded the fall, and only a few leaves had begun to turn. The bed of old, dead leaves through which the killer had dragged his victim, was from another year, another fall.

One of the STIC *techniciens* called out suddenly. He was crouched down on the west side of the shattered chestnut. With careful precision he lifted up between white-gloved fingers what looked like a discarded cigarette end. 'There're three of them,' he said. He sniffed at it. 'Fresh. If there's any saliva on these there's a good chance we'll get DNA.'

Enzo pursed his lips thoughtfully. DNA seemed like missing the point.

The *technicien* put the cigarette butts into separate ziplock bags, and labelled them each in turn.

Enzo said to Roussel, 'So how did you identify the victim?'

'I recognised him.'

'Really?' Enzo looked again at the shrunken, shadowed face of the corpse. 'I'm not sure I would have.'

'We were best pals when we were kids. When he was about ten he had a terrible biking accident. Front wheel caught in a railway line as we went over a crossing. Turned it right around and threw him over the handlebars. Nearly killed him. Fractured skull, depressed fracture of the cheek, broken jaw. He was a terrible mess. They just about had to rebuild his face. And didn't do a very good job. You could always see the scars.' He paused. 'Still can. Have to get his wife to make the official ID, though.' He looked less than thrilled at the prospect, and was lost for a while in private contemplation. Then he said, 'After we left school we sort of, you know, went our separate ways. But I still saw him. We had some good nights out. I always kind of found it hard to believe that he would just take off like that, without saying anything to me. But then I thought, if it had been me, would I have said anything to him? And I figured probably not.' He shook his head. 'But I never dreamt of anything like this.'

The adjutant from the STIC approached. He was a small man inside a tyvek suit that looked two sizes two big for him. The hood left only his face exposed, so Enzo could not see if he was bald. Or, if he had hair, whether it was dark, fair, silver. It was extraordinary how little you could tell about someone from the face alone. But he had thick brown eyebrows and looked to be a man in his forties. He glanced cautiously at Enzo then addressed himself to Roussel. 'There've been a lot of people tramping about here before we arrived, David. It's a shitty crime scene. Doesn't make our job any easier. But it looks like the kids disturbed him in the middle of trying to bury the body. The cigarette ends would indicate that he'd been here a while. Hard work digging a grave in ground as hard as this.'

'Hardly much of a grave,' Enzo said.

The adjutant turned hostile eyes in his direction. 'Who's this?'

'A forensic expert from Scotland. He's not here in any official capacity.'

The adjutant fixed him again with an unfriendly stare. 'So what's your point?'

'My point is he wasn't digging a grave at all. And the digging he did wasn't done tonight.'

Roussel turned towards him in surprise. 'How do you know that?'

Enzo said, 'It's a late fall this year.' He nodded towards the pile of earth and the leaves that had settled on it. 'Those leaves didn't just come down in the last couple of hours.'

Both men looked at the pile of earth, but neither of them said anything.

'He probably dug that up the night before.'

'Why?'

Enzo shrugged. 'Who knows? Probably preparing the ground before he brought the body.'

The adjutant's voice was laden with skepticism. 'So what did he bring the body here for if it wasn't to bury it?'

Enzo said, 'What does that corpse weigh, do you think? Seventy, eighty kilos? A lot for one man to handle. You can see that by the deep grooves left in the forest floor by the heels. So why would you go to the trouble of heaving it up into that tree cavity if you were just going to get it down again to bury it?' He made a point of meeting the adjutant's eye. 'But you're right about the cigarettes. He probably was here for quite a while. Waiting.'

'Waiting for what?' Roussel said.

'Someone to come. I mean, why would you choose to bury a body right next to a well-known lover's haunt? You'd pick somewhere a million miles from where anyone was likely to stumble across you. And even if you didn't realise it was a popular meeting place, and you suddenly heard people near-by, you'd hold your breath and not make a sound. But this guy went crashing off through the undergrowth, drawing at-tention to himself.' Enzo turned towards the path by which the body had been brought in. 'And, even if he'd panicked and wanted to make a getaway, it's a clear path out. No need to make all that noise.'

'I don't get it,' Roussel said.

But the adjutant from the STIC was nodding grimly, em-barrassed, but professional enough to admit that he had missed what Enzo hadn't. 'I do.'

'Well, what?'

The adjutant looked again at the leaves on the earth. 'He only wanted it to *look* like he'd been interrupted burying the body. He *wanted* to be interrupted. He *wanted* the body to be found.' He turned now towards the corpse. 'Propped up there for the world to see.'

As they walked back down towards the vehicles below, Rous-sel said, 'The adjutant from the STIC is going to be pretty pissed off at losing face like that, Macleod.'

'At me?'

'No, at me. For letting you anywhere near the place. There's going to be hell to pay. I can feel it in my bones.'

Enzo glanced at him. 'What rank do you have, Roussel?'

'Gendarme.'

'Just rank and file *gendarme*?'

'That's right.'

'So how did you get put in charge of a case like this?'

'I was the first officer on the scene.'

Enzo blinked in surprise. 'And that qualifies you to lead the investigation?'

Roussel became defensive. 'We are all trained in basic investigative and forensic techniques, monsieur. Of course, I answer to a higher authority, but I am perfectly well qualified to be the investigating officer.'

They walked in silence for a few steps before Enzo said, 'When I went through Raffin's notes, there were quotes from statements made to the Press by a police spokesman who wasn't you.'

There was a tension now in Roussel's voice, a hint of buried resentment. 'At the height of the inquiry, because it was such a high profile case, they appointed a PR officer from Albi to speak to the press. But he had nothing to do with the investigation.'

The group waiting down by the vehicles turned towards them as they heard their voices. Enzo stopped Roussel and lowered his. 'I don't know why the killer wanted us to find your friend tonight, Gendarme Roussel. But I figure it's his first big mistake.' Roussel waited for more. 'There has to be a link between Petty and this man. And maybe others in your missing persons file. It's just opened up a whole new avenue of investigation. We can't let it slip by us.'

'We?'

Enzo drew a deep breath. 'Alright. You.'

Roussel held him steady in his gaze. 'You don't think I'm up to this, do you, Macleod?'

Enzo considered his response. He said carefully, 'I think I can help you.'

CHAPTER EIGHT

The bedside lamp cast a pool of yellow light on the ceiling, and a circle of it spilled across her pillow. But the rest of the room seemed plunged into deeper shadow, dark and depressing.

Nicole sat on the edge of the bed ringing her hands, her nightdress hardly enough to keep her warm. Tears ran hot down cold cheeks, raising gooseflesh on her arms, and try as she might she couldn't restrain the sobs that bubbled up from her chest to break in her throat and part her lips. Her head ached and her eyes burned.

She looked up, startled by the gentle knock on her bedroom door, and a wedge of soft light fell into the room from the hall. Fabien's silhouette nearly filled the door frame. He stood there, hesitating on the threshold, and she could hear the bewilderment in his voice.

'Why are you crying?'

'You had no right to speak to Monsieur Macleod like that. He hasn't done you any harm.'

'He was coming to spy on us.'

'He's trying to find out who killed a man. Two men now.' Her breath trembled as she sucked it in. 'He's a good man. I owe him everything, and I've let him down. I don't know how I can face him tomorrow.' And fresh tears tumbled over her cheeks.

Fabien stepped into the room and pushed the door shut behind him. He hesitated briefly before sitting on the bed beside her. 'You don't understand.'

'I understand that I should never have come here. And when I discovered this was where Petty was found, I should have left immediately. I'll leave first thing in the morning.'

'You don't need to do that.'

'Yes I do.'

Fabien looked down at his hands, embarrassed and upset by her distress. 'Look, I'm sorry. Don't go. I don't want you to go.'

Which set her off on a fresh squall of sobbing. He seemed at a loss for what to do before putting a clumsy arm around her shoulder in an attempt at comfort. She didn't appear to notice, and so he left it there and they sat still for several minutes in a silence broken only by her sobs. Finally, she half turned towards him. 'Why did you hate Petty so much?'

'It wasn't him. It was the system he represented. A system that serves only one man's taste. That wants to deliver something as unvaryingly predictable as Coke or Pepsi. A system that's destroying diversity.'

For a moment, Nicole forgot her distress, startled by his intensity, impressed by his eloquence.

'Petty's been replaced by Parker, but nothing's changed. Winemakers talk now about "Parkerizing" their wines.

Making it to suit his tastes, trying to win his favour, pitching for one of his high ratings. Instead of following their own instincts, making wines that come from the heart and the soul. The critics are even telling us how to make our wines these days. Filter, don't filter. Micro-oxygenate. The wealthy *châteaux* are all employing consultants at hugely inflated fees just to make wines that'll please Parker, and Petty before him. Which leaves the rest of us, who don't have that kind of money, fighting for crumbs at the critics' table.'

'But if you make a good wine, surely people will recognise that?'

'What's a good wine? A wine that Parker likes? Does that mean one he doesn't like is a bad wine? Of course not. But these people don't want wines to be different. They want them to be all the same.' He was on a roll now, and Nicole was being carried along with it. 'You understand what we mean by *terroir*?'

'It's an area, a region.'

'In winemaking, *terroir* refers to the vineyard and how all the specific qualities of the land affect and change the wine. The type of soil, whether the vineyard is elevated or flat, whether or not it is south-facing. What weather systems affect it, even the microclimates that exist between one part of the vineyard and another.' Fabien shook his head. 'But there are people who refuse to accept the concept of *terroir*. They want to believe that they can make wines in California, or Chile, or Australia, that taste just the same as wines grown in Bordeaux, or Burgundy, or the Rhône Valley. *Terroir* doesn't exist, they say. Because to admit that it does means they will never make wines like the French. Which is what they all aspire to.'

'Don't *you* want to make wines that taste like Bordeaux?'

'Of course not. How can I do that? The soil is different here, the climate is different. We grow different grapes. I want to make good Gaillac wines.'

'But you also want people to know they exist.'

'Of course.'

'So people like Petty and Parker are important.'

Fabien just shook his head. 'Petty came here. But I wouldn't let him taste my wine.'

Nicole was astonished, her tears forgotten. 'Why not?'

It was a long time before Fabien answered her. And when he did, it was in a very small voice for such a big man. 'I was scared.'

'What of?'

'That I would get bad ratings.' He turned to meet her gaze of consternation. 'I took over the vineyard eight years ago, when my father died. He was very traditional. Made the same wine his father had made before him. In the same *chai*, in the same old concrete *cuves*. But there was a whole new generation of young winemakers at work in Gaillac, and I knew that to compete I would have to change things. Modernise, employ new techniques. So I borrowed. A huge amount of money, Nicole. I'd be scared to tell you how much. I mortgaged everything. The house, the farm. I built a new *chai*, installed stainless steel *cuves*, all the latest equipment. I went to

Bordeaux and Burgundy, to California and Australia, just to see how other people were doing it.' His eyes fell away to gaze at the floor. 'Petty was the first international critic to come and rate Gaillac wines. If he marked down the wines of La Croix Blanche, I'd never have been able to sell them. I'd have been ruined. Lost everything to the bank.' He glanced at her. 'How could I ever have faced my father in the next life?'

Nicole had no idea what to say. She became aware that his arm was still around her, and the warmth of his body had taken away her chill. Her tears had dried up, and her breathing had returned to normal, although her heart, perhaps, was beating a little faster. Gently, almost imperceptibly, she leaned into him, soaking up the comfort that he had intended his arm to give. She shook her hair out of her face and turned towards him. He turned, too, and his face seemed very close to hers. She could feel his breath on her forehead. Instinctively she tipped her head back as he dipped his towards her. And the bedroom door opened.

They were startled apart, the moment between them scattered like dandelion seeds in the wind. The formidable Madame Marre stood in the doorway. She did not fill it, as her son had done, but her presence was much more forbidding. She wore an old-fashioned nightcap over hair in curlers and pulled her flannelette dressing gown tightly around her bony frame. 'Time you were back in bed, Fabien. You're up at six.' It was an instruction, not an observation. Fabien stood up immediately. She was not a woman to be argued with.

*

Back in bed, curled up among the sheets, with the light out, Nicole wondered if they had really been going to kiss, or if it had been a figment of her imagination. She felt a tiny thrill of excitement run through her at the thought – and knew – that had he kissed her, she would have kissed him right back.

CHAPTER NINE

I

It had been a long night. And now Enzo needed coffee to keep him awake. He stood on the *terrasse* gazing out at the early morning shadows reaching towards him through the mist. The *pigeonnier* was wraithlike through its gauze, the sun a big, red orb rising above the line of the trees. But there was no warmth in it yet, no strength to burn off the tiny particles of moisture that filled the air and reflected its light.

Across the path, the *château* rose out of the *brume*, as if out of some timeless mediaeval mist, the east turret lifting above it to catch the light, white stone glowing pink.

The smell of the coffee reached him on the warm air from the house, and he turned back through the open door to watch Charlotte nursing the coffee maker. She wore a black, silk dressing gown embroidered with vividly coloured Chinese dragons. Her feet were bare, and he could see the curve of her calf narrowing to the ankle, and he had a brief recollection of the fragments of a dream. 'Don't go today,' he said.

She made no attempt to turn around. 'Okay.' No argument, no rancour, and he felt a surge of pleasure in that single, simple word. She filled two cups and carried them to the table, setting them down beside the sugar bowl and a couple of spoons. 'Come and get your coffee.' She dropped two lumps into his cup, knowing he preferred it sweet in the mornings. And he liked that she knew that. He sat down opposite her and took a sip.

'You know,' he said, 'the Chinese police look for everything else first. The who, the where, the when, and the how. Never the why. They believe that if you have accumulated enough evidence, the motive will become apparent.' He sipped again at the strong, sweet, black coffee. 'But it's always the first question we ask. And it's the question that's been nagging at me all night. Not just why he did it, but why he went to such lengths to show us. To display his handiwork.'

Charlotte cradled her cup in her hands, as if to warm them, and contemplated the steam rising from it. 'I think the Chinese are not without reason, Enzo. You need information to be able to answer the "why" question. Evidence. Although, by the same token, seeing a motive can help you look for that evidence in the right places.' She paused. 'But you're asking two questions. Two "whys". And they're probably related.'

'In what way?'

She took a first mouthful of coffee and closed her eyes. 'If we take your second "why" first, and ask why he would want to display his handiwork, then I'd say he was probably showing off. He's saying, "Look, I've committed two perfect murders, and you didn't even know." He wants us to know how clever he's been.' Another mouthful of coffee, and she opened her eyes and smiled.

Enzo was momentarily distracted. He loved her smile, the upturned corners of her lips, the creases around her eyes, the light emerging from their hidden darkness.

'There are lots of theories about why people commit crimes. Environment, stress, impulse, anger, low self-esteem, high self-esteem. I'd say our killer was neither modest nor self-doubting. He has high, rather than low, self-esteem. But the nature of the killings, and the way he has displayed his victims, would make me think that his motivation is compulsive in some way. That it derives from a character disorder, or a fantasy obsession, rather than some more conventional motive.'

'Because of his MO?'

'Partially. Although you shouldn't confuse his *modus operandi* with his signature. How he kills his victims is one thing – drowning them in wine, then preserving them in it for future disposal. There is a rationale and a logic to that. I would say that was his MO. And it is probably evolving as he perfects it. But the way he has subsequently revealed the bodies to us is his signature. Something that's not necessary for the accomplishment of the crime, but that the killer feels compelled to do to reach emotional fulfilment. And it probably has more to do with why he committed the crimes in the first place.'

'But the signature has changed, too, between the first and second murders.'

'You mean the robes and the hat?'

Enzo nodded.

'That probably only means that these things were available to him the first time, but not the second.'

And Enzo remembered the hot afternoon spent with Jean-Marc Josse in the shade of the old oaks at Mas Causse. The robes and hat of the *l'Ordre de la Dive Bouteille* would have been in limited supply. Passed into the possession of a family, only when one of the order's members died.

Charlotte drained her cup. 'The thing is, Enzo, I'd say that you were dealing with someone suffering from a serious personality disorder. Which means it won't be a simple matter to find reason in his motive.' She wagged a finger at him. 'So be careful. Nietzsche once warned about the dangers of duelling with devils. I read it years ago, in his work *Beyond Good and Evil*, and I've never forgotten it.' She took a breath and fixed Enzo with a look that told him she was serious. '*Whoever fights monsters should see to it that in the process he does not become a monster. When you look into the abyss, the abyss also looks into you.* It's a professional hazard of the forensic psychologist. And the cop. I've seen good men, and women, destroyed by it.'

The sound of a car door slamming made her turn to glance from the window. When she looked back at Enzo there was an unsettling smile on her face. 'Your girlfriend's here.'

His heart sank. However much Michelle might have inflamed his passions the night before, in the cold light of day he was glad it had come to nothing. For had there been any other outcome, the morning after would have cast cold light on their age difference and brought only regret. As it was, he was still embarrassed by what had passed between them. He left Charlotte at the table and went to open the door as Michelle arrived on the *terrasse*. 'Hi,' he said.

'Hey.' She looked pale and tired. 'I came to get my father's things.'

He nodded. 'I repacked the suitcase for you.'

She stepped into the room and cast a look of cool assessment in Charlotte's direction, lingering on the silk dressing gown and the bare feet. Almost involuntarily, she glanced then at the *clic-clac*, and saw that it had been slept on. Enzo thought he detected a small look of triumph in her eyes, and when she looked back towards Charlotte, it was clear that Charlotte had seen it too, and her unerring confidence seemed to waver just a little.

'They found another body last night,' he said, and Michelle whipped around, her face filled with consternation.

'Where?'

'Same vineyard where they found your father. It looks like he suffered the same fate. There'll probably be an autopsy today.'

'Who is he?'

'I don't know much about him yet. Except that he'd been missing for a year, and there doesn't appear to be any obvious connection with your dad.'

A knock at the door made them all turn to find Nicole standing there, flushed and apprehensive. But her initial anxiety was quickly replaced by bewilderment as she took in Charlotte and Michelle and Enzo still in his towelling robe. She made a hasty reassessment of an earlier conclusion that all his problems stemmed from the lack of a woman. She said, 'There are too many women in your life, Monsieur Macleod.'

Enzo looked around the three women in his *gîte*. 'Tell me about it, Nicole.'

Nicole looked over at the table and saw Petty's computer next to hers. 'Whose is the computer?'

'It was Gil Petty's. Michelle retrieved it along with his personal belongings. We've been through all the files looking for his Gaillac tasting notes, but we couldn't find them.'

Nicole's interest was piqued. She crossed the room, acknowledging Charlotte with the briefest, '*Bonjour*,' and sat down at the computer. 'It's an old one.' She pushed the power button to start it up and turned towards Michelle. 'Did he have a French server for internet connection and e-mail?'

'I don't know. I guess he must have. He was certainly sending and receiving e-mails while he was here.'

'Then it's possible he worked online and stored his notes on the server for security.'

The idea caught Enzo's imagination. 'You mean, they could still be out there in the ether somewhere? Even after all this time?'

'Sure,' Nicole said. 'It's just a matter of knowing where to look.'

Michelle had wandered across the room and was staring up at Enzo's whiteboard. 'Why have you written *Petit* under my father's name?'

Enzo had all but forgotten yesterday's revelation about Petty's ancestry. 'Because that was his family's name when they

lived here on the castle estate.' She frowned. 'In this very cottage. Petty was probably what the immigration official wrote
on their papers when they queued up to become American
citizens at the end of the eighteenth century.' He watched her
for a moment as she stared thoughtfully at the board. 'You
didn't know?'

She shook her head. 'I had no idea. I knew my mum's family
was German in origin, but I never knew anything about my
dad's side.' She had a sudden thought. 'Maybe that's why he
wanted me to have a French name.' It was like a revelation to
her. 'Michelle.' She spoke her own name as if hearing it for
the first time. It had taken on a whole new meaning to her,
and it seemed to bring back some of the emotions that going
through her father's things had provoked the previous day.

The moment was broken by Beethoven's Ninth. Enzo
fumbled in the leg pockets of his cargos to find his mobile. He
recognised Roussel's voice immediately and was aware of the
others watching him as he listened to the *gendarme*. 'Okay,'
he said. 'Ten o'clock.' He hung up and thrust the phone deep
into his pocket and glowered off into the middle distance.

'Well?' It was Charlotte who asked.

'Well, what?'

'What's at ten o'clock?'

'I've been summoned to the office of the *juge d'instruction*
in Albi.'

Michelle looked puzzled. 'What's a *juge d'instruction*?'

'He's the judge who directs the inquiry.'

'I thought Roussel was the investigating officer.'

'He is. But he takes his instructions from the judge, and reports to him on all aspects of the investigation.'

Michelle made a snorting sound. 'So much for the impartiality of the judiciary.'

Enzo shrugged. 'It's the French system.' He sighed. 'And I think the system is about to give my knuckles a severe rapping.'

II

The Tribunal de Grande Instance at Albi occupied an impressive building of brick and stone which had once belonged to the Church. Enzo wondered if it had been requisitioned by the State during the French Revolution for the more secular activity of administering justice. In any event, as he approached it across the Place du Palais, it inspired in him a sense of awe, befitting a building of such solemn purpose. It also filled him with a sense of apprehension.

He walked down the Rue du Sel and climbed steps to a side entrance where shady-looking characters hovered by barred windows awaiting summons to criminal hearings. Enzo loitered with them while his presence was conveyed to the judge somewhere within.

It was a full five minutes before a young woman emerged from a semi-glazed doorway, the click of her heels echoing off red tiles. She had shoulder-length auburn hair that fell to the collar of a conservative grey tweed suit, the hem of her skirt tailored exactly to the knee. Enzo couldn't help noticing the curve of her full calves tapering to narrow ankles. She was, perhaps, in her mid-thirties.

She smiled. 'Monsieur Macleod?'

He gave her his most charming smile. 'Yes.'

She held out her hand. 'I'm Madame Durand.'

Her hand felt warm and smooth in his. '*Enchanté*, Madame.'

'Would you like to follow me?'

'With pleasure.'

She led him down a corridor, past the Salle Pierre de Larboust, named after a former *procureur* of the *République* and through a doorway into the vaulted arches of an ancient cloister. 'The cloisters are open to the public during certain hours,' she said. 'But for the moment we have them all to ourselves.'

Enzo frowned his confusion. 'Aren't you taking me to see the *juge d'instruction*?

She smiled. 'Monsieur, I *am* the *juge d'instruction*.' She allowed a moment for his surprise to sink in. 'Is that so hard to believe?'

'With all due respect, madame, there is a belief abroad that Frenchmen are inveterate chauvinists. And I have noticed myself at times a certain patronising attitude to women.'

'Let me assure you, monsieur, it is a long time since anyone has patronised me.' There was a steel in her tone that left Enzo in no doubt that this was probably true. She eyed him appraisingly, something almost mischievous in her smile. 'You're not what I was expecting.'

Enzo grinned. 'Nor me you. Perhaps we should start again.' He held out his hand. 'I'm Enzo Macleod.'

She smiled and shook his hand warmly. 'Monique Durand.'

They set off at a sedate pace through arches that formed a square around a rose garden, their voices whispering back at them from the timeless red brick.

'You know why you're here?'

'To get my wrists slapped?'

She laughed. 'I'm sure there are places in town where men pay to have women slap them around.'

'But not here.'

'Not here, monsieur.'

'Just as well, or you'd have queues at the door.'

She turned towards him, her face creased by genuine amusement, and looked with curiosity into his eyes. 'You have very unusual eyes, monsieur. Have you ever been told how disarming they are?'

'Never by a judge.'

Her smile widened before slowly fading, and she turned away to draw and expel a deep breath that Enzo took to be something like a sigh of regret. They passed double doors leading to the Salle d'Audiences No.1. 'You know, I received an official complaint first thing this morning from the *Police Scientifique* at the STIC. Interference with a crime scene.'

'It's my speciality.'

'Interference?'

He chuckled. 'That, too.'

'I have spoken with Gendarme Roussel. And I have looked at your credentials on the internet. Very impressive.' She glanced at him. 'But I simply can't have someone without any official attachment to either the *Gendarmerie Nationale* or the IRCGN interfering with a police investigation. It's just not acceptable. And I have also made that very clear to Gendarme Roussel.'

'It wasn't Roussel's fault. I gatecrashed his investigation.'

She half-turned towards him and cocked a skeptical eyebrow. And almost as if he hadn't spoken, said, 'Which is why I am taking the highly unconventional step of inviting you to consult on this case, in an official capacity.'

His surprise drew him up short. He stopped, and she turned to face him. 'Why?'

'There are many reasons, monsieur, and I'm sure I am going to have to field some political brickbats. But you are clearly a man intent on solving Petty's murder. I'm aware of what you achieved on the Gaillard case. So I'd rather have you working with us, than against us. And, of course, sharing resources.'

'As well as the credit, if we find his killer. Preferable, no doubt, to my solving the case on my own and embarrassing the police yet again.'

She tipped her head to one side and regarded him carefully. 'They told me you were someone who likes to speak his mind. It can get you in trouble, you know.'

'Oh, I do. But diplomacy is not an attribute that has ever been associated with the Scots.'

'Nor modesty, if you are anything to go by.'

Enzo laughed. 'May I ask you something, Madame le Juge?'

'Of course.'

'Would you have dinner with me some night?'

She threw her head back and laughed out loud, her voice echoing around all the arches of the cloisters. He had taken her completely by surprise, but it was clearly not an unpleasant one. 'And you accuse Frenchmen of being chauvinists?'

'It's not chauvinistic to find a woman attractive, is it? Or to ask her out to dinner?'

She searched his 'unusual' eyes, one brown, one blue, and saw the twinkle in them. 'You know, I'm tempted to say yes. But I think my husband might have something to say about it.'

Roussel was waiting for him in the Place du Palais, nervously clutching his hat in his hand. His dark blue trousers had been freshly pressed, his black boots freshly polished. The sun slanted at an angle across the velvet stubble of his crew cut, and Enzo saw that there were silver hairs in amongst the black.

'Well?'

Enzo strode past him towards the police vehicle that had brought them, and Roussel had to hurry to catch him up and fall in step. 'She's officially invited me to consult on the case.'

Roussel stopped dead. 'You're kidding!'

Enzo turned and looked at him speculatively. 'Like you didn't know.'

Roussel shrugged. 'Well . . . not for sure.'

'Like you didn't suggest it.'

'Not in so many words.'

Enzo shook his head. '"We don't need your help. We have

all the expertise we require within the service." That's what you told me, isn't it?'

'Saves me getting into trouble with the STIC, or anyone else, when you come nosing around the investigation.'

'So what do I get? A badge and a gun?'

'You get a lift back to Gaillac. If you're civil.'

'And if I'm not?'

'You can take the train.'

III

Enzo hadn't noticed before the family photographs stuck up on the wall behind Roussel's desk. A little boy, aged two or three, playing on a tricycle. A young woman laughing at the camera. Plump, with an attractive smile. There was a child's drawing of a motor car made with coloured crayons. Pinned to the wall above the filing cabinet was a violet and white striped football supporter's scarf, and a banner for TFC – Toulouse Football Club. So Roussel had interests beyond Lara Croft.

Enzo said, 'Do you always have the shutters closed?'

'I think better in the dark. Sunlight's distracting. It just makes you want to be outside.' Roussel took his missing person's file from the filing cabinet and opened it carefully on his desk. He lifted up the sheaf of papers he had produced during Enzo's first visit and handed it to him. 'Serge Coste, aged thirty-four. Married. Childless. No longer missing. I guess I should be moving him into the Petty file. I broke the news to his wife just after first light.'

'How did she take it?'

He shook his head. 'Hard to say. She didn't cry or anything, not while I was there. She just nodded and bit her lip. I almost got the sense that she was relieved. He hadn't run off and left her after all. So, no loss of face. She asked me in and wanted to know the details. When I told her she seemed genuinely shocked. It's not an easy thing to describe, what we saw last night. Especially to a loved one.'

Enzo cast an eye over the file. Coste had been the manager of a DIY store, one of a national chain, on the outskirts of town. He had no apparent connection with the wine industry. He was born in Gaillac, grew up and went to school in the town. He had failed his *baccalauréat*, but still managed to get a place in a technical college where he had honed his skills in *bricolage* and got a job as a sales assistant in the store he would later manage. He had been married for eight years before disappearing without explanation one weekend twelve months ago. 'Had he ever been to the States?'

Roussel scratched his chin thoughtfully. 'Not to my knowledge. You know, a lot of people who're born here and die here, never venture any further than Toulouse. I don't know where Serge took his vacations, but he wasn't the type to go abroad.'

Enzo gazed sightlessly at Coste's file for several minutes, lost in deep contemplation. 'And you couldn't find any link between Coste and any of the others in your missing person's file.'

'To be honest, I wasn't looking. There was no reason to.

None of them was connected in life, there was no reason to look for connections between their disappearances.'

Enzo held out a hand. 'Can I have a look?'

Roussel handed him the file, and he started leafing through the cases. Roussel tucked his thumbs in his belt and tilted his chair back against the wall, watching Enzo as he absorbed the details of each. 'Until now, there wasn't any reason to look for a connection with Petty either. Not that I can think of anything anyway. Except maybe Robert Rohart. He was a good bit older than the others, an estate worker at one of the wine *châteaux*. But that's a pretty thin connection. A lot of people work in the wine industry around here.'

He continued to watch Enzo sift slowly through the papers in the file, as if somehow absolved now from all responsibility. Then he tipped his chair forward again and leaned his elbows on the desk.

'You know, I have this way of working. It's kind of conceptual. I see each case as being like a long corridor.' He held the palms of his hands six inches apart and moved them in parallel away from himself. 'There are doors off it to the left and right. So I stop at each door I come to. I go into the room, and I take account of everything that's in it. Then I shut that door and move on to the next. That way I miss nothing, and there's never any reason to go back. When I reach the end of the corridor, I have all the information I need to solve the case.'

Enzo looked up and found it impossible to mask his skepticism. 'What if there's a power cut?'

'What?'

'If it's dark in those rooms, there's stuff you won't see. Or in the corridor. You might miss a door. You might find a light bulb in the next room and go back to throw light on one you've already visited.' Enzo tapped the papers on his knee with his knuckle. 'In my experience, Gendarme Roussel, criminal investigations are never linear. You're constantly going back and forth and sideways, reassessing what you knew before in the light of what you've learned since. Looking again at what you've already examined because for sure there's something you've missed.'

Roussel's face reddened and he pushed himself back from the desk, folding his arms defensively. 'We all have our own ways of working.' He nodded huffily towards the missing persons file. 'So what have I missed in there?'

'A connection.'

Roussel seemed startled. 'Really?'

'But like you said, you weren't looking for one before. This is a classic example of going back to reopen a door you've already closed.'

'Tell me.'

'You've got four cases in here. All of them have disappeared over the last three years. Three of them share two things in common. The fourth shares neither of them, so let's take that one out for the moment.' He passed it to Roussel.

'Jeanne Champion.'

'She was sixteen. All her friends said she was pregnant, but her parents didn't seem to know. Classic hallmark of the teenage runaway. Disappeared April, 2004.'

'So what doesn't she have in common with the others?'

'Most obviously, she was a female. All the others were male.'

'And?'

'She went missing in the Spring. The others all disappeared on dates ranging between mid-September and mid-October from 2004 to 2006.' He waited for Roussel to realise the significance of the dates, but the *gendarme* simply looked perplexed. 'They all went missing when the grapes were being harvested. During the *vendanges*.'

The red of Roussel's cheeks darkened. 'Jesus.'

'And if Petty was still just a missing person, he would share those things in common with them. As it was, he was the first one to disappear. Serge Coste was the last. If you ask me, monsieur, I would say that the other two are probably curled up in barrels of wine somewhere awaiting disposal.'

'Or display.'

Enzo nodded his agreement. 'Or display.' He dropped the file back on Roussel's desk. 'But here's the scary thing. For all intents and purposes, there's been one a year for the last four years.' He paused for effect.

This time Roussel took his point. 'But there's been no one reported missing this year.'

'Yet.'

CHAPTER TEN

The hospital backed onto the railway line that ran between Albi and Toulouse, where it crossed the Avenue René Cassin on the road north out of town towards Montauban. The street which bordered its southern edge was appropriately named the Rue de la Maladrerie. Those who were unfortunate enough to be wheeled in or out of the hospital's mortuary were, however, more than *malade*. They were dead.

Enzo had attended many autopsies during his time with Strathclyde police in Scotland. Autopsy rooms all tended to be the same. White tiled walls, tiled floors, stainless steel autopsy tables, stainless steel counter tops. Clinical and soulless. The autopsy room in the morgue at Gaillac was no different. And, as always, Enzo found the accompanying perfume of death, of formic acid and formaldehyde, profoundly depressing.

The pathologist made them wear green aprons and surgeon's face masks. 'You never know what you might breath in when we're cutting through bone,' he said comfortingly. Doctor Garapin was a small man, but thickset, almost square. He was bald beneath his plastic shower cap, and the three inches of bare arm visible between the short sleeves of his gown and the plastic sleeve covers above his gloved hands were dense with wiry, black hair. He was the antithesis of the stereotypical tall, intellectual physician. He had a thick, local accent and would not have been out of place, Enzo thought, pruning vines at a *château* vineyard.

'The body is that of a Caucasian adult male. Age is estimated around mid-thirties. The body is identified as Serge Coste by a tag tied about the right ankle. The body weighs seventy-three kilograms, measures one hundred and sixty-three centimetres in length, and has been refrigerated and is cool to the touch.'

Garapin reached up to turn off the overhead mike. 'He's some colour. How the hell do I describe that? He's like . . . like rasperries soaked in *eau de vie*.'

Enzo thought it a very accurate description. Under the harsh lights of the autopsy room, the body did not seem as vividly coloured as it had in the woods the previous night. 'You didn't do the autopsy on Petty, then?'

The pathologist shook his head. 'No, monsieur. But I've read the report.' He turned his mike on again.

'The skin is a pale, grey-pink all over. The palms and soles, while still pink-stained, are paler and wrinkled.'

He switched off the mike once more. 'Just as if he'd remained in the bath too long. Only, in this case, a bath of red wine. What a way to go!' He grinned.

Enzo noticed that Gendarme Roussel had gradually moved away from the table, and was about a metre back from it. He was a bad colour. Worse than the corpse in front of them.

Garapin moved meticulously over the surface of the body,

noting contusions on the left shin, right knee, right fore-arm and an area of subgaleal haemorrhage on the left temple. With the help of an assistant, he manhandled the dead weight onto its front and examined the backs of the legs, the buttocks, the back, neck and head. He found more contusions on the left shoulder and another subgaleal haemorrhage on the head behind the right ear.

'Are these post or ante-mortem injuries?' Enzo said.

Garapin shook his head thoughtfully. 'Almost impossible to tell. They appear to be post-mortem. Bodies drowned in an ocean or a lake, for example, tend to have injuries, or damage, from rubbing on the bottom, or bashing against rocks after death.'

'The same kind of injuries you might sustain falling or being pushed into a fermentation *cuve* in a *chai*?'

The pathologist looked doubtful. 'There are a lot of contusions here. I'm not at all sure they would be consistent with falling into a *cuve*. And in any case, you would expect such injuries to be ante-mortem.'

'You said you couldn't tell whether they occurred before or after death.'

'That's right. See ...' He moved to the shoulder injury. 'There's no blood around here, which would lead you to think it happened post-mortem. But the victim went missing, what, twelve months ago? If he's been in wine all this time, which from the state of him seems likely, and these injuries were inflicted before death, then the liquid would have leeched the blood from around the skin wound, and it would have ended up looking pale and bloodless, like this, just as if it were post-mortem.' He turned away to the countertop behind him and leafed through a folder of photocopied pages. 'Yes, you see what's interesting is that Petty suffered very similar injuries, and the pathologist who carried out that autopsy wasn't able to decide whether they were post or ante-mortem either.' He turned back to the table and from his tool trolley lifted what looked to Enzo very much like a French chef's knife. 'Let's cut him open, shall we?'

With Coste laid on his back, head propped by a half-moon block placed below the neck, Garapin made incisions from either shoulder to the chest, and then down towards the pubis.

'The body is opened with a Y-shaped thoracoabdominal incision through the skin. There's subcutaneous fat measuring 3.7 centimetres thick at the level of the umbilicus. The pleural, pericardial, and peritoneal cavities are smooth and glistening, with no abnormal accumulations of fluid or gas, and there are no adhesions. All organs are present and in their appropriate positions.'

The first autopsy Enzo attended had been carried out by students, under supervision, on a preserved corpse at the University of Glasgow's faculty of medicine. The internal organs were subdued in colour, grey and pale, the blood dark and surprisingly unred. It had come as a shock to him, then, during his first post-mortem on a fresh body, to discover how vividly coloured it was inside. The fat was a bright yellow-orange, the blood dark red, muscle the colour of steak, and the guts very nearly white.

Coste's insides, however, bore a striking resemblance to that first, preserved corpse he'd seen in Glasgow. Except that the muted grey of the organs had a pink blush to them. And the overwhelming smell that rose from the open cadaver was that of stale alcohol, like a pub the morning after a drunken party.

Wielding a pair of what looked very much like garden shears, Garapin flexed thick muscles in his forearms to cut easily through the ribs, one at a time. Each one gave with a sickening crack. He took a knife to separate the breast plate from the diaphragm, and the fatty tissue sac that held the heart, before lifting the cage aside to get full access to the organs.

Holding the heart in one hand, he snipped open the pericardial sac looking for blood or excess fluid, but found none. Then he lifted the heart out for examination.

'The endocardial surface has a usual appearance and there are no mural thrombi. The valves are thin and pliable and are neither stenotic nor dilated. The coronary arteries have a usual distribution and show minimal atherosclerotic disease. There are no thrombi. The aorta is patent, without injury, and shows minimal atherosclerosis.'

'Meaning what?' Enzo said.

'That he didn't die of a heart attack.'

The pathologist moved on to the respiratory system, removing and weighing one lung at a time. They were grey-pink and spongy. He shook his head. 'Heavy. Waterlogged. Or should I say, winelogged. He wasn't getting any oxygen through these.'

'You're saying he drowned?'

'I'm not saying anything, except that there was wine in his lungs. Whether he breathed it in, or it seeped in over time, is impossible to tell.'

He sectioned them in turn, looking for giveaway particles, pieces of grape skin, fragments of seed, but found none, then turned to the gastrointestinal system and the stomach.

'The rugal pattern of the stomach is normal and there are no ulcers. It contains 300 millilitres of dark red fluid. An ethanol odour is noted.'

The pathologist flicked off his mike. 'No partially digested food material in there, just wine. So it had been some time before he'd eaten.' He chuckled. 'Should have known better than to drink on an empty stomach.'

Enzo was aware of Roussel's breathing becoming shallower behind him. He said, 'Gendarme Roussel was at school with the victim, Doctor Garapin.'

The pathologist glanced at the policeman. 'Sorry.' And he turned back to the job at hand, head down to examine the intestines. He cut the endless, looping tube from the fat which bound it, and slit it open from end to end releasing a thick, pungent odour that almost made Enzo gag.

Next, he removed the pancreas, liver, kidneys, spleen, and thyroid, and weighed and sectioned them on the countertop, describing each in turn, finding nothing unusual.

While he was bread-loafing the organs, his assistant incised the scalp from ear to ear behind the head, and rolled the scalp down over the face, like peeling off a mask. He warned Enzo and Roussel to stand back as he took a circular saw around the top of the skull, the noise of it filling the room, along with the smoky, sweet smell of burning bone.

When he finished, and pulled the skull cap away, it was with a sucking noise and a loud 'pop' as it disengaged from the brain. Then he pulled the brain itself gently back towards him, beginning at the forehead, transecting it from the cranial nerves and spinal cord, so that finally it plopped out into his cupped hands.

Garapin examined the damage to its frontal and temporal lobes. 'Small areas of subarachnoid haemorrhage,' he said. 'But not enough to kill him. Otherwise the brain is substantially normal.' He turned to Enzo and Roussel. '*Messieurs*, there's really nothing more for you to see here. If you'd like to adjourn to my office, I'll see you in about ten minutes, after I've showered.' Enzo noticed the sweat running in rivulets down Garapin's forehead and gathering in his thick, black eyebrows.

As they walked along the green-painted corridor to Garapin's office, Enzo said, 'Are you okay?'

Roussel was the colour of the walls. His hands were trembling. 'You know, as a cop, you see stuff. Stabbings, drownings, suicides. Horribly mutilated people in car wrecks. When I first started on the job, there were nights I came home and just lay on the floor shaking. You'd think you'd get used to it.'

'It's never quite the same when it's someone you know.'

'I kept thinking about Serge when we were kids. He was a character. Always getting in trouble at school. He wasn't much good academically, but he was clever, you know. Always had a comeback when some smartass teacher got sarcastic. The *profs* hated him for it.' He took a deep breath. 'What a shitty way to end up.'

In the end, Garapin kept them waiting nearly twenty minutes. They didn't speak much during that time, sitting staring at charts on the walls, diagrams of human organs, musculoskeletal structures, a multicoloured plan of the brain. Attending an autopsy always left Enzo feeling vulnerable. It was a very human response. Pathologists were somehow inured to it, able to separate the living from the dead. Enzo couldn't do that. It was invariably himself that he saw cut open on the table. A glimpse of the future, an acknowledgement of the inevitable.

Garapin smelled of shower gel and shampoo but, beneath the perfume, there lingered still the stench of death. 'Well,' he said, 'I have to tell you that unless toxicology comes up with something unexpected, I'm going to attribute cause of death to drowning. Not because I can prove that he drowned, but that, given all other factors, it's the most likely explanation.' He dropped into his chair and sighed, intent, it seemed, on trying to convince himself. 'Drowning is a diagnosis of exclusion, you see. There really is no specific pathognomonic or diagnostic sign. If you eliminate all other causes, and given the wine absorbed by his lungs, you're left with drowning.'

Enzo thought about it. It did seem like the only logical conclusion, but he was still concerned by the unexplained injuries, and whether they were inflicted before or after death. 'I suppose it's impossible to say how he came by those contusions.'

'Impossible,' Garapin agreed.

'What about the sample of wine retrieved from the stomach?'

'What about it?'

'He didn't drink that.'

'No, I think it seeped in there over time.'

'So it's the same wine he drowned in. The same wine he's been preserved in for the past year.'

'That's a reasonable assumption.'

'So a chemical analysis of the wine from the stomach could match it to the wine he'd been kept in.'

'Wait a minute.' Roussel was a better colour now. 'We don't know what wine he was kept in. There's probably a thousand red wines, maybe more, produced in Gaillac. You couldn't do a comparison with them all.'

'We could start with the wines of La Croix Blanche.'

Roussel scowled. 'You think Fabien did this? He'd have to be insane to dump the bodies in his own back yard.' And Enzo remembered Charlotte's words, 'I'd say that you were dealing with someone suffering from a serious personality disorder – which means it won't be a simple matter to find reason in his motive.'

Garapin interrupted. 'In any case, it's a moot point. The sample we have has been contaminated by stomach acid and tissue decay. We could never make a comparison accurate enough to stand up in court.'

Enzo nodded, conceding the point, then had a sudden thought. 'Its multi-elemental composition won't have changed, though.'

This time it was Garapin who conceded. 'Probably not.'

'What the hell's a multi-elemental composition when it's at home?' Roussel looked from one to the other, seriously out of his depth, and aware of it.

Enzo said, 'The minerals and elements that the grapes have absorbed from the soil while still on the vine. They would create a kind of identifiable fingerprint that would be passed on to the wine.' He was excited by the thought. 'There's been a lot of work done on this in recent years to try to prevent fraud in the wine industry. To stop crooks trying to pass off cheap plonk as Bordeaux or Burgundy. People get fooled by the label, you know. Even experienced wine tasters can be conditioned by what they read on the bottle.' He turned to Garapin. 'You've got a sizeable sample there. Could you keep me some?'

Garapin leaned back lazily in his chair. 'What are you going to do. Sniff and taste it and tell us the grape and the vintage?'

'No, but I know a man who might be able to tell us exactly where it came from.'

As they crossed the car park, Roussel said, 'I'm sorry to be thick about this, but you're going to have to explain to me how you can take a sample of wine and tell where the grapes were grown.'

Enzo opened the door of the *gendarme's* car and leaned on

the top of it. 'Each grape contains a unique and distinctive pattern of trace elements. These are absorbed by the grape through the movement of elements from rock, to soil, to grape, influenced of course by the solubility of inorganic compounds in the soil. But the point is the multi-elemental pattern of a wine will reflect the geochemistry of its provenance soil – that is, the soil that it's grown in. It will match it as accurately as a fingerprint.'

The light of understanding began to dawn for the *gendarme*. 'So you take a sample of soil, compare it to the wine, and if the *fingerprint* matches then that's where the grape was grown.'

'Exactly.'

'How would we know what soil samples to use?'

'We don't. We'll have to take samples from all the vineyards that Petty visited. Discreetly, of course.'

'And this guy you know will do the analysis?'

'I hope so.'

'Will he come here?'

'I doubt it. He's in California.'

'So you'll send them to him.'

Enzo shook his head. 'No. That could take weeks. And if there's a fifth victim marked up on our killer's list, then we don't have weeks. We might only have days – if that.'

'What'll we do, then?'

'*We* won't do anything, Gendarme Roussel. If my friend agrees to do it at all, I'll take the samples to him myself.'

CHAPTER ELEVEN

I

The smell of crushed, fermenting grapes was carried from the *chai* on the pungent edge of invisible carbonic gas escaping from the *cuves*. It filled the air with the heady scent of autumn wine, and reached Enzo on a light breeze as he walked across the grass towards his *gîte* in the fading evening.

Château des Fleurs seemed larger in silhouette against the setting sun, more substantial and imposing. Lights shone out from the cottage, casting shadows towards him from the *terrasse*. It had been a long day, and he had been away for hours.

A figure stood up from the table on the terrace and ran down the steps towards him. A slight figure, bursting with energy, hair streaming back through warm air. 'Papa!' She threw her arms around his neck and nearly knocked him over. She peppered his face and neck with kisses, then buried her head in his chest.

And his weariness was lifted by a surge of love and affection. 'Hey!' He put his arms around her and held her to him. 'Sophie, what are you doing here?' And even to his own ears his voice sounded strange, speaking English with a native Scottish accent that had remained unchanged across all the years. When they were alone together, he and Sophie always spoke English, and he loved to hear the soft, whisky accent he had given her, a legacy of a homeland she had never known. She could hardly have been more French. It was her culture, and her language, and she was a constant reminder to him of her mother. She looked like her. The same black eyes, the same infectious smile. Only the faint silver stripe that ran back through dark hair from her forehead betrayed the genetic link with her father.

She pulled away and pouted at him. 'Are you not pleased to see me?'

He grabbed her and nearly squeezed the breath from her lungs. 'Of course I'm pleased to see you. I'm just surprised to see you.'

'We thought we would come and help?'

'We?'

'Me and Bertrand. He's got someone looking after the gym for a week. He's a real wine expert, you know.'

'Sophie, a year as a trainee wine waiter doesn't make you an expert.' He put an arm around her waist and they climbed the steps together.

'Bet he knows more than you.'

As they reached the terrace Bertrand stepped out from the lit interior. Enzo could see his diamond nose stud catching the light, and the ring through his eyebrow. He was still gelling his hair into spikes, and wore a sleeveless tee shirt to show off the muscles cultivated during hours of patient weight-lifting at the gymnasium he ran in Cahors. He was not tall, but was very nearly perfectly formed. Enzo sighed inwardly. He had been forced by events to concede that there was more to Bertrand than he had given him credit for. But he was not what Enzo would have wished for his little girl. She was barely twenty. Bertrand was nearly twenty-seven. And worse, he was sleeping with her.

Bertrand shook his hand. 'Monsieur Macleod.'

'Bertrand.' And Enzo had a sudden thought. 'Where are you staying?'

'Here,' Sophie said.

'You can't. There's only one bed, and a *clic-clac* that's killing my back.'

'And two bunk beds up in the mezzanine.'

Enzo groaned inwardly. This was getting ridiculous. Four of them in a house with one bedroom and one bathroom. And he had yet to sleep in the bed. But, 'cosy,' was all he said.

Sophie missed his tone. 'Yeah, it's a great cottage. And a fabulous *château*.' Then she paused. 'So who's in the bed, then?'

'Charlotte.'

'Well, why aren't you sleeping with *her*?'

Enzo glowered at her. 'Don't even go there.'

They went inside, and Enzo was surprised to see Michelle sitting uncomfortably on the edge of the *clic-clac*. Charlotte was in the rocker, reading, and Nicole was tap-tapping at Petty's laptop. 'Have you been here all day?' Enzo found it hard to picture Michelle and Charlotte indulging in polite conversation.

'No, I only came back about half an hour ago to find out what happened at Albi.'

A tiny smile flickered across Enzo's lips as he remembered his conversation with Madame Durand. 'They made me an official consultant on the investigation.'

Charlotte looked up from her book. 'Are they paying you?'

'What do you think?'

'No, I thought not.'

'Shhhhh!' Nicole waved an irritable hand in their direction. 'I can't concentrate with all this chatter.'

Enzo crossed to the computer. 'What are you doing?'

'Right now I'm trying to get into Michelle's dad's webspace.' She sighed her annoyance and looked up at her mentor. 'But I wasted half the day trying to persuade Madame Lefèvre to let me run a phone extension up from the estate office. There's no Airport card in this computer. It's not configured for Wi-Fi.' She averted her eyes towards the screen again and added. 'She wasn't too pleased to discover we'd been tapping into their account.'

'We?' Enzo said, his voice rising in pitch with his indignation.

'You said you were going to tell her.' But before Enzo could respond, she added, 'Anyway, I'm beginning to make progress. Finally.'

Michelle got up and approached the table. 'What have you found?'

'Your dad was using a free server while he was in France. It's called Freesurf. Because he wasn't working from a single, fixed line, he was just paying for the calls as he went. But the thing is, he got a hundred megs of webspace with the account.'

'Was he using it?' Enzo peered at the screen to try to see what she was doing.

'Well, he's got a piece of software called *Fetch* in his Applications folder, which would suggest that he was uploading stuff to the internet. Normally you would save your username and password within the programme to make it quicker and easier each time you wanted to connect. But he doesn't seem to have done that.'

'And you don't know what username or password he was using?'

'I found a username in his mailer. Seems to be the same one he used for everything – gil.petty. But all his passwords are encoded.' She looked up at Michelle. 'I don't suppose you'd have any idea what he might have used as a password?'

She shook her head. 'I'm sorry. We weren't exactly on password exchanging terms.'

Nicole shrugged. 'Doesn't matter. It'll be somewhere in amongst his keychains. I've just got to figure out how to get in there. I know there's a way.'

'Try fishface,' Enzo said.

'Fishface!' Sophie laughed. 'What kind of password's that?'

Enzo glanced at Michelle and saw that she had paled. 'Just try it,' he said to Nicole, and he watched as she entered 'gil. petty' and 'fishface' into their respective fields and hit the return key. A new window opened up, full of folders they hadn't seen before.

Nicole clapped her hands in delight. 'We're in!' She scanned the screen with sparkling eyes. 'Gaillac ratings. Articles for the October 2003 newsletter.' She looked up at Enzo. 'How on earth did you know his password?'

'Lucky guess,' Enzo said, and he looked at Michelle to see eyes filled with tears she was trying hard not to spill. In his peripheral vision he was aware of Charlotte watching them.

But none of them had time to dwell on it. Nicole was opening folders one after the other. 'All the vineyards he'd visited,' she said. 'They're all here. Château Lastours. Domaine Sarrabelle. Château Saint-Michel. Domaine Vayssette. Château Lacroux. Château de Salettes.' She glanced up at Michelle, then looked back at the list, and for a moment her heart seemed to stop. *Domaine de la Croix Blanche*. He'd tasted Fabien's wines. But Fabien had told her that he'd turned Petty away.

'What is it?' Enzo said.

'Nothing.' She moved quickly on. 'There are subfiles with a *Word* document for each wine and each rating. Looks like he'd been to fifteen or twenty vineyards, tasted nearly a hundred wines. He did a lot of tasting in just a week.'

'*Sommeliers* and wine critics'll do that,' Bertrand said. 'I did a wine-tasting *stage* in Toulouse, and all the training was about identifying tastes and smells fast. Sniffing twice only, and keeping the wine in your mouth for as short a time as possible. That way you can taste a lot of wine without ruining your palate.' He shrugged. 'I don't know that I was very good at it. Our *prof* was a former French *sommelier* of the year. He could pick out and identify every flavour in even the most complex wines.'

Everyone turned at the sound of a cork popping, and Sophie stood holding an open bottle of red wine. 'Speaking of which, it's time for *apéros* don't you think?' She glanced at Enzo. 'You don't mind, do you, Papa?'

'What is it?' Bertrand said.

She looked at the label. 'Château Clément Termes. *Mémoire rouge*.'

Enzo gave her a sour look. 'You have the most unerring instinct, Sophie, for picking the most expensive wines.'

Sophie grinned. 'I have good taste, that's all. Must have got it from my mother.' She started pouring glasses.

Enzo displaced Nicole from her seat in front of the computer. 'Move.'

'Aw, Monsieur Macleod, you always get to do the good stuff.' She moved away from the table to take a glass from Sophie's outstretched hand, and sipped at it sulkily, in search of consolation. She brightened immediately. 'This is very good.'

'It ought to be. It cost enough.'

'Oh, don't be so Scottish, Papa.'

Enzo glowered at his daughter, then turned to scan the screen and open a folder entitled *Articles, October 2003*. There were several documents. *Wines of Gaillac. History. Cépages. GM Yeast. Editorial*. The unfinished content of a newsletter that was never published. Something drew him to the document entitled *GM Yeast* and he clicked on it. It was an article written for *The Wine Critic* by an American professor of genetics, revealing for the first time the widespread use of genetically modified yeast in the production of Californian wines. None of it made much sense to Enzo:

> The yeast ML01 was modified using a shuttle vector containing a chromosome integration cassette with genes for malolactic enzyme, malate transporter (permease), regulatory genes and a sequence directing homologous recombination at a chromosomal locus.

He wasn't sure Petty's subscribers would have made much sense of it either.

He turned to the document entitled, *Editorial*, and ran his eye down the text, leaping from sentence to sentence with a growing sense of disbelief:

> The Food and Drug Administration in the United States alone reviews and approves GM microbes such as yeasts used in food products. But international faith in the FDA is fast eroding because approvals are frequently influenced by political pressure, and the approval of wine yeast leaves fundamental questions to be answered. It is certainly premature to market GM wine yeast and, since the wines produced using GM yeast are not labelled in the marketplace, it is only prudent to avoid all US wines.

'Jesus Christ!' He looked up to find the others staring at him.

'What is it?' Michelle looked alarmed.

Enzo could still scarcely believe it. 'In his October newsletter, the one he never published, your father was going to
launch a campaign to boycott American wines.'

'Why?'

'Because of widespread use of genetically modified yeasts
that the consumer wasn't being told about. Yeasts approved in
June 2003 by the FDA following tests that he claims were . . .'
he searched for the quote, 'based on faith rather than
science.' He stared at Michelle and shook his head. 'This is
dynamite. A man of your father's influence. If he had published this stuff, it could have caused catastrophic damage to
the California wine industry.'

Charlotte pushed herself back in her rocking chair. 'And
provided a motive for any number of people to want to see
him dead.'

Sophie sipped her wine thoughtfully. 'But if it was never
published, and he kept all his notes hidden on the internet,
who would have known about it?'

'If we knew the answer to that,' Enzo said, 'we might be a
lot closer to knowing who killed him.'

It was Nicole who spotted the flaw in the logic. 'But whoever
killed Gil Petty also killed the man we found last night, right?'

Enzo nodded, the memory of the autopsy still only too
fresh in his mind. 'Almost certainly.'

'But you said this morning there didn't appear to be any
connection between them. Has that changed?'

'No. The second victim was a local man called Serge Coste.
He managed a *bricolage* store in Gaillac. No connection with
Petty, or the wine industry.'

'So wine wasn't necessarily the motive for the murders.'

Enzo inclined his head in acknowledgement. 'You might be right, Nicole. And it's certainly a danger that, if we focus too much on motive, we could miss stuff that's right under our noses. Which is why we'll carry on working our way, step by dull step, through every scrap of information we can dig out. Just like the Chinese.' He turned towards Sophie. 'Do I get a glass of my own wine or not?'

'Sure, Papa.' She brought him a glass and pecked him on the cheek. 'Me and Bertrand'll just go and get our bags from the car and get ourselves sorted out up the stairs.'

Enzo took a small sip of the *Mémoire* and enjoyed the silky vanilla texture of it on his tongue. Then he took a full mouthful and felt himself relax a little as the alcohol slipped back over his throat. He let the aftertaste fill his mouth and nasal passages for a moment before turning back to the computer screen. He selected a vineyard at random, Domaine Sarrabelle, and went into the folder. There were four wines reviewed in separate documents. The Saint-André that he and Michelle had drunk the previous night, a chardonnay, a syrah and a sweet *vin doux*. He opened the syrah review, and sat staring at it for a long time, lost in a deep, puzzled concentration.

'What's wrong?' Michelle's voice came to him through a fog of confusion.

He looked up. 'You said your father was obsessed with secrecy. Did you know he used a cipher?'

She looked at him blankly. 'No, I didn't.'

Enzo hit the print button, and the inkjet printer on the

bookcase chattered and spewed out a page. He lifted it up and crossed to his whiteboard and began copying onto it what he had printed out. The others watched in silence as his blue marker pen squeaked its way across the shiny, white surface. He wrote:

Domaine Sarrabelle – Syrah -2002
100% Syrah
Tile red
oh & nm. ky, ks & la
ky ms & nj. wjc. gf+ & lbj++
5-8
jb ca

As he turned around, Sophie and Bertrand came heaving huge travel bags in from the *terrasse*. Enzo eyed the bags in disbelief. 'I thought you were only here for a week?'

'We are,' Sophie said. 'I had to leave *so-o* much stuff behind.' She looked at the board. 'What's that?'

'It's Petty's review of Domaine Sarrabelle's 2002 syrah.'

She gazed at it for a moment. 'It's in code.'

Enzo grimaced. 'Well spotted.'

Sophie ignored his sarcasm. 'Great. A puzzle. You're good at those, Papa.'

Enzo looked at the board. Random groupings of letters and numbers in twos and threes. Petty had been a man of exceptional talent and intelligence. It was not going to be a simple matter, he knew, to unpick a code created by him.

II

Nicole lay on her back gazing up at the ceiling in the dark. She glanced at the bedside clock and saw that it was just after midnight. Her mind was a seething mass of facts and fears. Random pairs of letters swam in front of her eyes. Without a starting point, how could they ever crack Petty's code? She tried to focus on it, but the recollection of the folder entitled *La Croix Blanche* kept forcing its way into her thoughts. Why had Fabien told her that he had turned Petty away, when Petty had in fact reviewed his wines?

The reflected headlights of a vehicle in the yard swept across her ceiling, and she heard a car door slam shut. Fabien had not been home when she got back to the house, and she had received only a chilly greeting from Madame Marre.

She slipped out from between the covers and pulled her curtains aside in time to see Fabien, caught in the full glare of security lamps outside the house, striding across the yard and into the *chai*. After a moment, lights flickered on in the shed, and fluorescent light fell out into the night. Nicole made a very fast decision, and turned quickly to pull on her jeans and drag a warm, hooded sweatshirt over her head. She slipped into her training shoes and opened the door to the hall. A night light cast the faintest glow down its length. She listened for a moment and, hearing nothing, closed the door behind her and made her way carefully towards the stairs. The top step creaked loudly and she froze, listening intently for any indication that the formidable Madame Marre might have heard her. But all that broke the silence of the house was the heavy tick, tick of an antique grandfather clock in the downstairs hall.

She hurried down the remaining stairs and out of the front door to the garden. There she stopped and breathed the cool night air and was relieved to be out of the house. The lights were still on in the *chai*. Away to her left, agricultural machinery sat in the brooding shadow of a long, open shed with a rust-red tin roof. At the far end of the old farmyard, beyond the *chai*, was the shed where the wines of La Croix Blanche were ageing in new oak barrels. Its door stood open, and a wedge of light lay like a carpet in the approach to the entrance.

As she ran across the yard, the security lights came on and she felt very exposed. She jogged down the length of the *chai*, stopping only to gather her breath as she approached the shed where the barrels were stored. The lights went off again behind her, and she approached the open door with a great deal of nervous apprehension. She paused in the doorway and peered inside. Rows of barrels, stacked two high, ran off towards the back of the shed. The central strip of each barrel was stained pink between the cooper's bands of steel. Darker rivulets, like blood, ran down their bellies from cork bungs. The wine was still fermenting, and the smell of it in the air was thick enough to cut.

There was no sound, and no sign of Fabien. She stepped inside and saw an opening off to her left leading to another room filled with yet more barrels. There was an electric pump on the floor, and silver tubing coiled around it like a giant snake.

'What the hell are you doing here!' The sound of Fabien's voice startled her, and she turned in a panic, clutching her chest. He was standing in the doorway, wearing his ubiquitous baseball cap, glowering at her out of the darkness.

'I was looking for you.'

'This is no place for someone who doesn't know what they're doing. It's dangerous.'

Nicole almost laughed. 'Dangerous? Wine? Only if you drink too much of it.'

But he didn't laugh with her. He grabbed her hand and pulled her out into the yard. 'Come with me.'

Nicole followed reluctantly although, in truth, she had very little choice. 'Where are we going?'

'You'll see.'

He took her through the *chai*, where pumps were thundering in the still of the night to transfer freshly fermenting grape juice from one *cuve* to another. Past rows of brand new stainless steel tanks, and old resin containers from Fabien's father's time, to a large room through the back. There, the tops of sunken *cuves* rose fifty centimetres from the concrete floor. Fabien let go of her hand and knelt down at the nearest of them, and carefully removed the lid.

'Kneel down.'

'Why?'

'Just do what I tell you.'

Scared now, Nicole did what she was told and knelt down beside him.

'Take a sniff in there.'

She looked down into the *cuve* and saw the yellow-white frothing grape juice in full fermentation.

'Go on, smell it.'

With great apprehension she leaned over to smell the fermenting juice and felt her head snap back so suddenly that she was startled into calling out. She had recoiled from a smell and a sensation so extreme, that she'd had no control over her response to it. It had been entirely involuntary. She gasped, 'What in the name of God was that?'

He cocked an eyebrow at her as if to underline his earlier warning. 'Carbonic gas. A by-product of fermentation. It's not poisonous, but it'll kill you in the blink of an eye.' He took a cigarette lighter from his pocket, lit the flame, and then lowered it slowly into the neck of the *cuve*. As he did so the flame detached itself from the lighter, but continued to burn until the separation between the two was nearly ten centimetres and it was finally extinguished. 'No oxygen, you see.' He stood up and offered her his hand to help her to her feet.

She got up, and they stood for what seemed like a very long time, still holding hands, until he was overcome by self-consciousness and took his back. She desperately wanted to ask him about Petty, about his reviews of La Croix Blanche wines, but the words wouldn't come. And the longer they stood in silence, the more tense they both became. She started to be aware, for the first time, of how dark his eyes were, how long his lashes. And almost as if he knew what was in her mind, he averted his black eyes.

He said, 'About twenty years ago there was a lake somewhere in Africa that released cubic tons of the stuff into the atmosphere.'

She was taken aback by his sudden digression. 'Cubic tons of what?'

'Carbonic gas. The lake was in an old volcanic crater, and the gas must have come up from the volcano below. Probably over hundreds of years. It dissolves in water, you see.' He pointed to the grille-covered channels that ran through the concrete floor of the *chai*. 'We flush water through those gutters to collect and take away carbonic gas from the fermentation. It's heavier than air, so it sinks to the floor and dissolves in the water.'

Nicole followed the line of the gutter out into the yard.

'Anyway, the gas must just have been lying on the lake bed. Then, during a storm of some kind, there was a huge amount of rainfall, and they think that cold rainwater dropped to the bottom of the lake, displacing the carbonic gas and forcing it to the surface.' He shook his head, visualising it. 'Must have looked like the water was boiling. Except that it was the middle of the night, so no one would have seen it.'

Nicole was wide-eyed, imagining the scene as Fabien described it. 'So what happened?'

'The lake was way above sea level. So because the gas is heavier than air it just ran down the valleys, engulfing all the villages in its path. Most of the villagers were asleep in bed. Thousands died from asphyxiation.'

'Oh, my God, that's terrible.' Nicole was still wide-eyed, transfixed by the horror of his story, impressed by the breadth of his knowledge. It was not what she would have expected of a farmer's boy who made wine.

He fixed her again with his dark eyes. 'That's why you don't ever come in here on your own. Understand?'

She nodded mutely.

As they crossed the yard towards the house he said, 'So why were you looking for me?'

She was glad he couldn't see her face. She was not a good liar. 'It's just . . . you weren't there when I got back tonight.'

'There were cops crawling about the place all day. I got behind with things.'

As they passed beyond the security sensors, the lights went out, and Nicole saw the wash of moonlight over the hills that rose out of the river valley to the north, the silhouette of the old church starkly outlined against a jewelled jet sky.

'Is it still in use?' she asked.

He followed her eyeline. 'No, it's all boarded up. Which is a shame. It's a beautiful old building.'

'Why did they build a church way up there, anyway?'

'It used to serve the castle: then the castle was destroyed during the Albigeoise Crusades against the heretics of Cathar.' He looked at her. 'You know who the Cathars were?'

She shook her head with a growing sense of inadequacy. She was the university student, after all. Surely these were things she should know? 'I know they call this Cathar country. But I don't know why.'

'The Cathars were a religious sect in the twelfth and thirteenth centuries. They combined Christian and Gnostic elements. The thing that the Roman Catholic church regarded as heretical was their belief that the resurrection was a rebirth, rather than the physical raising of a dead body from the grave. So the Cathars were slaughtered in their thousands and driven out of towns and villages all over south-west France.'

'How do you know all this?' She gazed at him in wonder.

He shrugged. 'I read a lot. It's interesting. Though it was the legend of the *source* that first caught my imagination. Forbidden love. A Cathar princess from the castle, and the son of a Roman Catholic knight who was intent on destroying the heretics. They met secretly at the *source*, up there in the woods, until the night the crusaders marched on the castle and destroyed it. Both their fathers died in the battle, but, according to the legend, the young couple escaped to the north, where they married and raised a family.'

'And lived happily ever after?'

'Who knows? Does anyone?' She saw the moonlight catch the crinkles around his eyes as he smiled. 'But the *source* became regarded as a place where star-crossed lovers could change their luck. All the kids around here go up there at some time.'

'Did you ever go up there with someone?'

'Once. A long time ago.'

'It didn't change your luck, then?'

'Oh, yes it did. I had a narrow escape. She's married now with four kids and makes the poor man's life hell.'

They both laughed. But their voices seemed inordinately loud in the quiet of the early morning, and they quickly stifled their mirth.

They stood for a minute or more staring up at the church, which seemed to shimmer in a haze of warm, silvered air, before walking back in silence to the house. And it was with a slight chill of apprehension that Nicole realised it would take someone with very specific local knowledge to know that a body left up by the *source* would be discovered sooner rather than later.

III

Enzo selected 'send' from the toolbar, and a sound like a soft jet engine passed from one speaker to the other to signify the despatching of his e-mail into the ether. He put the laptop to sleep and folded down the lid. As he stood, he stared out from the pool of lamplight around the table to the reflected light on his whiteboard and those mysterious groupings of letters and numbers that made no sense. He glanced up towards the mezzanine and heard the gentle purr of heavy breathing. Sophie and Bertrand were asleep. He turned out the lamp and crossed the room in the dark to the open door and the candle-light on the terrace.

Charlotte looked round. 'You want a glass?'

'If there's any left.'

'There's plenty.' As he sat down she poured him a glass from a bottle of Château de Salettes *Vin des Arts* and refilled her own. 'Who were you writing to?'

'A guy called Al MacConchie. I was at university with him in Glasgow. He went off to the States about twenty-five years ago and is now a big shot wine consultant in California.'

'Wine? What was his major?'

'At university?' Enzo laughed. 'Chemistry. He believed that the problems of the universe could be answered by chemical analysis. And statistics. Now he's applying his philosophy to the making of alcoholic beverages.'

She turned eyes filled with curiosity in his direction, waiting for further explanation. But he just shrugged.

'I need a favour from him.' He was too weary to go into it now. He took a sip of the *Vin des Arts*. It was freshly acidic, with soft tannins, and filled his mouth with the taste of raspberries. 'Nice wine. Must get a case of it.'

They sat for some minutes, sipping the fermented juice of red grapes and gazed out over silver grass wet with dew. The shadows cast by the chestnut trees were almost impenetrable.

Candlelight flickered over all the soft surfaces of Charlotte's face as she turned it towards him. 'There was another reason I came down here to see you.'

Something in her tone rang warning bells. He turned his head sharply. 'What?'

She hesitated for a long moment, as if undecided. Then she said, 'Enzo . . . Roger's seeing Kirsty.'

He could not have said why this news filled him with such dark foreboding. Except that there was nothing about it that seemed right, or natural. Enzo was only just on speaking terms with his daughter after their years of estrangement. She was raw and vulnerable, and he knew instinctively that a relationship with Roger Raffin was wrong.

Raffin was an intelligent and successful Parisian journalist in his mid-thirties who had been motivated to write his book on France's seven most notorious unsolved murders by the failure of police to find the killer of his own wife. When Enzo began his investigation into the first of those killings, he and Raffin had reached an arrangement on shared publication rights. At that time Raffin had just ended an eighteen month affair with Charlotte, and the separation had been acrimonious.

'I suppose that means he's not jealous about you and me any more.'

'He's never stopped being jealous, Enzo. And him being with Kirsty doesn't change anything.'

He looked at her very directly. 'I know why *I* don't like the idea of Kirsty and Roger. Why don't you?'

'Because I know him too well. He's not right for her, Enzo. He's . . .' She looked away, and he could see the tension gathered all along the line of her jaw. She finished her thought with a shadow in her tone. 'There's something dark about Roger, Enzo. Something beyond touching. Something you wouldn't want to touch, even if you could.'

*

It was a full five minutes after Charlotte left him to go to bed, and the light went off in the bedroom, that he turned at the sound of movement in the doorway.

Sophie stood there, in the dark, barefoot in her nightdress, her hair a tangle, and he had a sudden memory of her as a little girl standing in the dark of his bedroom telling him about the monsters under her bed, and how she wanted to spend the night with him. And how he'd led her back to her own room, and shown her there was nothing under the bed, and tucked her in again. He'd had to read to her for nearly half an hour before she finally drifted away, her little hand still clutching his so tightly he'd had to pry her fingers gently free.

'I thought you were sleeping.'

'Couldn't get to sleep for the monsters under my bed.'

He looked at her in astonishment. Had she read his mind? And then he realised that, of course, it was a shared memory. As vivid for her as for him. Something in the moment must have evoked the recollection for them both. He smiled and held out his hand. She took it and sat on his knee, tipping her shoulder into his chest and tucking her head up under his chin, just as she had always done as a child.

'Don't go interfering in Kirsty's life,' she said.

He tensed. 'How . . . ?'

'Voices carry in the dark.'

He sighed. 'He's not right for her.'

'That's for her to decide.'

After a long moment, he said, 'Do you see her?'

'I've seen her a couple of times. Up in Paris.'

'You never told me.' The half-sisters had met for the first time only very recently, each regarding the other with deep suspicion, even jealousy.

'I don't tell you everything in my life.'

'You used to.'

'I'm not a child anymore.'

'What difference does that make?'

'*You* don't tell *me* everything.'

'That's different.'

'Why? I ask you about Charlotte and all I get is, "Don't even go there."'

She did such an accurate parody of his gruff Scottish voice that he couldn't help but smile. Then, after a moment, 'So you knew about Kirsty and Roger?'

'It's none of your business, Papa.'

He tipped his head down and kissed the top of her head.

'I love you,' she said.

'I don't have to tuck you in and read to you tonight, do I?'

She sat up grinning. 'No, it's alright. If there're any monsters, Bertrand can get them.'

And as she padded off into the house he thought, with a pang of regret, about how the baton of responsibility for daughters as they grew up always got handed on from fathers to lovers.

But where Kirsty was concerned, despite Sophie's warning, he did not want to pass that baton on to Roger Raffin.

CHAPTER TWELVE

I

Nicole could smell coffee on the cool morning air as she climbed the steps to the *gîte*. She had been awake early, to find La Croix Blanche blanketed in a fog that had risen up from the river. Without waiting for breakfast, she had left the house and climbed the hill to the old church, emerging from the autumn *brume* into brilliant sunshine, finding the church and hilltop like an island in a sea of mist. A studded wooden door closed off an archway of stone and brick, and standing on the steps she'd had a view out across the ocean of cloud below. It seemed to lap through the vines at the very foundations of the church.

Then, as she'd followed the path down to Château des Fleurs, the mist had simply melted away, rising on air warmed by the sun to evaporate and reveal a sky of the clearest, palest blue.

But her good spirits, which had risen with the mist, ended abruptly as she entered the *gîte*, and Enzo turned towards her from his whiteboard without so much as a *bonjour*. His brow was furrowed in concentration. 'I've been thinking, Nicole.

You can't stay at La Croix Blanche. In fact, if I'd thought about it, I wouldn't have let you go back there last night.'

Her hackles rose. 'Why not?'

'Because Fabien Marre has made it perfectly clear that he had nothing but antipathy towards Petty. And since both bodies were found on his vineyard, he has to be considered a suspect.'

'No!'

Her abrupt response startled him. 'No, what?'

'You're wrong about Fabien.'

'Nicole . . .'

She did all but stamp her foot. 'I'm staying at La Croix Blanche, Monsieur Macleod. And if you don't like it, then I'll just go home. You're not my father. You can't tell me what to do.'

Charlotte turned from the kitchen worktop where she was grilling toast, and she and Enzo exchanged glances.

Enzo shrugged. Long experience had told him that when Nicole was in this frame of mind, rational argument was wasted on her. He raised his hands in self-defence. 'Okay, okay. Just don't come crying to me later telling me what a terrible mistake you made.'

Nicole did not consider this worthy of a response and instead installed herself noisily at the computer and hit the start-up button.

A creak on the stairs made them all look up, and Bertrand came down wearing only a pair of boxer shorts. Enzo was aware of both Charlotte and Nicole eyeing him with interest.

He was stunningly well-built, smooth, tanned skin stretched over taut muscles, and Enzo suffered a moment of irrational jealousy. It was a long time since women had cast such lascivious eyes in his direction. If ever. He had certainly never had a body like that.

Bertrand was clutching an old, well-thumbed copy of Gil Petty's newsletter which had been among Enzo's papers. There was a spontaneous exchange of compulsory *bonjours* before he waved the copy of *The Wine Critic* at Enzo. 'I've had an idea about how to crack the code.'

Enzo eyed him skeptically. A well-developed body often reflected a less well-developed brain. But Bertrand had surprised him before.

'I've been looking at his old reviews, and they all follow the same pattern.' He reached the foot of the stairs and crossed to the whiteboard.

A sleepy-looking Sophie emerged from the mezzanine above him and looked down into the room, sweeping the hair out of her face. 'What's all the noise?'

But Bertrand ignored her. He pointed to the first line of the coded review, which was not in fact coded at all. *Tile red*. 'Okay, he starts with the colour. That's clear. Then he sticks his nose in the glass and describes what he smells.' He stabbed a finger at the second line – *oh & nm. ky, ks & la*. 'So these groupings of letters must represent the smells he's going to describe when he writes up his review. Strawberry, oak, vanilla, whatever they might be.'

Enzo shuffled patiently, stifling a mild irritation. All of this seemed rather obvious, and had occurred to him almost immediately the night before. He couldn't see how it helped.

'The next line represents the taste, or the texture of the wine in his mouth, and then the finish.' He ran his finger down to the next line – 5-8. 'That's not code at all. He's just telling us how many years the wine can be laid down for. Then the last line, of course, is his rating. Which, I guess, was the thing he was most concerned about keeping secret.'

Enzo tried not to sound patronising. 'I had thought through most of this already, Bertrand. What's your point?'

The young man didn't seem in the least dismayed. He beamed. 'It's obvious, isn't it? All we have to do is get a bottle of the wine he's describing and taste it for ourselves. If we can identify the smells and the flavours, and then cross-reference them to other reviews and taste those wines, we should be able to figure out what some of these codes represent.'

Enzo glanced towards Charlotte and saw the tiny smile playing about her lips. She cocked an eyebrow at him, and he found himself revising his opinion of Bertrand yet again. It wasn't a bad idea. If they could identify even two, or three, of those flavours or smells, and relate them to Petty's code, then it would give them a starting point for breaking it.

'Neat, huh?' Sophie beamed down at them from the mezzanine, basking proudly in the reflected glory of her *petit ami*.

'There's just one drawback.' Everyone turned towards Nicole, and she blushed. 'I mean, Monsieur Macleod's an experienced drinker of wine. Everyone knows that.' Enzo glared at her. 'But Bertrand's the only experienced *taster* among us.'

'Not a problem.' Sophie padded down the stairs and lifted a flyer from the selection of leaflets and tourist guides that Madame Lefèvre had left in the *gîte* for her *locataires*. 'I was just looking at this last night. They run daily wine-tasting courses at the Maison du Vin in Gaillac. It's just a couple of hours. We could all do it. It would be fun.'

II

The table was covered in clear plastic, then white butcher's paper. With fastidious care, Enzo laid out the red cape on the paper. It smelled of damp earth and stale alcohol and death, and its black trim was marred by a fine cast of green mould. The three-pointed red hat was bashed and stained. There were still hairs clinging to the interior of its black headband. Enzo wondered if they had belonged to Petty, or to its original owner.

He looked around to find Roussel watching him, plastic evidence sacks piled on the chairs beside him. Space at the *gendarmerie* was at a premium, and so the police officer had acquired a room at the town's medical *laboratoire* for Enzo to examine the evidence from the Petty case. He had been to Albi early that morning to collect everything from the *parquet*, the prosecutor's office.

'Were there any notebooks found amongst Petty's things at the *gîte*?'

Roussel shook his head. 'No. I thought that was odd at the time. Because everyone said he took notes when he was tasting. Always in a small, moleskin notebook. But there was nothing.'

Enzo thought about it. Petty's murderer must have taken it. Or destroyed it. Why? Might there have been something incriminating in it? They could only speculate. He turned his attention back to the hat. 'Was there any attempt to establish if this was Petty's hair?'

Roussel nodded. 'There was Petty's hair and hair from at least two other people. Unidentified.' He stooped to lift a hefty document from his leather briefcase, and handed it to Enzo. 'That's the report from the lab in Toulouse.'

Enzo took it, and glanced at the policeman. He looked terrible. There were penumbral shadows beneath his eyes. He seemed tired, and drawn, diminished somehow, almost as if he had lost weight overnight. And Enzo was certain that he could smell stale alcohol on his breath. 'You okay?'

Roussel eyed him for a long time. 'Not really.'

Enzo waited for him to elaborate.

Roussel couldn't hold his gaze. He sighed. 'I loved this job, you know. Gave me a position in society. Big shot cop in a small town. I had such self-confidence. In my own ability. In my own instincts. I coped with everything, from burglary to arson, road deaths to domestics. I knew how to deal with people, how to work the system. I had respect on the street.' He shook his head. 'Then Petty comes into my life. Celebrity wine critic. Disappears into thin air. I can't find him. Then he turns up dead. I can't find his killer. I get big pressure from upstairs. They appoint people over my head. I start to lose confidence.'

He looked at Enzo. 'Then you show up. A real pro. And I begin to look like what I am. Big fish in a little pool. Small time cop in a dusty country town.' His eyes became glazed, faraway thoughts making them cloudy, like cataracts. 'You take one look at a missing person's file and see what I never saw in four years.'

'Only because you had no reason to look.'

Roussel shook his head sharply. 'No. That's just an excuse. I should have seen it. If I had, then maybe poor old Serge would never have gone missing. Maybe he and his wife would have agreed, finally, on adoption. They might have had a kid by now. Instead, he's all hacked up in a refrigerator in the morgue, because I never saw a connection.'

Enzo realised there was nothing he could say to ameliorate Roussel's pain. He was inflicting it upon himself, self-castigation for his own perceived failures, when perhaps the failure was systemic rather than personal.

He crossed the room to the countertop where Roussel had laid out the police photographs taken of Petty at the scene of his discovery. The colours of the cape and of Petty's wine-stained skin seemed more lurid caught in the flash of the camera, the night a black backdrop to the grotesque arrangement of corpse and cape. Although he had been tied by the wrists to a stout wooden cross driven into the ground, the image of Petty was not at all like a crucifixion – more like a scarecrow prominently placed in a newly seeded field to frighten the birds. The shrivelled face beneath the pointed hat seemed almost comical, like a Halloween mask.

Enzo followed the outstretched arms, draped in long, red sleeves, to white gloves dragged on to hands that were too big for them. He paused and looked carefully at the gloves. The thumbs had not even made it into them; the glove fingers were empty. The gloves were no more than dressing, there for effect and to reflect the detail of the costume worn by the *l'Ordre de la Dive Bouteille*.

He turned to Roussel. 'Do we have the gloves there, too?'

Roussel nodded and removed them from one of the sacks. Enzo took them in his own latex-gloved hands and turned them over, examining them in great detail. They were dirty, as if perhaps they had never been washed, and purple stained from the wine. So Petty had been taken fresh from his liquid preservative, still wet when his killer had dressed him. What trouble to go to, every minute spent dressing the body and transferring it to the vineyard increasing the risk of discovery.

Enzo could see why the murderer had been unable to get Petty's hands fully into the gloves. They were tiny, and must have belonged, originally, either to a very small man – or to a woman. He remembered seeing at least two women amongst the members of the *Ordre* in Josse's photograph album. So it was not unheard of, even if it was uncommon. He said to Roussel, 'There's a good chance these gloves belonged to a female. You should be able to get a list from Jean-Marc Josse of all the women members of the *Ordre* since its inception. Just the dead ones. There can't have been many. That could seriously narrow the field for us, in terms of identifying families with access to old robes.'

Roussel nodded grimly. It was almost as if each fresh thought of Enzo's was another nail in the coffin of the *gendarme's* self-esteem. Belief in himself was visibly ebbing.

Enzo returned his focus to the gloves and carefully pushed the fingers of each into their palms and teased them inside out. The backs and palms were wine-stained from Petty's fingers, but the fingers of the gloves themselves were almost pristine white. He examined the end of each one in turn, stopping only when he reached the ring finger of the left hand. He slipped his reading glasses down to the end of his nose and brought the glove up close to his face to examine it. 'Ah-hah!'

'What?' Roussel moved closer to see what Enzo had found.

Enzo pointed to a tiny, dark-stained fleck close to the top of the back of the finger. 'Almost certainly blood.' He smiled. 'It's amazing how often you'll find it inside the fingers of a glove. A little tear in the cuticle, a tiny bit of bleeding. Happens to us all. Can't be Petty's though, because his fingers never got up there.'

'How on earth did the lab at Toulouse miss that?'

'You'll have to ask them. But I suspect it's because they didn't look. Or, at least, didn't look carefully enough.'

'Is there enough to get a DNA sample?'

'Should be. Though it's almost certainly not the killer's blood. Like Petty, he'd never have got his hands in there. But it'll mean we can confirm a family connection if we get ourselves a suspect.'

Roussel nodded. 'I'll make a call right now. Arrange to have it couriered to Toulouse this afternoon.'

When he'd left the room, Enzo took a look at the other plastic evidence sacks. The first label he looked at was marked 'Contents of Bin'. He cleared away the robe and hat from the table and emptied the sack on to the white paper. Every item was separately bagged in clear plastic ziplocks. Enzo sifted through them. An empty toothpaste tube, a used razor head, pieces of toilet paper scrunched up around what looked like dried mucus. There was a bloodstained wad of some kind. Enzo held it up to examine it more closely and realised it was a used sanitary pad. He crinkled his nose in distaste and moved on to find an empty pop-out pack of Hedex painkillers, several open plastic sheaths for haemorrhoid suppositories, a piece of chewing gum wrapped in tissue paper.

He stopped suddenly, realising where these items must have been found. The Hedex, the suppositories – these were things he and Michelle had come across in Petty's toilet bag. These discarded medications and toiletries must have been recovered from the bathroom wastebin at the *gîte*. Then consternation drew his brows together in a frown. A used sanitary pad?

The door opened, Roussel returning from his phone call. 'It's all arranged. A dispatch rider will take the gloves to Toulouse later today.'

Enzo held up the bag containing the sanitary pad. 'Might be an idea if he took this, too.'

'Why?'

'Didn't it strike you as odd that a man living on his own would have a soiled sanitary pad in the wastebin of his toilet?'

'Of course it did. But there was no evidence of anyone else staying there. And neither the Lefèvres nor anyone working at Château des Fleurs, saw Petty with a woman, or even saw a woman coming or going to the *gîte*.'

'You didn't think to DNA-test it?'

'Why would we? We had nothing to compare it to.'

'I'd like it tested now, please.'

'Okay.' Roussel snatched the bag from him, his earlier self-pity turning now to irritation. 'Anything else, Monsieur Macleod?'

Enzo was thoughtful for several moments. 'Yeah. There is.' He cast an eye over the contents of Petty's bin strewn across the table. 'How come you kept the contents of his bin, when you didn't know he'd been murdered until a year after his disappearance?'

'Because by the time he'd been missing for a week, alarm bells had started ringing.'

'You told me people go missing all the time.'

'They do. But not famous people. Not celebrities. You or I, we could disappear into the ether. But someone like Petty?' He shook his head. 'Not so easy just to vanish when half the world knows your face.'

'So alarm bells began to ring . . .' Enzo prompted him.

'Missed appointments, conference calls he never logged in for. His agent started hassling us. Then the US embassy. We started taking it more seriously. He'd booked the *gîte* for a month. There were still ten days of the rental left, and he'd been missing for well over a week. All his stuff was still there, including the contents of the bathroom wastebin. So we bagged it all, as a precaution.'

'Did *something* right for once.'

Roussel turned sullen eyes away from Enzo's. 'Anything else we can do for you, monsieur?'

'Yes, there is.' From his shoulder bag, Enzo took the ziplock bags containing the samples of Petty's hair, and the gunk from his razor. They were labelled and dated, and he held them out to Roussel. 'It would be useful to have a sample of Petty's DNA as well.'

III

From the lab, in its tiny, hidden square in the heart of the old town, Enzo walked through to the Église Saint-Pierre. The repeating pattern of arches in an elaborate stone doorway were reflected in the red brick architecture of its towering façade. Coloured fragments of sunlight, glimpsed beyond the half-open door, fell in through stained-glass windows to cast light in the gloom of its vast, echoing interior. But Enzo did not go inside. Neither prayer nor confession were high on his list of priorities.

He turned left into the Rue Portal and followed the narrow, cobbled street up between oddly canted apartments to the big, leafy Place de la Libération, where sunlight danced in the shade of tall chestnuts whose leaves were stirred by a light wind. All along its length, old people sat on benches watching leaves fall and time slip away.

Sophie and Bertrand were sitting at a table outside the Grand Café des Sports with Nicole, Michelle, and Charlotte. As soon as he joined them, Enzo became aware of an unspoken tension between Charlotte and Michelle – aware, too, that he was probably the cause of it. He was neither flattered nor pleased by the thought, reflecting only that his life would be much less complicated if there were fewer women in it. Sophie was being extra bright in an attempt to gloss over the discordant atmosphere.

'We went to the Maison du Vin,' she said. 'They've got an amazing tasting room down in the cellars of the old *abbaye*. Rows and rows of sinks for spitting your wine into.'

Nicole humphed. 'A waste of good wine.'

Sophie ignored her. 'Trouble is, Papa, we're out of season now, and they're only doing tasting classes on Thursday nights.' She delved into her bag. 'But we got these.' And she produced a sheaf of photocopied documents. '*Les étapes de la dégustation*. Everything you need to know about tasting wine.' She thrust them at her father, and he flicked through sheets of paper with illustrations of wine glasses being looked at, sniffed, swirled, and quaffed. *La vue. Le nez. Le goût*. There was a list of colour nuances for red, white, and rosé wine, categories of smells and tastes, an illustration of the human tongue with its clusters of taste buds capable of distinguishing everything from sweet to acid to salty to bitter.

'And I used to think wine was easy,' he said. 'You drank it, and you liked it. Or you didn't.'

'There's much more to it than that, Monsieur Macleod,'

Bertrand said earnestly. 'It's full of subtlety and variety. And once you've trained your palate, you know, there's no going back. Drinking wine will never be the same again.'

'Hmmmph.' Enzo was not convinced. He felt something tugging at his feet. 'What the hell . . . ?' He looked under the table in time to see a brown puppy dog pulling at his laces before dancing away across the pavement.

Nicole laughed. 'It's just Braucol. Shoelaces are his party trick. We've been watching him go round all the tables.'

'Braucol?'

'Yeah, that's what they've christened him here.'

'Well, they should teach him not to bother the customers.' Enzo stooped to retie his laces.

'Oh, he doesn't belong to the café. He's a stray.'

Enzo glared at the dog, which cocked its head and seemed to be smiling at him. He waved his hand at it. 'Go on, bugger off!'

'Papa!'

But Braucol seemed to take Enzo's dismissal as a sign of encouragement and came racing back to the table to put his front paws up on Enzo's thigh and thrust a big head and floppy ears into his lap.

'He likes you, Monsieur Macleod.' Nicole reached over and tousled the puppy's head.

But he only had eyes for Enzo. Big, soft, irresistible brown eyes which he turned up towards what he clearly took to be the leader of the pack. Enzo sighed and gave in, scratching behind its ears, before pushing it back down on to the *terrasse*. 'On you go, shoot the craw!'

Michelle frowned. 'Shoot the craw?'

'An old Scottish expression,' Enzo told her. 'For . . . for . . .'

'Bugger off?' Sophie suggested.

'Something like that.' Enzo turned to Bertrand. 'So what do you suggest?'

'Well, we should still go ahead and do the tasting.' He riffled through the notes. 'This is all pretty much what I got taught anyway.'

Enzo felt a tugging at his feet again. 'Jesus Christ!'

Braucol went scampering off amongst the trees, having successfully undone the pack leader's shoelaces again.

As he bent to tie them for the second time, Enzo saw the puppy go chasing down the sidewalk after a middle-aged lady wearing pink cut-off trousers with laced-up slits at the side of either calf. She was what Enzo's mother would have described as mutton dressed as lamb. She tried to avoid the dog dancing around her legs, then stumbled on precariously high heels and sat down abruptly as Braucol succeeded in grabbing one of her laces.

'Braucol!' Enzo shouted admonishment at the dog, and it immediately turned and raced back to their table. The woman glared in their direction, humiliation flushing her face as pink as her trousers. She got to her feet and strode over to the gathering of would-be wine tasters.

'Is this your dog?' she demanded of Enzo.

'Well, actually . . .'

But she wasn't waiting for an explanation. Her hand swung unexpectedly from somewhere beyond her handbag, and its open palm caught Enzo squarely on the side of the face. It made a very loud slapping sound. 'You should learn to keep your animals under control.' And she strode off, dignity restored, leaving Enzo speechless, face stinging.

There was a moment of shocked silence around the table, before they all burst out laughing. Except for Enzo. And Braucol began dancing around Enzo's chair, barking his delight.

The dog sat next to their table all through lunch, gazing up, wide-eyed and expectant, as Nicole and Sophie, to Enzo's annoyance, threw him scraps of skin and fat from their *poulet farci*.

'You'll only spoil him,' Enzo growled.

But no matter who it was who fed him the scraps, it was always to Enzo that he came back with upturned eyes.

'Look, see, he only has eyes for you, Papa.'

Enzo glared at the dog. 'Go away!'

Braucol smiled. And when, eventually, they paid up and left, crossing the square to the Place d'Hautpoul, where they had parked their cars opposite the *mairie*, he followed. Initially at a safe distance, before getting bolder, and diving around their feet, rubbing himself against Enzo's legs. But despite several gentle attempts by Enzo to discourage him with the toe-end of his training shoes, Braucol was determined to remain a part of the group.

When they reached Enzo's 2CV Michelle broke her long silence. 'Would you drive me back to Château de Salettes please, Enzo?' She had left her rental car at the hotel after taking her father's belongings from the *gîte*, and come down with them to Gaillac in the back of Bertrand's van.

'Of course,' Charlotte said quickly. 'We'd be happy to.' She smiled sweetly at Enzo. 'Wouldn't we?'

Enzo flicked her a dark look. 'Of course.'

And as he opened the door for Michelle, Braucol jumped up on to the backseat and dipped his head to peer out at them from under the curve of the roof.

Sophie laughed. 'He's definitely adopted you, Papa.'

'He can't come with us,' Enzo insisted. 'We've got nothing to feed him.'

'Don't worry, me and Bertrand'll stop and get some dog food and a bowl at Leclerc's. I'm sure the Lefèvre's won't mind a dog at the *gîte*. They've got one of their own, haven't they?'

Michelle slipped into the backseat beside Braucol and ruffled his ears. Charlotte got in the passenger side. Enzo sighed and got in behind the wheel. He flipped up the window and called to Sophie as the three youngsters made their way across the car park towards Bertrand's van. 'You'll have to take him home with you when you leave. I can't look after him here.'

Braucol curled up next to Michelle, his head on her lap, as they drove north and east out of Gaillac, heading in silence up into the hills towards Cahuzac and the Château de Salettes. Although the sky was still clear, the wind had risen, warm and humid, redolent with the sense of approaching rain. The weather was on the change.

Sun slanted off the angles of red roof and white stone as

they drove into the compound outside the walled gate of the *château*, dust rising from crushed *castine* on the edge of the wind, to be whipped away across a sea of fibrillating green and red vine leaves. Enzo left the engine running as Michelle got out of the car. She hesitated, eyes concealed by her sunglasses, and tossed her hair back from her face. She seemed to be looking beyond Enzo towards Charlotte, before switching her focus back to him. 'Could we talk?' she said. 'Privately.'

Enzo hesitated, then turned off the ignition and stepped out of the car, suspension dipping dangerously. He leaned in the window. 'I'll be back in a minute.'

He followed Michelle through the open half of a wooden gate into the courtyard beyond. The walls seemed to press in around them in the heat of the afternoon. There was no one else about. Michelle stopped at the entrance to reception. She took off her sunglasses and turned disconcerting green eyes towards him, holding him in their gaze. 'I'm sorry things turned out like this.'

'Like what?'

She smiled sadly. 'Like you don't know?' She nodded towards the gate, and the unseen Charlotte somewhere beyond the walls. 'I never meant to go trespassing on anyone else's territory.'

'You didn't. I'm not anyone's territory.' He raised a rueful eyebrow. 'In any case, nothing happened between us.'

She nodded. 'I know. I never did get to taste whisky on the lips of a real Scotsman.'

'That sounds very past tense.'

'I'm leaving, Enzo.'

'Why?'

'Because.'

'Michelle, we haven't found your father's killer yet.'

She shrugged her regret. 'I'm sure you will. And I'm sure you'll tell me when you have. But as long as she's around, I'm going to feel like I'm in some kind of competition. And this is all stressful enough without that kind of complication. You know, I only ever intended to come and get his things. To close a door on that part of my life for good. Move on.'

He wasn't sure if it was the heat of her body he felt, or the sun reflecting off the stone. But she was standing very close to him. Almost touching. And her eyes still held him in their relentless, searching green. She put a hand on his arm. It felt cool.

'You know, they say when one door closes another opens. I thought, maybe, that night at Le Romuald, that you were that other door. You're different, Enzo. Special.' She pushed herself up on tiptoes to kiss him. A soft, moist caress of the lips. 'But I guess it wasn't meant to be.'

He swallowed hard. 'I'm too old for you, Michelle.'

She smiled and shook her head. 'No you're not. It's my fault. I'm too young. I wish I were older.'

'No. You shouldn't ever wish your life away.' He cupped her face in his hands, and it felt very small and delicate in his palms. He stooped to kiss her softly, before enveloping her in strong arms to hold her tightly for several moments.

Moments in which neither of them heard the slamming of a car door in the carpark.

When he let her go, her eyes were moist and her cheeks flushed. She gazed up at him for a long time, searching for words. And when none came, she reached up to kiss him again. A short, sweet kiss. 'Goodbye, Enzo.'

She turned and hurried off into the shuttered cool of the stone-tiled reception, and he stood for nearly a minute before turning to find Charlotte leaning against the arch of the gate watching him. She cast him a very curious look, before pushing herself away from the wall and walking back across the *castine* to the car. She was sitting staring straight ahead when he slipped into the driver's seat beside her, and the car rocked on big, coiled springs. He put his hands on the wheel and held it for some time without speaking. Finally he said, 'So how much did you see?'

'Enough.'

'She's leaving, Charlotte.'

'That makes two of us.'

He stared at her very hard, but she refused to turn and meet his eye. 'Because of Michelle?'

'Because I have patients.'

And he knew there was no point in discussing it further. He looked over his shoulder to find Braucol watching him with big, sad eyes. Almost as if he had understood. Enzo breathed silent frustration through his teeth and turned the key in the ignition. The one reliable thing in his life turned over, as it always did, the characteristic tinny purr of the two horsepower engine idling patiently, waiting for him to engage first gear.

Sophie followed Charlotte around the *gîte* as she collected her things. 'But *why* are you going? It's because of her, isn't it?' She glared at her father. With a woman's instinct, she had gone straight to what she perceived to be the heart of the matter. Bertrand gave Enzo a sympathetic smile, and Enzo found himself grateful for even that small crumb of support in this conspiracy of the sexes which he knew would always cast him as the villain.

'No. I have patients.' Charlotte wasn't playing the game. 'I have no reason to be jealous of anyone in relation to your father, Sophie. Least of all a child like Michelle Petty.'

Sophie looked towards Nicole at the computer, in search of an ally. But Nicole just shrugged. 'In my limited experience, women are always fighting over him. I can't think why.'

'I am still in the room, you know,' Enzo said.

When, finally, Charlotte emerged from the bedroom with her case packed, Bertrand stepped smartly forward to relieve her of the burden. 'I'll take that for you.'

Enzo glowered at him. A look that said, *traitor!* And grabbed the handle before him. 'I might be nearly twice your age, Bertrand, but I think I can still handle a suitcase.'

After Sophie and Charlotte had kissed goodbye, Enzo followed the psychologist across the grass to her car and heaved her case into the boot. She banged the lid shut, and they stood looking at each other. He wanted to take her by the shoulders and shake her, and tell her if only she would commit to him he would have no need for any other woman in his life. As if she could read his thoughts from the frustration in his face, her eyes softened suddenly, and a slight smile curled up the corners of her mouth.

'If you go to California, you'll be flying from Paris?'

'Probably.'

'Stay over at my place before you go, then.' She slipped cool fingers behind his neck and gently pulled his head down so she could kiss him. And then she stepped into the car, backing up before accelerating away on the long drive through the trees to the road.

He watched her go, filled with love and frustration and anger, and wondered if he would ever understand her.

A tugging at his feet drew his eyes down, and Braucol sprang away, never tiring of his party trick, eyebrows pushed up in anticipation of admiration or admonishment. Either would do.

CHAPTER THIRTEEN

I

'Hold still!'

Enzo sat in the chair with his tongue sticking out, and struggled to prevent it from twitching involuntarily.

Bertrand held his head back with one hand, and with the other squeezed the rubber nipple of his eye-dropper to let the blue food dye drip on to the tip of Enzo's tongue.

'Now keep your tongue out, don't swallow.'

Enzo gurgled incoherently as Bertrand pressed the punched hole in a sheet of paper on to the end of his tongue and brought a magnifying glass up to his eye. He started counting the fungiform papillae visible in the hole.

'Twenty-seven,' he said. 'Which puts you bang in the middle category. A taster.' He gave Enzo his tongue back, and watched as the older man pulled a face and washed away the food dye with a glass of water.

Bertrand had explained the experiment before dropping dye on to each of their tongues in turn. The tongue would take up the dye, he told them, but the small round structures of the fungiform papillae, or taste buds, stayed pink, allowing them to be counted. Fewer than fifteen, concentrated in the seven millimetre hole in the sheet of paper, classified you as a nontaster. Fifteen to thirty-five, as a taster. And more than thirty-five made you a supertaster.

Nicole had been delighted to learn that she was a super-taster, until Bertrand told her that this wasn't necessarily a good thing. 'If you're too sensitive to taste, then you can end up with flavour overkill. Things are too sweet, or too bitter, or too salty.'

Bertrand, Sophie, and her father all had average counts in the fifteen to thirty-five middle range.

'We can only perceive five different tastes.' Bertrand was warming to his subject, revelling in his knowledge. 'Sweet, salty, bitter, sour, and *umami* – which is a Japanese word that translates as meaty or savoury.'

Enzo looked at the young man with renewed admiration. He really did know his stuff. However, this was an area about which Enzo also knew a little. 'But we're sensitive to thousands of smells,' he said. 'Although we can only identify up to a maximum of four odours at any one time in any mixture, regardless of whether it's a single molecule odour, like alcohol, or something more complex, like smoke.' He grinned. 'So the next time you see some flamboyant wine review, extolling the virtues of a half dozen or more wonderful aromas, you'll know just what bullshit it really is.'

Bertrand took up the baton again. 'The hardest thing, though, is to identify the smells. The olfactory epithelium . . .'

Sophie pulled a face. "All factory what . . . ?'

'Epithelium,' Enzo said. 'The tissue that traps and identifies smell molecules.'

Bertrand ignored the interruption. 'The olfactory epithelium in humans is only about a fifth as sensitive as cats, and we just don't live in the same smell universe as dogs.' He looked at Braucol, who cocked his head and looked back at him. 'If dogs could taste wine, Robert Parker would be out of a job.' He turned back to Enzo. 'What made Gil Petty almost unique, was his ability to remember smells, to classify them in some way that allowed him to associate them with words.'

Enzo nodded. 'Michelle said he had the smell equivalent of a photographic memory.'

Bertrand started lining up bottles and glasses. 'It's much harder than you think to identify a smell. The first day of my training course, they gave us little bottles of clear liquid infused with different odours. Some were easy, like peach, or strawberry. Others were impossible. You recognised the smell, but couldn't for the life of you say what it was. Until the *prof* would tell you it was ground pepper. And immediately you thought, of course it is! Why the hell couldn't I tell that?' He turned to face the others. 'It's a long, hard learning process.'

'It can't be that hard, surely?' Nicole said. 'I mean, we've all got the same sense of taste and smell. Except for me, of course. I'm a supertaster.'

Bertrand started pouring a little wine into each glass. 'They did this experiment in Italy with something called fMRI. I'm not sure what it stands for.'

'Functional magnetic resonance imaging,' Enzo said.

'It's an MRI scan specifically applied to the brain. It allows scientists to actually see the brain working.'

'Well, anyway, they did this experiment taking seven professional *sommeliers* and seven other people matched for age and sex, who didn't have any specific wine-tasting abilities, and scanned their brains while they fed them different wines.'

'Hmmm, I'd have volunteered for that,' Sophie said.

Bertrand tipped her a look of mild annoyance. 'While the wine was actually in the mouth, it stimulated activity in the same area of the brain in all fourteen participants.'

Nicole let a little explosion of triumph escape her lips. 'Like I said, we've all got the same sense of taste and smell.'

But Bertrand shook his head and raised a finger. She was being premature. 'No, you're wrong, Nicole. Because there was another area of the brain that showed activity only in the *sommeliers*. And then during the aftertaste phase, when they'd swallowed the wine, the *sommeliers* had brain activity on both sides of the ... the ... amagama hippo something ...'

'Amygdala-hippocampus?' Enzo suggested.

'That's it. Well, the professionals showed activity on both sides of that, and the others only on the right side.'

'So what's your point?' Nicole was impatient to get on with the tasting.

'Well, the experiment showed that the professional tasters were accessing parts of their brains that the non-professionals weren't, almost certainly consulting database material accumulated through training and experience.

You can't just walk in off the street and be a professional wine-taster, you know. It's a learned art, and it takes time.'

'Not much point in us even trying then, is there?' Nicole was skeptical.

'Well, let's see,' Enzo said.

Bertrand spread the tasting information sheets from the Maison du Vin across the kitchen worktop and handed them each a glass. 'Okay, this is how we do it. We hold the base of the glass between thumb and forefinger, and tip it away from us, preferably towards something white. We're looking for the colour here, and how the light strikes through it.'

In silence they all did as they were told, peering at the wine through tilted glasses.

'Okay, so this is the Sarrabelle syrah. Petty described the colour as being tile-red. Like terracotta tiles on a roof. You can see what he means. It's a good, strong red, but if you look around the edges of it, there's a slightly brownish quality that gives it a sort of brick colour. That comes with age and oxidation. This wine's five years old now, so it'll be browner than when Petty looked at it.' Bertrand glanced up at Enzo's whiteboard. 'He also suggested that it would have a drinking life of five to eight years. So it should be perfect for drinking right about now. Let's see if he was right.'

He dipped his head, putting his nose right into the glass, and breathed deeply.

'This is important. The first smell. Don't shake the glass or disturb the wine.' He watched as the others followed his example. 'So what do you think? What do you smell?'

No one had any immediate thoughts to offer. Nicole looked disappointed. 'I don't really smell anything. I thought I was supposed to be a supertaster.'

Bertrand shook his head. 'No, you smelled something. You just haven't identified it. Try again.'

They all tried again.

'Fruit,' Enzo said.

'Yeah, fruit,' Sophie agreed.

'Yes, but what kind of fruit?'

'Plums.' Nicole looked pleased with herself. 'Red plums.'

'No, I'm getting strawberries,' Sophie said. 'And maybe something a little more tart, like blackcurrants.

'Could be rasperries there,' Enzo said.

'Yeah, and ripe melon.' Nicole was on a roll now.

Bertrand sighed in exasperation. 'Sounds like you've found a whole fruit salad in there.'

'Okay, smartass, what do you smell?' Nicole thrust her jaw at him.

Bertrand sniffed again. 'Strawberries certainly. Rasperries, maybe. Red fruit, for sure. But we need to swirl the glass and smell again?'

'Why?' Sophie asked.

'To get oxygen into the wine and release more of the smell molecules.'

So they all swirled their glasses and hung their noses over the rims once again.

'Big fruit,' Enzo said. 'And something meaty, maybe. *Gibier*. Like game. That . . . what was it, *umami* smell?'

Bertrand canted his head doubtfully. 'I don't know. I'd say it was more . . . woody. Oak, maybe.'

'Liquorice!' Nicole looked pleased with herself. 'I can smell liquorice.'

Sophie breathed deeply from her glass. 'Me, too.'

Enzo began counting on his fingers. 'Okay, so now we've got strawberry, raspberry, red plum, ripe melon, black currant, meat, liquorice and oak. That's eight different smells.' He looked up at the whiteboard. 'Petty lists five.'

'I thought you said we could only smell four things at the same time,' Nicole said.

It was Bertrand who responded. 'Yes, but we've had two tries at it, the second time after oxygenation. So we're picking up different things.'

'Too many things,' Enzo said. 'I'm not sure this is going to work, Bertrand.'

But Bertrand was not to be deterred. 'We've still to taste it, Monsieur Macleod.'

'About time.' Nicole raised her glass with relish.

Bertrand lifted his own glass to his lips. 'Just take a small mouthful, then let it flow back over your tongue. The front of the tongue is more sensitive to sweet tastes, the back of it will pick out the sharper notes. And while the wine is still in your mouth, suck in a little oxygen to help the wine release its flavours.'

They all gurgled and slurped, and Nicole nearly choked.

Bertrand kept up his commentary. 'The first thing you experience is the attack. That initial flavour and texture in the mouth. Then as the complexity of the wine develops, you should start being able to distinguish all the flavours. And after you've swallowed, there'll be an aftertaste – what's called *the finish*. The longer that lasts, the better. Provided, of course, that it's a pleasant taste. Then, really, we should spit it out.'

'I'm not wasting wine this good.' Sophie rolled her eyes dreamily. 'It's fantastic. Smooth and silky. And I'm not getting any of that meat that you were smelling, Papa. But I'm still getting strawberries.'

'And liquorice,' Nicole chipped in.

'And soft, soft tannins,' Bertrand said. 'And vanilla from the oak.' He smacked his lips noisily several times. 'And the finish just goes on forever.'

But Enzo was looking at the board again. 'Petty lists codes for six flavours. We've come up with three.'

'Yes, but he's also describing textures, tannins, acidity, complexity, finish,' Bertrand said. 'Just look at any of his reviews. And those pluses, and plus-pluses alongside the codes probably translate as something like *very* and *extremely*, or words to that effect.'

Enzo shook his head. 'All of which means, we're wasting our time here. There are too many variables. We've hardly agreed on a single smell, or flavour.'

'Can't we even just *try* the other wines?' Sophie said, disappointed.

'Or even just finish this one.' Nicole held out her glass for Bertrand to fill it up.

'Apart from drinking them for the pleasure of it,' Enzo said, 'I don't see the point. Like Bertrand said, you can't just walk in off the street and be a professional wine taster. It would take an experienced professional to identify the smells and flavours we're looking for.'

Bertrand sipped thoughtfully at his syrah. 'And I know a man who might be able to do just that, Monsieur Macleod.'

CHAPTER FOURTEEN

I

The old man shuffled slowly across the *grande salle*. Ancient wooden floorboards, supported on centuries-old oak beams, creaked and dipped beneath his feet. An enormous *cheminée* of white sandstone was set in a blackened wall, rising to a ceiling transected by yet more oak beams.

The last golden light of the day was fading to pink, seeping in through *portes-fenêtres* that opened on to a covered *terrasse* perched high up on the gable elevation of this fifteenth-century gothic residence. Enzo and Bertrand and Sophie followed the old man out on to the *terrasse*, Braucol trotting obediently at their heels.

The climb, in fading light, up through the steep, cobbled streets of the thirteenth-century *bastide* town of Cordes-sur-Ciel, had left Enzo breathless and perspiring. What little breath remained was taken away completely by the view that opened out before them from the *terrasse*. To the north, Puech Gabel rose high above the valley of the silver-pink Cérou river. To the east and west, the Saint Marcel heights extended towards the horizon and the brooding dark line of the Forest of Grésigne. A patchwork of green fields smudged dark by trees and villages, lights twinkling sporadically in the fading day. Immediately beneath them, a jumble of tiled roofs fell away to the market square two hundred feet below. Woodsmoke rose in the still air, carrying with it the first portents of winter.

Shortly before his retirement, Jacques Domenech had been awarded l'*Ordre national de la Légion d'honneur*, by Président Chirac, for his services to the French wine industry. In his day he had been, quite possibly, the best known *sommelier* in France. When, finally, he had sold his string of Michelin-starred restaurants and bought this extraordinary house, he retreated here to gothic retirement, perched high up above the rolling hills of the south-west.

'For centuries,' he said, 'this town was known only as Cordes – a word of Indo-European origin, by the way – meaning rocky heights. It was only recently that they changed the name to Cordes under The Sky. But it's not until you live here that you see why. In spring and autumn the surrounding valleys fill with mist, and one wakes to the illusion of floating in the sky above the clouds. It is almost as heady as good wine.'

He regarded Bertrand with affection, and put a hand on his shoulder.

'My boy, you haven't changed a bit. Except for those bits of metal in your face. Is this your girlfriend?' He peered at Sophie.

'My daughter,' Enzo said.

He looked at Enzo and nodded. 'Lucky man.' Then turned towards Bertrand. 'Best pupil of his year, you know. Could have been a professional *sommelier*, had he chosen to.' He sighed. 'But that would have been a long, hard road, Bertrand, eh? And you were too impatient.' And to Enzo, 'He's like all the youngsters these days. They want everything now. And who knows, maybe they're right.' He raised a finger in the air and quoted, '*All things come to those who wait, I say these words to make me glad, but something answers soft and sad, they come, but often come too late.*' He chuckled. 'I had a long and very successful career as a *sommelier*. But it wasn't until I retired and got bored and agreed to do a little teaching at Toulouse, that I discovered the rewards of imparting wisdom to others. Too late.' He waved a hand towards the chairs set around a long, wooden table. 'Take a seat.'

Half a dozen bottles of fine Bordeaux were set out with a dozen or more tasting glasses. A Château Cheval Blanc, Enzo noticed, and a Château Lafite Rothschild. His eyes widened. These were wines you tasted rarely in a lifetime, if ever. There was a large basket of hard-crusted bread cut into thick chunks, and three bottles of still mineral water. Several yellowed and well-thumbed editions of Petty's *The Wine Critic* lay open, pages separated by pink Post-its.

'Have you brought the Gaillacs?'

Enzo put his carrier bag on the table and lifted out the three bottles.

Old Domenech examined them each in turn. 'Syrah, eh? Classified as a *vin de pays* because it doesn't contain the minimum quantities of the prescribed grapes to qualify for the Gaillac *Appellation Contrôlée*. Stupid system. Making French wines uncompetitive in a changing world.' He looked at the faces turned towards him in the twilight. 'You know, ten years ago France exported three times as much wine as the so-called New World countries. Today we sell fifteen per cent less than they do. We're making wine we can't sell. Even in Bordeaux there are tankers queuing daily outside distilleries to take advantage of government subsidies for turning unsold wine into industrial alcohol. What a waste!'

He moved on to the next bottle. 'Domaine Vayssette. Cuvée Lea 2001. Don't know it.' And the next. 'Château Lastours, Cuvée Spéciale 2001. Ah, yes. A fine wine. You have Petty's codes?'

Enzo placed the computer printouts on the table. 'It's a matter of trying to identify flavours and smells and cross-referencing them between different reviews.'

'I understand the principle, monsieur. But I can't make any promises. I met Petty a few times. Didn't know him well and didn't like him much. His tastes and mine were somewhat different. But it's a challenge. Since young Bertrand called, I've been going through some of Petty's old newsletters from my files and I went down to my cellar to dig out some of the Bordeaux he reviewed. That way we can make a direct comparison between what I taste and what he's already described.' He beamed. 'But first, a few glasses of wine amongst friends for pleasure, eh?'

He reached for the Cheval Blanc, and Enzo's heart nearly stopped. It was a 2005, and probably cost somewhere in the region of five hundred euros.

As old Domenech went through the ritual of opening

the bottle and pouring a little of the wine into each of their glasses, he said, 'You know, it's odd how few female *sommeliers* there are. Most wine critics are men, too. Yet, all the research shows that women are better tasters than men and have a particularly heightened sense of smell during ovulation.' He passed a glass to Sophie. 'So our young lady should have the honour of tasting first.' He grinned. 'Although it's not compulsory to tell us whether you're ovulating or not.'

Sophie blushed deeply, and took a sip of the wine to cover her embarrassment. In an evolution of only two or three seconds, her expression changed completely. 'Oh, my God!' Her voice was almost a whisper. 'I've never tasted wine this good.' She immediately revised her statement. 'I've never tasted *anything* this good.'

Domenech beamed his pleasure.

II

Nicole tried to avoid the scowling face of Madame Marre as she used her bread to mop up the last of her sauce. Roast veal sliced and served in its own *jus*, accompanied by sliced potatoes fried in duck fat and garlic and lathered in cream. What Fabien's mother lacked in the social graces, she more than made up for in culinary skills. Nicole had been disappointed to discover that Fabien was not eating with them tonight, and so they had partaken of dinner in a depressing silence surrounded by floral wallpaper and lace doilies and large pieces of dark, antique furniture squeezed into a room too small to accommodate them. Madam Marre, it seemed, was intent on perpetuating the tastes of a generation long since passed away.

Ten minutes before, Nicole's spirits had lifted briefly as Fabien came in from the *chai*. But he had merely nodded before heading on up the stairs. She had heard him moving about in his bedroom, the floor creaking overhead, like footsteps in wet snow.

'Is Fabien not eating with us?' she'd asked.

Madame Marre had glared at her. 'He's going out.' Conversation over.

Nicole sighed, and wished she had gone with the others to the *sommelier's* house at Cordes-sur-Ciel. As soon as she was finished, she excused herself from the table and hurried upstairs to her room, in the hope perhaps of bumping into Fabien in the hall. What she had not been expecting was the sight that greeted her through the half-open door of his bedroom.

Fabien stood in front of a full length mirror, flowing crimson and black robes draped from the shoulders of his ample frame almost to the floor. He was adjusting his red triangular Rabelaisian hat with white-gloved hands. Nicole was unable to suppress a gasp of astonishment, and he turned at the sound, only for his face to flush as red as his robes. They stood staring at each other for several long moments.

Nicole finally found her voice. 'What are you doing?'

'I'm going to a meeting of the *Ordre*. A *chapitre* at the abbey.'

'I didn't know you were a member.'

Fabien shrugged, still cowed by the weight of his embarrassment. 'It's a family tradition.'

Nicole smiled. 'Have you any idea how ridiculous you look?'

Fabien blushed again. Only now there was a defensive tone in his voice. 'It was good enough for my father, so it's good enough for me.'

'Is that his outfit?'

'No. His stuff would never have fitted me.'

'Can I come with you?'

'No, you cannot. It's a private meeting.'

'Oh, go on. I'll wait for you in the car.'

'No.'

'I've nothing else to do all evening. I'll just be sitting on my own in my room.'

'You could sit with my mother.'

Nicole gave him a look, and the point was conceded without a word passing between them.

'It could be a long wait.'

'I don't mind. I could take a wander around town.' She put on her most appealing face. 'Please, Fabien. It's really depressing here on my own.'

'What about your *friends*?'

'Oh, they're off tasting wine somewhere.'

Fabien straightened the collar of his shirt. 'So how's Monsieur Macleod's investigation going?'

His enquiry was just too casual, and Nicole became suddenly guarded. She remembered Enzo's admonition: *Fabien Marre has made it perfectly clear that he had nothing but antipathy towards Petty. And since both bodies were found on his vineyard, he has to be considered a suspect.* Not that she believed it for a moment. But she was determined she would not commit any further errors of indiscretion. 'Fine,' was all she said. 'So I can come with you, then?'

His sigh of resignation told her she had bullied him into submission.

It was more than twenty minutes since Fabien had disappeared through the arched gateway into the complex of offices, with its *salle de dégustation* and wine museum, that comprised the Maison du Vin. The abbey next door had lost its pink quality in the dying light and huddled darkly now on the banks of the river until floodlights snapped on to throw it into stark relief against the darkening sky in the east.

Nicole was bored. She watched the faithful coming and going to confession through a small doorway in the entrance to the abbey. Whispering dark secrets to a hidden listener behind a latticed screen, then emerging minutes later muttering Hail Marys, absolved of all responsibility for life.

It was a long time since she had been to church. It brought back memories of her childhood. Squirming on uncomfortable pews next to her mother and father, listening to the cants and criticisms of the *curé*. Words that meant nothing to her then or now. But it made her think of her mother, and she felt a sudden stab of guilt. For two days she had barely given her a second thought. Except for a call the previous night to her father to ask how she was. He had been his usual uncommunicative self, and their brief conversation had left her depressed, bringing back the memory of sunlight splintering around the closed shutters of her mother's bedroom, the air hot and heavy with the scent of impending death.

She decided to go into the abbey to light a candle and say a prayer for her.

The vast, vaulted space of the Abbey Saint-Michel was gloomily lit. She passed down the central aisle and crossed to the Madonna and Child, where candles burned and spilled their wax. She dropped some coins into the box, took a fresh candle, and lit it from one already burning. Then she knelt in front of the Virgin Mary and closed her eyes. She had no idea what to do. It was so long since she had prayed, she had forgotten how. She concentrated her thoughts and hoped with all her heart that her mother would be delivered from her suffering quickly and without further pain.

When she stood up again, she realised she was alone in the church. The confessional was empty. And yet she could hear voices. A babble of them, some raised in what sounded like anger. Away to her right, on the curve of the apse, a door stood ajar, and she crossed the nave to listen at it. The voices were louder, though still distant, and so she was unable to hear what they were saying. She glanced around, self-conscious and indecisive. There was still no one else in the church. And so after a moment's hesitation, she pushed the door open and stepped into an ante-room with coat hangers and an antique *armoire*. An old stone staircase spiralled down into darkness, to the vaulted cellars below.

The offices of the Maison du Vin, and the museum, were all part of the original abbey, interconnected by its cellars. And aware that she was probably hearing the assembled dignitaries of *l'Ordre de la Dive Bouteille* in mid-meeting, she started tentatively down the stairs, drawn on by curiosity.

She felt the temperature drop as she descended into darkness, with only a rope handrail for a guide. The air was suffused with a smell of damp. Light bleeding down from the abbey above was quickly snuffed out and she became enveloped by an impenetrable black that swallowed all shape and form. It occurred to her that there was probably a light switch at the top of the stairs and she stopped, wondering whether or not to go back. But the voices were louder now. And as her eyes adjusted, she became aware of a faint glow coming up from below. She pressed on, following the spiral curve of the wall, until the world took shape again in light, and she found herself stepping into a vaulted *salle* with freshly pointed brickwork and tiled floors. Black triangular uplighters on the walls echoed the flaming torches that once would have lit this underground place. An unlit corridor led off south, towards the river. The voices of the assembled dignitaries of the Order of the Divine Bottle echoed along it. Nicole took the first tentative steps towards them, leaving the light behind her again. Guiding herself with fingertips on rough brick, she turned left and then right and saw light again ahead of her.

It spilled through a glass door in a closed archway, and from the obscurity of darkness, Nicole could see through it into a large vaulted meeting room, where the crimson-robed members of the *Ordre* were assembled on chairs facing a top table. Most of the dignitaries appeared to be older men, although there were three or four younger ones, Fabien amongst them, and two women.

The dominant voice was Fabien's. He was on his feet, red-faced again. Only this time, from anger and indignation. 'I've worked damned hard all year. And then this. Just as I'm harvesting the fruits of my labour, some foreigner playing amateur detective comes snooping around my vineyard, disrupting my *vendange*, threatening my livelihood. You know, he even sent one of his spies to rent a room at my house!' He stopped to draw breath. 'I can't take issue with an official police investigation. A man was found dead yesterday on my land. But Petty's murder was years ago. This Macleod character is just reopening old wounds. And for what? I've read about him in the newspapers, like everyone else. This all started with a bet. He doesn't care about Petty. He doesn't care about us. All he cares about is his own reputation – and winning a wager. Well, he's not going to do it at my expense.'

There was a chorus of murmured agreement, and Fabien pressed on.

'We all have livelihoods at stake here. The reputation of the wines of Gaillac. The whole point of our *Ordre* is to protect and promote those wines. I don't think we should be cooperating with this Macleod. It's not in any of our interests.'

The wall at Nicole's shoulder seemed to give just a little. There was a click, and the corridor was flooded with sudden light. She realised, to her horror, that she had leaned against a light switch. As heads in the meeting room swung towards her, she fumbled to switch it off again, and ran back the way she had come, training shoes squeaking on shiny tiles.

She reached the *salle* at the foot of the spiral staircase, and plunged herself again into darkness. Running up and round, burning her palms on the rope rail, stumbling on the stairs as profound blackness wrapped itself around her once more. And then there was light again, from above, and she emerged finally, gasping for breath, into the ante-room with the *armoire*.

She stood for a full minute, breathing hard, perspiring in the gloom, trying to regain her equilibrium. But her legs were like jelly, and her breath trembled in her chest each time she filled her lungs. Try as she could, straining to listen above the rasp of her breathing, she was unable to detect any sound from below. There were no voices. Nothing. And she knew she had to get out of there.

With as much composure as she could muster, she peered out into the abbey. There were a couple of elderly ladies kneeling before the Virgin, but there was no sign of the *curé*, and so she slipped out into the whispering vastness of the nave and hurried towards the back of the church.

The night air felt soft and warm as she emerged into the cobbled square. She walked quickly amongst the parked cars until she reached Fabien's four-by-four, and slipped into the passenger seat with a huge sigh of relief. In the reflected light of the abbey's floodlamps she saw that her hands were trembling, and she leaned her head back against the headrest and closed her eyes.

The members of the *Ordre* emerged into the abbey square from the light of the arched tunnel of the Maison du Vin, a flood of crimson and black, dispersing to their vehicles and swallowed by the night.

Fabien peered in at Nicole before opening the door and removing his hat to throw it in the back.

She did her best to smile naturally. 'How did it go?'

'Fine.' He slipped off his gown to reveal that he was wearing jeans beneath it, and folded it carefully to place it on the back seat. He pulled his shirt out from his jeans, where it was stretched in tight around the waistband, and he seemed to breath more easily. In the glove compartment, he found a baseball cap which he pulled on over his shock of curls, and slipped in behind the wheel. He glanced at Nicole. 'Not too bored?'

'No.'

He started the motor and turned on the lights. But she knew she couldn't pretend for much longer.

'Why are you so much against Monsieur Macleod?'

His head snapped around, eyes full of sudden anger. 'It was you down in the cellars.'

She nodded. 'Yes.'

'Spying.' He almost spat the word at her.

'Oh, yes, that's what I do. I'm a professional spy for Monsieur Macleod. I'm spying on you at your house, I'm spying on you at your meeting.'

'But you were.'

'Not on purpose. It was an accident.'

'Oh, so you're an accidental spy?'

She gathered her indignation around herself like a cloak. 'I was in the abbey saying a prayer for my mother, and I heard voices. I was curious, that's all. I didn't mean to spy on you, but I couldn't help but hear.'

'Then you *know* why I'm against him poking around my vineyard.' He paused to gather his cool. 'And he suspects me of some involvement in all this. I can see it in his face.'

Nicole stared at her hands in her lap for a long time, frightened to meet his eyes, before finally she said, 'What happened to your father's old costume?'

She heard his deep sigh of frustration, and turned to see him grasping the steering wheel, his knuckles white with tension. 'So you think so, too?'

'No, I don't. But it's a reasonable question.'

He turned and glared at her. 'Is it?'

'Yes it is, Fabien. And if you've nothing to hide, then you've no reason not to answer it.'

He looked away again. 'I don't know.'

'Don't know what?'

'What happened to my father's outfit. My mother probably cannibalised it for her rag bag. Spending money on clothes has never been a big priority in our family. My mother's handy with a needle and thread. She makes things last.'

They sat for several more minutes without saying anything.

Then Fabien made a decision and slipped the vehicle into first gear and pulled out of the square into the street.

They drove up through the town in silence. The Place de la Libération was deserted, benches empty beneath the gloom of the chestnut trees. A bunch of teenagers stood smoking and laughing outside the DVD shop, the brightly lit interior of the pizza restaurant next door revealing that all its tables were empty. A bored chef leaned on the countertop in front of his oven reading a newspaper.

The outskirts of town, heading west, had a seedy, neglected air before they reached the commercial park with its gaudily lit stores and hypermarket. And then they were out amongst the vines, heading towards the hills that rose to the north, the dark shapes of *pins parasols* outlined against a sky awash with moonlight.

In the yard at La Croix Blanche, Fabien pulled up outside the house and cut the motor. Neither of them had spoken during the drive back, and now neither of them made any attempt to get out of the car.

Fabien said, 'Why were you saying a prayer for your mother?'

'Because she's dying.' She heard him turn to look at her.

'I'm sorry.'

'I never prayed for her before. All this time I should have been praying for a miracle. That she wouldn't die. And then when, finally, I do say a prayer it's for an end to it. For death to come quickly and without any more pain.' She turned to look at Fabien, tears brimming in her eyes. 'What's scary is, I'm not sure if I was saying the prayer for her or for me.'

He leaned over and put an arm around her, and she let her head fall against his shoulder, and they sat like that for a long time. Only now, the silence between them was easier, without tension. A gentle hand brushed the hair from her face, and she tilted her head to look at him.

'Take me to the *source*,' she said. 'I know we're not lovers or anything. But, well, maybe it would change our luck. Maybe it would be better than praying.'

He seemed embarrassed. 'I don't know, Nicole.' He dipped his head to peer out of the passenger window towards the house. 'She'll know we're back.'

Nicole looked, too. All the ground floor windows were shuttered, but she was certain that she saw a curtain twitch at an upstairs bedroom. She looked back at Fabien. 'Are you scared of her?'

'No!' His denial was fierce.

'Then don't use her as an excuse. If you don't want to take me to the *source* just say so.'

He responded by taking his arm from around her shoulders and leaning forward to start the car. The engine seemed very loud in the still of the night, and there was no doubting now the movement of curtains at the upstairs window.

Fabien accelerated out of the yard and turned up towards the foothills of the Plateau Cordais, headlights raking across acres of silent vines.

III

Enzo emerged unsteadily onto the steeply sloping cobbles of La Barbacane. He saw moonlight glistening on a surface slick with dew and felt his feet sliding from under him. Strong hands stopped him from falling. He turned to look into Bertrand's smiling face, pointless pieces of metal glinting absurdly in the moonshine.

'You've had too much to drink, Monsieur Macleod.'

'No more than you.' Enzo heard his words slurring, as if they were coming from someone else's mouth.

'Bertrand was spitting, Papa. You were drinking.'

'You can't spit out wine of that quality. That Cheval Blanc was probably about ten euros a sip.'

'Some of us have to drive, Monsieur Macleod.'

'And some of us can hold our wine better than you, Papa.'

Enzo shook himself free of Bertrand's grasp. 'I can manage perfectly well, thank you.' And he promptly sat down heavily on the wet cobbles. '*Merde!*'

Bertrand helped him to his feet again and looked down the two hundred feet of incline they would have to negotiate to get to the van. The streets were narrow and dark and treacherous. He made a face at Sophie and shrugged.

'Look, Papa, why don't you stay here with Braucol. I'll go with Bertrand to get the van.'

Enzo glared at her. 'If you can get the van up here, why didn't we bring it up in the first place?'

'Because we didn't know,' Bertrand said. 'Monsieur Dome-nech says there's a back road up that's easier.'

They helped Enzo up over the crest of the hill to the for-tified battlements of the original thirteenth-century enclo-sure at the Porte du Vainqueur. From here, there was a clear view out south over the dew-glistening layers of surrounding countryside. The autumn mist that old Domenech had spoken of earlier was already gathering in the river valley, luminous and ghostly. Enzo sat on the stone retaining wall and shivered. 'Be quick, then. It's getting cold.'

When they had gone, he looked down at Braucol looking up at him and smiled at the absence of disapproval. Certainly, he had drunk too much, but Braucol wasn't making any judg-ments. The wines had been wonderful. And now he had in his pocket the annotated outcome of old Domenech's tasting. He was certain they had managed to marry three or four flavours to Petty's lettered codes, so he was anxious to start looking for ways of deciphering the rest. But he was not so drunk that he didn't realise he was in no condition to do it tonight. He closed his eyes and felt the earth move beneath him. When Braucol sighed he opened them again to find the puppy still staring at him. 'It's alright for you, Braucol. You don't have a daughter who disapproves of your drinking. Or a lover who won't commit to a relationship. Or a woman half your age who wants to take you to bed.' He snorted. '*Putain*! I should be so lucky.'

He closed his eyes again and drifted off into an alcohol-induced torpor. He felt himself swaying, then heard the dangerous, throaty rumble of Braucol's growl. A bark startled him awake. He opened his eyes in time to see Braucol disappearing into the shadows. Then nothing. Not a movement. Absolute silence.

He called out. 'Braucol?' But there was no response. To his right, the cobbles meandered unevenly between houses shuttered and dark. Clumps of grass and weed grew all along the stone gutter. The walls of the battlement rose steeply into the sky. Every gateway and alley was mired in the deepest shadow. To his left, the narrow road fell away to the west. Ahead of him, a tall archway opened into a tunnel devoured by darkness. Something moved. A fragment of something shiny catching the light. A sound, like the scuff of a leather heel on stone.

Enzo felt the perspiration gathered across his forehead turn cold. It was only three nights ago that someone had tried to kill him. But who would even know he was here? He stood up. 'Who's there?'

No reply. His mouth was dry from sudden fear and too much alcohol.

'God damn you! Come out of there, will you!' The bellow of his voice echoed around the ramparts. He was no more than a hundred metres from the safety of the house where they had been drinking wine all evening. But it was down the steepest of inclines, and he doubted if he would make it. And up here, on the top of the hill, there wasn't another soul around. No light, no sign of life. He felt absolutely alone and horribly vulnerable. Why in the name of God had he let

Sophie and Bertrand go off without him? And where the hell was Braucol? Just the presence of the dog might have given him courage.

A sudden movement, and a clatter in the shadows, provoked a surge of adrenalin to fuel the opposing instincts of fight or flight. He was in no condition to fight, so turned instead and ran. Slithering over the cobbles on shaky legs. He heard sounds of pursuit behind him, but was afraid to look round. The street ahead dipped away into darkness, and he was afraid that if he went that way he might be lost in it for good. Beneath the wall on his right, where he had been sitting just moments earlier, a slope thick with shrubs and bushes fell away to a lower street transecting the hillside. It was caught in full moonlight and seemed like the safer option.

He scrambled over cold stone and felt fresh air beneath his feet as he dropped into the bushes below. It was not as soft a landing as he had hoped for. Jagged branches and thorns tore at his clothes and face and hands. Then he began tumbling uncontrollably down the slope. Even as he fell, he was aware of a streak of movement off to his left. But he was unable to focus on it, as the world turned over again. He came to a cushioned halt, cradled in the branches of a young tree. Branches that creaked and dipped, and broke beneath him, to dump him unceremoniously into the middle of the street below.

The fall took away his breath, and pain shot up his arm from his elbow. He heard his head crack hard on the cobbles, and his whole universe was shot through with light. A roaring sound filled his ears, to be replaced by a sudden squealing.

He screwed up his eyes against the light and saw that it came from two blinding orbs no more than a metre from his face. He lifted an arm to shield his eyes and a car door slammed.

'My God, Papa, what are you doing?' To his great relief, Sophie loomed out of the darkness, her silhouette crouching against the light.

'Someone was trying to kill me.'

'What?'

'Up there.' He waved an arm vaguely through the air. 'There was someone up there.'

Bertrand dipped into the light and helped him up off the road. 'Did you see them?'

'Well . . . no. But there *was* someone.'

'Where's Braucol?' Sophie said. And almost as if he had heard her, Braucol came haring out of the undergrowth, growling and barking, a streak of black cat ahead of him, just inches beyond his reach.

With three agile leaps, the cat mounted a wall, a window ledge, a roof, and sprinted away across the tiles. Braucol was left barking in frustration below the wall.

Sophie shouted at him. 'Braucol, shut up! You'll wake the whole town.'

Enzo wondered if there was anyone in the whole town to wake. It had seemed so impossibly deserted just minutes before.

And as Braucol flapped big paws and crossed the cobbles to join them, disconsolate and defeated, Sophie said, 'So that was who was trying to kill you, then? A cat?'

Enzo shook his head and found that it hurt. Surely it wasn't just a cat that had spooked him. 'There was someone up there,' he repeated, but with less conviction than before.

'We'd better get you home,' Bertrand said.

IV

Fabien parked his four-by-four at the top of the rubble track where the police had left their vehicles the night before. An abandoned length of black and yellow crime scene tape was the only evidence that they had ever been there. He gave Nicole his hand to help her up the slope towards the trees.

'I used to play up here all the time when I was a boy,' he said. 'The woods were my world. I fought battles against the crusaders, hid from the Germans, got shipwrecked. The cellars of the old Cathar *château* still exist, right below the hill. Just bits of broken-down wall and the remains of a flagstone floor. But it became my *château*, my hideaway. I loved it.' He stopped and breathed deeply. 'And the smell of the woods takes me back every time.' He looked at Nicole. 'Almost as if all the years between then and now had never been.' His face shone with some distant, happy memory. Then a shadow crossed it, like the moon slipping behind a cloud. 'That tree, where they found Serge Coste. I used to climb it, and hide in the hollow where the killer put the body. It was *my* tree. Seeing the body there like that, I felt . . . violated.'

They turned at the treeline and looked back down the vine-covered slope towards the flood plain below. The moon was a bright globe in a star-encrusted firmament, turning night almost into day. They heard the wind moving through the treetops, brittle leaves whispering to the night. Fabien still held her hand, and she felt a strange, aching sensation in the pit of her stomach. Not unpleasant but accompanied by a sense of apprehension verging on fear. She could feel the beat of her heart, and it seemed to be in her throat.

'Anyway, the *source* is up here.' Fabien turned and led her along a well-beaten path through the trees to a small clearing where stones had been set into the earth centuries before to protect the precious water.

'This is it?' Nicole was disappointed. She had been expecting more, although she was not sure what.

'There hasn't been much rain in the last six weeks, so the water table's low. When she's in full flood, she bubbles out of the ground like she's alive.'

And still he held her hand. She could feel his anxiety through it. Shattered moonlight fell among the trees to sprinkle them with bits of silver. Beyond the *source*, the forest seemed dark and impenetrable. Nicole looked up into Fabien's face and thought how much she liked its soft cadences and the dark of his eyes. 'What age are you, Fabien?'

He shifted uncomfortably, unsettled by her question. 'Thirty-one.'

'Why have you never married?'

This brought a tiny smile of regret to his face. 'There have been one or two close things. I guess I never met the right woman.' His smile turned wry. 'Certainly, my mother thinks so.'

'So do you think twelve years is too much?'

He frowned. 'Too much what?'

'Of an age difference.'

She was certain he blushed, but his embarrassment was masked by the night. 'What do you mean?'

'Between you and me.'

He laughed. 'When I was twenty, you'd have been eight. A primary school kid.'

'I'm a big girl now, though.' And then, realising what she'd said, added self-consciously, 'Too big, most people seem to think.'

Fabien took her other hand and stared earnestly into her face in the dark. 'I think you're lovely.'

She could barely hide her pleasure. 'A lovely spy.'

'A beautiful spy.' He let go of her hand and slipped his arms around her, drawing her tenderly towards him. She put her hands around his neck and stretched up to meet his lips as he bent to kiss her. For such a big, clumsy man, he was very gentle. The aching in her belly had spread to fill her whole body. She wished he would put his hand on her breast. Men were always looking at her as if they wanted to, but few of them had ever had the courage to actually do it. And Fabien was much too much of a gentleman. So slowly she drew one of his arms out from behind her, and slid his hand up to cover one of her breasts, an erect nipple pushing hard against the taut cotton of her tee shirt. She felt his tension, and then an almost uncontrollable wave of desire as she pressed her body against his to feel his passion pressing right back.

V

Enzo had sobered up a good deal by the time they got back to the *gîte*, forty minutes in the passenger seat of Bertrand's van, the window down, cold air blowing in his face, the best part of a litre of mineral water poured down his throat.

He could feel the swelling at the back of his head where it had cracked off the cobbles, and his elbow was distended and stiff where it had broken his fall. He had no idea, now, whether he had simply imagined everything on the hilltop at Cordes, or whether in fact there had been someone there. But it left him feeling unsettled and vulnerable again. For there was no doubt that someone had tried, and failed, to kill him on his first night here. Why wouldn't they try again?

Bertrand drove past the line of parked cars opposite the *chai* and pulled his van up at the foot of the steps. Enzo climbed stiffly down on to the gravel and shrugged aside offers of help from Sophie. 'I'm fine,' he said tetchily, and climbed up to the *terrasse* to unlock the door.

The room was filled with the glow from his computer screen, and he crossed to the table to switch on the desk lamp and drop into the seat in front of it. He got rid of his screensaver and saw that there was an e-mail waiting for him. He opened up his mailer. It was from Al MacConchie in California.

Hey, Magpie . . .

It was a long time since anyone had called him that. It was the nickname schoolfriends had given him when, as a teenager, his Waardenburg syndrome had manifested itself in a silver stripe running back through dark hair from his temple.

Bring your samples. I'll see what I can do. Let me know what flight you're on and I'll pick you up at the airport.

'We're going to bed, Papa.' He looked up as Sophie and Bertrand climbed the stairs to the mezzanine. 'You should, too.'

'I've got to book a flight.'

'Where to?'

'California.'

She stopped mid-step, and Bertrand nearly bumped into the back of her. 'Why?'

'I'll explain tomorrow.'

He waited until the light went out upstairs and he thought they might be sleeping before he got up to pour himself a small whisky sprinkled with a dash of water.

'You're not having a drink, are you?' Sophie's voice came out of the dark like a reproach from the gods.

'Sophie!' He tried to imbue her name with all the gravitas of an adult chiding a child. If he was going to make this booking tonight, he needed something to keep him awake. He heard her sighing.

It took him nearly half an hour of internet searches, and a dozen small sips of whisky, before he found a flight that wouldn't bankrupt him. Paris to San Francisco with Air

France in four days' time. Non-stop. Eleven hours and forty minutes. He groaned at the prospect. Then he remembered Charlotte's suggestion that he stay over with her the night before flying out, and his stomach flipped over.

He sent an e-mail back to MacConchie with his flight details and put the computer to sleep. His head was throbbing and his eyes felt full of grit. He turned off the light, and waited for his pupils to dilate before standing up and making his way to the door. The moon was still dispensing its light across the lawn and through the glass. He opened the door and stepped out on to the *terrasse* to breath in fresh air. The night was filled with the sound of warm wind in the trees. He could see the dark shape of them swaying against the sky.

A movement distracted him and drew his eyes towards the line of parked cars beyond the *pigeonnier*. And with a shock he realised there was someone sitting in one of them, a flash of white face caught in the moonlight. Alarm bells began ringing in his head and he was about to call for Bertrand when the car door opened, and by its courtesy light he saw that it was Michelle. She stepped out of the car and stood looking across the grass towards him.

He closed the door of the *gîte* and went down the stairs. They met beneath the *pigeonnier*, the child's swing turning in the wind. Her hair blew about her head, and she swept it back out of her face. She seemed very pale.

'How long have you been sitting there?' He searched her face for some clue as to what might be in her head, but there was an opaque quality in it, an evasive cloudiness in her green eyes.

'Most of the evening.'

'Why?'

'I was waiting for you.' She glanced towards the *gîte*. 'Where's Charlotte?'

'She's gone back to Paris. I thought you were leaving.'

'So did I.' She scuffed the gravel with the toe of her shoe. 'Then I got to thinking. About that kiss. Up at Château de Salettes. And about whether I really wanted to go or not.' She looked up from her feet, into his eyes, and reached up to touch his face.

He shook his head. 'I'm old enough to be your father.'

'My father's dead.' Her voice was flat, emotionless. 'I'm not looking for another one.'

She pushed herself up on tip-toes towards him and her nose crinkled in a smile.

'I smell whisky.'

CHAPTER FIFTEEN

I

It was his first night in the bed. After the *clic-clac* it had been soft and warm, enveloping him in quilt and mattress, to relieve aching and weary bones and draw him down into a deep sleep. Now sunlight spilled in through the unshuttered window, lying hot across the bed, and he felt Michelle's breath in his face. She kissed him. A soft, wet kiss, her tongue dragging across his lips and nose. He reached over and ran a hand over her smooth, hairy body. And an arrow of consciousness pierced his slumber, startling him awake.

Braucol gazed lovingly into his face and licked him again.

'Jesus!' Enzo sat up spitting and spluttering, then groaned as pain flooded his head. There had been way too much alcohol the night before. But where the hell was Michelle? And then he remembered. He wrapped a sheet around his nakedness and hurried through to the bathroom to slunge cold water on his face. She had been reluctant to spend the night as long as Sophie and Bertrand were there.

'Sophie doesn't like me,' she had told him.

'Nonsense. Why wouldn't she like you?'

'Because she likes Charlotte, and Charlotte doesn't like me.'

Women, Enzo reflected, always seemed aware of things that passed him by. And so he had spent the night alone. Again. Waking up to the dog on the pillow next to him. He brushed his teeth with extra vigour, then found his towelling robe and went through to the *séjour*. Sophie and Bertrand were heating *croissants* in the oven. The room was filled with the smell of their savoury sweetness and the aroma of fresh coffee.

'*Bonjour,*' Bertrand said brightly. Sophie scowled at her father, then turned away to pour herself a coffee. She was in a mood with him. Enzo raised his eyebrows towards Bertrand in silent question, but Bertrand just shrugged and made a facial apology in silent response.

'I need your help collecting soil samples today,' Enzo said.

For a moment, Sophie forgot her mood and turned around, coffee raised to her lips. 'What for?'

He explained the principal of wine fingerprinting and told them they would need samples from every vineyard Petty had visited. 'We know where he went from his tasting schedule. I'll draw up a list after breakfast and we can divide them up among us. I doubt if any of the *vignerons* are going to welcome us with open arms, so we'll not tell anyone what we're doing. Nicole can collect a sample from La Croix Blanche.'

'And Michelle? I suppose she'll be helping too?' Sophie cocked a disapproving eyebrow at her father.

'Any objections?'

Bertrand said, 'I think I'll just go and take my shower.' He hurried out of the room, leaving father and daughter in awkward silence.

'Look, if this is because I had one little whisky last night—'

'I saw you,' Sophie said. 'You and Michelle Petty out there by the *pigeonnier*.'

'You were spying on us?'

'No, I was worried about you. I heard you going outside.' She drew a deep, indignant breath. 'It's disgusting, Papa.'

'What is?'

'You and that . . . that girl. She's less than half your age. Younger than Kirsty, for God's sake!'

Enzo gasped in frustration. 'I don't believe I'm getting lectured on my love-life by my own daughter. It's none of your business, Sophie.'

'You're my father!'

'You're my daughter. And you've made it abundantly clear that it's none of *my* business who *you* go out with.'

'That's different.'

'No, it's not. We're all adults here. We make our own choices in life. I've been twenty years on my own, Sophie.' He choked back a sudden surge of self-pity. 'Sometimes a man needs the company of a woman.'

'What about Charlotte?'

'Good question. One I've asked *her* often enough. I'm still waiting for an answer.'

They stood glaring at each other, but the flame of their anger was subsiding as quickly as it had flared. And with two steps Sophie extinguished it completely, throwing her arms around her father's waist and burying her head in his chest.

'I'm sorry, Papa. I just worry about you. I don't want to see you hurt.'

He drew her to him. She was all he really had in the world. The only one he could count on for unconditional love. And he hated it when they fought.

They broke apart at the sound of the door opening and turned to see Nicole hesitating on the threshold. Her eyes were red-rimmed and raw, her face the colour of chalk. It was clear she had been crying, and now tears gathered again in stinging eyes, like rain in clouds.

'My God, Nicole, what's happened?' Enzo reached her in three strides.

Her lip quivered as the tears burned tracks down her cheeks, and she looked up into his face. 'My mother's dead.'

II

The *gendarme* was young, attractive, with short dark hair, and black Mediterranean eyes. She smiled at Enzo across the desk and told him that Gendarme Roussel had taken several days' leave. Enzo nodded through the open window towards the other side of the courtyard.

'Does he stay in the apartments?'

'No, he and his wife moved out when they had their second kid. They live in his family home near Lisle-sur-Tarn.'

Enzo nodded thoughtfully. 'The pathologist in the Serge Coste case has a sample for me to collect. But they won't release it without the proper paperwork. Gendarme Roussel was going to take care of that for me.'

Her smile widened. 'He did. If you'll hold on a minute . . .'

She disappeared through an open door, and Enzo heard distant music and voices raised in laughter. Out in the court-yard, where a group of *gendarmes* stood smoking, the shadows of clouds raced across the gravel, the advance guard of rain-clouds approaching from the south-west.

He couldn't shake off the depression of Nicole's news. He had never met her mother, but he knew her father, and knew too how hard it was for a man on his own. Nicole had been inconsolable. No matter how prepared you think you are for the death of someone close, it always comes harder than you could ever imagine. He had sent her straight home, and made her promise to call him once they had fixed a date for the funeral.

'Here you are.' The smiling *gendarme* emerged holding a large buff envelope. She handed it to him. 'He left it for you.'

As he buzzed the gate open to step out into the street, he saw how dark the sky was beyond the river, sunlight cutting tile-red roofs sharp against the black. He felt the wind strong in his face and smelled the change of weather in it. The rain would not be far behind. He would need to hurry. He did not want to be digging up earth samples in the wet.

The first drops of it fell as he tipped the last trowelful of sandy earth into his plastic carrier bag. When he had first crouched between the vines to dig deep into crumbling, dry soil, the wind had been fierce, whipping through the leaves on either side of his head, filling his ears with a sound like rushing water. Which was probably why he had not heard the motor of the approaching vehicle. Now the wind had dropped, and the rain was starting to fall. He turned his face up towards a sky swollen with cloud and felt it splash warm on his skin. He tied the bag shut and stood up, turning abruptly into the shadow of Fabien Marre. The young man was blocking his way out from between the rows.

They were both big men, and their eyes met on a level. Enzo was startled. He had not heard the other man approach. But he stood his ground, determined to brazen it out. The rain began to fall in earnest, so that within seconds they were both soaked, rain streaming down faces carved in stone.

'What the hell do you think you're doing?' Fabien's eyes dropped to the carrier bag and the dripping trowel in Enzo's hands.

'None of your business.' Enzo moved to push past him, but Fabien shoved a big hand into his chest.

'It's my land. Which makes it my business. What's in the bag?'

In his day, Enzo could have met Fabien on an equal physical footing. But although he kept himself fit, there were twenty years between them. He would be no match for the younger man. 'Nicole says you told her you refused to let Petty taste your wines.'

'So?'

'We found his reviews. He tasted five wines from La Croix Blanche.'

Lightning crackled somewhere over the other side of the hill, followed seconds later by an explosion of thunder.

Fabien shrugged. 'He didn't get them from me. You can buy my wines in any supermarket or *cave* around here.'

'Why would he do that?'

'You'd have to ask him.'

'I would. Only someone murdered him.'

Fabien held him in a steady, unblinking gaze, face streaming. His change of subject took Enzo by surprise. 'So, when's the funeral?'

More lightning, more thunder. Enzo frowned. 'What do you mean?'

'Nicole's mother.'

Enzo felt anger rise up his back like bristles on a porcupine. 'What's it to you?'

'I thought I might go.'

Confusion diluted anger for just a moment, and Enzo stared at Fabien through narrowed eyes. 'Why would you do that?'

'Me and Nicole, we have . . . an understanding. I think she'd appreciate my support.'

Enzo shook his head. 'You stay away from Nicole. That's the only thing you need to understand. You go anywhere near her, you answer to me.'

'I'm shaking in my shoes.' Thunder burst above their heads, so loudly that both men ducked involuntarily, momentarily chastened by an anger greater than their own before recovering their dignity and resuming their stand-off. Fabien tipped his head towards Enzo's carrier bag. 'Are you going to tell me what's in the bag?'

Enzo glared at him and sounded much braver than he felt. 'No.'

'Looks to me like you're stealing my land.'

'Does it?'

'And you're trespassing.'

Enzo thrust out his jaw. 'You know, in Scotland there is no law of trespass. Because we figured out a long time ago that nobody owns the land. We inhabit it for a short time. And when we're gone, other people inhabit it. The land is forever, we're just passing through.'

'Semantics.'

'That's a big word.'

'I read a lot.'

'Well, read my lips. Stay away from Nicole.' As Enzo tried to move past him, Fabien's wet hand pushed into his chest once more. Enzo looked down at it, a hand that could do him a great deal of damage if its owner chose to use it for that purpose. Then he looked into the young man's eyes. Their faces were only inches apart.

'I could take you any day, old man.'

'Maybe you could. But you'd suffer a lot of collateral damage in the process.'

The two men stood dripping in the rain, staring each other down, like animals in the wild. Each daring the other to make the first move. Each knowing that whatever the outcome, it would be bloody for them both. A few moments seemed to stretch into eternity. Then Fabien's hand dropped to his side, and Enzo pushed past, their shoulders bumping, ungiving and hard, neither man wanting to lose face.

Fabien turned and watched, impassive, as Enzo got into his 2CV, backed it out around Fabien's four-by-four, and headed back towards the road, down a track which had become a stream. Wipers smeared a fly-stained windscreen. Lightning flashed again across the valley, but the thunder had retreated beyond the hill. Like the threat of violence which had passed, its fury was spent and its roar muted.

III

Enzo pulled out eight inches of plastic from the roll in the machine and drew the cutter across it to make a plastic bag big enough to take a small trowelful of earth. Then, carefully, he placed the cut edge inside the machine and hit the *start* button. The plastic crinkled around the soil as the machine sucked out the air to create a vacuum before heat-sealing the bag.

He passed it to Sophie for labelling, cut another bag from the roll, and poured in the last of the eighteen samples they had collected.

There was a knock at the door. Michelle opened it, shaking her umbrella out on to the *terrasse* and propping it against the wall before stepping inside. 'Hi.' She tried to sound bright, but there was a tension behind her smile. 'The rain's really bad. Nobody's picking grapes in this.'

Enzo had seen the harvesters out earlier, a frenzied attempt to strip as many of the vines as possible before the deluge. Now the vineyards were empty, harvesters abandoned, dripping in the rain.

Sophie cast Michelle a look, then turned back to her father who was concentrating on the final seal. 'This is the one from Château Lacroux?'

'Yes, the *argile calcaire.*' It was a stony, chalky texture.

'Hi,' Bertrand said to Michelle. He was doing his best to ignore the atmosphere that Sophie was doing her best to create.

Michelle gave him a smile of appreciation and crossed the room to see what they were doing. She brought the smell of damp clothes with her and looked at all the bags laid out on the table. 'Are those the soil samples?'

Enzo nodded as he hit the *start* button for the last time. 'Yeah.'

'I thought I was going to help with that.'

Without looking at her, Sophie said, 'Some of us manage to get out of our beds earlier than others.'

Enzo glared at his daughter, remembering all the weekend mornings he'd had to tip her out of her bed in time for lunch. 'We had to move fast before the rain started,' he said.

The machine sucked the air out of the bag, then buzzed as it heat-sealed it shut.

'Wow, where'd you get that?' Michelle said.

Enzo straightened up and stretched his stiffening back.

'At the hypermarket in town. It's a food saver, for vacuum-sealing foodstuffs. Ideal for preventing contamination of the soil samples.'

'How are you sending them to the States?'

'I'm not. I'm taking them myself.'

Michelle pursed her lips. 'Do you have official permission?'

'Why would he need permission?' Sophie glowered at her.

'Because you can't just go carrying soil samples with you on an airplane into the United States. Americans are paranoid about contaminants being brought in from other countries. Bugs and bacteria and viruses. They're even scared you might carry something into the country in the treads of your shoes. That's why you have to sign a form on the plane saying you haven't been on a farm before travelling.' She looked at Enzo. 'You do have permission, don't you?'

Sophie gazed up at her father with concern. 'Do you?'

Enzo shrugged dismissively. 'It could take weeks to get the paperwork sorted out for something like this. We don't have the time.'

'So how are you going to get them through customs?' Bertrand said.

'I'll pack them into the lining of my suitcase. They're not going to show up on the x-ray.'

But Michelle was shaking her head. 'You know, these days the TSA are going through almost every bag. They find these things in your suitcase, not only will you lose them, you'll be in deep shit.'

'What'll you do, Papa?' For the moment, Sophie had forgotten her feud with Michelle.

'I'll think of something,' Enzo said, as if thinking of something might be the easiest thing in the world. While, in truth, he hadn't the least idea of what it was he would do. He turned instead towards his whiteboard and the coded review he had scrawled across it the day before. 'Right now, we need to concentrate on breaking Gil Petty's code.'

IV

The rain had not yet reached Lascombes but, as she drove up the winding track towards the farm, Nicole could see the clouds gathering on the distant horizon. The wind breathed through the hills in gasps and sighs, gathering in eddies where mountain streams cut through rock as old as time, shaking leaves from trees and lifting them up to carry them off on its wayward path.

Everything seemed so normal. The tractor stood in the yard, a chainsaw lying beside the wooden trestle where her father cut the logs. The dogs came running to greet her as they always did, oblivious to the death in their midst, recognising the pitch of the old Renault 4L that her father had bought for her at the car market. As she got out of it, the wind whipped about her face, and the dogs danced, barking, about her legs. She barely noticed them. She looked towards the stoop, where they had sat so often on warm summer evenings, her mother reading to her from the books she borrowed each week from

the library van that came to the road's end. And as the door of
the house opened, she found it hard to believe that it would
not be her mother who stepped out to greet her. Harder still
to accept that it never would.

Her father stood in the doorway looking at her. Still with
his old flat cap pushed back on his head, dungarees torn and
stained from his labours on the farm, big boots caked with
mud and shit. He looked miserable, desolate. Diminished
somehow.

Tears sprang to her eyes again, and she ran across the yard
and up the steps to throw herself into his arms. They stood for
a long time holding each other, holding onto every memory
they'd ever had of the woman they both loved, in case they
might slip away just as she had. When, finally, she looked up
into his face, she saw no tears in his eyes. Men like her father
did not cry. They just bled inside and suffered in silence.

The *séjour* was dark, the remnants of oak logs smoulder-
ing in the *cheminée*, the smell of stale cooking hanging in
still air. Her aunt took her in her arms and kissed her. She,
too, was dry-eyed, but Nicole could see in them that there
had been tears. There was a limit to how much crying you
could do.

It was with an awful sense of dread that Nicole pushed
open the door to her mother's bedroom to see her laid out
on the bed, candles burning on bedside tables at either
side of her pillow. Their flames threw flickering shadows on
the bloodless skin of her mother's face, the only warmth in
the blue-white chill of death. But the lines etched around her

eyes and mouth by months of pain had gone. She looked at peace now, a strange serenity about her.

The air was filled with the scent of burning wax and something medicinal, like disinfectant in a hospital. Her mother's hands were folded together in her lap. Nicole approached the bed to take one of them in hers. She was shocked by how cold it was. Shocked, too, by how little like her mother this dead person was: all animation and personality removed, life and laughter long departed. Leaving only the vessel that had borne them. Not really her mother at all.

She closed her eyes and thought again about kneeling in the abbey the previous night, praying for a quick and painless departure. She could not help wondering, irrationally, as she had through all the long drive from Gaillac, if she was somehow responsible for her mother's death.

They walked in silence together up to the old abandoned farmhouse, past the piles of logs heaped up along the track, canvas covers whipping and billowing in the wind. Cloud had obliterated the sun. They could see the rain now, sweeping across the distant hills like a fog. Lightning flashed across the horizon, and they heard the far-off rumble of thunder. They stopped to watch for a moment, knowing that it was only a matter of minutes before the rain would reach them.

Her father scratched his head with fingers that were black from harvesting walnuts. 'Can't do it on my own,' he said.

Nicole turned her face up to look at him, puzzled.

'Do what, Papa?'

'Run the farm. With Marie gone . . . I can't do it on my own.'

Nicole sighed. Her mother had done so much on the farm, as well as keeping house, cooking for them, doing the laundries. Her father was right. There was no way he could do it all himself. 'Can't you get help?'

He shook his head and avoided her eye. 'Can't afford it.' He was silent for a long time. Perhaps it was only the first spots of rain blowing in their faces that precipitated his final confession. 'See, it was always a struggle, Nicole. Putting you through university. Paying your digs in Toulouse.' He turned big, sad, guilty eyes to meet his daughter's. 'Can't do it and pay someone to help. You'll need to come home. Take your mother's place.'

CHAPTER SIXTEEN

I

'Cryptography,' Enzo said. 'From the Greek. *Kryptós*, meaning hidden, and *gráfo*, meaning to write. Once described by the cryptographer Ron Rivest as being all about communication in the presence of adversaries.'

He set himself tipping back and forth in the rocking chair, all the while gazing thoughtfully at his whiteboard. In his hand he clutched the tasting notes of old Jacques Domenech. He was looking for a starting point.

Michelle sat on the stairs, a half-drunk glass of red wine on the step beside her. She pulled her knees up under her chin, arms hugging her shins, and stared at the code her father had created. She had no idea where to even begin to try to break it. Sophie had taken Nicole's place at the computer. Bertrand stood behind her, a glass of wine in his hand, pointing and prompting as she pulled up different sites on the internet.

'Wikipedia,' he said, and she tapped some more.

'Okay.' She read aloud. 'One of cryptography's primary purposes is hiding the meaning of messages. Not usually the existence of such messages.' She puffed up her cheeks and blew through her lips. 'Talk about stating the obvious.'

'No, no.' Enzo interrupted her. 'The obvious is what we so often miss. So it does no harm to state it.'

Sophie's fingers rattled over the keyboard, annoyed at being put down by her father in front of Michelle. 'Here's a book called *Between Silk and Cyanide*,' she said. 'About code-breaking during the Second World War.'

'I've read it,' Enzo said. 'Agents used poems they'd written themselves as the basis for their codes.' He grinned. 'There was no way the Germans could possibly guess the next line in a piece of doggerel which began, "Is de Gaulle's prick twelve inches thick?"'

'Papa, that's disgusting!'

'That was the point. The more crude or absurd, the more impossible for someone else to crack it.'

'It doesn't sound like my father,' Michelle said.

Enzo nodded his agreement. Petty, it seemed, had been a pretty humourless individual. 'But in any case, he wouldn't have needed to make his code that difficult. He was guarding against accidental discovery. I don't think he ever imagined that anyone would be making a concerted effort to break it. I guess it was almost like a kind of shorthand. More for himself than anything else.'

'Did your father speak another language?' Bertrand glanced towards Michelle.

'French. Some Spanish. I don't think he was particularly fluent in either.'

Sophie looked up at the board. 'oh, nm, ky, ks is not French. It's not like any kind of Spanish I've ever seen either.'

'No, but it's a good thought,' Enzo said. 'What's another language, except another set of words for the same thing? A French-English dictionary, for example, is just two lists of corresponding words, one of which is alphabetical.'

'I see what you mean.' Michelle lifted her glass and sipped pensively. 'So you think my dad just made a list of the terms he uses to describe wines, and set them against another list of some kind.'

'A poem, maybe?' Sophie chipped in. 'The first and last letters of each word.'

'I doubt it.' Enzo shook his head. 'Too complicated. It would have to be something he could remember quite easily, without reference to something written.' He caught Sophie glaring at him and felt a stab of guilt at having dismissed her so easily. 'But it's a good thought.'

The damage, however, had been done. Sophie confined her frustration to a single, audible tut. She turned back to the computer and the chatter of the keyboard reflected her annoyance as she typed another search into Google. Her eyebrows shot up in sudden surprise and she looked at Michelle. 'Did you know your dad's website's still up on the net?'

Michelle shrugged. 'There wouldn't have been anyone to remove it. I guess there are probably thousands of websites out there belonging to dead people.'

Bertrand stabbed a finger at the screen. 'There. What's that?'

Sophie peered at the screen. 'It's a link to something called a taste wheel. What the hell's a taste wheel?'

Michelle said, 'It's a wheel divided into flavour segments. Just a graphic representation of tastes and smells. It was the department of oenology at UC Davis that first came up with the concept. My dad published his own version of it in a book he wrote about wine tasting.'

Sophie clicked the mouse and waited a moment. 'And he put it right up here on his website.'

Enzo eased himself out of the rocker and rounded the table to have a look. The wheel was divided into multicoloured segments. An inner wheel was separated into the ten perceived categories of taste and smell, the largest of which was *Fruit*. It then ranged through *Sweet, Wood, Spice, Savoury, Herbal, Floral, Nutty, Mineral*, and *Dairy*, which was the smallest. Each category was allotted a different colour, subdivided through the outer wheel into individual flavours represented by tonal variations of that colour. *Fruit* was split into red and green and went from apple, pear, and lemon, through to prune, fig, and jam. *Spice* was pink and included tobacco, smoke, and liquorice; while *Dairy*, which was yellow, comprised only butter and cream. In all, there were sixty-four flavours.

Enzo shook his head and marvelled at the smells and flavours people were able to discern in wine. Ground coffee. Leather. Cut grass. Toast. Stones. And yet, they were all things he had perceived himself in one wine or another over the years. Violets, cherries, grilled nuts. Some were appealing, others less so. Earth, green pepper, petrol. He screwed up his face at the very thought.

Bertrand said, 'Look, he also lists the words he used to

describe the sensual qualities of wine in the mouth.' He pointed to an alphabetical list of seventeen words below the wheel. They went from *Astringent*, describing mouth-puckering tannins, through *Firm, Heavy* and *Sharp*, to *Thin*, representing a lack of flavour and body.

'Okay,' Enzo said, 'print all that out for me.' He felt a *frisson* of excitement. Things were starting to fall into place. 'This gives us pretty much his full flavour vocabulary, describing what he smelled in a wine, tasted in a wine, and how it felt in his mouth. These are almost certainly what he created the codes for.'

'As well as his ratings,' Sophie said.

Bertrand nodded. 'A through to F and 1 through to 5.'

'Which means . . .' Enzo did a quick mental calculation. ' . . . we're looking for a total of ninety-two codes.' He lifted the pages from the printer as it fed them out through the inkjet and crossed to the whiteboard. He wiped off Petty's coded rating for the Sarrabelle Syrah and started listing the flavours in columns, beginning with *Fruit*. Then he moved on to the one-word sensual descriptions, and finally the ratings. It took him nearly ten minutes, and the others watched in silence as his marker pen squeaked its way across the shiny white surface. 'Okay.' Enzo stood back and looked at the lists before picking up the notes they had made at old Domene-ch's house the night before.

He scrutinised his scribbles, frowning in concentration. His writing had become less and less legible as the night wore on.

'There,' he said at last. 'The 2001 Petrus Pommerol that we had. Domenech agreed with Petty's published description of a wine with strong hints of liquorice and vanilla.' He ran a finger down through his notes, stopping and tapping near the foot of the page. 'Now, when he tasted the three Gaillac reds that we only have the coded notes for, he discerned vanilla and liquorice in the Sarrabelle Syrah, and vanilla in the Cuvée Léa.' He held out a hand towards Bertrand. 'Give me the printouts.'

Bertrand handed him the coded reviews of the three wines they had taken to Cordes-sur-Ciel, and Enzo pinned them to the wall beside the board. He stood scanning them studiously before exasperation exploded in a breath from pursed lips. 'Trouble is, there are too many repeating codes. There are codes unique to each one, but there are several. We have no way of knowing which one might be *liquorice*. And of the ones that repeat, which one might be *vanilla*.' He slumped into the rocker and let his notes fall into his lap. 'Shit! The sample's too small. We'd need to go on tasting wines until we found a unique flavour to match a unique code, or multiple codes that repeated so often that we could be sure of the match.'

Sophie cocked an eyebrow and grinned. 'Well, I'm all for tasting more wines.'

But Enzo was adamant. 'No. It's not the way.' He glanced semi-apologetically at Bertrand. 'It was a good idea, but it's not how we're going to break the code.'

'Well how are we going to break it?' Sophie cocked her head at her father.

'*We* are not going to do anything. *You* are going to leave me in peace to think about it.' He cast a rueful look at Michelle. 'All of you.'

Sophie stood up. 'Well, there's no point in arguing with him. When my Papa makes up his mind about something, that's it.' She took Bertrand's hand. 'Come on, let's go to town and find a café.' She flounced out with Bertrand in tow. Enzo saw that the rain was still falling from the heavens.

He sighed and turned to Michelle. 'You can stay if you want.'

But Michelle shook her head. 'No. You need to think. I understand that.'

'I'm sorry about Sophie.'

'I understand that, too. Maybe if I was her, I'd feel the same way.' She got up from the stairs and crossed the room to plant a gentle kiss on Enzo's forehead. He smelled her perfume and felt her warmth, and for a moment was tempted to forget about codes and killers and take her through to the bedroom. But the thought that someone else might be about to go missing, that someone else was in danger of suffering the same fate as Petty and Coste, and probably the others in Roussel's file, weighed on his conscience, and he knew that Michelle would have to wait. He gave her hand a squeeze, and felt a rush of regret as she went out onto the *terrasse* to recover her umbrella and brave the rain.

He got up and crossed to the wine rack and took out a bottle of Château Lacroux 2001 Vignes de Castellan. He uncorked it and poured himself an inch of it before swirling the deep, rich red around inside the glass. The wine was at perfect room temperature and gave off the distinctive Gaillac aromas of the duras and braucol grapes. Which made him think of the puppy for the first time in hours, and he looked in vain around the room before spotting him curled up fast asleep under the table. Enzo smiled. Daughters and dogs, he thought. Endless trouble. But always worth it. He took a mouthful of wine. Red fruits, a hint of black cherry, liquorice.

He carried the bottle over to the rocking chair, sat down, and filled his glass. As he sipped at the wine, he gazed at all the flavours he had written up on the board, until they blurred and swam in front of his eyes. He refilled his glass and turned his attention to the coded reviews:

ky, ms and nj. wjc. gf+&lbj+++
jmo, zt&nm, with a little nj
giving way to ky, la&ma

The letters were always in groups of two or three. Some of them made words, like *la* and *ma*. Others made no sense at all. *jmo* or *hh*.

He drank some more wine and closed his eyes. But the codes were still there, etched by light on his retinas. There had to be a simple logic to it. He thought back to his own allusion to the French-English dictionary. Two lists of corresponding words, one of which was in alphabetical order. And something began to chip away at his consciousness from somewhere below the surface. Something nagging, insistent, like a woodpecker drilling holes in trees. His head hurt at the thought, and he wondered irrationally, if woodpeckers ever got headaches. He felt his glass slip in his hand, and he put it down on the floor before he dropped it. There was something there. Something just beyond reach. Something that someone had said. Something right in front of his eyes. A key to unlocking the code. But he was so, so very sleepy.

He was a long way down. It was very dark here, and strange creatures floated through the murk, skulking in the shadows, bulbous eyes staring at him through fronds that waved about in the eddies and currents of cold, cold water. There was a tug on his line, and he realised that there was very little oxygen left. He could hear a voice, from somewhere very far above, calling him back to the surface. He had found something down here, and he wanted to tell them. But he knew he mustn't make his ascent too quickly, or he would lose it.

He pushed off towards the voice, mud and sand rising all around him. He tipped his head back and saw the light and heard the voice again, and found himself rising at an alarming rate. Too fast. He broke the surface gasping for breath.

'Papa!' Sophie glared at him. 'You've been drinking.'

Enzo frowned. 'Only a couple of glasses.'

The door opened from the *terrasse*, and Michelle came in. Sophie turned to look at her. 'Where were you?'

'I waited in the car until I saw you coming back.'

'Well, the great mind here, who wanted us to leave him alone so that he could concentrate, drank some wine and fell asleep. That's what old men do, you know. Fall asleep in chairs.' She flashed Michelle a very purposeful look, just in case she'd missed the point.

'What time is it?' Enzo ignored his daughter's barb.

Bertrand looked at his watch. 'Nearly six. You've been out for a couple of hours, Monsieur Macleod.'

Enzo stood up stiffly and focused on the whiteboard; then he ripped one of the coded reviews from the wall and blinked at it, trying to remember. And then he did. He turned to find three faces looking at him expectantly, and he smiled and waved the piece of paper in the air. 'It's quite simple, really.'

'What is?' Sophie took the review from him and looked at it.

'The code.'

'You broke it? In your sleep?'

'Maybe I was asleep, maybe I wasn't.' He turned towards the whiteboard and lifted his marker pen. The others watched, filled with sudden curiosity, as he wrote up *l*, *b* and *j*, then turned back to them. A smile split his face. 'What do these letters mean to anyone.' They all looked blankly at the board. 'Okay. Let's capitalise them. It makes a big difference.' He wrote up *LBJ*. 'Come on. You've got to see it.' Still nothing. 'Okay, maybe you were too young. But in the sixties, during the Vietnam war, these were initials on everybody's lips.' He said them out loud. 'LBJ.'

Which was when the penny dropped for Michelle. 'Lyndon B. Johnston. He was sworn in as President after the assassination of Kennedy.'

'Good girl.' He turned back to the board and wrote up *WJC*.

Now Michelle couldn't keep the smile off her face. 'William Jefferson Clinton. They're all Presidents of the United States!'

But Enzo waved a finger of admonishment. 'Not all of them. There haven't been ninety-two Presidents.' He held open palms out towards her. 'You told me yourself the other night, Michelle. Your dad's party-piece when he was a kid.'

Realisation dawned on her like sunlight breaking through dark cloud. 'States!' she said. 'Presidents and States.'

Enzo wrote up KY.

'Kentucky.'

Then NJ.

'New Jersey.'

He beamed at them. 'The most common of all codes. Ones that get used by millions of people every day. Post codes. It's so simple. His parents made him commit to memory all the States and all the Presidents when he was just a kid. He wasn't ever going to forget them. So every flavour on the wheel got assigned to one of them.'

'In what order?' Sophie said.

Enzo shrugged. 'The States would be alphabetical, the Presidents chronological. All we have to do is figure out where on the taste wheel he started.'

Sophie said, 'We need a list of States and Presidents.' And she rounded the table to the computer and tapped a quick search into Google. A smile spread across her face. 'Fifty States, and forty-three Presidents. Actually, forty-two, because one of them served twice. Isn't the internet a wonderful thing?' She clicked a couple of times with her mouse, then hit the print button, and the printer started spewing out a list of US States and American Presidents.

Michelle was looking at the coded scores given to the three wines they had tasted, then glanced up at Enzo's whiteboard. 'This doesn't match, Enzo.'

'What do you mean?'

'Well, if the A to F and the 1 to 5 were the last things to be coded, then you would expect them all to be recent Presidents. But they're not. Look.' She pointed to the score her father had awarded the Château Lastours 2001 Cuvée Spéciale. 'ALI and CA. That's got to be Abraham Lincoln and Chester Arthur.'

'We've got them the wrong way round, that's why.' Everyone turned to look at Bertrand. 'Look at the sensory descriptions of the wine in the mouth. WJC. LBJ. GE.'

'Bill Clinton, Lyndon Johnston, Gerald Ford,' Michelle said. 'All right down at the most recent end of the list.'

'So we work backwards through the sensory descriptions,' Enzo said. 'Starting with George W. Bush.' He wrote up *GWB* against *Thin*.

Sophie said, 'How did Gil Petty describe *Thin* again?' She pulled up the page of Petty's flavour and sensory listings, then burst out laughing. 'Lacking flavour and body.' She scrolled up the list. 'And his father? GHWB? *Simple*. A sound, drinkable wine of no great distinction. Two Bush presidencies summed up to perfection.' She looked at Michelle, grinning. 'Do you think you're father matched these on purpose?'

'I doubt it somehow. More like happy coincidence.'

'What about Clinton?' Bertrand said. 'What's his sensory adjective.'

Sophie put the two together from the separate lists and could hardly speak for laughing. When, finally, she managed to control herself, she said, 'William Jefferson Clinton comes under the category of *Smooth*.' Which brought a spontaneous eruption of laughter from around the room. Braucol woke up and started barking.

'Maybe your father had a secret sense of humour after all,' Enzo said. He took the printout of Presidents and States and, starting from the bottom of the board, worked his way back through the list of sensory descriptions, ratings and flavours, putting initials against each. 'Some of these Presidents had the same initials as States, or each other, so it looks like he's added the second letter of the surname to distinguish them.'

As he reached the tastes that he had copied down from the flavour wheel, Sophie said, 'How do you know where he started listing the flavours?'

'I don't. But let's assume that, like me, he started with the biggest grouping, *Fruit*. We'll assign the initials to the order in which I've written them down, then see how they match up with our own tastings.'

It took several more minutes for him to finish writing State postal codes against flavours, finishing with *AL* against *Apple*. He riffled through a confusion of papers to retrieve his notes from the Domenech tastings.

'Okay, so *oak* would be *NM*. We tasted that in the Last-ours and the Sarrabelle.' He checked the two coded reviews and found *NM* in the taste lines of both. 'So far so good. We also found *vanilla* in both the Cuvée Léa and the Sarrabelle Syrah. Which means we should find *NJ* in their taste lines.' He checked. 'And there they are.'

'And *liquorice*?' Bertrand said. 'We found that in the Syrah, too.'

Enzo looked at the board. '*Liquorice* is *OH*.' He checked it against the review. 'And there it is.' He looked up, beaming his satisfaction. 'By George, I think we've got it!' He pulled the review of the Château Lastours Cuvée Spéciale 2001 off the wall and held it up in front of him, so that he could switch focus between the whiteboard and the paper. His mobile began to ring. 'Get that will you Sophie? I want to translate this.'

Sophie took his phone out on to the *terrasse*, and Enzo began to translate the coded review in front of him.

'Colour – dark red with brick tones. Nose – smoky oak with wild fruit, following up with strong crushed strawberries. Mouth – soft tannins, velvety and round. Long finish. Longevity – five to eight years. Score – B1.' He looked at Michelle. 'No doubt he made it a little more colourful when he wrote it up for the newsletter, but that's his basic description of the wine.' He picked up the review of the Sarrabelle Syrah. 'And it looks like he found his Holy Grail here in Gaillac. He's given the Syrah an A1.'

Sophie came back in and shut the door gently behind her. Enzo saw immediately that she had paled.

'What's wrong?'

She took a tremulous breath, trying to hold back her

emotion. 'Oh, just, you know . . . We're here, having a laugh, drinking wine, cracking codes . . .' She shook her head. 'That was Nicole. Her mother's funeral's the day after tomorrow.'

CHAPTER SEVENTEEN

I

Rain wept from a dark sky, steady and slow. Black umbrellas jostled for space above the heads of mourners. Grass turned to mud underfoot, splashing black shoes which had been polished to a shine just that morning. The marble slab that covered the family tomb had been slid to one side by red-faced professionals with ropes. Fetid air rose from the concrete hole below. There were other coffins down there. Nicole's grand-parents. Nicole watched as coffinbearers, straining arms and faces, lowered her mother into blackness. One day her father would join his wife. And Nicole would join them both when her turn came. It was salutary for a young girl, looking down into the gaping darkness of eternity, to know that this was where her future lay.

The sight of her mother disappearing into the dark brought fresh tears to eyes that had fought to stay dry, and she felt the comfort of Fabien's arm as it slid around her shoulder. She looked up and saw Enzo standing at the other side of the tomb, his mouth set in a grim line, his eyes full of sadness. She knew that Scotsmen often wore their kilts to weddings. She'd had no idea that they wore them to funerals, too. And she was moved that Enzo had taken the trouble. He made a striking figure with his white shirt and black tie, black dress jacket, and the eight metres of pleated tartan wool that made up his kilt. Silver trim on a black leather *sporran* gleamed dully in what little light the sky let through. There were small, thoughtful touches, too. The black flashes on either side of long, dark socks that stretched over sturdy calves and folded down below the knee. Black shoes laced up above the ankles. His black hair, pulled back in its habitual ponytail and held by a black ribbon. But it seemed greyer somehow, its white flash less distinctive.

And then it was over, mourners drifting away from the graveside among the tombs and headstones of this tiny *cimetière* in the shadow of the hills. Past the old stone chapel with its faded stained-glass windows, out on to the narrow road that wound through the jumble of mediaeval houses gathered around this final resting place. Acorns fallen from a towering oak beyond the wall crunched underfoot, the only sound to break the shuffling silence as they left.

Nicole took her father's arm as they walked towards the car. He was a big man reduced by loss, stooped and defeated. He looked awkward and uncomfortable in a suit that didn't fit him, that would not button shut across a belly that had expanded since last he wore it.

Enzo stood back and watched father and daughter with an ache in his heart. Sadness for them, discordant memories for him. He became aware of someone stopping at his side and turned his head to find himself looking into Fabien Marre's cautious black eyes. Anger displaced melancholy. He kept his voice low. 'I thought I told you to stay away from Nicole.'

'And I'm supposed to listen to a man in a skirt?'

If they had not been at a funeral Enzo would have taken him down with a swift left hook. In his imagination, at least. He contained his anger by making and unmaking fists at his side, then shoved his hands into his jacket pockets to keep them under control. He thought about all the hours they had spent decoding Petty's Gaillac ratings. Enzo had been keen to read what Petty had written about Laurent de Bonneval's Cuvée Spéciale, since he had tasted it himself. But it hadn't been among the coded reviews downloaded from the server. The wines of La Croix Blanche, however, had. He said, 'We decoded Petty's reviews of your wines.' And saw Fabien tense.

'Oh?'

'Don't you want to know how he rated them?'

'I don't give a damn what Petty thought.'

'Three A2s and two B1s. We figure he must have been planning to change his value ratings for the Gaillac wines, otherwise they'd all have been 1s. There's hardly a single wine that costs more than fifteen euros.'

Fabien said nothing.

'He liked your wines, Monsieur Marre. If he'd published those ratings, you'd have been selling them all over America by now.'

'So why would I want to kill him?'

Enzo looked at him thoughtfully. 'I don't know that you would. But, then, you had no way of knowing he was going to rate you at all, if we're to believe that you threw him off the vineyard.'

'It doesn't matter to me what you believe.'

'And what about Nicole? Does it matter to you what she thinks?'

A frown gathered the young man's brows into a knot. 'Why don't we just leave Nicole out of this?'

'You're the one who's bringing her into it. You're the one who's here.' He glanced towards the line of cars and saw Nicole's father and aunt driving off, leaving her standing in the road. She turned and looked back at Enzo and Fabien, and her concern was clear for them both to see. 'You shouldn't have come to the funeral, Marre. You've no business here.'

And as he walked across the small car park towards Nicole, he realised that the rain had stopped and he lowered his umbrella. He took her in his arms and held her for a long time, before releasing her with unexpected tears in his eyes.

She said, 'Thank you for coming, Monsieur Macleod.' She reached up and touched his face briefly with cold fingertips. A tiny expression of gratitude and affection. 'When do you leave for America?'

'I fly out tomorrow. I'm going up to Paris this afternoon.'

She nodded almost imperceptibly towards Fabien, who remained standing, a lone figure, by the cemetery gate. 'I hope there's no trouble between the two of you, Monsieur Macleod. I really do.' She avoided his eye, focusing somewhere off into the middle distance. 'I think he's really special.' And she flicked a quick, apprehensive look at Enzo to gauge his reaction.

But he remained impassive. 'Be careful, Nicole,' was all he said.

Then she took both of his hands in hers and stared studiously at the ground. She took a deep quivering breath and turned her face up towards him. 'There's something you should know.' He saw the pain in her eyes. 'I won't be coming back to university, Monsieur Macleod.'

The yard was still crammed with vehicles, and the house full of mourners eating the *quiche* and *petits fours* that Nicole's aunt had made the previous day, drinking the wine that Fabien had brought in the back of his four-by-four. Nicole's father had changed out of his suit as soon as he got back to the house. Now he was comfortable again in his dungarees and cloth cap, anxious to move on, to fill his head with work and leave no room for thought or memories. He and Enzo followed the track up the hill above the house to where he had walked with Nicole the day she got back. A warm breeze had sprung up out of the south to sweep the sky from the tops of the hills. The worst of the rain had passed. Battered and torn clouds let fragments of light break through to rush in ever changing shapes across an undulating landscape, messengers bearing the promise of better weather to come.

'It breaks my heart, Monsieur Macleod. It really does.' The dogs went barking off ahead of them, scattering a gaggle of hens around the boarded-up remains of the abandoned farm-house at the top of the hill.

'She's a smart girl, Monsieur Lafeuille. Brightest of her year.'

Her father raised his hands in a gesture of guilt and frustration. 'I know, I know. She deserves better. And I appreciate everything you've done for her, I really do.' He shook his head helplessly. 'But I just don't have the money.' He waved an arm vaguely in the air. 'The farm is all I have. It's how I make my living. I have no choice but to work it. And I just can't do it on my own. God knows, I might even have to let a few fields to my neighbours. We did that once before, for a season, after I nearly cut my foot off with a chainsaw.'

They stopped at the top of his world and looked out over the land that bound him as well as fed him. Land that demanded not only his life, but that of his daughter.

'The one bright spot for Nicole in this dark place we're in, Monsieur Macleod, is young Fabien Marre. He arrived yesterday. He's been a great support to her. A nice lad.' He managed to raise a smile and turned it towards Enzo. 'And he's of the land. Just like us.' He shook his head. 'And there was me thinking she was never going to find herself a man.'

Enzo nodded. Whatever doubts he had about Fabien Marre, this was neither the time nor the place to voice them. But where Nicole's father saw the young winemaker as light in their darkness, Enzo feared he might only be casting ever deeper shadows. He hoped he was wrong.

II

A dusky, pink twilight fell like a veil across the Paris rooftops. The rain in the south-west had not touched the capital. The air was autumnal soft, vibrating to the sounds of traffic in the boulevards. People sat at tables outside cafés enjoying an Indian summer, sipping chilled wine, animated chatter fusing with the sounds of birds that dived and swooped in darting clouds between the buildings.

Enzo walked up the Rue de Tournon from the Boulevard Saint-Germain towards the *Sénat*, the floodlit stone of the Upper House painted gold against blue fading to red. He stopped outside huge green doors that opened into a hidden world of Parisian courtyards, and hesitated for just a moment before tapping in the entry code.

From the courtyard beyond, he could see that Raffin's windows were open to the night. Soft classical music from a stereo drifted in gentle evening air, carried on the light that fell from unshuttered windows across the cobbles. The indignation that days before had fuelled his determination to speak to Raffin, gave way now to a nervous apprehension.

Raffin, too, seemed nervous. He had been hesitant about his availability to see Enzo that night. But Enzo had stressed that it would be their only chance to meet, and so he had cancelled an engagement and called back to tell Enzo to come to the apartment.

There was a bottle of wine open on the table and two glasses set beside it. Raffin wore immaculately pressed, pleated trousers that gathered around brown suede Italian shoes. His white shirt looked freshly starched, open at the neck, collar turned up to where soft brown hair grew to meet it. It was longer than when Enzo had last seen him. His sharp, angular jaw was shaved smooth and still carried the scent of some expensive aftershave that Enzo couldn't identify and probably couldn't afford. Raffin lit a cigarette, which he held between long fingers, and looked at Enzo with pale green eyes. 'You'll take a glass?'

Enzo nodded and sat down uncomfortably at the table.

Raffin poured two glasses. 'So how's the investigation going?'

'Well. I hope this trip to America is going to help me crack it.'

'Will you be away long?'

'A couple of days.' Enzo took a sip of his wine and glanced at the bottle. Of course, it was something good. A Clos Mogador 2001 Priorat. An inky-purple Bordeaux with rich, full tones of blueberry and raspberry and toasty new oak. Enzo thought that it probably cost fifty euros, or more.

Raffin sat down opposite. 'Tell me.'

And so Enzo told him everything. About Petty's coded ratings, and how they had broken the code. About his article on GM yeasts recommending a boycott of American wines. Which drew a whistle of astonishment from Raffin. About the attempt on Enzo's life in the vineyards of Château Saint-Michel. Jean-Marc Josse and the l'Ordre de la Dive Bouteille. Gendarme Roussel and his missing person's file. The discovery of Serge Coste who, in the space of one evening, had moved from the missing person's folder to a murder file all on his own. And, of course, Fabien Marre, whose vineyard had played host to two corpses, and who seemed consumed by an unnatural hatred of Gil Petty.

Raffin listened in silence. 'And the trip to America?'

'I'm taking soil samples for analysis. If we can match them to the wine taken from Serge Coste's stomach, it might well lead us to our killer.'

'Any thoughts?'

Enzo shook his head. 'Not really.'

'What about this Fabien Marre?'

Enzo pursed his lips grimly. 'I hope not, Roger. Nicole seems to have formed a real attachment to him.'

Raffin raised an eyebrow in surprise, but Enzo didn't elucidate. 'And that's it? That's what was so important for you to come and tell me? You couldn't have briefed me by e-mail?'

Enzo nodded. 'I could.'

'So what are you really here for?'

Enzo returned his unblinking gaze. 'Kirsty.' He saw Raffin's jaw set.

'I thought as much. How did you find out?' But he raised a hand to pre-empt Enzo's response. 'No don't tell me. It was Charlotte, right? She come down to see you in Gaillac?'

'I had a right to know.'

'It's none of her damned business!' Raffin's voice raised itself in anger. 'Jealous bitch!'

'That's not how she tells it.'

'No. Well, she wouldn't, would she?'

'She figures you're the one who's jealous of me and her.'

Raffin flashed him a dark look. 'The way I heard it, there is no you and her.'

'Well, you might be right there. But I didn't come to talk about me and Charlotte. Or you and Charlotte.'

'Kirsty's a big girl now, Enzo. She doesn't need her daddy vetting her boyfriends.'

'I don't want you seeing her, Roger.'

'Why?'

'Because I don't think you're right for her.'

'Why?'

Enzo stared at him and struggled to find an answer. It wasn't their age difference, which was only seven years – no more than the gap between Enzo and Pascale. So what was it? Roger was a successful journalist. A good-looking young man. Widowed, so he was available. As much as anything it was what Charlotte had said: *There's something dark about Roger, Enzo. Something beyond touching. Something you wouldn't want to touch, even if you could.* 'You're just not.' Even to Enzo, it sounded like the most feeble of reasons.

'Oh, fuck off, Enzo.' There was no rancour in it, just a weary dismissal. Raffin stood up, but Enzo reached across the table and held his wrist.

'I'm not asking you, Roger . . .'

'Well, that's really rich coming from you!' Her voice startled him. He turned around to find her standing in the bedroom doorway. Enzo could see himself beyond her in the mirrored doors. He could see the shock on his own face.

'Kirsty.' He flicked an angry glance at Raffin. 'You bastard, you set me up.'

'No.' Kirsty stepped into the room. 'I set you up. I couldn't believe it when Roger said he thought you might be coming to warn him off.' Her long, chestnut hair fanned out over square shoulders. She wore a powder blue shirt knotted at the waist above cut-off jeans. She was tall and elegant, and Enzo thought her quite beautiful.

He stood up. 'Listen, Kirsty—'

But she wasn't listening. She moved into the room. 'I couldn't believe that the man who didn't care about leaving his seven-year-old daughter would turn up twenty years later telling her who she could and couldn't see. I didn't believe anyone would have that kind of gall.' She issued a tiny snort of self-disgust. 'Shows you what I know.' She looked very directly at her father. 'Certainly not you, anyway.'

'Kirsty, I'm not trying to tell you what to do.'

'No?'

'I'm just concerned, that's all.'

'Well, you know what, *father*? I never needed your advice in all the years you weren't there. I don't need it now.'

The three of them stood in a tense silence, and from one of the other apartments they heard someone playing the piano. Some jolly ragtime romp that seemed only to mock them.

'I think you'd better go,' Kirsty said. And when Enzo made no move to leave, she added, 'I'm not asking you . . .'

III

'I can't believe you did that, Enzo!'

'You sound just like her.' He was huffy and defensive.

'I'm not surprised.'

'Anyway, it was you that told me about them. What did you think I was going to do?'

Charlotte shook her head, eyes wide with disbelief. 'I didn't think for one minute you'd go charging in there to lay down the law. These are two grown people, Enzo. You don't have the right.'

'Why did you tell me, then?'

'Because I thought you had the right to know.'

Enzo breathed his anger and frustration through clenched teeth. He looked down into the street from Charlotte's kitchen window and saw a man walking his dog. Otherwise the Rue des Tanneries was deserted beneath the street lamps of this slightly seedy *quartier* in the thirteenth *arrondissement* where mills and tanneries once poured their industrial bile into the river Bièvre.

Charlotte had made her home in the offices of a former coal merchant, creating an indoor garden and atrium in the one-time courtyard, where she now consulted with her patients. Galleries on each floor looked down into the garden and opened onto bedrooms like fishbowls behind walls of glass. Its eccentricity reflected the character of its owner.

He turned away from the window to face her. 'I think maybe I also have the right to know what it is about Roger that so concerns you.' He took her by the shoulders and made her look at him. 'Something dark, you said, Charlotte.'

She pulled away from him and crossed to the work counter to refill her wine glass. 'I can't.'

'You mean you won't.'

'No, I mean I can't. It's not something I can point a finger at and say, "it's this," or "it's that." It's just a feeling.' There was pain in her face. The pain of searching and failing to find a way of expressing something felt deep inside. 'I lived with him for eighteen months, Enzo. It was a feeling that grew on me. That sense of something dark in him, something hidden. In the end it overshadowed everything that had ever drawn me to him, his charm, his humour, his intelligence. I grew to dislike him so much I could barely stand to be in his company. It's why I left him. It's why I told you about him and Kirsty.'

Enzo threw his hands out to either side of him. 'So what am I supposed to do?'

'Nothing. There's nothing you can do. Except be aware, and be there when she comes to you, as one day she will, and says, Papa, you were right.'

He straightened the waistband of his kilt, fastened the buckles, and carefully clipped it to its hanger. Then he crossed the bedroom to hang it from the rail. His suitcase lay open on the bed, clothes and toiletries strewn about it. He felt a tiny worm of apprehension, maybe even fear, turn over inside him. If he was caught . . . But he didn't want to think about it. If he did, he would probably be unable to see it through. From the far side of the bed, he looked through glass to the darkness beyond and had the uncomfortable sensation of being watched, as he always did here. Of someone being out there on one of the galleries, made invisible by darkness, while he was exposed to full view by the light. He invariably felt vulnerable until he turned off the lamps, and then, with moonlight spilling through the glass above the garden, would lie and watch strange things take shape in the dark. He had never understood how Charlotte could live on her own in this place, with its ghosts and shadows and obfuscations.

A movement in his peripheral vision made him turn, startled. Charlotte leaned in the doorway watching him. She was wearing her black silk dressing gown with the Chinese dragons. It was very loosely belted at the waist, and he could see that she wore nothing beneath it. She had an odd, predatory look in her eyes. 'You don't *have* to spend the night in the guest room.'

He turned back to his packing and sighed wearily. 'You feel like sex, and I'm supposed to just sit up on my hind legs, stick out my tongue and pant for it. Is that how it works?'

'If you like.' She was quite unruffled.

'I'm not going to do it, Charlotte. I'm not going to be your occasional sleeping partner. I'm not going to be your occasional anything.'

'You don't want to sleep with me?'

He whirled around. 'Of course I want to sleep with you! You're a beautiful woman. You do terrible things to my libido.

But you also do terrible things to my head. And I can't deal with that. I need more than just sex.'

'Is that your feminine side speaking?'

'No, it's my lonely side speaking. I spent twenty years on my own, Charlotte. Sex lasts minutes, an hour, a night if you're lucky. Lonely lasts a lot longer.'

He returned to his packing and there was a long silence, broken finally by the swish of silk as she moved into the room. 'I didn't know you had a kilt.'

He glanced round to see her examining his kilt hanging on the rail. She touched the pleats, felt the wool between her fingers, and then ran them down the tartan.

'It's heavy.' She looked at him. 'Are you taking it to America?'

'I wore it for the funeral.'

'It'll get crushed in your case.'

'I'm not putting it in my case. It cost nearly a thousand euros, Charlotte. I'm not entrusting it to the vagaries of airline baggage handlers. I'll wear it for the flight.'

She raised an eyebrow. 'That'll make you a bit conspicuous at customs. And give the cabin crew something to look at.' She smiled. 'Both sexes.'

He shrugged. 'Americans like the kilt. A lot of them have Scottish roots. If they're looking at me, they're less likely to look at what I'm carrying.'

She frowned. 'What are you carrying?'

'You don't want to know.'

She regarded him thoughtfully for several moments before

a tiny smile turned up the corners of her mouth. 'One thing I would be interested to know, though . . .'

'What.'

'Something I've always wondered. Probably most women do.' She paused. 'You know . . . what it is a Scotsman wears under his kilt.'

'There's a standard reply to that.'

'Which is?'

'There's nothing worn under my kilt. It's all in perfectly good working order.'

She grinned. 'Which doesn't answer the question.'

He straightened up and looked at her very directly. 'You really want to know?'

She nodded. 'I do.'

He looked down at the floor with a sense of resignation, then up again to meet her eye. Somehow they had got very close, and he could smell her perfume rising on the heat of her body. He let his hands slide over smooth silk until they cupped her buttocks, and he pulled her towards him. She moved her hands behind his head and undid the ribbon to release his hair, and her robe fell open. Full breasts swung free. He dipped his head to kiss the hollow at the base of her neck, and as his hair tumbled across his shoulders to brush her skin, she shivered. 'You'll have to promise never to tell a soul.'

'I promise.' Her voice was a whisper.

'Because, you know, it's a national secret. I could be hanged from the gibbet at Edinburgh Castle.' He moved his mouth across all the curves and angles of her face, peppering it with kisses until he found her lips and then her tongue, and he pushed himself hard against her belly.

She moaned and drew her head back, breathing in short bursts. 'I thought you weren't going to be my occasional sleeping partner.' His own words came back to him with the full force of her irony and his regret.

But libido had triumphed over lonely. The tumescence between his legs told him he had gone beyond the point of no return. 'I won't tell anyone if you don't.'

CHAPTER EIGHTEEN

I

It was the humiliation that had robbed him of his fear. The girls in uniform giggling behind the Air France desk at Charles de Gaulle airport. His embarrassment. Was there a problem? And when they'd shown him his ticket, he saw the misprint – *Mrs Enzo Macleod* – they had fallen into fresh paroxysms of laughter, looking pointedly at his kilt. What else would you call a man in a skirt but *Mrs*?

And so he had passed through airport security in a fug of mortification, almost forgetting that the slightest misstep could lead him to a police cell somewhere, a full body search, awkward questions that he couldn't answer.

Now, with the drone of jet engines filling his head, and a coach class seat too small for his big frame, he tried with difficulty to make himself comfortable for the long hours that lay ahead. He opened his eyes at the sound of clinking bottles, and found a pretty air hostess smiling at him. The twinkle of amusement in her eyes made him think that she, too, was probably in on the joke. He glowered at her. 'Whisky,' he said. 'No ice. Water. In fact, make it a double.'

*

The immigration hall was busy. Several flights had landed within half an hour of each other. Lines of travellers, accustomed to delays, stood patiently waiting to be called forward by humourless immigration officers. Enzo was clutching the forms he had filled in on the flight promising that he wasn't a terrorist, or a Nazi war criminal, or someone with recidivist tendencies. He wondered if anyone ever admitted they were. He was happy to fill his mind with anything that would stop him thinking about what could happen in the next few minutes. He drew a deep breath and felt it trembling in his chest. A film of cold sweat pricked his forehead. He stepped up to the yellow line. He was next. As he glanced around, he was aware of people looking at him. The kilt, of course. He kept forgetting. Men in skirts were not a common sight in the United States.

'Next!'

Enzo looked up to see the officer signalling him forward to the desk. He was a large man with a shaven head. He wore a white shirt with sleeves rolled up and took Enzo's passport in big hands. He looked at it carefully, then at Enzo, then passed it through a code scanner. There was an electronic fingerprint reader on the counter, and the officer said, 'Put your right finger on the pad.'

Enzo looked at his hands and frowned. Then looked at the immigration man. 'My *right* finger?'

The officer gave him a dark look. 'Your right finger,' he repeated slowly.

Enzo's confusion persisted. 'I'm sorry, which finger's my *right* finger?'

The look darkened. 'The index finger of your right hand.' It was clear he suspected insolence.

'Oh, right.' Enzo laughed nervously and held up his right index finger. '*Right* finger.' He pressed it on to the electronic reader to register his fingerprint.

'Purpose of your visit?'

Enzo felt a sudden, irrational panic. 'Em . . . a holiday.'

The immigration officer tipped his head and narrowed his eyes. 'What holiday?'

Enzo looked back at him, mystified. And then light dawned. 'Oh,' he said. 'Not a *holy* day.' He remembered suddenly what Americans called it. 'A vacation. That's what you say, isn't it?'

By this time the immigration officer had obviously concluded that Enzo was insane. He sighed, shoved the green entry card inside his passport and thrust it back across the counter. He regarded Enzo thoughtfully for a moment, and then something almost like a smile appeared in his eyes. 'You're a varr,' he said.

Enzo felt panic returning. 'I'm sorry?'

'You're a varr.'

Enzo knew he was not a stupid man, but however many times he processed this statement he could make no sense of it. 'I'm sorry, I don't know what you mean.'

The amusement melted away from the man's eyes, to be replaced by an irritation reflected in his voice. 'Yo – ra – varr.'

And suddenly Enzo heard it. 'Oh,' he said. '*Au revoir!* You're speaking French. Because I've come from Paris.' He grinned. 'Only, I'm not French. I'm Scottish.'

The immigration man looked down at the kilt, and looked up again, a looming certainty in his eyes that *all* Scotsmen were probably insane. After all, they wore skirts, didn't they? He flicked his head. He'd had enough. Enzo was dismissed.

Enzo walked across the concourse to the luggage carousel with legs like jelly. How could he have been so stupid? He was attracting all the wrong kind of attention to himself. And he knew the worst was yet to come.

He retrieved his suitcase after a short wait and began the impossibly long walk through the customs hall towards the gate marked 'Nothing to Declare'. Customs officers stood at desks watching everyone as they passed with darting, suspicious eyes. They always made Enzo feel guilty, even when he really had nothing to declare. Today all eyes were turned in his direction.

A woman with large breasts, barely constrained by the navy blue uniform blouse tucked into her trousers, signalled him to stop. She had a US customs badge on one breast, a name tag on the other. She was Enzo's age, perhaps older, wiry ginger hair piled up and held in place by clasps. She had a granite face and unblinking blue eyes.

'Good day, sir. Would you lift your bag on to the counter top?'

'Sure.' Enzo tried to be casual. But his heart had pushed up into his throat and was nearly choking him.

'Open it, please.'

He unzipped the case and threw back the lid. His clothes had been disturbed, unpacked and rearranged. There was a printed sheet tucked into the containing belt informing him that his bag had been opened and searched by officers of the Transport Security Administration. The customs lady looked at the case, then signalled Enzo to move closer. She leaned towards him confidentially.

'Don't worry, sir. I only stopped you because ... well, I always wanted to ask.' An unexpected smile split the granite. 'Are you, you know, regimental under there?'

Enzo frowned. 'Regimental?'

Her smile became coy. 'You know. You wearing anything under the skirt?'

And Enzo had a sudden memory of the night before, the sweet smell and touch of Charlotte in the dark. His apprehension dissolved, confidence returning. He gave the customs lady his best eye contact and smiled back. 'If you want to give me your number, maybe we could arrange a private viewing.'

She flushed with pleasure and was hardly able to stifle a giggle. 'You'd better get out of here before I drag you next door for a body search.'

It was with an enormous sense of relief that Enzo saw Al MacConchie waiting for him on the other side of the barrier. He hadn't laid eyes on him in over twenty-five years and was shocked by how he had aged. He was still tall and thin, though slightly stooped now, his boyish good looks long vanished. Most of his hair had gone, too, but still grew in reasonable abundance around the sides, where he had pulled it back and tied it behind his head in a silvery knot. It looked more like a little curly pig's tail, than Enzo's thick, bushy ponytail. But he looked prosperous and suntanned, casual in baggy jeans, chequered cotton shirt, and tennis shoes. One leg of his sunglasses was hooked over the top button of his shirt. He thrust a bony hand into Enzo's and grinned. 'Jeez man, what happened to you?'

'What do you mean?'

'You were such an ugly boy. Must have grown into your looks.'

'Cheeky bastard.'

'And what's with the kilt, Magpie? We'd better get you out of here fast. You'll be turning heads. Most of them male. This is San Francisco, after all.' He grinned and relieved Enzo of his hand luggage and let him wheel his suitcase across the concourse himself. 'Couldn't you get a connecting flight to Sacramento?'

Enzo shook his head. He had not wanted the stress of going through security one more time. 'Afraid not.'

'Man, it was a three hour drive down here. You're going to have to get yourself a rental on the way back.'

Enzo noticed how MacConchie hadn't fully lost his Scottish accent. Nor had he fully adopted an American one. It lingered somewhere in mid-Atlantic. 'I appreciate it, Al, I really do.'

'Don't worry about it. The gasoline's going on your bill.' There was a shuttle bus waiting out front. 'It's just a five minute ride to the parking lot.'

They headed south and west to the Burlingame airport parking lot on the 101, spectacular views across the Bay off to their left, afternoon sun coruscating across diamond blue water liberally sprinkled with the white sails of myriad small boats. It seemed extraordinary to Enzo that he had left Paris midmorning, had flown for more than eleven and a half hours, and it was still just early afternoon in San Francisco. Fatigue, he knew, would catch up with him quickly.

The shuttle dropped them at MacConchie's car and Enzo put his bags in the boot. They sat inside and MacConchie turned the key in the ignition. Then he turned and looked at his old friend from university and cocked his head. 'You got the samples with you?'

'Of course.'

'Man, you must have moved mountains to get the paper-work through this fast.'

'I didn't.'

MacConchie frowned. 'Well, how'd you get them through customs?'

Enzo grinned and lifted up his kilt to reveal an underskirt of plastic sample bags strung together with thin plastic cord. 'I'm always getting asked what I wear under there, but no one ever dares to look.'

II

Sonoma was a small town of one and two storey buildings in brick and clapboard siding at the southern end of one of the most famous wine-growing valleys in California. It was a town of church spires and picket fences and a population of just over nine thousand. Its tree-filled downtown square had once been the sacred meeting ground of the Pomo and Miwok Indians.

'Home of the last mission in California,' MacConchie said. 'It was the Franciscan monks in the missions who laid the foundations for wine growing in California, you know. They planted and cultivated the first vines, though it was mostly brandy and fortified wines they made back then.'

He turned along Napa Street on the south side of the square and headed west until they reached Sixth Street, and he took a right and pulled into a parking lot in front of a low, single-storey building. A large sign planted in the lawn read 'OENOPHILES INC.'

MacConchie said, 'Of course, the Americans don't know how to spell. When I first had the sign painted, I had to have to the guy come back and put an "O" in the front of it.'

Enzo sipped on a mug of stewed, watery coffee and wondered how people could drink it like this. He had taken the wine sample from the bottle of aftershave in his toilet bag, and MacConchie had put it in a refrigerator in the lab. Then he had removed his underskirt of soil samples to pile them up on a table by the window in MacConchie's office. A G5 Macintosh computer on a worktop next to it ran constant checks on incoming e-mail. MacConchie leaned his elbows on a desk devoid of papers, his own reflection looking back at him from polished wood, and said, 'People think I'm a heretic because I don't go for all this flavour wheel, cherry-berry bullshit. Wine is science. What we consider good, we can quantify scientifically.'

'How?' Enzo was curious.

MacConchie grinned. 'Trade secret.'

'Aw, come on, Al. It's me you're talking to.'

'You know, Magpie, I've got nearly a hundred clients paying me fifty grand a time to share my secret. You got that kind of money?' Enzo did the calculation, and MacConchie enjoyed the expression that wrote itself across his face. 'Come a long way from the east end of Glasgow, huh?'

'How in God's name did you get involved in the wine business, anyway, Al?'

MacConchie shook his head. 'Never meant to, Magpie. Came out here with a degree in chemistry looking for a job in industry. Ended up working one summer at a winery painting barrels with mildicide and stayed on for the crush.'

'The crush?'

'The *vendange* you guys call it. The harvest. Anyway, that's where the interest started. I went back to university, did a PhD, and got myself involved in a discipline called chemical ecology, which studies the interrelation of environment and plant biochemistry. That led me to some research already done by the Japs and others into the chemistry of grapes. Ended up sifting through the hundreds of chemical compounds you'll find in fermented grape juice. You know, tannins, phenols, norisoprenoids, that kind of stuff. Identified eighty-four of them that comprise those flavours, and smells, and colours that make wine special. Thirty-two in reds and fifty-two in whites. Put them together in the right quantities and you'll end up making wine that's going to get a ninety score or better from Parker or the *Wine Spectator*. Or an A or B from Petty in his day.'

'But how do you do that? How do you know what makes a great wine?'

MacConchie smiled. 'Easy. Choose one that everyone agrees is great, like a 2003 Petrus Pomerol, and take it apart, molecule by molecule. Once you know its chemical profile, it's not so hard to recreate it.'

Enzo shook his head in wonder. 'That would be *anathema* in France.'

'Sure. They make great wines there because they have hundreds of years of tradition and experience behind them. Plus great *terroir*. And, hey, I'm not one of those that thinks *terroir's* not important. The weather, the temperature, the lie of the land, the chemistry of the soil.' He waved a hand at Enzo's 'underskirt' lying on the table. 'Those samples you brought. Each and every one of them will produce a different wine from the same grape. I'm just using science and technology to achieve the same effect.' He grinned. 'You know what the main difference is between any one of my clients and a French wine producer? The French guy's driving a tractor. My guy's driving a Porsche.'

'You're still not letting me into the secret.'

'Hey, Magpie, a secret's a secret. But I'll tell you this much, it's mostly about number crunching. Facts, figures, statistics.' He nodded towards his computer. 'They're all in there. In the database. Most winemakers decide when to harvest the grape by using a hydrometer to measure sugar content. You know when the hydrometer was invented? 1768. Shit, man, talk about old technology! My clients send me their grapes once a week. I crush them, process them, run them through a liquid chromatograph connected to a spectrometer that feeds direct into my computer. And they get to pick their grapes at the moment of perfection. It's not a judgment call; it's science.

'And, you know, it doesn't stop there. Once it's in the barrel, I run tests at regular intervals. Wines are hard to taste in the early days, but I can measure the key compounds, and can make a quality judgment from the facts and figures in my database. We can then make virtual blends between barrels and run the figures through the computer to see how they'll taste. That way, you don't actually have to mix the wine until you *know* it's going to be good.'

He laughed. 'I had dinner with a client the other week. He produced a bottle of his best wine. I told him I would be really interested to taste it. I'd only ever tried it on my computer screen.' He leaned confidentially across his desk. 'These wine critics ... Petty, Parker and the rest. They're so goddamned predictable. I say to them, this is what you like? Okay this is what I'll make. In a blind tasting I'll predict nine times out of ten the score they're going to give. And do you know what kind of power that gives me, Magpie? It's like knowing today what a stock'll do tomorrow. It's inside info.'

And Enzo thought of the lengths that Petty had gone to just to keep his ratings secret. Of the alchemy that Laurent de Bonneval had talked about at Château Saint-Michel when Enzo first arrived in Gaillac. MacConchie was exploding it all. The myths, the mysticism, and two thousand years of tradition. His secret for success was a marriage of Silicon and Napa Valleys; his wines constructed from the building blocks of molecules. And Enzo couldn't help but wonder if, in all this science, the fundamental human component might be missing. The instinct, flair, and sophistry of which Bonneval had spoken. That element impossible to define by maths or science – the personality of the winemaker.

But he said none of this to MacConchie. There was no point. Whatever it was he was doing, it was working for him. A hundred clients on his books and a turnover of five million a year. A lifestyle that a boy from a housing scheme in Glasgow's deprived east end could hardly have dared to dream of. He'd had a brain, and used it. Enzo regarded him thoughtfully across the desk, and couldn't help but admire him. They'd both come a long way in the thirty years since they'd first met. And very different paths had led them, strangely, to meet again in this place in the heart of California wine country, thousands of miles and millions of dollars away from where they had started.

'You know, if Petty hadn't been murdered, he was going to publish an article urging a boycott of American wines.'

MacConchie looked at him in disbelief. 'What?'

'Unlabelled use of genetically modified yeasts. He thought it was unethical. And dangerous.'

'Jesus, Magpie. If he'd published that he could have put us all out of business!'

Enzo cocked his head. 'Which reduces my list of suspects to a mere few thousand.' He paused. 'So how will you treat the samples?'

MacConchie leaned forward, concentrated on the question. 'I figure I'll dry the soil samples in an oven up to a constant weight. Sieve the stuff through nylon nets to fraction and homogenise it, then digest it with concentrated HNO_3 by high pressure microwave.'

Enzo looked at him. 'Can you translate *any* of that into English?'

MacConchie grinned. 'Chemistry never was your strong suit, Magpie, was it?' He stroked his chin thoughtfully. 'You know, it's not easy to explain this in layman's terms. High-pressure microwave digestion for the soil, UV irradiation for the wine. Then, I figure, inductively coupled plasma mass spectrometry for both.'

Enzo sat back shaking his head. 'I guess the simple answer to my question was "no". Here's another one. How long will it take?'

'A while. This is my busiest time of year.'

'Could be that a man's life is dependent on it.'

MacConchie nodded thoughtfully. 'Okay. Two, three days. When do you fly back?'

'Tomorrow.'

'I'll e-mail you the results.' He leaned back and grinned. 'But tonight you'll meet my surgically perfected wife and taste my virtually perfected wines, and wallow in envy.'

But somehow Enzo didn't think he would.

III

The hot California sun beat through the windscreen of his rental car as he cruised slowly through The Shores housing development in the Natomas district, north of downtown Sacramento. The houses on the north side of Hawkcrest Circle were built along the shores of a man-made lake where wild birds now mated and nested. It was only a short drive to the airport from here, and had he arrived by plane, Enzo would have seen the sun reflected in the water of the flood plains that stretched between the Sacramento River to the west and the American River to the south. This was where Gil Petty had bought his home when the money started coming in. It was where his marriage had foundered, a relationship malnourished by long and frequent absences.

Enzo blinked to try to stay awake. He had barely been able to keep his eyes open during dinner the night before, a problem not aided by the rich, red wines poured by the hand of Al MacConchie. Then, infuriatingly, he had been awake most of the night. And now, he was once again almost overcome by fatigue. Jetlag was the curse of the modern age.

He drew up outside a large house with wisteria growing

around the gate to a courtyard entrance. Shrubs were in flower all along a bed below shuttered windows that faced out to the street. People preserved their privacy here. He walked up a short drive to the gate and pressed the bell. It rang somewhere distantly inside the house. He waited for what seemed like a very long time before the gate opened, and a small, sallow-skinned woman in black peered out at him from the shade. Beyond her, he could see a paved courtyard, shallow-pitched roofs sloping down to semi-tropical flowers. At the far end, a door opened into a large, airy room with a floor to ceiling view out across the lake.

'Enzo Macleod for Mrs. Petty. She's expecting me.'

Linda Petty was smaller than he had been expecting. Small but perfectly formed, and he saw where Michelle had got her looks, if not her height. She wore jeans that tapered to her ankles, and white, high-heeled sandals. Her cream top dipped low to show off the deep cleavage of her silicon implants and was cut short at the waist to reveal her tanned belly. Although still an attractive woman, her face had that stretched quality created by plastic surgery which drew loose flesh up behind the ears, leaving unnaturally high cheekbones and almond-shaped eyes. Her skin was too smooth, almost shiny, like plastic. Blond-streaked hair was cut short and tucked, like her face, behind her ears. Only the brown spots on the backs of veiny hands betrayed her age.

He followed her through into the dining room, and noticed her trim buttocks and narrow thighs, wondering how much of that was down to exercise and how much to lipo-suction. The theme of floor-to-ceiling glass continued here, like a giant screen showing constant re-runs of the lake beyond. One complete wall of the dining room was divided into beechwood pigeonholes behind glass, a giant wine rack filled with priceless bottles.

'It's sealed and refrigerated,' she said. 'Kept at a constant twelve degrees.' She smiled condescendingly. 'Celsius, of course. He liked to think he was so European. His wine wall, he called it. Broke his heart to lose it in the divorce settle-ment.' She slid open glass doors and stepped out on to the deck. It was north-facing here, so shaded from the sun. Steps led down to a small pleasure boat bobbing on the water. She eased herself into a cushioned mahogany sun chair and lifted her legs on to an equally cushioned footstool. She lit a ciga-rette and blew smoke at the sky. 'What is it you think I can tell you, Mister Macleod?'

Enzo squatted down on the edge of another cushioned footstool. 'Who might have killed him.'

She smiled. 'Not me, if that's what you're thinking. After the divorce, I had everything I'd ever wanted. It was my daughter who inherited the leftovers. But, of course, you said you'd met her.'

Enzo nodded. 'She's in France to recover her father's belongings.'

Linda Petty looked unimpressed. 'Is she? Took her time, then.'

'Did you ever go with him on any of his wine tastings abroad?'

'In the early days, yes. It was fun, then. We had a laugh and got drunk a lot. But the novelty soon wore off. He was quite obsessed, you know. And, frankly, I was more interested in a vodka martini than wine.' She glanced back through the glass towards the wine wall. 'Oh, I open a bottle occasionally. Something he'd have treasured. But I only ever have a glass and usually pour the rest of it down the sink.'

It was clear to Enzo that this was something that gave her pleasure. An ironic, bitter, retrospective revenge on her dead husband.

'What about Michelle?'

'Oh, she was obsessed, too. Not with wine. With her father. She always thought it was something personal. That he rejected her because of something she'd done. She never could grasp that it was nothing to do with her or me. That there was no way for either of us to compete with his precious wine.' She took a long pull at her cigarette and flicked ash towards the water. 'I suppose that's why she followed him to France.'

Enzo frowned. 'What do you mean?'

'The year he went to Gaillac. She flew out to France the week after he left. She said it was a trip to Paris to see friends. But I never believed her. She just couldn't let it go.' She snorted her derision. 'And then, of course, he goes and vanishes. Murdered, as it turns out. And she never did get to have it out with him.'

Enzo found himself taking short, shallow breaths, and

everything he thought he'd known about Michelle went up in flames around him, conviction buried beneath the ash of sudden uncertainty.

'But the obsession's never left her, Mister Macleod. Since her father's death there have been a string of older men in her life, almost as if by making them love her she's proving to herself that it wasn't her fault that her father didn't.' She glanced at Enzo. 'Of course, all that these men are really interested in is sex. Imagine. Men your age. Older. With a young girl like that. It's disgusting.'

And Enzo felt himself slide from uncertainty into guilt and shame.

CHAPTER NINETEEN

I

It was late by the time he got back. And dark. Distant lightning lit up a brooding sky.

He had stopped several times on the long drive south from Paris, pouring coffee down his throat to try to stay awake. Now he was suffering from caffeine overload, his head buzzing, his hands shaking. He had flown out of San Francisco late afternoon, unable to sleep throughout the flight, and landed in Paris with almost a full day ahead of him.

He turned into the driveway leading up through the trees to Château des Fleurs. An enormous wave of fatigue washed over him. Like a runner at the end of a long race, the sight of the finish line almost robbed him of his ability to reach it.

All he wanted was to fall into bed. But it crossed his mind that Sophie and Bertrand might well have occupied it in his absence. He would probably have to make do with the clic-clac. Again. They would, no doubt, be asleep by now, and he didn't have the heart to wake them.

There were no lights on in the *château*. The Lefèvres had told him that they would be away when he got back. The *gîte*, too, was in darkness, and he groaned as the prospect of the *clic-clac* beckoned. He drove past the parking area to the foot of the steps. He would get his stuff out of the boot tomorrow. Lightning flashed closer, a shorter gap now before the following thunder.

It was on the second or third step that his foot slid from under him, pitching him forward. He grazed his hands trying to break his fall. He cursed under his breath. Someone had spilled something slick on the stairs. Something like oil. It was profoundly dark, but he could see something darker pooling on the steps, sticky and wet. It was on his clothes and hands. Lightning flashed again and by its light the spillage looked almost black. He made his way up to the door, fumbled for his keys with sticky fingers and unlocked it. He reached inside and turned on a light. With a shock he saw that his hands were red. He looked down and saw that his trousers were stained the same colour. For a brief, irrational moment he thought someone had spilled red paint on the steps. Then the realisation that it was blood hit him with the force of a baseball bat catching him full in the chest.

'Sophie!' He shouted through the open door into the house, seized by a sudden and almost paralysing fear. But he was greeted only by silence. He could see that the bulk of the blood had run down from one step to the other, before being smeared over the gravel path at the foot of the stairs as if something, or someone, had been dragged across it.

He hurried back down the steps, careful this time not to slip. The blood was still a vivid red. Fresh. Not yet the rust brown it would turn when dried and oxidised. He could see it in the grass now, a bloody trail leading away from the house towards the trees and the shadow of the *pigeonnier*. He could hear the approaching storm moving through the trees above him. The light from the *terrasse* made little impression on the night. Beyond its circle of illumination, the castle parkland seemed even more obscure. But the blood almost glowed. Caught in a sudden flash of lightning it was like the ghostly trail of a giant slug.

Enzo had forgotten his fatigue, all rational thought displaced by an all-consuming fear for his daughter. The thunder crashed ever closer. He ran across the *pelouse*, leaving tracks in wet grass, and could see the drag of other footprints left there, straddling the path of the blood. Into the impenetrable shadow beneath the ancient *pigeonnier*, and smack into something soft and heavy suspended from the beams overhead. With fingers made clumsy by fright, he fumbled to switch on the penlight on his keyring and shone it in front of him.

'Jesus!' The blasphemy slipped involuntarily from his lips, as he felt bile rising from his stomach. More lightning threw the image in front of him into stark relief against the black beyond.

Braucol was strung up by the neck. His killer had used the child's swing as a gallows rope, and slit the puppy's stomach open from neck to pubis. Tears stung Enzo's eyes, like the coming rain. He could imagine Braucol greeting the stranger on the steps, trusting and playful, trying to untie his shoelaces. Quite unprepared for the thrust of the knife coming out of the dark. The amount of blood on the steps and the trail of it through the grass told Enzo that the first blow had not been fatal. Braucol had still been alive when his murderer strung him up and slit him open.

Revulsion fuelled anger and incomprehension. Why would someone do something like that? Then fear returned, and he looked back towards the *gîte*. A sudden, dreadful picture filled his head. Tangled bedsheets soaked in blood. Sophie and Bertrand murdered as they slept. He sprinted back through the night, powered by panic, a dread desire to banish the image from his mind's eye, to know that it wasn't true. Lightning ripped through the night, and thunder struck like a blow almost immediately overhead. He took the steps two at a time, calling their names aloud as he burst through the door into the bedroom. A flick of the light switch revealed the bed neatly made up, undisturbed. He stood for a moment, staring at it blindly, then ran back through to the *séjour* and up creaking stairs to the mezzanine. Both bunk beds were empty.

Confusion filled his head like a fog. Where were they? Why weren't they here?

And why in God's name would someone slaughter a defenceless dog. Poor Braucol.

'Bastard!' He roared his frustration into the night after the retreating thunder, then froze on the spot. Through the window at the back of the *gîte* he saw a light moving along the gallery at the top of the *château*. It flashed through the dark in the direction of the cottage and was then extinguished as suddenly as it had appeared. Sheet lightning crossed the sky, illuminating the shadow of a figure leaning on the rail of the gallery looking across the gardens towards the *gîte*.

For the briefest of moments Enzo wondered if it might be a burglar in the castle, a thief taking advantage of the absence of its owners. But a burglar wouldn't have killed and strung up a puppy. And Enzo knew with an absolute certainty that Braucol was a calling card, an unmistakable message. The light in the gallery flashed on again, for several seconds, and then off. Whoever was up there was letting Enzo know it. Banking on anger dispensing with caution. Making Enzo come after him. Luring him into the dark halls and corridors of the *château* where his adversary would have every advantage. And though all of that rationale passed through Enzo's mind in just a fraction of a second, the red mist that Braucol's killer had foreseen robbed him of his reason.

He hurried down swaying steps to the kitchen and drew a long, sharp chef's knife from the block. Someone was waiting for him up there. Someone who had tried to kill him in the vineyard, someone who had murdered a defenceless animal just to inflame his anger. It was time to put a stop to it, one way or another.

On the gravel path, he slipped past the narrow shadow of a poplar, ducking beneath the low hanging branches of the chestnut trees that framed the approach to the *château*. Granite chippings crunched beneath his feet as he ran beyond the abundance of carefully nurtured flowers and shrubs that grew all around the walls of the estate office. Overhead, an exhalation of the passing storm parted clouds, allowing moonlight to burst through. Still lightning flashed as it moved beyond the far hills, and Enzo felt the first spots of rain on hot skin.

Silver light bled all colour from the *château* gardens, lying now illuminated before him. Manicured lawns and low hedges laid out in repeating patterns towards an avenue of *pins parasols*. There was no point in stealth. His would-be assailant was probably following his progress, watching unseen from the shadows of the gallery sixty feet above.

Enzo glanced up to the line of stout oak beams protruding from the wall to support the gallery. Brickwork filled in the walls around criss-crossing timbers. Black windows in white stone were like missing teeth in a wide smile. A smile that mocked. It seemed like a very long way up.

He stopped at the door and listened. In the distance he heard the hooting of an owl, and the rumble of the passing storm. It had been short-lived, violent. Its legacy of rain began now in earnest. As the moon vanished again behind raincloud, he felt the night, like a living thing, close in around him. The rain obliterated any sound the intruder might make. The left half of double doors that should have been locked stood ajar. Opening into blackness. And for the first time since the rush of blood to his head, Enzo questioned the wisdom of what he was doing. Surely it would make more sense to stand guard out here in the rain and call the police? If the intruder wanted to come out, then they would at least meet on equal terms. He checked his mobile and cursed softly as rain splashed on its blank display. He hadn't charged it during his trip to America. The battery was spent.

But almost as if his adversary could read those thoughts from his hesitation, there was another blink of light. This time from a second floor window. Just the briefest of glimpses that seemed to say, *Come on, you coward. Come and get me.* It gave Enzo renewed motivation to push open the *château* door. It creaked loudly, and the castle breathed cold damp air into his face. The sound of the rain retreated as he stepped inside.

He remembered Paulette Lefèvre, just a few days before, leading him up to the *grande salle* on the second floor. The broad stone staircase, sunlight falling in through narrow windows. He tried to remember how the castle was laid out. Off to his left was the dining hall, where he had looked at Pierric Lefèvre's photographic record of the restoration. To his right, off a narrow hallway, were the couple's living quarters. A salon, a kitchen, a study, a reading room. Immediately above it was the Lefèvres' bedroom. That was where he had last seen the light. The central staircase divided the *château* into two equal halves. Up one level, opposite the bedroom, was the dusty, cluttered *grande salle* where Pierric had uncovered Petty's roots among the *château* archives. Up one more level was the gallery, running right around the top of the castle, doors opening off it into rooms beneath the roof, the one-time living quarters of serving staff. The gallery was contained by low, brick walls, and beams that supported the roof. Where the wall extended to the roof itself, there were unglazed windows exposing the long corridor to the night. It would be freezing up there in winter, and suffocatingly hot in the summer.

Enzo stood in the dark of the hall, listening for the slightest sound. Then he heard the creak of a floorboard, the clatter of something fallen or dropped. A soft curse. The intruder was in the *grande salle*.

In that moment, when he knew where his adversary was, Enzo sprinted up the staircase to the half landing and pressed himself against the stone wall, trying to stop his own breathing from drowning out other sounds. He was in the deepest shadow here. Distant lightning flashed through the windows on the floor above, to zigzag down the steps towards him and then vanish, and Enzo ran swiftly up to the second floor while the image of the stairs was still burned in his mind's eye.

One hand pressed against the wall to guide him, he worked his way along to the huge studded door of the *grande salle*. It stood open, but the density of darkness beyond it was suffocating. He reached a hand inside the door to feel for the light switch. It clicked loudly in the vast stillness of the room. But there was no light. He did not have the courage to venture into the darkness, and retreated to the landing, where he stood for several long minutes, reflecting on his stupidity. He had been suckered in here on someone else's terms, someone who knew exactly where he was. Someone who knew exactly what their next move would be, while he could only guess at it. But it was not too late for Enzo to change the rules, withdraw from the game. It was not too late for common sense to prevail.

More lightning briefly illuminated the staircase, and he saw a shadow move from the landing above him, the rasp of leather soles on stone. And the memory of Braucol dangling, bloody and dead, from the rafters of the *pigeonnier*, fuelled fresh anger.

'You bastard! Come out and face me like a man!' His voice echoed back at him from cold stone and died in the dark. With his knife held at arm's length ahead of him he began up the final two flights of stairs to the top of the *château*, one soft step at a time.

From the half landing he looked up towards the gallery and saw the faintest moonlight edging broken clouds in a ragged sky beyond. But the rain was still falling, heavy now, relentless, drumming on the roof, drowning out all other sound. With barely enough light to see by, Enzo edged himself up the last of the steps, moving out and onto the gallery, just as the far-off lightning underlit a turbulent sky and cast momentary flickering light all along the open corridor. Tiled floors. Wattle and daub walls, bleached timbers. The blade of his knife flashed briefly in the dark. And a shadow rose up in front of him. A shadow without face or form. And pain shot up his forearm to his elbow as his knife went clattering away across the tiles. He had no time even to call out before something dark and heavy swung out of the night to catch him square on the side of the head. He dropped to his knees and fell face-forward to the floor. A boot sunk into the soft muscle of his stomach and robbed him of his ability to breath. He rolled over, away from the pain, and looked up as his attacker raised a blade level with his head. The final gasp of the storm breathed light across the sky behind him, and he saw the killer in full silhouette as he crouched down to deliver the final, fatal blow. The lightning passed in a moment, and darkness absorbed him again into obscurity. The rain still hammered on the roof.

Enzo's outstretched hand found the handle of his dropped knife. He grasped it and, in desperation, lunged towards where his opponent had been. He felt contact, the sound of his blade slicing through soft flesh and heard a scream. In an unexpected flood of moonlight, he saw his attacker recoil and turn around as a second figure appeared behind him. For several ludicrous moments both men appeared almost to be dancing, locked in furious embrace, each grunting from the effort of trying to gain ascendancy over the other. Then they took several forced steps backwards and toppled to the floor in a tangle of arms and legs. Enzo heard the sickening crack of skull on terracotta, a gasp of pain, and then one man detached himself from the other to fly past Enzo, heading for the stairs. Even above the thrum of the rain Enzo could hear his panicked retreat down the staircase. Rasping breath, a sob of pain, footsteps clattering on stone. The other man groaned.

The nausea which had filled Enzo's world for several long moments retreated, and he managed to get to his feet. With shaking hands he found his penlight and snapped it on. The figure on the tiles rolled into the tiny pool of yellow light thrown by the torch, and Enzo saw with a shock that it was Bertrand.

II

Floodlights on the *chai* illuminated the forecourt, casting the long shadow of the *pigeonnier* towards the trees. The rain had washed away most of the blood on the steps and the grass, except where it had pooled in the shelter of the *pigeonnier*. The *gendarmes* had untied Braucol and removed the body, evidence in a criminal investigation. The child's swing stirred gently in a current of damp air. The night was sticky warm. The storm and its rain had passed, and mist rose now from all around the castle grounds. A police van was parked beneath the trees, its blue light flashing hypnotically. All the lamps outside the *château* had been turned on and, through the back window of the *gîte*, Enzo could see the two *gendarmes* who guarded its entrance, installed for the night, smoking and talking in low voices that carried on the *brume*.

'Hold still, Papa!' Sophie's face was close to his, dabbing disinfectant on the grazing at the side of his head. He could see her tear-stained eyes, and was unsure whether she had wept in grief for Braucol or in relief because her father was safe. Both, perhaps, or maybe it was just the shock. 'You poor thing,' she said. 'I hate that man! He could have killed you.'

'I think that was his intention, Sophie.'

'He could have killed us both.' A subdued Bertrand held a bag of frozen peas to the back of his head.

'You're perfectly capable of looking after yourself,' Sophie told him. 'But my Papa's an old man.'

'Thank you, Sophie,' Enzo said. 'That makes me feel so

much better.' He was sitting on a chair in the *séjour* in his boxer shorts, having stripped off his blood-soiled clothes and washed his hands. But he still felt dirty.

The *gendarmes* had spent nearly an hour taking statements. Enzo had half-expected to see David Roussel, but of the *gendarmes* who appeared, none was familiar. Bertrand had described to them how he and Sophie had returned late from a meal out to find Enzo's car at the foot of the stairs, blood on the steps, the dead dog. And then seen lights and heard shouting from the *château*. If it hadn't been for his intervention, Enzo's would-be assassin might well have succeeded in killing him.

But Bertrand was still furious with himself. 'I had him,' he kept saying. 'I was stronger than him, I could have taken him.' And Enzo thought how Bertrand was probably stronger than most men he knew.

But when they had fallen, it was Bertrand who had struck his head and was momentarily disabled. All that he had been left with, when Enzo's attacker made his escape, was a handful of blood-stained material torn from a jacket pocket. Enzo had told him to keep that to himself when the police arrived. He did not want the piece of pocket disappearing into some repository in a rural *gendarmerie*, where it would probably languish, wasted evidence, for weeks, months, or even years.

He asked for it now, and Bertrand handed him the scrap of torn green fabric. 'Linen,' he said, as he held it up to the light, and winced as Sophie dabbed more disinfectant in his face. There was the remains of some embroidered emblem along one edge, unidentifiable with its shreds of ripped and broken thread. 'And good silk thread. He's not short of a few euros, our killer.'

'Is it his blood, do you think?' Bertrand said.

'Probably. I definitely cut him. Although it could be Braucol's. But it won't be hard to establish if it's human or animal.' He reached for his shoulder bag and took out a clear plastic ziplock evidence bag and dropped it in. He closed his eyes, and the image of the puppy dangling on the end of the rope was still there, engraved in his memory. 'This man's a psychopath. And every one of us is going to be in danger until he's caught.'

He opened his eyes to find Sophie looking into them, concern etched all over her face. 'Oh, Papa, I don't like this.' She sat on his knee, as she had so often as a little girl, and put her arms around him.

'No, I don't like it either, Sophie. Which is why you and Bertrand are going back to Cahors first thing in the morning.'

She pulled away. 'No!'

'We can't leave you here on your own, Mister Macleod.' Bertrand stood up, pushing out inflated pectorals, as if somehow his youthful macho posturing would make the old buck back down.

'That's exactly what you're going to do, Bertrand. I'm putting Sophie in your care. Anything happens to her, you'll have me to answer to.' And he raised a quick finger at Sophie to pre-empt her protests. 'This is not up for discussion, Sophie. You're out of here. Both of you. First thing.'

CHAPTER TWENTY

I

Early sunlight fell in wedges between buildings, casting the shadow of Christ across the warm tarmac in the Place Jean Moulin. Enzo squeezed his 2CV into a blue zone parking space and set the dial on his permit for the maximum hour and a half of free parking. He stepped out to breathe air freshened by the storm, and felt the sun warm on his face.

The events of the previous night had, like a nightmare, retreated with the clearing of the sky and the rising of the sun. He had watched Bertrand's van disappearing down the *château's* tree-lined drive towards the road, Sophie's continued protests still ringing in his ears. And when they were gone, he had turned back to the *gîte* with a deep sense of depression that even the yards of sailor blue sky above him could not lift.

Now he turned down the Avenue Jean Calvet towards the electronic gate of the *gendarmerie*. The same attractive *gendarme* with the Mediterranean eyes greeted him at the *accueil*, but this time she wasn't smiling. When he asked for Gendarme Roussel she told him to wait.

It was several long minutes before she returned and instructed him to follow her. The sway of her hips ahead of him, emphasised by the movement of the holstered gun on her belt, was hypnotising as he trailed her upstairs and into a long corridor. Halfway along it, she knocked on a door and opened it into a large office. Enzo saw the plaque on the door. *Adjutant Brigade*. And he began to get a bad feeling.

A secretary showed him into the *adjutant's* office, and a tall man in full uniform turned from the window to cast a cold eye of assessment over him. His office was bigger than the one Roussel shared with two other officers downstairs. His desk was enormous and groaned with papers and files, all stacked and grouped in meticulous piles. On the wall behind it was a large chart of the *Gendarmerie Départementale du Tarn*, with the *Groupement* at Albi at the head of a pyramidic command structure. The *Compagnie* at Gaillac was highlighted in orange, as were the eleven *communes* that it controlled.

The adjutant offered Enzo a cursory handshake. 'You seem to be very popular with would-be assassins, Monsieur Macleod.'

'*Failed* would-be assassins,' Enzo told him.

The *adjutant* raised an eyebrow, then rounded his desk to drop into a well-worn leather swivel chair and balance a pair of reading glasses on the end of a thin nose. As he opened a file in front of him, he waved a hand vaguely in the air. Which Enzo took to be an invitation to sit. So he drew up a chair and sat down to wait expectantly. It gave him a moment to weigh up the senior ranking officer of the *Compagnie*. The hair was almost all gone from his crown, the remaining growth from around the sides slicked across it in a poor attempt to disguise his baldness. Where it had gone grey, black hair dye had taken on a ginger hue. He had long, feminine hands, with immaculately manicured fingernails. His face was shaved to a shiny smoothness, and Enzo could smell the lingering traces of his aftershave. That he had been brought here at all was worrying to Enzo. The *adjutant*'s hostility was evident in his body language, and Enzo knew that vanity like his meant he would never willingly put his rank to one side.

The *adjutant* dragged his eyes away from the file. 'What do you want with Roussel?'

This was not a question that Enzo had anticipated. 'You're aware that the *juge d'instruction* at Albi has made me a lay consultant on the Petty murder.'

'I am.' His disapproval was apparent in the curl of his lip.

'Gendarme Roussel sent several samples to Toulouse for forensic examination. At my request. I was looking for the results.'

The adjutant reached across his desk, lifted a large buff envelope and slid it towards Enzo. 'Preliminary reports came back yesterday.' He watched as Enzo took the envelope, pulled out a sheaf of stapled papers and gave them a quick glance. 'Do you have any idea where he is?'

Enzo looked up, surprised, and let the papers fall back into their envelope. 'What?'

'Gendarme Roussel.'

'I'm sorry, I don't understand.'

The *adjutant* removed his reading glasses and folded his hands on the desk in front of him. 'Gendarme Roussel took several days leave at short notice for what he described as personal reasons. He was due back the day before yesterday. Which is when I discovered that his wife had been here looking for him the day before that. Several of his colleagues suspect marital problems. I thought you might be able to throw some light on his whereabouts.'

Enzo was very still, hardly daring to think the worst. 'He's gone missing?'

'Officially, he is absent without leave. Which means he will be arrested the moment he turns up.'

It was a short walk down to the roundabout, and the Place de la Libération, but Enzo took every step as if he carried the weight of the world on his shoulders. And it seemed like a very long way. He moved like a man in a trance through the dappled shade of the chestnut trees, leaves and chestnuts falling around him, drying in the morning sun and crunching underfoot. And he slumped into a chair under the yellow awning of the Grand Café des Sports and gazed out across the square with eyes that did not see.

It barely seemed credible that Gendarme Roussel should have become one more case in his own missing persons file. Enzo had feared that someone else would go missing during this year's grape harvest, but had never for one moment thought that it might be Roussel. He tried to convince himself that it was just coincidence. That there would be some rational explanation. But although he knew that life could throw up some extraordinary coincidences, he never believed in them when it came to an investigation. There were always reasons. For everything.

He searched through his mind for connections between Roussel and the other missing persons in the file. They were not hard to find. Like all the others, Roussel was a local man. He had been personally acquainted with one of them. And he had gone missing at the same time of year. But there had to be something else. Something he wasn't seeing. His colleagues thought it was a simple case of domestic disharmony. But that's exactly what Roussel himself had thought about Serge Coste. And Coste had ended up pickled in wine, just like Petty.

The thought of Petty took Enzo back to the day in the *grande salle* at Château des Fleurs when Pierric Lefèvre had dug out the American's family records from the old archive. In a strange sort of way, that made Petty a local, too. Or, at least, his antecedents. But it made no sense, for it had been Petty's first trip to Gaillac. His only connection to the place was historical.

Enzo's reflections were interrupted by a young waiter with dark, curly, gelled hair shaved close around the sides of his head. '*Bonjour monsieur. Je vous écoute.*'

Enzo glanced up. '*Un petit café, s'il vous plaît.*'

The waiter cocked his head. 'You're the guy that went off with Braucol.' He grinned, shaking his head, some affectionate memory of the puppy dog coming back to him. 'How is the little guy?'

Enzo didn't have the heart to tell him. 'Doing good.'

The waiter laughed. 'He was a pain in the ass, you know. But I kind of miss him.'

And as he went off to get the coffee, Enzo thought how he would miss him, too. He turned quickly to the envelope the *adjutant* had given him from the *Police Scientifique* in Toulouse, and drew out the preliminary report. He ran his eye down the text, nodding to himself as it confirmed what he had suspected. Petty's DNA sample did not match the sample recovered from the speck of blood inside the glove. The chances were that if the blood in the glove did not belong to the killer himself, then it belonged to a relative. But if they got themselves a suspect, familial DNA matching could still secure a conviction. *If* they could find a suspect.

He flipped over a page and felt sudden goosebumps rise up all across his shoulders. He felt his face sting as if he had just been slapped. He stood up as the waiter arrived with his coffee, and dropped a couple of coins on the table.

'Give it to someone else.'

II

She was sitting at the table where he had first seen her. She was reading, just as she had been then. But she greeted him somewhat differently. When his shadow fell across her book she looked up, irritation replaced immediately by a smile that broke like sunshine across her face. 'You're back. I'm so glad. I had a thought about my dad, and those vineyards he visited ...'. She took off her sunglasses, green eyes flashing and stood up to kiss him.

His recoil was almost imperceptible, but it was like a shutter dropping between them. Her smile was gone in an instant. 'What's wrong?'

He dropped the buff envelope on the table and sat in the free chair opposite, leaving her to stand looking down at him. He glanced out across the shimmering green and red vines. The harvesters were out again after the rain to gather the last of this year's *récolte*. Then he looked up to meet the concern in her eyes and remembered how attractive she was. Clasps held chestnut hair clear of her face. Her lips were pale in a lightly tanned face, and he remembered the feel of them against his. Soft, sensuous. And he recalled her mother's words in Sacramento: *There have been a string of older men in her life, almost as if by making them love her she's proving to herself that it wasn't her fault that her father didn't.*

'Why have you been lying?'

Her skin paled beneath her tan, and she sat down. 'What do you mean?' Her voice was small and uncertain.

'Four years ago when your father came to Gaillac, you followed him here. You went to see him at the *gîte*.'

But she wasn't going to admit it easily. 'How can you know that?'

'Familial DNA matching, Michelle. It was in my mind for quite another reason, even before I read the report.'

Her self-confidence was evaporating as he looked at her. 'I don't understand.'

'Back in 2003, in the UK, a kid dropped a brick from a bridge on a motorway. It smashed through the windscreen of a car and killed the driver. Forensic scientists managed to salvage a sample of the kid's DNA from the brick. The British have got the biggest DNA database in the world. More than three million people in it. The kid wasn't one of them. But a relative was. They matched sixteen points out of twenty, and secured a conviction in March 2004. The world's first conviction using familial searching.'

He could see that she made no sense of this.

'Michelle, when you went to see your father it was . . . how can I put this delicately? It was that time of the month. You left a used sanitary pad in a plastic bag in the trash can in the bathroom.' He saw realisation breaking over her like an ocean wave. 'For some reason, the police kept the contents of the bin as evidence. I sent the pad for DNA testing, along with those samples of your father's that we found among his things. And guess what . . .'

But he didn't need to elucidate further. She shook her head despondently. 'You don't think I killed him?'

He looked at her for a long time, searching those green eyes, trying to divine what complexity they masked. Then he sighed. 'No. No, I don't. But I know you lied, Michelle, then and now. And I want to know why.'

He watched as tears bubbled up in her eyes, and she tried hard to control them. 'I wanted to confront him. I wanted to make him meet my eye and tell me why. Why some goddamned bottle of fermented grape juice was more important to him than his own flesh and blood. But even then, even to my face, he wasn't going to give any part of himself away. It was the same old blind he always drew on his emotions. He accused me of being like my mother. Possessive and territorial. He said that marrying her had been the biggest mistake of his life. And by implication, I was just an extension of that mistake. He couldn't even see me as being a part of him, of belonging to him. I'd have given anything . . .' She broke off, her voice cracking, and she clenched her fists on the table in front of her, fighting hard to control her emotions, to sublimate them again behind cool, green windows of obfuscation. And Enzo thought how like him she was. How for all her feigned affection, she hid everything real behind the same blind her father had always drawn.

She rediscovered her control, and Enzo saw her expression harden. It was not attractive.

'We just shouted at one another. And I stormed off. Then, when he went missing, it crossed my mind that maybe he'd killed himself. Because of me; because of our row.' She laughed, a sad, bitter little laugh without humour. 'But I should have known better. That might have meant he'd cared.' She drew a deep breath. 'Anyway, I never told anyone I'd been there. And when he turned up dead, murdered, it was twelve months too late. And wouldn't have helped anyway.'

She examined his face for a response, and whatever she saw there brought with it a look of resignation. Her eyes flickered away from his. It was as if she suspected that he had seen her truly for the first time, and that there was no longer any point in pretending with him. She gazed away across the valley, the hum of insects filling the air around them, the distant sounds of the harvesters carried on the warm *vent d'autan*.

'So where does that leave us?' she said.

'There is no us, Michelle.' And he was struck by the irony of the words that Charlotte had used so often with him. 'It's very flattering for a fifty-year-old guy like me to have some young girl half his age fawning over him, offering him sex, giving him back maybe just a little of his lost youth. But there's no future in it for you. Go home. Get yourself a real life. Someone of your own generation. Forget your father. Sometimes people are just flawed.' And his own daughter's voice rang around his head: *I couldn't believe that the man who didn't care about leaving his seven-year-old daughter would turn up twenty years later telling her who she could and couldn't see.* He shook his head sadly. 'Even dads.'

III

The road curved up around the edge of the hill, the land falling away to the left, a dramatic sweep of empty vines straddling the slope. Beyond, the vast flood plains of the Tarn shimmered away into a distant haze, the river snaking lazily through it, towns and villages in red brick dotted along its banks.

Enzo's 2CV strained against the gradient and then picked up speed as it reached the top of the hill. Suspension rocked and rolled through the narrow streets of a tiny stone village, before the road swooped down again towards the church on its distant promontory.

A chalk white track left the road to curl around the hillside, past the towering apse of the twelfth-century Église de Verdal, depositing Enzo finally in the shade of the oaks that clustered around its ancient forecourt. He got out of the car and felt the wind whip warm in his face. The three bells in the church tower swayed in gentle acknowledgement of its rising strength. Vines dropped away on all sides, and from here the view to the south was an unbroken panorama. You could almost believe that on a clear day you might see all the way to the Mediterranean.

He found himself looking down on the cluster of buildings that was Domaine de la Croix Blanche, perhaps a kilometre away, in the valley below. He could make out the *chai*, and the *salle de dégustation*, a group of red-roofed barns, and the Marre's house on the far side of the yard.

He turned away to look at the old church. The stained glass in tiny arched windows high up on the wall had somehow survived intact. Windows at ground level were all boarded up, wooden shutters bleached and rotten. Concrete rendering was crumbling to reveal golden stone walls beneath it. A sign on the door told *randonneurs* that the *église* was a stop on an historic walk, and that Lisle-sur-Tarn was ten kilometres away.

Enzo had come here to escape from people, to breathe and to think, to try to focus on the myriad *morceaux d'informations* he had accumulated in the last two weeks. To see where they fit and how they related, to visualise in his mind's eye the picture they might create if only he could make sense of them.

But he was finding it hard to get Michelle out of his mind. The pain she felt at her perceived rejection, the lies she had told, her seemingly endless capacity for self-deception. And always that tinge of regret that he had not, in the end, slept with her, even if it would have left him with a bitter aftertaste of guilt. For a fleeting moment, he wondered what it was she had been going to tell him at Château de Salettes before he confronted her about her lies. But he knew he would never know.

He walked down to the highest edge of the vineyard, closed his eyes and let the wind fill his mouth. It tugged at his shirt and his cargos, carrying to him the distant sound of a motor car. He opened his eyes and saw it following the road up from the river towards La Croix Blanche. Even from here he could tell that it was an old vehicle, a muted grey-green. One of those old French cars that just seem to go on forever. Like the Citröen 2CV, or the Renault 4L. And he felt a sudden stab of apprehension. He ran back to his car to retrieve a pair of binoculars from the parcel shelf, and returned to his vantage point on the edge of the hill. As he brought the vehicle into focus, it pulled up in the yard at La Croix Blanche and a familiar figure stepped out.

'Shit!' Enzo lowered his binoculars. What the hell was Nicole doing there?

IV

Dust rose from the *castine*, quickly dispersing on the edge of the wind, as Enzo pulled his 2CV in behind Nicole's 4L. Several vehicles sat around the yard. A tractor stood idling in the shade of a barn with a corrugated red tin roof. He could smell the fermenting juices of this year's harvest coming from the *chai*. But there was no sign of life. Enzo started up the path towards the house, past an old stone bread oven. Apple trees were dropping ripe red apples in the grass. As he reached steps leading up to the front door Fabien emerged from the *cave* below, dragging a coil of yellow plastic tubing.

He stopped when he saw Enzo. 'What the hell do *you* want?'

'To see Nicole.'

'Maybe she doesn't want to see you.'

'Well, why don't we ask her?' Enzo's eyes dropped to the coil of yellow tubing, and he saw that Fabien's right hand was heavily bandaged. Fresh white gauze wrapped around the thumb and palm. Blood had seeped through lint from the fleshy area at the base of the thumb and dried a dark brown. 'What did you do to your hand?'

Fabien seemed surprised by the question and looked down at the bandage. 'I cut it.'

'Doing what?'

'None of your damn business!' He dropped the tubing and pushed past Enzo to start up the steps. 'If you want to talk to Nicole, you'd better do it. Then get off my land.'

Enzo followed him into the cool of the shuttered house,

past the disapproving glare of Madame Marre, and up creaking stairs to the landing. Nicole turned in surprise as Fabien moved aside to let Enzo step into her bedroom doorway. The large suitcase that accompanied her everywhere lay open on the bed, the wardrobe doors stood ajar, and clothes were strewn over chairs and pillows. 'What are you doing here, Monsieur Macleod?'

'That's just what I was going to ask you.' He turned towards Fabien. 'In private.'

Fabien gave him a long, surly look, then headed back along the landing. Enzo heard him on the stairs, and closed the bedroom door behind him.

'For heaven's sake, Monsieur Macleod! What's all the drama about? When I got the call about my mother, I never even stopped to pack. I'm just back to collect my things.'

'And to see Fabien?'

She bristled. 'That's my business.'

'Mine, too, Nicole.'

She thrust defiant breasts at him. 'I don't see how.'

'I'm responsible for you being here at all. And Fabien Marre's still very much in the frame for these killings.'

'Oh, don't be ridiculous.'

'Someone tried again to kill me last night.'

Which took the wind out of her sails. Her voice shrank in size. 'What happened?'

So he told her, and it seemed to him that she was almost more upset about Braucol than about the attempt on his life.

'It couldn't have been Fabien.' She was filled with self-righteous certainty.

'Why not?'

Her conviction crumbled just a little. 'Because . . . because he's not like that.'

'And you know him so well.' Enzo couldn't hide his skepticism.

'I've known him nearly two weeks, Monsieur Macleod!' And after a moment, 'And in ways you couldn't possibly.'

Enzo looked at her, shocked, uncertain what she meant, and afraid to ask. 'Nicole, whoever it was that attacked me last night, I slashed him in the dark with my knife. Fabien's got a badly cut hand. You must have seen the bandage.'

Nicole wavered now towards reluctant uncertainty, but remained defiant. 'That doesn't prove anything.'

And Enzo cursed inwardly. A simple DNA test on the bloodied piece of torn pocket would prove it one way or another. But for that to happen he would have to admit to the investigating *gendarmes* that he had withheld evidence from them. 'Go home,' he said. 'Now. Please, Nicole. Until we know for sure who's responsible for these killings, we're all in danger.' He flicked his head towards the bed and sighed at the sight of her enormous suitcase. He knew how heavy it would be. He had carried it often enough. 'Finish packing, and I'll take your case down to the car.'

'I don't need your help, thank you, Monsieur Macleod. I have someone else who'll carry my suitcase these days.' She returned to the packing of it, making it clear in tone and body language that their discussion was at an end.

Enzo contained his frustration. She was a stubborn girl, filled with the certainty of ignorance. Her experience of the world was naïve and second-hand, selectively assembled from surfing the internet and watching TV. The things he knew, the things he had seen in his life, would be incomprehensible to her, shocking beyond belief. And yet, she would always know better.

Fabien was waiting for him at the foot of the stairs. Through the kitchen door, Enzo could see his mother hovering by the sink. He lowered his voice. 'Anything happens to that girl—'

'And what, old man?'

Enzo squared up to him and saw Fabien almost wince in the face of his intensity. 'They'll need DNA to identify your remains.'

Nicole stood silent, listening at the top of the stairs. Something in Enzo's tone scared her more than any argument he could ever have made. Mr. Macleod was such a gentle big soul, she was both touched and shocked by his threat to Fabien. She drew back into the shadows as Enzo pushed past the young man and out of the front door. Fabien didn't move. He remained standing in the downstairs hall for a long time after Enzo had gone. Perhaps he had been as shaken by Enzo's words as Nicole. She moved forward now to try to catch a glimpse of him through banister uprights, and the floorboards creaked beneath her feet. Fabien turned a pale face towards her and caught her watching. There was nothing for it but to carry on down.

As she reached the downstairs hall, Madame Marre appeared in the kitchen door behind her son. Fabien and Nicole looked at each other for several long moments. Then her eyes fell to his bandaged hand. 'What did you do to your hand, Fabien?'

CHAPTER TWENTY-ONE

I

A glob of spittle transferred itself between upper and lower lip. His face was pale and angry. 'I'm sorry, but I want you out of here, Monsieur Macleod. ASAP.'

Paulette Lefèvre stood behind her husband pink-faced with embarrassment. But she said nothing. Lefèvre himself was puffed up with anger and indignation. He had just removed the bloodied swing from beneath the *pigeonnier* and put down sawdust to soak up any remaining blood from the damp earth below. They stood in a knot of confrontation outside the estate office.

'There have been nothing but women coming and going at all hours of the day and night since you got here. You've vandalised the interior of my *gîte* by drilling holes in the wall for your precious whiteboard. And now this! Break-ins, the ritual slaughter of animals. *Gendarmes* crawling all over the estate.

Enzo regarded him thoughtfully. 'Who else knew you wouldn't be at home last night?'

Lefèvre was pulled up short. He glared at Enzo. 'What's that supposed to mean?'

'Whoever was waiting for me here knew that the place would be empty.'

'Well, *you* knew. You should be asking yourself who *you* told. After all, it was *you* they were waiting for. Not us.'

Enzo ran his mind back over the past few days. Who might he have told? But, then, he dismissed the thought. 'It doesn't matter who I told. Certainly not anyone who might want to kill me. You're the only ones who knew for certain the place would be empty. And you knew when I'd be coming back, because I told you.'

The globs of spittle on each lip had grown in size and seemed permanently connected as Lefèvre exploded in indignation. 'Are you suggesting I broke into my own home and lured you in to attack you?'

'No, I'm just speculating about who knew what, and when.' Enzo glanced towards the *chai*. 'How come Petty never tasted your wines, Monsieur Lefèvre?'

'Who says he didn't?'

'He didn't review them.'

Paulette said, 'We always leave a bottle in the *gîte* for our *locataires*. We left one for you, if you'll recall.'

Enzo did. And recalled, too, that it wasn't bad. 'So why didn't Petty review it? You'd have thought it might have had some resonance for him, since this is where his family originated.'

'You'd have to ask him that.' Lefèvre finally got rid of the spittle, flicking it away on the tip of a lizard-like tongue. And Enzo tried to remember who it was who'd suggested exactly the same thing. Fabien Marre. That's who. He had used almost exactly the same words, too. The day they confronted each other in the rainstorm at La Croix Blanche.

'I would,' Enzo said, echoing his own response from that day. 'Only someone murdered him.'

'I want you out of the *gîte* by the end of today.'

'Monsieur Macleod has paid until the end of the week, Pierric.' Paulette Lefevre was trying very hard to soften the blunt edge of her husband's ire.

'Midday Saturday, then. And you can take your whiteboard with you!' Pierric Lefevre stormed off into the estate office. His wife hovered for an apologetic moment, an appeal for forgiveness in her eyes.

'I'm so sorry,' she said, and hurried after her husband.

II

The voices of men rang out across the cut green grass, the smack of hands on leather, the thunder of studs in turf. Enzo sat high up in the empty stand watching the first team regulars battling it out with the reserve team in a training match. One or two diehard fans leaned on the white painted rail around the pitch watching their heroes sweep towards the far posts, the oval ball switching from one set of hands to the next, to be carried across the line in a diving try. On match day, it would have brought a roar from fanatical crowds jamming this tiny stadium. Today it brought a shouted reprimand from the trainer. Where the bloody hell was the full back?

Gaillac was, after all, in the heart of rugby country. Catholicism came a poor third to the twin religions of wine and rugby.

Enzo had stayed away from the *gîte* for the rest of the day. It would, in any case, have been depressingly empty without Sophie and Bertrand, and Nicole and Michelle. And Braucol. Braucol was dead. The others he had sent away. His isolation was self-inflicted. He was treading treacherous water on his own until MacConchie e-mailed him the results of his sample analysis. He was pretty sure he would not sleep tonight.

A large banner flapped in the wind at the far side of the stadium, *Allez GAILLAC tes Supporters sont là*, distracting him from his thoughts. He became aware of the players trooping off the field, to dressing rooms beneath the stand, steam issuing from hot showers, young men's voices rising in laughter to ring around the tiles. The sun was beginning to dip, and the first golden pink was discernible on the far horizon.

Enzo walked among the handful of cars in the huge parking lot to find his 2CV. Kids were playing basketball on the asphalt, voices shrieking in the late afternoon. Murders were being committed. Men dying, others gone missing. And still the world turned. As if none of it mattered. And in the context of time, and space, and history, Enzo thought, perhaps it really didn't. All he knew was that it mattered to him.

The southerly wind had died away again, and swung around to blow down from the north-west. Although the sky was still clear, Enzo could feel a chill in the air. The first breath of coming winter. The temperature would fall tonight. There might even be frost.

Nicole's car was parked opposite the *chai* at Château des Fleurs, and she was sitting waiting for him at the table on the *terrasse* of the *gîte*. Another coming and going for Lefèvre to complain about. 'Monsieur Macleod, where on earth have you been?'

'Nicole, I told you to go home.'

She ignored him. 'I've been waiting for you for ages.'

He brought out his keys and unlocked the door. 'You should have been back at the farm by now.'

She followed him in. 'Don't you want to know why I'm not?'

'No. I just want you to go.'

'Monsieur Macleod, you're a stubborn man!'

'*I'm* stubborn?' He sat down at the computer and hit the space bar to wake it from sleep. 'Nicole, whatever it is you've got to say, I don't want to know. I want you to get into your car and drive.'

'I'm not leaving till you know the truth about Fabien.'

This drew his eyes briefly from the computer screen. But a *ting* announcing that he had mail drew them back again. He opened up his mailer and saw that there was an e-mail in the box from MacConchie. He felt his heart rate quicken and clicked on it.

'It wasn't Fabien who attacked you last night. He was at home with his mother. And that cut? He did it in the *chai*, on a broken bottle. His mother was there when it happened. It was her that dressed it.' She glowered at him. His attention seemed fixed on the screen. 'Are you listening to me?'

He looked up. 'It doesn't matter how he cut himself, Nicole. It was Fabien Marre who killed Petty and Coste.'

She shook her head in anger and frustration. 'You've just got it in for him, haven't you? Right from the very start.' But there was a still centre to Enzo as he sat behind his computer looking steadfastly back at her. It scared her, and her voice tailed away. With less conviction she said, 'How can you know that?'

'Because the multi-elemental profile of the soil we took from La Croix Blanche is the same as the sample of wine taken from Serge Coste's stomach. It's like a matching finger-print, Nicole. There's no doubt. The grapes that wine came from were grown on Fabien Marre's vineyard.'

For once there was no retort, no protest of innocence on Fabien's behalf, no petted lip or metaphorical stamping of the foot. The blood drained from her face, and she was shocked to silence. And in that moment, he felt a sudden surge of pity for her. Whatever she felt she knew about Fabien, whatever she thought she had found in him, had been dashed on the rocks of science. All certainty shattered.

His phone rang. It was still on the charger and he saw that there had been several calls, all from the same number. The caller was ringing him again.

'Enzo Macleod.'

Her voice was taut with barely controlled tension. 'Monsieur Macleod, I need your help.'

'Who is this?'

'Katy Roussel. David's wife. I'm so scared for him, monsieur. They won't believe me at the *gendarmerie*. They think we've had a row, and that he's left me.'

'How do you know that he hasn't?'

'Because I *know*. David's the most loving man. Even if we had fallen out, he'd never leave his kids. He adores them . . .' Her voice cracked, and he could tell that she was having trouble controlling it. 'I know he thought highly of you, monsieur. He thought he'd failed in his investigation. That's why he took time off. To bring his missing persons file home. He was spending nearly all his waking hours on it.'

'And did he get anywhere with it?'

'He thought he'd found something. A connection between Gil Petty and the others.'

'What is it?'

'He wouldn't tell me. He was really secretive.' He heard her breath trembling at the other end of the line. 'Something's happened to him. He wouldn't go off like this, he just wouldn't. Please, monsieur, please help me.'

'Give me your address, Katy.' He wrote it down as she gave him directions. 'I'll be there as soon as I can.'

He hung up and looked over the computer to see tears rolling silently down Nicole's face. He stood up and took her in his arms, and felt her shaking as he held her.

'I'm so sorry, Nicole. I really am.' He disengaged and took her face in his hands, turning it up towards his. 'Please. Go home.'

III

From the roundabout on the west side of Lisle-sur-Tarn, the single track road meandered through acres of flat farmland, tall cornstalks rattling in the cool north-westerly, red-turning leaves fluttering along row after row of vines. Everywhere you looked there were *châteaux* and *chais*. So much wine and not enough people to drink it. Even in France. Enzo had read somewhere that there was a worldwide glut, production increasing by fifteen per cent a year. Everyone was overproducing, and not everyone would survive. He passed an *à Vendre* sign. Someone, perhaps, had got the message, and was selling up before the going got worse. Wine was a tough business to be in these days.

The road divided and he took the left fork, heading towards the distant hills and the dusky sky beyond it. The Roussel's family home was a single-storey Roman-style brick villa hidden behind high hedges and a copse of protective trees. *Pins parasols* and tall, blue-green conifers. He drove through the gate into an overgrown yard and parked in front of a terraced veranda. Weeds poked up through the *castine*. There were swings and a children's paddling pool. A punctured football nestled, squashed and useless, amongst the growth at the foot of the steps. Shredded netting hung from a basketball hoop above the garage doors. There was a seedy air to the place, of peeling paint and neglect. A husband too occupied with his job, a wife too busy with their children. Eyes that stop seeing.

The interior, by contrast, was clean and tidy, almost spartan. The children were not anywhere in evidence. Staying with friends, perhaps. Katy Roussel offered no explanation. She was too distressed. An attractive woman gone to seed, like the house. It was the same neglect. She was overweight, but not fat. A once carefully styled haircut had been allowed to grow out, and was clumpy and unkempt. The roots were showing grey. She wore a voluminous shirt over black leggings, and Enzo wondered whether she might be disguising another pregnancy. But he was frightened to ask in case he was wrong. There was no trace of make-up, and her eyes were red from the shedding of tears.

She shook his hand, and he noticed that the skin of hers was rough and dishwater red. 'Thank you for coming, Monsieur Macleod. I think I'd have lost my mind if you hadn't. I've no one else to turn to.'

'When did he go missing?'

'Three days ago. He'd brought those damned files home with him. He wasn't supposed to. Nobody at the station knew what he was up to. He just shut himself in his study. Well, it's a spare room, really. But it's where we keep the computer. He was on the internet for hours, sitting up into the small hours every night. The day before he disappeared he told me he was going to the library in town. But not why.'

'What happened?'

'Well, nothing. The next morning he said he was going out to the vineyards. That there was somebody he needed to talk to.'

'He didn't say who, or where?'

She shook her head. 'He said he would be back for lunch.' She bit her lower lip so hard, Enzo saw blood oozing through her teeth. 'He never appeared. I haven't seen him since.'

'You went to the *gendarmerie*.'

'The next day, yes. I was beside myself by then. But he was still officially on leave, so when I showed up looking for him, they jumped to all the wrong conclusions. His *friends*. I could see it in their faces. David takes leave for personal reasons, then his wife shows up looking for him. Of course, there's been some kind of bust up, and he's taken off. Maybe with another woman. They didn't say as much, but that's what they thought.'

Enzo hesitated. 'At the risk of repeating myself, you're absolutely certain he hasn't?'

'I'd stake my life on it.' And then, to underline her conviction. 'I'd stake my children's lives on it.'

'Those files he was working on. Are they still here?'

She nodded. 'I've had a look through the stuff, but I can't make any sense of it.'

'May I see?'

'Of course.'

And he followed her down a shadowed hallway.

IV

It was almost dark when Nicole drove into the yard at La Croix Blanche. She was dry-eyed and determined. But behind that determination, there was a disconcerting sense of apprehension. Her mouth was dry, and her heart rate increased as she stepped out of the 4L. There wasn't a light anywhere. Not in the *chai* nor in any of the sheds. Nor at the house. Security lamps that would normally have responded to the arrival of a vehicle remained stubbornly dark.

She stood listening, but could only hear the tick of her radiator as it cooled in the falling temperature. The wind filled her flimsy jacket, and she shivered beneath her tee shirt. She drew her hair from her face and fixed it behind her head with a rubber band and started up the path to the house.

The front door was not locked, but the house beyond lay choked in a darkness that swallowed her voice when she called into it. The only response was silence. She tried the light switch, but there was no light, no reassurance. Apprehension now verged on fear. She had been determined to confront Fabien. There had to be some logical explanation. But something was wrong. Where was his mother? Why was everything dark?

She retreated from the house, scared by its unnatural silence. On the far western horizon, the last light was dying in the sky. Fiery red fading to black. A flash of electric light drew her eye towards the *chai*. Double doors opened into blackness stabbed by the beam of a flashlight. There was someone moving around in there.

She wrapped her courage around herself to stifle rational thought and started across the yard towards it, clinging to the memory of the night with Fabien at the *source*. He had been so gentle with her. So affectionate and loving. She just knew he wasn't capable of murder.

And then his conversation with Enzo at the foot of the stairs replayed itself in her mind:

Anything happens to that girl . . .

And you'll what, old man?

They'll need DNA to identify your remains.

And the night they found Serge Coste up in the woods, and Enzo and Fabien had their first confrontation: *If you want to know what I think, whoever killed Petty deserves a medal.*

Conviction diminished with every step, to be replaced by fear and uncertainty. She stopped at the entrance to the *chai*. Double rows of stainless steel *cuves* disappeared into darkness. She hesitated. There was no sign of the flashlight now, or its owner. She called out in a feeble voice. 'Hello? Is there someone there?'

As at the house, she was greeted only by silence. And then a loud *clunk* came from somewhere deep within. From the *pressoir* maybe, or the shed with the sunken tanks. It was followed by a dragging sound, and then a feeble blink of distant light from the adjoining shed. And then silence and darkness again.

She moved cautiously into the *chai*, and felt herself consumed by the dark. The smell of fermenting wine carried on falling carbonic gas was almost suffocating. As she reached the opening between *cuves* that led to the next shed and the *pressoir*, she stopped to listen. There was no sound, no light, no hint of any human presence. But she knew there was someone there.

A sudden light in her face blinded her, and she screamed. A startled, terrified scream that echoed back at her from every stainless steel surface. And almost as if triggered by the scream, unexpected light washed down from the roof, and Fabien stood no more than a foot in front of her, his flashlight still directed in her face. Fluorescent tubes buzzed and flickered all around the *chai*.

'What in the name of God . . . ?' Dilated pupils had turned Fabien's eyes even blacker than usual. He looked pale and startled.

'Fabien, what are you doing here in the dark?' Her own expression, she was sure, was as startled as his.

'We had a power cut. There's been no electricity for nearly an hour. Must have been the wind. A cable down somewhere. I've been checking temperatures in the *cuves*. If they'd got any warmer I'd have had to start up the generator.' He looked around the *chai*. 'But we've got power again now.' He turned off his flashlight. 'I thought you'd gone home, Nicole.'

'Where's your mother?'

He frowned. 'She made soup and took it over to Pappy's.' He gave her a long look. 'Nicole, what's going on?'

With the light, a little of her confidence had returned. But she still needed reassurance. Her feet planted firmly on the concrete, she summoned all her courage and decided to confront him head on. 'The wine those people drowned in. You know, Petty and Coste. It was made from grapes grown on your land, Fabien.' She saw confusion furrow his brow. 'How is that possible?'

V

The light from the desk lamp seemed unnaturally intense. Black letters swimming on white paper, until he could barely look at them. And from all of these papers that covered the desk, a blinding blizzard of conflicting information, some kind of awful sense was finally emerging from confusion.

Roussel had been busy. There were photocopied extracts from historical documents he had found in the library. Pages marked up in several books on local history, whole paragraphs highlighted with diagonal orange lines. There were printouts from the internet. Genealogical searches, Roussel's own family tree, several articles on the French Revolution, a piece downloaded from Wikipedia about something called *The Great Fear*.

When he first sat down, Enzo hadn't had the least idea where to begin. So he had started randomly reading, before the logic of Roussel's researches had finally dawned on him, and he began retracing the *gendarme's* footsteps in the order they had been taken. Now he just sat staring without seeing, words burning out in front of him. He knew now who had killed Petty, and why. And Coste. And probably Roussel. And all the others in the file. And he knew, too, that these were not the actions of a sane man.

An absurd French wordplay entered his head, a *jeu de*

mots that seemed somehow horribly apposite. Winemakers usually left a portion of the vineyard unharvested during the *vendange*. The grapes remained on the vine, sometimes until November, when withered and frosted, they were almost like raisins, super-concentrated with sugar. These were the grapes they used to make the *vin doux*, the sweet white wine that was drunk with *foie gras*. The late harvest was known as the *vendange tardive*, but Enzo couldn't get it out of his head that what Roussel had discovered was a case of *vengeance tardive*. Belated revenge.

'Can you make any sense of it?' Katy Roussel's voice crashed out of the darkness beyond the ring of light. He had almost forgotten she was there, and he was nearly overcome by his own sickening certainty that her husband was dead. But there was no way he could tell her that. And as long as there was no body, there was always hope.

He turned to see concern burned into a face washed out by worry. 'Do you know what *The Great Fear* was?'

'I saw the article on the desk. But I didn't read it. We learned something about *The Great Fear* at school. It was part of the French Revolution, but I don't really remember.' Her confusion was clear in her eyes. 'Is it important?'

Enzo nodded. 'It's where madness began, and is still feeding it.'

She shook her head. 'How?'

'*The Great Fear* took place in July and August of 1789, right at the start of the French Revolution. There were rumours circulating among the peasantry that the nobles had hired bands of thugs to march on the villages and destroy their new harvest. In response, the peasants formed themselves into gangs and sacked the castles of the nobles, and burned all the documentation recording their feudal obligations.' He turned towards the papers strewn across the desk. 'What your husband discovered was the thing that linked Petty and the others in his missing persons file. That they were all descendants of a group of vigilantes who rampaged through Gaillac that summer more than two hundred years ago. A notorious gang who committed dreadful atrocities. They beat up the local nobility, sacked their estates, and in some cases set their homes on fire.'

Her frustration bubbled over at Enzo, almost as if he was somehow responsible for it all. 'I don't understand. What are you saying? Why has David disappeared?'

Enzo sought resolve in a deep breath. For he knew that his next words would amount to a pronouncement of death on the man she loved. 'He was one of them, Katy. Directly descended from one of that group of vigilantes. Everyone knew who they were at the time. With Church and State records now widely available on the internet, it would have been a relatively easy matter to trace the lineage of each and every one of them.'

'You mean someone's been killing these men because of what their ancestors did? That's insane!'

'Madness takes many forms. Sometimes all you need is to give it an excuse.' He drew one of the open books towards him and focused on a paragraph marked out in fluorescent orange. 'It seems the gang went too far one night. Maybe they'd been drinking, whipped themselves up into some kind of crusading frenzy. But they marched on a *château* just outside of town, dragged its owner into the courtyard and beat him to death in front of his wife and children. Then they set the place on fire.' He looked into the desolation in her eyes. 'Nearly two hundred and twenty years later, someone's been exacting a very belated revenge.'

CHAPTER TWENTY-TWO

I

There was light somewhere in the *chai*. But Enzo could not pinpoint its source. It was some kind of nightlight. So dim that he could see only far enough to stop himself bumping into things. He heard wine fermenting in the *cuves*, bubbling and frothing and producing the carbonic gas that that he could smell all around him. Pungent, nearly overpowering. Rivers of it, unseen, washing around his feet, carried away by water running through drainage channels in the floor.

He stumbled, nearly knocking into a makeshift table. Planks of wood raised on empty barrels, strewn with papers and charts. Empty bottles grouped together rattled, the chink of glass on glass echoing around the vast empty spaces of the winery. The air was so thick he could almost feel it on his skin, brushed soft by the hidden light.

The dark shapes of *cuves* towered around him as he made his way towards the back of the *chai*. Again he stumbled, this time tripping over something on the floor, and he fell to his knees. His curses whispered off into the dark. He felt about the floor with his hands and found coils of rubber cable leading to a handheld inspection lamp with a wire mesh guard. It was what had caused him to fall. Enzo fumbled for the switch and turned it on. He had seen winery workers hanging these lamps down inside the *cuves* to check levels when juice was being pumped from one to the other.

He looked around him, but the lamp didn't throw its light very far. Outside its circle of illumination, it seemed even darker than before. But he could tell that he was still in the old brick-built *chai*, extended now to the west through huge sliding doors. Rows of abandoned resin tanks faded into the gloom. He stood up and raised the lamp above his head, realising for the first time that light would pass through the fibreglass. He could see that the nearest tank was more than three-quarters full, the level of the dark, red wine it contained clearly visible just below the rim. And he wondered why, if it was no longer used to ferment wine, it was nearly full. Perhaps these old tanks were simply used for storage. Or maybe their owner had found a more sinister use for them.

At the end of the row, metal steps led up to a grilled walkway that gave access to the tops of the tanks. Enzo checked the length of his cable. There were metres of it coiling off into darkness. Holding the lamp ahead of him, he made his way along to the steps and climbed carefully up to the overhead catwalk. The old, rusted structure rattled and swayed in the dark. He felt it trembling beneath his heavy frame as he clung to the handrail and made cautious progress, just below the angle of the roof, towards the row of disused fibreglass tanks. Black pipes which had once fed cold water to cool fermenting wine ran level with his head.

He stopped at the first tank. Its pulley system enabled a large, flat lid to be lowered in to the level of the wine, forcing oxygen out of the *cuve*. Enzo hung his lamp over the rail and pulled on a rope that lifted the lid clear of it. He held the rope, braced in position with one hand, and retrieved the inspection lamp with the other. He swung the lamp out over the tank, and peered down into its sharp, red limpidity. The pale upturned face of David Roussel stared back at him, eyes wide, suspended just below the surface.

A startled cry escaped Enzo's lips quite involuntarily, and he recoiled from the *cuve* letting go of the rope. The lid dropped back into place, expelling air with a loud *whoosh*. The inspection lamp fell from his hand and swung back and forth, suspended by its cable from the rail. Shadows lurched crazily about the *chai*. Enzo grabbed the cable and pulled the lamp back up with shaking hands. He remembered Roussel the day he had met him, arms folded across his chest, U2 playing on the computer, Lara Croft watching them from the wall. *People go missing all the time,* he had said. He himself had been missing for only a short time compared to the others. And now he had transitioned from missing to murdered in the blink of an eye. Enzo was having difficulty controlling his breathing.

He moved along to the next tank and hauled up the lid. The wizened face of a middle-aged man, his mouth gaping, gazed up at him from the wine, coruscating *rouge* shot through with reflected violet light. His arms were extended to either side, hands floating outstretched, legs fading off into dark, impenetrable red. Enzo lowered the lid and moved to the next. Another face, a younger man this time, a strange, sightless appeal for help in eyes floating like clouds.

Enzo let the lid drop back into place. There was one last tank, at the end of the row. As far as he knew, there was no one else missing, so there was no reason to expect that there might be another body. But something drew him on. Some sixth sense, a premonition that filled him, unaccountably, with a dreadful foreboding. He moved along the catwalk holding up the lamp, steadying himself with his free hand on the rail. He let it go to grab the rope hanging down from above and pulled hard to raise the lid. This time he secured it by tying the rope to the rail, before leaning forward to hold the inspection lamp over the tank.

Her hair was fanned out all around her head like an aura, chestnut stained red. Her head was tipped back, the striking green of her eyes staring up at him, magnified by the wine. For a moment he thought he saw a rebuke in them. Why hadn't he listened to her? She'd had something to tell him, and he hadn't given her the chance. And then he realised that there was no rebuke there. Only his own guilt. And an enormous rush of pain and regret that rose in his throat to almost choke him. Poor, neglected, dead Michelle. The tears that pricked his eyes were held at bay only by the anger that threatened to overwhelm him. It took him several moments to control the urge to bellow his anguish at the top of his voice. And then it passed, leaving him weak and trembling.

He had seen enough. It was time to go and get help. And

right now, there was no way he could get out of there fast enough.

He hurried back along the walkway. It swayed and rattled beneath him. When he reached the steps he turned to climb down backwards. But as he grasped the rail, the electric cable caught on something unseen, and the inspection lamp was pulled from his grasp. It went tumbling off into space. In as much time as it took him to look down, it struck the floor with a loud crack, and the lamp shattered. Darkness closed around him like a glove.

'Shit!' He heard his own whispered imprecation snuffed out like a flame.

Anxious not to lose his footing, he moved slowly downwards, one careful step at a time, until he felt concrete solid and safe beneath his feet. There was more light now than he remembered. The dark shadows of *cuves* and bottling plant, of pumps and barrels, seemed less ill-defined. And he became aware of light bleeding faintly from an open door further down the shed. It was a strange, feeble, flickering light. But it washed around the *chai* in barely perceptible waves and guided him to the door, which groaned softly as he pushed it open. He saw the red rail around the edge of the pit, the insulated necks of *cuves* set in cement, like so many ceramic chimney tops. He had been here before. Had made an almost fatal mistake. A misstep in ignorance, his life saved by a man who had killed without pity. Revenge for a murdered ancestor.

He stepped into the room and saw a candle flickering on the top step of the stairs. It had only just been lit, molten wax not yet pooling in its holder. He peered down into the maintenance pit to the tiled floor below. There was no one there. No one living, at any rate. He moved along the rail to the top of the steps and peered beyond them into darkness. He could see a ladder leaning against the wall, pipes snaking around the concrete apron. The scrape of a shoe echoed in the gloom, and Laurent de Bonneval stepped into the candlelight. He looked down at Enzo from the apron two feet above, his face chiselled from gneiss, hard and expressionless.

Enzo said, 'Your wife told me I'd find you out here.'

Bonneval fixed him with emotionless eyes. 'You know, don't you?'

'Yes.'

A barely audible sigh. 'He was going to ruin us, you know. He didn't like our wines.'

'He told you that?' Enzo found it hard to believe.

'Not at first. But I could tell. The little questions he asked after each barrel-tasting. His lack of conviction as he scribbled in his notebook.' His pause was momentary. 'I burned it afterwards.'

'How did you know what he was going to write?'

'Normally he wouldn't have told me, I know that. But when I accused him of trying to finish off what his ancestor had started, he pretended not to know what I was talking about. Then when I confronted him he laughed and told me not to be ridiculous. He said if he was going to give my wines a poor rating it was because they were too thin, that they lacked the body and maturity that he expected of a good French wine.'

Bonneval shook his head. 'No one should have that much power, Monsieur Macleod. One man's taste determining another man's fate.' He drew a long breath, and Enzo wondered if he detected regret in it.

'So you killed him.'

'I couldn't let him leave. Do you have any idea how much I have invested in this place? In its future? The future of my son? He would have destroyed my family all over again. Just like his forebears did two hundred years ago.'

'How long had you known about that?'

'I discovered the details of the full, sordid story about ten years back. Old family diaries locked away in a bureau, in a room that had been shut up for decades. It was my grandfather who had gathered the records, pieced together the whole history. It was shocking, Monsieur Macleod. I was truly shocked.'

Some unrecorded memory flickered across his face. 'Petty gave me an excuse for taking my revenge. But when Coste showed up the following year, I knew it wasn't going to be possible to stop there. The man had been working on a family tree and was looking for my help. It was only a matter of time before he found out the truth. Before people made a connection between me and Petty that went way beyond wine. I realised then that they all had to go.'

He gazed off into some distant landscape that only he could see, a landscape stalked by the twin devils of madness and revenge.

'Hubert de Bonneval was a great philanthropist. No one

treated his workers better. He was a major contributor to the local community. He opened a brick factory to provide bricks for the enlargement of the *château*, and jobs for the people of Gaillac. He paid his grape pickers well at harvest time.' The descendant of the murdered man breathed out in anger. 'And they rewarded him by killing him in front of his own family. His son wrote about it decades later. Watching his father clubbed to death, his mother abused and beaten, his home robbed of everything valuable, and then set alight. You could feel his pain on the page, Monsieur Macleod. I wept when I read it.'

Some *courant d'air* stirred the flame of the candle, and it dipped and dived and nearly went out. Almost as if the ghost of Hubert de Bonneval had drifted past, dragging cold air in his wake.

But Laurent de Bonneval was only momentarily distracted. He focused dull, dark eyes on Enzo. 'Fortunately, it was only the east wing that was destroyed by the fire, the original *chai*. Most of the *château* survived intact. But it damned near ruined my family. It took them two generations to get back on their feet, to rebuild and restore the *château*, to produce wine they could sell and recover their wealth. And Hubert's murderers walked free, laden with the riches they had stolen.'

'It's a sad story, Monsieur de Bonneval,' Enzo said. 'But I don't see how two hundred years later you can blame the actions of these men on their descendants.'

'I didn't. At least, not until Petty started trying to do it all over again . . . and I remembered my bible. Exodus chapter twenty, verse Five. "I the Lord God am a jealous God, visiting the iniquity of the fathers unto the third and fourth generation of them that hate me." There was justice in it.'

Enzo shook his head. 'Romans. Twelve. "Avenge not yourselves, but give place unto the wrath of God: for it is written, vengeance is mine, saith the Lord."'

A slight smile cracked the gneiss. 'You know your bible, too, then, Monsieur Macleod.'

'I know that it is a dangerous tool in the hands of people who twist and corrupt its words to justify their own ends.'

Sudden anger flared in the winemaker. 'My ancestor was brutally murdered in cold blood, my family cast into the wilderness. And, because of a quirk of history, his killers escaped justice, and their descendants lived to profit from their sins. Comfortable little men leading comfortable little lives. Well-fed, well-mannered, well-meaning progeny of murderers! And here was Petty, like the ghost of his own ancestor, coming back to finish the job.'

There was no reasoning, Enzo knew, with madness. He looked at the man and wondered when and where and how the balance had tipped that way. Bonneval had known the story of what had happened during the French Revolution, and had chosen to sublimate whatever feelings it had wakened in him in the hope of receiving Petty's blessing, and the financial rewards that would bring. And when it had become clear that this was not about to happen ... 'Why Michelle?' Enzo closed his eyes and saw her face staring back at him from the wine, before anger forced them open to focus on the killer who stood in front of him. 'What possible reason could you have for harming her?'

'Because she figured it out. She came to see me this afternoon. You found his reviews, it seems. If Petty had come to taste my wines, why had he not reviewed them?' And he seemed almost amused at the pain of realisation that he saw in Enzo's face.

Enzo's voice seemed tiny in the dark. 'Because yours was the last vineyard he visited. He never reviewed the wines of Château Saint-Michel because you killed him before he ever got the chance.' How could he not have seen it? Why hadn't he listened to Michelle instead of accusing her of lying? 'She didn't deserve this. None of them did. You're deluded, Bonneval!' He heard his own voice rising in anger.

But Bonneval shook his head, and looked down into the pit. 'The girl ... well, there was a kind of poetic justice in that. She was Petty's daughter, after all. But I did nothing. They took their own lives, monsieur. All of them. Through ignorance. Going down there to their deaths of their own free will. Stupid, unsuspecting men. And women.' And Enzo realised now how Petty and Coste had sustained the contusions found during autopsy. Overcome by gas as they went down into the pit, they had fallen the rest of the way. Bonneval turned back to him. 'And you people couldn't even tell. I didn't drown them. They filled their lungs with carbonic gas. The wine was just a convenient place to keep them until I could dispose of the bodies.' He allowed himself a wry smile.

'Petty may not have liked my wine. But he was damned well going to drink it for eternity.'

'Why in God's name did you present him to the world like that? All dressed up and staked out like a scarecrow?'

There was a wry smile on his lips. 'My father's old gown and hat from *l'Ordre de la Dive Bouteille*. It was rather appropriate, wasn't it?'

Enzo shook his head. 'Until then, nobody even knew Petty was dead.'

'But that was just the point. Nobody knew. And people needed to know. That justice had been done. To understand that their sins will always find them out.'

He seemed to have forgotten that the real reason he'd done it was because Petty hadn't liked his wine. 'But you certainly didn't want anyone to know that it was you who'd been the instrument of that justice.'

Bonneval smiled. 'No. No one ever needed to know that.'

'I know.'

He nodded. 'And so did Roussel. His timing was perfect. He was the last one. It was his turn. But, like both him and Michelle Petty, I don't think you'll be sharing it with anyone else, monsieur.' He turned to the wall and unhooked a rope that strained up into darkness.

Enzo watched with a mixture of alarm and incomprehension. Then heard a soft, swift current of air as Bonneval released the rope. He turned as something dark and heavy swung out of nowhere and knocked him from his feet. His head hit concrete with a resounding crack. And in the moment before blackness consumed him, he found himself looking into the flickering flame of the candle, red-painted steps descending beyond it to eternity. Into the abyss of which Charlotte had warned him. He saw his own blood making a pool around his head. And he knew with an absolute certainty that there was nothing he could do to stop Bonneval from pushing him down the stairs to his death.

II

His whole world was filled with a rushing sound so all consuming that he could hear nothing else. His eyes were open, but he was blind. He could move, but only slowly, his entire body constrained by a softness he could sense but not feel. He had no conception of time or space. Only pain. A pain so intense he thought his head would burst. He remembered the flickering flame of the candle. The red stairs descending into light. Was this what lay at the foot of the steps? Was this death?

And yet he felt so very much alive. If only he could find some shred of comprehension, grasp some reference to a world he might understand. He fought through pain in search of illumination and found it in the air he breathed. Thick and sweet and filled with the fragrance of freshly crushed fruit. Grapes. His feet found solid form beneath him, and he tried to stand up. But a solid stream of heavy, wet liquid knocked him over again. And now it filled his nose and mouth. He tasted the sweetness of the grape juice, the pulp of its flesh, and realised he was completely submerged in freshly pressed *must*.

In panic he pushed up and broke the surface. The jet of crushed grape broke over his shoulder, and he spun away from it, hands outstretched, until he found the round smooth stainless steel wall that contained him. He followed it round, defining in his brain the limit of his circular prison, and understanding broke over him like the juice that thundered down from above. He was in the bottom of a *cuve*. The *must* had not yet begun its fermentation, otherwise the oxygen would already have been displaced by carbonic gas.

But why had Bonneval not simply pushed him into the pit? And even as the question formed in his mind, Enzo knew the answer. The killer would only have had to haul him out again. And Enzo was a big man, bigger than Bonneval's other victims. It would have been hard enough for him to drag the dead weight of the Scotsman across the *chai* and bundle him into the *cuve* through the access hatch.

The thought of the hatch gave him fresh hope. It was, doubtless, how he had got in. It might be his way out.

He crouched down, submerged again, and felt around until he found the hatch and the seal around it. But to his disappointment realised that there was no way to release it from the inside. He broke the surface once more, and became aware that he was almost up to his neck now. There was no way he could float in something this dense. Once it was over his head, he would drown in it. And there was nothing he could do.

Blind fear gripped him. And he craned his head back, peering desperately into the darkness above. There had to be light.

The lid must be off to allow the tube access to the *cuve*. He could hear the motor now above the thunder of the juice, pumping it under pressure. From the *pressoir*? From another *cuve*? Enzo had no way of knowing. But at last he found light. The merest trace of it. And only in the sense that it gave vague dark form to the stream of juice that gushed down from above. Seeing it, he realised that halfway down the jet divided into two streams. That there was something there. An obstruction *mid-cuve*. He couldn't see it. He reached up and couldn't touch it. It was too far above his head. But in his soul he knew that it was his only salvation. He crouched down, submerged again beneath the heavy, sweet, thick juice and pushed up with all his might. He stretched and stretched into darkness and his fingers touched something cold and solid, before he slipped back into the *must*. And he realised in that moment what it was. One of the wafer-thin radiators, feeding cold water through black tubing, that they lowered into *cuves* to cool fermenting wine. If he could somehow get a hold of the thing, it just might be a lifeline. Literally. But it seemed the most slender of threads on which to hang his life. He roared his anger and frustration into the void and prepared himself to jump again, with barely any remaining hope to sustain him.

III

Nicole saw the floodlit façade of the *château* at the end of its long avenue of trees. Dust rose up in the night all around them from the wheels of Fabien's four-by-four. It had been his suggestion they come here after they had failed to find Enzo at the *gîte*.

As they circled the lawn in front of the main entrance, Nicole pointed with excitement to Enzo's 2CV parked outside the *chai*.

'He's here!'

Fabien pulled in beside it and they jumped out on to the gravel forecourt. Nicole started for the *château*, but Fabien grabbed her arm. 'There's a light in the *chai*. I can hear pumps going.'

They followed the old brick wall of the *chai* along to a door that stood open, bleeding feeble light out into the night. The crumbling brickwork of Hubert de Bonneval was patched and repaired with pebbles from the river. Fabien pulled the door wide, and they stepped over the tube that fed carbonic gas up from the maintenance pit below the *cuves*.

Laurent de Bonneval looked up, startled, as Nicole followed Fabien inside. He had failed to register their arrival above the thunder of the pumps. He was crouched at the top of the steps with a bucket and brush, scrubbing at the concrete. Beyond him, a sack of sand dangled from the roof on the end of a rope. A candle burned on the apron above him, down now to its last inch. Dull fluorescent strip lights flickered overhead. Bonneval stood up and climbed quickly on to the apron.

'What do you want?'

Fabien stared him down. 'It was you who killed Petty and Coste, wasn't it?'

Bonneval gave a small snort of derision. 'Why on earth would you think that?'

'Because the mineral fingerprint of the wine taken from Serge Coste's stomach shows that the grapes were grown at La Croix Blanche.'

Bonneval raised an eyebrow. He seemed almost amused. 'Do they? In that case it must have been you who killed them, Fabien.'

'That's what Macleod thought.'

'Did he?'

'But what he didn't know, that you and I do, is that I didn't make any wine the year Petty went missing. I was re-equipping my *chai*. Remember? You should, because I sold all my grapes to you.'

Nicole stepped forward, fearful and aggressive, and Fabien held her arm. 'Where's Monsieur Macleod?'

'I have no idea.'

Fabien said, 'His car's outside, Laurent.'

'What were you doing when we came in?' Nicole pulled free of Fabien's grasp and moved towards the stairs that led to the pit. She looked down at the bucket. Soapy water on the floor around it was marbled with veins of red, seeping across the cement and spilling onto the top step. 'That's blood.' She swung towards Bonneval. 'What have you done?'

There was a strange, sick smile on his face, but he said nothing, and then looked startled as she lunged for him. He stepped back to avoid her and caught his feet in a tangle of coiled tubing. The moment hung in the air, as if some unseen finger had pressed a *pause* button. Bonneval glanced behind him, as he tried to catch his balance. There was no containing rail here along the edge of the apron, only a sheer drop into the pit. His arms windmilled as he fought to prevent the fall. Wide eyes stared at Fabien, a silent plea for help. But there was nothing the young winemaker could do. And, as if the *pause* had been released, he toppled backwards into space. Nicole's scream filled the room, before they heard the smack of his body as it hit the floor below.

'Oh, my God, I've killed him!' She jumped down from the apron, and started down the stairs.

Fabien covered the distance between them in four quick strides and grabbed her wrist. 'Don't go down there!'

'Why not?'

He jumped down beside her and lifted the candle. 'I showed you before, remember?' And he pushed her aside and started slowly down the stairs, holding the candle ahead of him. He had gone only three or four steps before the flame separated from the candle, and he dropped it, retreating quickly to the top of the stairs, grabbing fast lungfuls of air. He looked down into the pit where Bonneval's body lay at an oddly twisted angle, blood pooling slowly across the tiles around his head. 'It's full of gas down there. He was probably gone before he hit the ground.'

Nicole was in shock. Chalk white. 'It's my fault. I killed him.'

'He killed himself, Nicole. And God knows how many others.'

And the memory of fear replaced guilt. 'Monsieur Macleod! What's he done with him?'

Fabien's face reflected a grim acceptance of the worst. But he didn't express it. 'I don't know.' He cocked his head, listening for a moment to the sound of pumps thundering in the *chai*. He took her hand. 'Come on.'

They ran through into the old shed and Fabien flicked a row of switches, one after the other. Strip lights hummed and flashed overhead, and they realised that the sound of the pumps was coming from the next shed along.

Three pumps roared in the narrow aisle between two rows of stainless steel *cuves*. Pink tubing, like giant worms, lay around the floor, feeding in and out of red plastic tubs. Yet more pumps sat idle on trolleys. Nicole glanced helplessly at Fabien as his eyes darted around the *chai*, following tubes up to the metal catwalk above them. 'He's pumping *must* from one *cuve* to the other.' He frowned, and then clarity filled his eyes. 'Jesus. Macleod must be in the tank.'

He let go of her hand, and she ran after him, as he sprinted for the stairs that led up to the access grilles. By the time she had climbed up after him and run along the walkway, he was crouching down at the neck of a *cuve*. She could see the dark *must* pulsing through the semi-translucent plastic of the tube and heard the sound of it crashing into the tank. Fabien held an inspection lamp over the open edge of the neck and they peered inside. The foaming red juice was nearly up to the top. Nicole's face was creased with anxiety. She turned to look at him, but he wouldn't meet her eye.

'If he's in there,' he said. 'He's dead.'

A small cry of anguish broke from her lips, just as an arm broke the surface of the *must*, streaming red fingers grasping for the black pipes that fed water to the radiator. Enzo's upturned face, mouth open, gasping for air, followed it for the briefest of moments before disappearing again into the froth.

Fabien grabbed for the hand as it lost its grip on the pipes, and Nicole watched in horror as fingers slipped through grasping fingers. And then somehow, at the last, formed a bond, and Fabien reached further in to seize his wrist. He braced himself against the neck of the *cuve* and pulled with all his might.

Enzo broke the surface once again, and this time his free hand grasped the lip of the neck. Nicole reached over, and between them she and Fabien pulled him free of the *cuve*. He scrambled for footholds and toppled over the rail, to lie gasping on the catwalk, stained red by juice that seemed to stream from every pore.

Nicole was sobbing with relief. She knelt beside him, repeating his name over and over again. He opened his eyes, and for a moment met Fabien's, a world of misunderstanding still between them. And as he pulled himself up on one elbow, Nicole threw her arms around him and pulled his head into the cleavage between large, quivering breasts. Where he was sure, for several long seconds, that he was going to suffocate.

CHAPTER TWENTY-THREE

I

Nicole sat watching the President's secretary copying a document and wondered why she was there. She had informed the university in writing that owing to personal circumstances she would be unable to continue her studies at the department of biology this year. She had been clear and unambiguous. But the summons from the university President had been equally clear. Her presence was required at two-thirty on Thursday afternoon. And she had begun to fret that perhaps they were going to demand compensation for loss of fees. Which would be something that neither she nor her father could afford.

Well, if she couldn't pay, she couldn't pay. They couldn't make her. Only Monsieur Macleod could get blood out of a stone.

She sighed and glanced through an open door to the mezzanine where students stood around in animated groups, talking and laughing, drinking coffee and making the most of whatever time they had between lectures. And she envied them. She missed student life already, and nothing she could do at home seemed to please her father. No one, it appeared, could live up to the impossibly high standards set by her mother. And there was no way she could escape the daily comparison.

She was thoroughly miserable.

From behind the closed door of the President's office, she heard men's voices raised in what sounded like anger, and she was sure that she could hear Monsieur Macleod's strange, Scottish-accented French among them.

'I object to being ordered here like some schoolboy to be dressed down by the headmaster!' Director Frauziol was red-faced with indignation. 'This university has no jurisdiction over the *Police Scientifique*. We chose not to participate in your department of forensic science for the simple reason that we refuse to work with amateurs.' He looked pointedly at Enzo.

Monsieur le Président was the personification of calm, pouring oil on troubled waters. 'Now why don't we all just relax, gentlemen? You were not ordered here, Monsieur le Directeur. Your presence was requested. Isn't that correct, Monsieur Gineste?'

Everyone looked towards the representative from the Ministry of Justice. 'Absolutely, Monsieur le Président. We are here to find a means of facilitating cooperation between the Toulouse laboratory of the *Police Scientifique* and the University of Paul Sabatier. At the *request* of the Garde des Sceaux. We are all here at his pleasure.'

'Well, I find it rich,' Enzo said, 'being called an amateur by an idiot.' He glared at Director Frauziol.

Frauziol was unruffled. 'An amateur is what you are, Macleod.'

'*Monsieur* Macleod, if you don't mind. And in my case, the only reason you can't call me a professional is that I don't get paid for what I do. But I'm better qualified than you are.'

'Qualifications that are not recognised in France.'

Enzo stabbed a finger at him across the room. 'Well, let me tell you what the French press and public will recognise very quickly when they see it. And that's incompetence. Yours.'

'Gentlemen, gentlemen, there's no need for this.' Monsieur le Président looked longingly from the window towards the Lycée Bellevue at the far side of the Route de Narbonne. It was clear he wished he were somewhere else.

'Yes there is,' Enzo said. 'The *Police Scientifique* is a publicly funded body, with a responsibility towards future generations of forensic scientists.'

'We don't have the time or manpower to waste sending trained scientists to talk to students, monsieur.'

'Well, you'd better find both.' Enzo leaned over and opened his canvas satchel. He pulled out a plastic evidence bag containing a white glove. 'You'll recognise this?'

The Director paled. 'That was an oversight.'

'An oversight? You call something that might well have cost men their lives an oversight? I would call it professional ineptitude.'

The *fonctionnaire* from the Ministry leaned forward to peer at the glove. 'I'm sorry, I don't understand.'

Enzo said, 'A vital piece of blood evidence on an inside

finger of this glove, which was missed by the lab in Toulouse, could have led to an earlier resolution of the murder of Gil Petty, and prevented the killing of others, including Petty's daughter and Gendarme David Roussel. It belonged to Laurent de Bonneval's father. Who, by a strange quirk of fate, gave a DNA sample, along with dozens of other men in the area, to rule himself out of a criminal investigation into a rape shortly before his death. That sample is still on the DNA database, and familial searching could have led us to his son at least two years ago.'

The *fonctionnaire* and the President turned to look at the Director. He remained resolutely silent.

Enzo said, 'There's not much any of us can do about it now. And if I can stop taking this personally for a minute, I'll admit that I don't blame Monsieur Frauziol *per se*.' He turned towards Frauziol. 'But as Director the buck has to stop with you.' The dark cloud of depression left by David Roussel and Michelle Petty's deaths still hung over him.

'I have instigated a system of checks and balances to ensure that no such oversights occur in the future.'

Enzo said, 'And I'll tell you what else you're going to do. You're going to delegate an adjutant forensics officer to spend one afternoon a week lecturing to my students. *And* you're going to give each year's students access to your labs to see how the professionals are supposed to do it.'

'Or what?'

Enzo held up the glove. 'Or you might just be reading about your *oversight* in tomorrow's edition of Libération.'

The long silence which ensued ended with a discreet clearing of the throat by the representative from the Ministry. 'I think, Monsieur Frauziol, you might be well advised to arrive at an accommodation with the university. For all our sakes.'

Monsieur Frauziol looked as if he'd swallowed a golf ball. He stood up. 'You'll have to put your request in writing.'

Monsieur le Président got to his feet, all smiles. 'Excellent, excellent. I always knew we'd find some mutual agreement, some common ground.'

Enzo remained in his seat. 'There *is* one other thing . . .'

And they all turned towards him expectantly.

Nicole stood up as the grim-faced adversaries filed out of the President's office. Frauziol strode past her without acknowledgement. The *fonctionnaire* nodded politely. Monsieur le Président poked his head around the door. 'A moment, please, Amélie.' His secretary grabbed her notebook and hurried into his office, closing the door behind her. Which left Enzo standing smiling fondly at Nicole.

'Hello, Monsieur Macleod.'

'Hello, Nicole.'

'I don't suppose you'd know why I'm here?'

'Actually, yes. I do. It was a bit of a subterfuge really. It wasn't the President who wanted to see you. It was me.'

She looked at him in astonishment. 'But you can see me any time. I didn't have to come here.'

'That's true. But I thought I might have news for you after my meeting today.'

She frowned. 'You did? I mean, do you?'

'Yes.' He scuffed his foot idly on the carpet. 'You haven't cancelled the lease on your student digs yet, have you?'

'I'm going to see the landlord this afternoon.'

'Well, don't.'

She shook her head, mystified. 'Why?'

'I just had an interesting conversation with the head of the forensics lab here in Toulouse. He's agreed to provide us with lecturers and lab facilities.'

'Oh?' she said, trying to sound enthusiastic. 'That's good.'

'He's also agreed to find money in his budget to provide an annual scholarship for the best student of the year. As recommended by me, of course.' He couldn't stop the smile spreading across his face as her eyes widened. 'And guess who I'm recommending for this year . . .'

II

Enzo walked Madame Durand across the Place du Palais past the three arches that once opened into the entrance hall of the Tribunal de Grande Instance before they turned right down the Rue Du Sel. Albi glowed brick pink in the autumn sunshine. But all the warmth had gone out of the air, and the cool wind had started taking leaves from the trees. The *juge d'instruction* again wore a conservative cut of business suit, this time in dark grey, and her auburn hair streamed out behind her as they walked. Enzo cast her an admiring glance.

'Still married, Madame le Juge?'

She smiled. 'Don't you ever give up?

He shook his head. 'Never.'

They climbed the steps and entered into the hall *d'accueil*. He followed her upstairs and along a wood-panelled corridor to her office. They had met several days before at Gendarme Roussel's funeral, and she had asked him to drop by.

She laid her bag on a desk piled high with files, and dropped into the high-backed leather chair behind it. She found reading glasses in a breast pocket and slipped them on, then opened a folder in front of her.

Enzo dug into his satchel and pulled out a bottle of red wine. 'By the way, I brought you a present.'

She looked up. 'Wine?'

'Petty's only Al. His Holy Grail. A bottle of Domaine Sarrabelle's 2002 Syrah. Can't find it for love or money these days. But I'm told the 2003 is just as good.'

She turned the bottle to look at the label. 'I've never tried it.'

'There's always a first time.' Enzo took two glasses and a *tire bouchon* from his bag. 'Be prepared, I always say.'

'I'm not sure I should be drinking in the office.'

'I wouldn't worry. I've heard the judge around here is a woman. A real soft touch. I don't think she'll bother us. And I won't tell her if you don't.'

Madame Durand pursed her lips to contain a smile, not sure whether to be amused or offended. But Enzo just grinned and opened the bottle, pouring them each a generous glass. He raised his. 'To your very good health, Madame le Juge.'

'*Santé.*'

They both sipped the wine and she raised an eyebrow. 'Hmmm. I'm impressed.' Then her face clouded, and she laid down her glass. 'But maybe we shouldn't be celebrating too soon.' She turned back to her file. 'That piece of material your daughter's boyfriend tore from your assailant's pocket at Château des Fleurs . . .' She peered over her reading glasses at him. 'You know, you could have been in serious trouble for not handing that over straight away.'

Enzo shrugged and took another sip of wine. 'What about it?'

'I ordered a DNA test on the blood, and we did a comparison with a sample taken from the body of Laurent de Bonneval.'

Enzo frowned. He couldn't see where this was going. 'And?'

'They didn't match, Monsieur Macleod. Whoever tried to kill you up in the gallery at Château des Fleurs, it wasn't him.'

Enzo's frown deepened to a furrow. 'But that doesn't make any sense. If it wasn't Bonneval, who was it?'

The *juge* shook her head. 'We have no idea. But whoever it was, he's still out there.'

Read on for an exclusive preview of

BLACKLIGHT BLUE

CHAPTER ONE

Paris, February 1992

Yves watched the traffic in the boulevard below come to a standstill in the frigid Paris morning. The *bouchon* stretched as far as he could see, to the next traffic lights and beyond. He could almost feel the frustration of the drivers trapped in their cars rise to meet him like the pollution that spewed from smoky exhausts. The city air was not good for him. It was time for a change.

The long, repeating monotone in his ear was broken by a man's voice. 'Yes, hello?'

'*Salut.* It's me.'

'Oh, okay.' The voice seemed tense.

Yves was cool, relaxed. Each word delivered with the easy assurance of a soldier with an automatic weapon pumping bullets into an unarmed man. 'I'm sorry I didn't call yesterday. I was out of the country.' He wasn't quite sure why he felt the need to elaborate. It just seemed more casual. Conversational. 'Portsmouth. In England. A business trip.'

'Is that supposed to mean something to me?' Clear irritation in the other man's voice now.

'I just thought you'd wonder why I hadn't called.'

'Well, you're calling me now.'

'I was going to suggest tomorrow afternoon. Three o'clock. If that's okay with you.'

'Where?'

'Your place.'

He sensed the other's reticence in his hesitation. 'I prefer somewhere public, you know that.'

'Listen, friend, we need to talk.' If there was a threat in the forced intimacy of the word, 'friend,' it went unnoticed. He heard a sigh at the other end of the line.

'You know where to find me?'

'Of course.'

'Three o'clock, then.'

'Fine.' He retracted the aerial of his mobile phone and saw that the traffic had not moved.

Lambert's apartment was on the second floor of a recently renovated building in the thirteenth *arrondissement*. A newly installed electronic entry system was designed to cut costs by doing away with the need for a concierge. Which meant that no one but Lambert would witness his arrival. And no one, not even Lambert, would know when he left.

'Yeh?' The speaker in the wall issued a scratched rendition of Lambert's voice.

'It's me.' Yves never used his name if he didn't have to. The buzzer sounded, and he pushed the door open. Lambert was waiting on the landing. A gaping door opened into the apartment behind him. He was a strange young man, abnormally pale, sparse blond hair shaved to a cropped fuzz. Penumbral shadows beneath darker eyes punctuated a skeletal face, and bony fingers clasped Yves' gloved hand in a perfunctory greeting. 'Come in.' He glanced towards the stairs as if concerned that someone might be watching.

The bay windows in the salon looked out towards the park, bearing out Yves' assumption that the room was not overlooked. A well-worn sofa and armchairs had seen better days, hiding their tawdriness beneath colourful, fringed throws. Yves smelled old garlic and stewed coffee coming from the open kitchen door. And the whole apartment was suffused with the stink of stale cigarette smoke. Yves felt it catching his throat and, as Lambert took out a fresh cigarette, he said, 'Don't do that.'

Lambert paused with the cigarette halfway to his mouth, and cast wary eyes towards his visitor. Then, reluctantly, he tapped the cigarette back into its packet. 'Coffee?'

'Why not?'

Lambert disappeared into the kitchen. Yves perched on the edge of the sofa and saw motes of dust hanging still in the slabs of weak winter sunlight that fell at angles through the window. He heard his own breath as he forced it in and out of contracting lungs. His blue eyes felt gritty at first, then watery. His tension was palpable.

Lambert reappeared with small cups of black coffee and placed them on the table. Yves leaned forward to drop in a sugar lump and poke it with a coffee spoon until it dissolved.

'Aren't you going to take off your coat?' Lambert sat opposite, in the armchair, keeping his eyes on his visitor as he raised his coffee cup to his lips.

'I'm not staying.'

Lambert's eyes dropped to his guest's hands. 'You can take off your gloves, surely?'

'I have a form of psoriasis,' Yves said. 'It affects my hands. When I have a flare-up I have to rub them with cream. I keep the gloves on to protect them.' He took a sip of his coffee. It was bitter and unpleasant, and he wished he had declined the offer. It was only putting off the moment.

'So what is it we need to talk about?' Lambert seemed anxious to get this over with.

But Yves wasn't listening. The tightness across his chest had become vice-like, and his lungs were reluctant to give up spent air. His throat was swelling, and he felt the rapid pulse of blood in his carotid arteries. Tears spilled from reddening eyes as did his coffee as he tried to replace the cup on the table. The sneezing and coughing began almost simultaneously. His mouth gaped, his eyes stared, and panic gripped him. His hand shot to his face, a politeness dinned into him during childhood years by a smothering mother. *Cover your mouth when you cough! Coughs and sneezes spread diseases!* For a moment, he thought that Lambert knew why he had come, and that there had been something in the coffee. But the symptoms were only too familiar.

It was nearly impossible to breathe now. In a world blurred

by tears he saw Lambert get to his feet, and heard the alarm in his voice. 'Are you alright? What the hell's wrong with you?'

He sucked in a breath and forced it out again. 'Do you . . . do you keep pets?'

Lambert shook his head in consternation. 'Of course not. In God's name, man, what's wrong?'

As Yves struggled to his feet, Lambert rounded the table to stop him from falling. It was now or never. Yves clutched the outstretched bony arms and threw his weight forward. He heard Lambert's gasp of surprise, and then the air exploding from his lungs as both men toppled over the coffee table and crashed to the floor. Yves was on top of him, but could barely see, mucus and saliva exploding from his mouth and nose as his body fought against the toxins with which his own immune system was attacking his airways.

Lambert was screaming and flailing beneath him. Yves' gloved hands found the younger man's face, then his neck, and he squeezed. But his physical powers were failing, and he released his hold on the neck to seek out the head. He felt Lambert's barking breath in his face, before his hands found that familiar grip, one hand spread across the face, the other at the back of the head. And then it was easy, in spite of everything. A quick twist. He heard the pop of the disarticulated vertebra, and almost felt the sharp edge of the bone, released from its cartilage, slice through the spinal cord. Lambert went limp. Yves rolled off him and lay fighting for breath. If he blacked out now, there was a good chance he would never wake up. This was as bad as he had ever known it.

It took a superhuman effort to force himself to his knees. He fumbled in his coat pocket to find the bottle of pills and closed desperate fingers around it.

He had no idea how he managed to reach the kitchen, or how it was even possible to force the pills down a throat that was swollen nearly closed. He heard the sound of breaking glass as the tumbler fell into the sink, and the rattle of pills as they spilled across the floor. But none of that mattered. If he didn't get out of here now, he would be as dead as the man he had come to kill.

ACKNOWLEDGEMENTS

I would like to offer my grateful thanks to those who gave so generously of their time and expertise during my researches for *The Critic*. In particular, I'd like to express my gratitude to pathologist Steven C. Campman, M.D, Medical Examiner, San Diego, California; Professor Joe Cummins, Professor Emeritus of Genetics, University of Western Ontario, Canada; Gaillac winemakers Hubert and Pierric de Faramond of Château Lastours, and Fabien and Laurent Caussé of Domaine Sarra-belle, for allowing me unfettered access to their respective vendanges; Alan and Laurence Geddes for their gîte and fabulous Château Mayragues; Patrice Leconte for his insights into the workings of the Gendarmerie Nationale; Jacques Auque, President of the Ordre de la Dive Bouteille, and win-emaker extraordinaire; the Commission Interprofessionnelle des Vins de Gaillac; Leo McCloskey of Enologix, Sonoma, California, for his fascinating introduction to the cutting-edge science of winemaking; and all the winemakers of Gaillac whose reds and rosés, sparkling mousseux, wonderful chilled whites and vin doux made the research for this book such a pleasure.

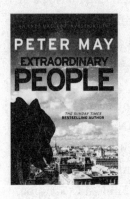
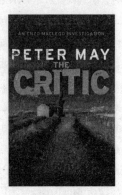

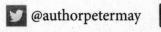 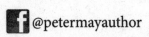